WHAT'S NEW, PUSSYCAT?

Alexandra Potter

HODDER

First published in Great Britain in 2011 by Hodder & Stoughton
An Hachette Livre UK company

A version of this book was first published in paperback
in 2000 by Fourth Estate Limited

1

A CIP catalogue record for this title is available from the British Library

B format Paperback ISBN 978 0 340 91960 6
A format Paperback ISBN 978 0 340 99385 9

Typeset in Plantin Light by Hewer Text UK Ltd, Edinburgh

Printed in Great Britain by Clays Ltd, St Ives plc

Hodder & Stoughton policy is to use papers that are natural, renewable
and recyclable products and made from wood grown in sustainable
forests. The logging and manufacturing processes are expected to
conform to the environmental regulations of the country of origin.

Hodder & Stoughton Ltd
338 Euston Road
London NW1 3BH

www.hodder.co.uk

For Mum and Dad, Kelly and Pete

ACKNOWLEDGEMENTS

Thanks a million to my agent Stephanie, my editors past and present – Arabella and Isobel – and everyone at Hodder for their enthusiasm and vision in republishing this new updated version of my first ever book. A very big thank you to my wonderful mum, amazing sister Kelly and to Pete, who always believed I could write this book and encouraged and supported me from the very beginning.

And finally in the age-old tradition, I've saved the best to last – My Dad – whose unique sense of humour, spirit of adventure, sense of fun and wonderful gift for story-telling, have all helped make me the writer I am today. He truly was, and forever will be, the best dad in the world and I'm forever grateful and proud to be his daughter.

Thanks Dad, for everything and a whole lot more.

Prologue

London is basking in blue skies and sunshine. It's the weekend and the first warm spring day has brought the city to life, waking it from its winter hibernation and tossing off its grey layers of heavy clouds, woollen coats and gloomy faces. There's a celebratory mood. Across the capital people are digging out their shorts and summer dresses, slipping pale feet into flip-flops and smiling at each other. Empty parks are filled with children squealing on swings. Cafés spill out onto pavements.

And in a small corner of West London, a handful of streets are awash with bubblegum-pink blossoms, designer boutiques and an explosion of tourists. This is Notting Hill. Made famous by the movie, its pavements are thronging with day-trippers, laden down with cameras, maps and souvenirs from the renowned Portobello Market.

Amongst them is a woman wearing faded blue jeans and a simple white T-shirt, her hair is long and loose and her face is half-hidden under a straw hat. Which is just as well. Because that woman is me and I didn't have time to put any make-up on this morning – saying that, I can't remember when I *did* have time in the morning to do any more than drag a comb through my hair – and you can see the freckles on my nose and the beginnings of a few pencil lines around my eyes.

Damn, my sunglasses, I suddenly remember. I forgot them. Squinting in the sunshine I think about running back into the flat and getting them, then realise I don't have time. I'm late already. Unchaining my bicycle, I hop on and begin weaving in amongst the crowds. The air is filled with the scents of cherry blossom and espresso, the sounds of taxi-cabs, chatter, a cacophony of foreign accents. As I cycle along it's like tuning a radio; French, Russian, German, American . . .

Slowly I make my way along Westbourne Grove. In the old days I would whizz down here in my old VW Beetle, but that was before the traffic got so bad, not to mention the tourists crossing the road and always looking the wrong way. 'Hey, watch out!' I brake sharply, narrowly missing a young Japanese girl stepping out to take a photograph.

But then so much has changed since I first moved here. It was, what? Ten years ago? No . . . even longer . . . It was 1999 and the movie had just come out. Back then it was the first time anyone had ever heard of the Travel Bookshop or the Blue Door, and people were always stopping you in the street asking where Hugh Grant lives (he doesn't live around here by the way, he lives in Chelsea and the famous door is now painted black to stop the legions of fans knocking on it).

It was before the last greasy spoon disappeared and was replaced by a fashionable restaurant. Before the rows of designer boutiques selling clothes you can't afford. Before you had to win the lottery to buy a house around here. I glance at the rows of pillar-fronted houses, at the sunlight bouncing off the smooth white stucco like icing on a cake, and think about my tiny little flat. I adore it, but it's about the size of a postage stamp. You could probably fit it ten times into one of these big swanky houses.

And yet, despite everything, I can't imagine living anywhere else. I've been here so long it's like I have Notting Hill running right through me like the words in a stick of Blackpool rock. I grew up here.

I fell in love here.

I smile at the memory. Gosh, that was all so long ago. Before the millennium . . . before I met Sam, or Charlie . . . before I'd even heard this place existed . . . before everything . . .

Like the spokes on my wheels, my mind starts whirring backwards, back to Bradford, back to when it was just me, a skinny whippet called Fatso, and my Tom Jones records.

Back to where it all began.

Chapter One

What would you do if your boyfriend proposed? Shout yes, grab the diamond solitaire and take out a subscription to *Brides* magazine, or panic and buy a one-way ticket to Outer Mongolia? Delilah did neither. She looked down at Lenny, clutching a red velvet jewellery box and balancing on one knee on the kitchen lino, and said nothing.

'So, what's your answer?' he urged, shifting his weight from one knee to the other.

Delilah bit her lip.

'Come on, Dee, what's it to be?'

A sequence of wedding pictures sprang to mind: white meringue dress with tulle netting and mutton sleeves; a golf clubhouse full of pissed elderly relatives feasting on sausage rolls and cheap bubbly; Uncle Stan and his band launching into another rendition of 'The Birdie Song'. And the small matter of a lifetime with Lenny.

Delilah winced. It wasn't that she didn't love Lenny, but it was more of a habit than a passion – rather like wearing the same eyeshadow for years, even though the colour doesn't suit you anymore. She'd known Lenny since she was seventeen and he'd given her driving lessons; after six months of clutch control and reverse parking she'd passed her test and lost her virginity. Fast forward a decade and they were ensconced in a three-bedroom semi, complete with mock-Tudor windows and an all-weather conservatory.

'Well, forget it then.'

Delilah stopped daydreaming. 'What?'

'If you don't want to get hitched we might as well call it a day.'

'Lenny . . . wait.'

Lenny stood up, sucking in his stomach and bringing himself up to his full height of five foot seven and a half. He sported a little extra poundage (due to his addiction to takeaway chicken vindaloos and extra poppadoms) and tried to conceal his swelling waistline in a daily uniform of stripy rugby shirts (with the obligatory collars-up), chinos and the kind of slip-on, crêpe-soled shoes that are meant for yachting, but are always worn by blokes who only see the sea on a fortnight's holiday to Ibiza.

'I'm off to the pub . . . don't wait up.' He opened the door, then turned and flung the ring across the table. It bounced against the microwave and landed in the dog's bowl. 'Take it, you might as well have the bloody thing anyway.' The door slammed.

Delilah sighed. Everyone thought Lenny was a great catch. He was the manager of Forty Winks, a large store in Bradford specialising in pine beds, quilted headboards and king-size mattresses, was popular at the local pub and had even recently swapped his beaten-up Mini Metro for a top-of-the-range Vauxhall. What more could a girl want?

Excitement. Delilah was bored. Bored of Lenny, bored of Bradford and bored of life. She needed a new one, but unfortunately a life wasn't something she could find ready-made on a shelf in Marks & Spencer – complete with a full guarantee so that she could take it back and swap it if she didn't like it. And that was the problem. Delilah wanted to change things but didn't have the balls.

But she hadn't always felt this way. In fact it didn't seem that long since she'd been over the moon at the thought of moving into Lenny's poky rented flat above the fish-and-chip shop on the high street in Shipley, a small village on the outskirts of Bradford. Back then she was an unhappy teenager, arguing with her dad and his new wife Sandra, the wicked stepmother, halfway through her A levels and waiting for the day when she could escape to art college. Which she probably would have done, if Lenny, her boyfriend of eight months, hadn't altered the course of her life by taking her to the posh Italian in town and, over a plate of tiramisu with extra whipped cream, asking her to live with him. For as soon as he did all thoughts of exams and a career were forgotten in the throes of romance and the wonderfully heady realisation that she could escape from whingeing Sandra and her dad's strict curfews. She was young and slap-bang in the middle of her first love affair, and nothing was going to come in its way.

So, ignoring the advice of her teachers who begged her to stay on in the sixth form and finish her A levels, she swapped her textbooks for tables and got herself a waitressing job at a motorway café paying £2 an hour. During the day she served fry-ups to randy lorry drivers who filled the greasy air with cigarette smoke and sexual innuendo. Hiding her embarrassment she'd laugh at their dirty jokes and concentrate on counting her tips. Long-distance lorry drivers were generous tippers and she was glad of the money. It meant that by night she could start transforming Lenny's grotty little flat into their very own love nest, decorating it with bright splashes of paint, carefully chosen pictures and second-hand furniture she'd found at jumble sales, then stripped and rubbed with sandpaper until her fingers were sore. This was her very own flat, and she relished the opportunity to make it feel like a real home.

Delilah had never been happier, despite a slight pang a year later when her best friends disappeared off to college and university. At first she wrote to a few, but she soon lost touch. After all, they had nothing in common, their lives seemed so childish – living off government grants, getting up at midday for lectures, getting pissed at the student bars and pulling a different bloke every week. Her life was a grown-up one: having a job, paying the rent, cooking Lenny huge bowls of spaghetti bolognese or shepherd's pie (the only two recipes she knew), and snuggling up with him in front of the little black and white portable TV her uncle had given her, waggling the coathanger they'd rigged up as an aerial, trying to get a better picture.

But somewhere over the years – she wasn't sure whether it was before or after they'd moved into the new house, or what triggered it – things changed, or rather they didn't but she did, and she'd started to feel dissatisfied. To hanker after something else. At first she dismissed her feelings – it was just one of those days. But then one of those days turned into one of those weeks, which turned into one of those months. And the boredom began to spread like a disease, infecting her relationship with Lenny, her home, her whole life.

She thought about her daily routine. It was just that. A routine. At 8 a.m. the alarm would go off and she'd have a quick shower before going downstairs and fixing two boiled eggs for Lenny who would sit glued to breakfast TV. Not even looking from the screen to smash off the tops and dip in his soldiers, he'd chew them slowly as he watched the weather forecast. But it hadn't always been like this. They used to eat breakfast together, giggling as they buttered the toast, giving each other strawberry-jam kisses and playing footsie under the table. But now she was lucky if she got a couple of grunts out of Lenny, who wouldn't move until the end of the show was signalled by the childish theme music, and then he'd hum along, wiping his mouth, hoisting himself up from the sofa, straightening his tie in the mirror in the hall, fiddling with his hair – Lenny could be quite vain, despite his lack of interest in what he looked like underneath his clothes – until, finally satisfied, he'd shout 'Ta-ra, luv. See you at teatime,' before grabbing his distressed, elasticated bomber jacket circa 1987 and heading off down the drive, still humming that bloody theme tune.

She'd clear up the plates and get ready for another day at the restaurant where she now worked. Gulping down two cups of strong black instant coffee she'd rummage through a hundred pairs of tights, cursing her inability to throw any away due to an ill-founded belief that one day they'd come in useful: 'I'll wear them with long dresses' (what long dresses?) or 'they'll be perfect under jeans in winter' (who the hell wears tights under jeans? Apart from women who favour American tan ones with drainpipes and work in launderettes). Finally she'd find a pair wedged at the back of the drawer, throw on her waitress uniform and stroke Fatso, her six-year-old whippet, who'd lick off her blusher with his doggy-breath tongue, and leave at exactly ten minutes past ten. It should be ten on the dot, but she was always exactly ten minutes late, even when she tried getting up exactly ten minutes earlier. Which meant she had to sprint for the 636 bus as it pulled out of the terminus, but she always caught it and she'd sit on those high seats above the wheels: the ones that have the hot-air vent under your feet.

Perched on the orange and black tartan seat, she'd lean against the window reading a magazine as the bus made its slow journey into Bradford town centre, occasionally looking up to see the queues of grumpy pensioners, young Asian girls in brightly coloured saris, mums grappling with toddlers, push-chairs and bulging carrier bags, struggling to get on board. Gloomily she'd watch them, women in their late twenties, looking harassed and miserable, and wonder if that was going to be her in a couple of years' time. Is that what her future held? A double baby buggy and trips to Mothercare?

At L'Escargot, Pascal, the *maître d'*, would be waiting for her, rocking on the built-up heels of his polished shoes, cocking his skinny peanut-shaped head from side to side like a budgie and tapping his watch with his long manicured fingernails. As usual she would mutter her insincere apologies, grab her white frilly pinafore – the management's pathetic attempt to titillate the lunchtime expense accounts into leaving hefty tips, which would bypass the staff and go straight into their expensive suit pockets – and start covering the tables with white linen table-cloths and clipping on paper coverings. Her shift covered the boozy businessman lunches and she'd serve artery-clogging dishes of steak au poivre doused in rich, shiny sauces, bread rolls, small silver dishes piled high with cholesterol-choked butter curls and pour large glasses of thick, warm red wine to wash it all down with. None of the customers had any idea it all came out of packets, frozen and ready-made. Blissfully ignorant, they quaffed and smacked their lips together, loosening their belts and collars, mopping their brows with the white starched napkins, lighting cigars and laughing thick resonant chortles about that disagreeable chap in the finance department, or the size of the new secretary's breasts.

She'd worked at L'Escargot for less than a year. It was one of those chain restaurants, pretending to offer traditional home-cooked French cuisine, and paid better than most waitressing jobs. And the customers were less aggro. It was easy money. Especially since she'd learnt how to fiddle the drinks with the aid of Matt behind the bar. Not that she liked waitressing but what else could she do? She'd tried temping in offices, but her typing was crap and she hated being stuck behind a desk all day, trying to transfer phone calls that she always seemed to cut off and struggling to make sense of the complicated computer systems. She'd once toyed with the idea of retaking her A levels, maybe even trying to get into college like she'd planned to before she met Lenny, but she soon gave up on that idea. She couldn't afford to – it would take years and they needed her wage – and anyway, Lenny was probably right. He said she was living a pipe dream – whoever heard of anybody making a career out of interior design in Shipley? That was what those poncy presenters did on the telly, not people like her.

She picked up the ring and rinsed it under the tap. It twinkled under the new Ikea lights; a sapphire surrounded with little diamonds – a Princess Di engagement ring. The temptation was too much, there was no harm in trying it on and she squeezed it onto her finger. She wriggled her hand in front of the mirror and practised some regal waving.

Her reflection waved back: a twenty-seven-year-old dressed in faded Wranglers and a Gap Kids T-shirt, with long crumpled chestnut hair and a smattering of pale freckles on her small, slightly upturned nose. She leaned forward and stared at herself. She didn't look like wifely material. Well, not Lenny's anyway.

'What am I doing?' she muttered. This is how a girl gets enticed up the aisle and married to the wrong man for thirty years. She tried to pull the ring off. It was stuck. 'Shit,' she cursed, frantically tugging on her finger. The ring refused to budge. Delilah grabbed some Fairy Liquid and squirted it liberally over her hand. It lathered up nicely but had no effect on the ring, apart from loosening one of the 'diamonds' which promptly swirled down the plug hole.

Normally Ms Laid Back, Delilah started to feel nervous – her finger was beginning to turn a strange lilac colour. What if they can't get the ring off? What if they have to cut my finger off? What if . . . Her mouth felt dry. A bizarre thought flashed through Delilah's mind: what if this was a plot masterminded by Lenny – to leave her with no wedding-ring finger, ensuring that if he couldn't marry her, no one else could. She dismissed the idea as quickly as it had appeared. Lenny was more *Wheel of Fortune* than *University Challenge*: he had trouble setting the video let alone concocting a plot that would leave her in the clutches of singledom. Delilah deliberated. She couldn't drive with her finger swelling up like a balloon, so she had two choices: either wait for Lenny's return – drunk and useless after the pubs had shut – or she could take a trip to Casualty. She looked at her left hand. The finger was beginning to take on the appearance of her Uncle Stan's nose: purple and bulbous. There was nothing else for it. Furiously, she dialled 999.

Chapter Two

Within five minutes a faint siren could be heard. Delilah looked through the wobbly glass of the porch. The siren became louder – embarrassingly louder – until she saw a distorted vision of an ambulance and flashing blue lights turn into the close. The neighbours are going to love this, she thought, as she saw curtains twitching and Mrs Bennett from Number 42 standing on the doorstep in her sheepskin slippers and pink quilted dressing gown. The ambulance screeched to a halt. Delilah opened the front door. Two men in bright green jumpsuits were running up her drive. 'Delilah Holdsworth?' barked the one with a moustache, looking distinctly annoyed that Delilah wasn't writhing around on the floor in agony.

'That's me . . . look.' Delilah held up her finger which had doubled in size, resembling a small root vegetable. 'I've got this ring stuck, it was my engagement ring, but I didn't want to be engaged, I just wanted to try it on, it looked all sparkly and . . .' She could feel the tears welling up. Her voice trailed off as they hurriedly bundled her into the back of the ambulance.

Fifteen nerve-wracking minutes and several screeching tyres later, Delilah arrived at Bradford General Hospital and was briskly strapped into a wheelchair and manoeuvred into a pastel-curtained cubicle where she was greeted by a sturdy-looking nurse in Scholls and a pinny: Sister Hamish.

'Female, twenty-seven, ring constricting blood supply on left finger, needs to be cut off.' Sister Hamish read loudly from her notes in a sing-song voice reminiscent of Miss Jean Brodie. She looked up and beamed at a blotchy-eyed Delilah.

Delilah felt as if she was in some kind of conspiracy. All these people smiling and nodding at her. Everybody was so cheerful – perhaps Lenny really had plotted the whole thing, even to the point of bribing the hospital staff. She stopped herself. She was being neurotic.

Sister Hamish wielded a shiny pair of miniature secateurs and, without further ado, grabbed the engorged digit. Delilah couldn't bear to look and covered her eyes with her free hand. She heard a sudden snap, and felt a twinge, followed by a weird tingling sensation. One by one she wriggled her fingers, one, two, three, four, five – all present and correct. She peeked between the fingers of her right hand and held up her left. The mutant finger had lived to fight another day. She wasn't going to be forced into early spinsterhood.

She stood up, slightly dizzy with relief, and pulled back the curtain. 'I think I'd better be going.'

'Aren't you forgetting something?' Sister Hamish held out the mangled ring.

'Ah, yes.' Delilah forced a smile. 'The ring.' She stuffed it hastily into her coat pocket and tried to dart for the exit.

'And make sure you sign out at reception.'

Delilah grimaced. The nightmare was nearly over.

She elbowed her way to the front of the queue. 'I need to sign out,' she grumbled to a decidedly unsmiley person in a cerise sweater behind the counter. Obviously smiles only came with the uniforms and not nasty pink mohair sweaters.

'Excuse me, I think I was before you.' A male voice with Pierce Brosnan overtones came from behind her. Delilah bit her lip in annoyance. The last thing she needed was some smart-arse bloke trying to push in. She turned round ready to give him a bollocking. 'Sorry about all this, but we're in the middle of making a fly-on-the-wall docu-drama and I've got to sort out some extra lighting.'

She swiftly changed her mind. Standing before her was a gift from God. Chocolate-brown hair and baby-blue eyes packaged in six-feet-two of tight black T-shirt and faded Levi's. The gift smiled and held out his hand: 'I'm Charlie Mendes, assistant producer with LLB – Living London Productions.'

Delilah smiled weakly, while silently screaming profanities. Why was it that every time she met a sexy bloke she was guaranteed to have opted for the ungroomed, bare-faced look – piggy eyes, blotchy skin and a chin full of coverstick-free zits? Never, ever did she meet this elusive species when she'd spent three hours with her make-up bag, a paddle brush and a bottle of hair serum. Instead, it was when her lash-building mascara had formed crusty rivers down her cheeks, transforming her into a dead ringer for Alice Cooper.

She took a deep breath and shook his hand. 'Hi, I'm Delilah.'

'As in the Bible?' asked Charlie, staring sexily into her blood-shot eyes.

'As in the Tom Jones song. My mum was a big fan.' She stuffed her hands into her pockets, feeling her face flush with embarrassment.

Charlie grinned. 'Hey, my mum used to be into Engelbert Humperdinck, but luckily my dad's royalist tendencies won her over and I got Charles instead.'

Delilah laughed. Charlie was nice. Nice *and* sexy – an unusual combination in a bloke.

'So, do you live near here?' He was looking at her intently.

'Er, yeh, just a few miles away. I had an accident earlier and had to come down so the doctors could take a look.' She stopped, suddenly realising she was standing in the middle of the casualty department on a Friday night, happily telling a stranger all about herself. But she couldn't help it. There was something magnetic about Charlie. Something about him that rooted her to the green-tiled floor of Accident and Emergency.

'Really?' Charlie wrinkled his tanned brow and looked concerned. 'What happened?'

'Oh, it was nothing. I just sprained my wrist.' Delilah surprised herself. Why hadn't she told him the truth? Why hadn't she told him about the accident with the engagement ring? She caught his gaze and took a sharp intake of breath. That's why she didn't tell him. Because he was gorgeous, and she fancied the bloody pants off him. Her cheeks burned. It felt as if her libido had been asleep for God knows how many years and Charlie had come along like Prince Charming and woken it up. She didn't want him to know about the ring, or Lenny. In fact, she wanted him to think she was single. Single and very available.

'Are you okay?'

'Yeh, fine.' Delilah swallowed, trying to hide her raging hormones. Charlie was staring at her, really staring at her and, if she didn't so look awful and he didn't look so handsome, she would have sworn he fancied her. God, what was she thinking? Being with Lenny for so long had made her forget how to read the signals. Charlie didn't fancy her. He couldn't fancy her. *Could he?*

He carried on staring. Mesmerised, Delilah stared back. She looked deeply into his big black pupils, wishing she knew more about him. No doubt he lived in a trendy flat, in a trendy part of London, and lived a trendy life, full of exciting clubs and exciting friends. He wouldn't eat boiled eggs and watch break-fast telly, or spend his evenings down the pub with his mates. He wouldn't drive a Vauxhall Cavalier and wear rugby shirts. And he certainly wouldn't be boring.

'So, you're here filming?' She forced out the words, trying to sound cool, as if meeting an assistant TV producer was an everyday occurrence, when in reality it was about as rare as winning money on one of those newspaper scratch cards, or discovering your suitcases are the first on the airport carousel. A once-in-a-lifetime event.

'Yeh, we're putting together a documentary about real-life casualty units. We're just here in Bradford tonight and then we move on to Birmingham.'

Suddenly Delilah twigged. So this was why all the hospital staff looked oddly cheery. *A documentary*. Now it all made sense. Being on telly is more powerful than anything you can snort, smoke or pop – point a camera in someone's face and hey presto! It's a miracle. A grumpy sod is transformed into a grinning idiot.

'Look, I'd better make a move. Some drunken guy's been brought in with a broken ankle and I've got to set up the cameras.'

Delilah's stomach did a quick flamenco. He was leaving. The horniest guy to ever drive north of Watford was about to do a disappearing act.

She tried to look cool. 'Sure, I'd better be making a move anyway.'

'Meeting up with some friends?'

'Yeh, we're going to this groovy new club in Leeds,' Delilah lied. Not convincingly.

'Oh, so you're a bit of a clubber?' He smiled at her as if they were members of an exclusive club. A club with only two members – Charlie and Delilah.

'I guess so . . .' *Clubber?* The nearest Delilah had been to a club in the last eighteen months was the golf club to watch Uncle Stan sing with his band. Still, she didn't want Charlie thinking she was completely unhip.

'So, do you ever come down to the clubs in London?' He cocked his head on one side and raised his eyebrows. Delilah felt as if she was dreaming. Perhaps she was getting crossed wires here, but he looked almost hopeful.

'Erm, no, but I'd love to.'

'Well, look,' Charlie reached into his back pocket, 'here's my card. If you're ever in London, look me up. I'll take you out and show you some great places around town.' He winked. 'And we can finish our chat.'

Delilah took the card. She ran her thumb over the expensive embossed lettering (definitely not a product of one of those design-your-own-card booths you find in train stations and bus terminals). 'Thanks,' she spluttered. Stringing a sentence together was difficult when your long intestine was doing the Riverdance. 'I just might take you up on that.'

'Please do.' Charlie smiled his deliciously crooked smile and turned to chat to the receptionist who, hoping she was going to be on telly, was now grinning like a Cheshire cat.

Delilah floated towards the exit.

'Catch you later, Delilah.'

Yes please, she thought, catching her breath. As they'd been chatting she'd mentally packed her bags and moved into his minimalist *Elle Decoration* loft in Soho. She could see herself now, wafting around in Calvin Klein undies, grating parmesan and placing daisies in little test-tube vases. Living the kind of life she'd dreamed about as she read those glossy magazines on the bus on her way to work. And then of course there was the man himself. Charlie was exciting. He worked in TV and spent his evenings at trendy clubs, not in front of the telly with a chicken vindaloo or propping up the bar with a pint and a packet of pork scratchings. He was gorgeous and funny and had *SEXY BASTARD* written all over his forehead. Delilah didn't usually imagine having sex with men she'd just met, but Charlie was different. She bet he'd be fabulous under the duvet as well, and she wouldn't mind finding out. Sex with Lenny had long since waned in enthusiasm and frequency. It had become a monthly chore, on a par with defrosting the fridge. Rest assured, carnal knowledge with Charles Mendes would involve a lot more than a bit of nipple tweaking and five minutes of fumbling in her knickers.

Delilah turned and waved. As she did, the ring fell out of her pocket and rolled into the drain, where it made a sad tinkling noise and vanished. She suddenly felt herself breaking into a grin. Who cared? She'd lost a ring but she'd finally found her balls – or, more to the point, she'd found somebody else's.

Chapter Three

It was Saturday and L'Escargot was packed with hordes of hungry shoppers, taking a break from blowing their wages at the high-street mall. Saturdays were always busy. Friday was pay day and instead of the usual McDonald's people liked to treat themselves to a slap-up lunch at a fancy restaurant. Unfortunately, this Saturday the restaurant was short-staffed, and Pascal hopped from one built-up heel to another, swearing and snapping irritably at what staff he did have. Namely Delilah, who walked around in a daze, mixing up orders, dropping cutlery, forgetting drinks. Not that she could help it. Her mind was on other things – Charlie. Since last night she hadn't been able to think of anything else – his pale-blue eyes, his sexy crooked grin, his casual invite to call him if she was ever in London.

In between courses she'd escape Pascal's foul temper and sneak into the cloakroom, grab her wallet, and lock herself into one of the cubicles in the ladies' loos. Sitting on the cold toilet seat, she'd take out Charlie's business card and run her fingers over the lettering, reading: *Charlie Mendes, LLB Productions, 163 Kensington Villas Road, Notting Hill, London W11,* and the digits of his telephone and mobile numbers, just to prove to herself that he had been for real, he really did exist and wasn't just a figment of her vivid imagination. He was somewhere – probably in Birmingham filming – right at that moment. She wondered if he was thinking about her. Last night she'd left the hospital determined to change things, dreaming of leaving Lenny and following Charlie to London. But that was last night, when her common sense had taken a back seat to her racing hormones. Now, in the bright lights of the ladies', she was having second thoughts. It was a crazy idea. Wasn't it?

'Delilah, is that you in there?' It was Amy, one of the waitresses, rapping on the door.

'Yeh, what's up?' Delilah hurriedly shoved Charlie's business card back into her wallet and rattled the loo-roll dispenser to add a touch of realism.

'It's Pascal, he's going nuts out there looking for you.'

Delilah muttered irritably. 'Tell him to sod off.'

Amy was shocked. At just seventeen this was her first job since leaving school and she treated Pascal as if he was her headteacher, even calling him sir. 'I can't do that,' she gasped, alarmed. Was Delilah being serious?

Delilah sighed wearily. 'Okay, tell him I'll be out in a minute.' She sat on the toilet seat, not wanting to budge, listening to Amy scuttling thankfully out through the swing door. Slipping her feet out of her shoes she leaned her head against the cubicle wall. The radiators were jammed on full power and the toilets were invitingly warm and smelled of a mixture of bleach and air freshener. Sleepily she closed her eyes and thought about Charlie. Funny, kind, sexy Charlie. His image juxtaposed sharply with the one of Lenny, who'd reappeared from the pub at midnight, pissed and peevish. He'd woken her up by stumbling loudly into the bedroom, switching on the light and collapsing onto the duvet reeking of Tetley's bitter and garlic naan bread. She'd watched him for a few moments, mouth hanging loosely open, snoring heavily, before grabbing a pillow and a spare blanket from the airing cupboard and going to spend the rest of the night in the uncomfortable single bed in the spare bedroom. He'd still been asleep when she'd left for work that morning.

Her head lolled forward and she was just on the brink of nodding off when her body jolted itself awake. She opened her eyes and forced herself to stand up – if she sat there any longer she really would get fired. Flushing the loo, she emerged from the cubicle and stared hard at her baggy-eyed reflection in the mirrors, lit with an unforgiving overhead bulb. A knackered twenty-seven-year-old, dressed in a bloody silly waitress uniform, stared back. Delilah frowned. She wasn't thrilled with her appearance at the best of times, but now she liked it even less.

Tying her hair into a ponytail she rummaged around in the bottom of her rucksack and applied a bit more black eyeliner. Pascal hated the waitresses to wear make-up. Good, she thought, smiling wickedly and adding two little black curls to the outer corner of each eye. He was already angry with her and this would annoy him even more. She was fed up with taking orders from Pascal, fed up with her poxy waitressing job. Scowling, she straightened her frilly pinafore. Quite frankly she felt like telling him to stuff his job up a duck à l'orange's arse.

'Delilah, what 'ave you been doing in there?' Pascal cornered her as she left the toilets. He stood, hands on hips next to the freezers, his head twitching up and down and side to side in agitation.

'Having a pee. What do you think?' snapped Delilah, letting the toilet door swing loudly behind her, dislodging the metal figure of a Victorian lady in a crinoline nailed to the door. It swung backwards and forwards, keeping time like a metronome.

Pascal sniffed. 'You are 'eading for trouble.' He picked a hair off his jacket sleeve and adjusted his cufflinks. 'If you are not very, very careful you will 'ave plenty of time to spend in zee toilets because you will not 'ave a job.' He threw back his head with a flourish and folded his arms, smug in his threat. 'And then what will you do?'

Delilah deliberated. Out of the corner of her eye, she could see Amy and the rest of the waitresses watching with bated breath at the kitchen door. For a split second she thought about backing down and apologising, but was stopped by an image of

Charlie which suddenly flashed into her mind. Gorgeous
Charlie with his exciting job in TV. She stared back at Pascal. 'I
don't know what I'll do, but anything has to be better than
working here.' Unfastening her pinny, she slowly folded it in
two, pressed her foot on the pedal of the wastebin so that the lid
sprang open, and calmly dropped it inside. 'The job's crap, the
money's terrible, but the food's even worse. Call yourself a
restaurant? It's all boil-in-the-bag and microwaved rubbish.'

Pascal's face seemed to shrivel up. He seemed to have difficulty in finding his tongue, which had disappeared into the
back of his throat. Perhaps it was for the best, as before he'd had
a chance to say one single French expletive – and he had a fine
repertoire – she'd turned, flicking her ponytail in his face, and
waltzed happily out of L'Escargot for ever.

It was only on the bus on the way home when the adrenalin
stopped pumping and Delilah floated down from her high, that
she realised what she'd done. It was all very well telling Pascal
to stick his job, but what now? Jobs weren't that easy to find, not
even waitressing ones. She sighed gloomily. She was supposed
to be meeting her Uncle Stan that evening at the Dog and
Duck. He and his wife were off to Benidorm to stay with some
friends they'd met there the year before – the doctor had said it
would help his arthritis – and they weren't due back until the
summer. He'd invited a few friends along for a farewell drink
– which, in Uncle Stan's language, meant getting completely
legless by last orders.

Delilah leaned against the window of the bus as it rattled its
way down the high street, past the ice rink that had closed years
ago but still had part of its name spelled out in bulbs; the Odeon
with a few people spilling out on the steps after the matinée;
Bombay Paradise, the large warehouse selling a thousand
different kinds of sari material. Ignoring the familiar buildings
she closed her eyes, a faint smile playing on her lips as she
thought about her uncle. He was her mum's big brother and
Delilah was the spitting image of him when he'd been younger.

Not that you'd see the resemblance now. He was as bald as a coot and as round as a barrel, with small, watery green eyes, ruddy cheeks and big fleshy ears. But it was his nose that was the *pièce de résistance*. Swollen and purple from years of downing pints of bitter and his favourite tipple – Scotch on the rocks – Delilah remembered being mesmerised by it as a child, staring up his hairy nostrils, inspecting the clusters of tiny veins that spread across it like a spider's web, marvelling at how it was shaped like a parsnip from repeatedly being broken when he was a teenager and trained as a featherweight boxer.

He was married to Shirley, a small sparrow of a woman who dyed her hair copper-red, wore too much face powder and smoked Benson & Hedges from one of those tortoiseshell cigarette holders. Shirley had pleated lips from a forty-year nicotine habit and during the day her lipstick would slowly seep upwards and outwards in the cracks, making her mouth look like a raspberry-pink ink spot. She'd met Stan when he'd turned up at her parents' house one winter's morning in 1959, a painter and decorator in paint-splattered overalls. He'd chatted her up as she'd made him cups of strong tea and offered him lemon slices, and asked her out on a date before the first coat of matt emulsion was even dry. Next year was their ruby wedding anniversary. Theirs had been a very happy marriage, despite their sadness when they realised they couldn't have children. Not that they'd ever felt sorry for themselves. Instead they'd compensated with a menagerie of stray dogs and a couple of tabby cats – and then of course there'd been Delilah.

They treated Delilah as the daughter they'd never had, taking her out, spoiling her with presents, giving her more love than any child would know what to do with. When she was little she'd spend hours at their house, playing happily with scraps of leftover wallpaper and pots of discarded paint, and as she'd grown up Uncle Stan had let her accompany him to odd jobs. She'd sit crosslegged on dustcovers, eating Aunt Shirley's corned-beef sandwiches and watching him transform houses into palaces of wallpaper and vinyl gloss, learning the art of painting a wall, creating a mood with different colours, or opening up a space. As a kid she didn't know what 'interior design' meant, she didn't even know it existed, but she knew all about colour and shape, space and light, and she knew that that was what she wanted to do when she grew up . . .

The Dog and Duck was busy. Saturday lunchtime stragglers who'd had one too many merged with early evening boozers. Delilah stood on tiptoes, straining her neck to see over heads and through the air hanging heavy with tobacco smoke and stale beer. She hoped Lenny wouldn't be there, but there was a pretty good chance that he would be. Stan had invited him too, and Lenny never turned down the excuse for a piss-up – not on a Saturday night.

She spotted Shirley round the side of the bar sipping a port and lemon and chatting to Vera the landlady. Glancing up, she caught sight of Delilah and waved her cigarette holder in the air. Delilah smiled and pushed past a rowdy group of teenage girls having a few drinks before they went out on the town. Despite the sub-zero temperatures outside, they were dolled up in tiny Lycra miniskirts and vest tops, their bare arms and legs white and goosepimpled.

'Hello, luv,' cooed Shirley, planting a raspberry-lipstick kiss on the side of her face. She smelled of hairspray and setting lotion. 'Your uncle will be chuffed you could make it.'

'Of course I could, do you think I'd let you both go to Spain without saying goodbye?' She smiled and gave Shirley a hug. God, Spain! Even her retired aunt and uncle had a more exciting life than she did.

'Dee, luv.' Uncle Stan appeared with an empty pint glass and patted her head with his large sandpapery hand. 'It's great to see you.' He beamed, slightly gassed, and patted her head again. 'You're looking luvely tonight. Isn't she looking luvely, Vera?' The landlady smiled and nodded, as Delilah flushed with embarrassment. When Stan was drinking, his compliments flowed as freely as the beer. He plonked his glass down on the sodden beer mat. 'Same again, luv, and whatever Dee and Shirl want.'

'Where's Lenny?' Shirley sucked on her cigarette holder and drained the last of her port, fishing out the slice of lemon and chewing the flesh from its rind.

'Oh, I'm not sure. I came straight from work,' answered Delilah vaguely. The last thing she needed right now was to be quizzed about Lenny's whereabouts. She prayed he'd stayed at home. Her prayers went unanswered.

'Lenny's here, look,' shouted Stan, waving heartily as Lenny appeared through the side entrance. 'Hello, son, what are you drinking?' He put his arm around Lenny's shoulder and beamed proudly. 'This 'ere lad is going to be part of the family soon, aren't you!' He winked over his shoulder at Delilah, who groaned inwardly. Stan was always trying to move things along when it came to her love life. As a teenager he'd vetted any boy she'd had a crush on and shared with her the wisdom of his courting experiences by giving her lots of advice on men and how to get the one you want. According to Stan it was the same as fishing: lots of patience and a little bit of skill.

'When are you going to make an honest woman of our Dee, then?'

Lenny looked up at Delilah and their eyes met. A mixture of sadness, regret and anger. 'You'll have to ask Dee that.' Lenny put her on the spot.

All eyes were on Delilah.

'Well?' Lenny stared at her. The question was loaded. He was giving her a second chance. It was now or never.

'Aren't we supposed to be celebrating Stan and Shirley's trip to Spain?' Ignoring both him and the question, Delilah turned pointedly to Shirley. 'What time's your flight tomorrow?' As Shirley happily launched into details of her holiday, Delilah saw Lenny's face set hard like cement and he grabbed his pint from the bar, downing it in one.

'You're thirsty, lad,' laughed Stan heartily, unaware of what had just occurred between Lenny and Delilah. ''Ere, have

Alexandra Potter

another.' He passed Lenny a pint of bitter that Vera had just pulled, its frothy head spilling over the side of the glass.

'Thanks, I need it,' he grunted, throwing Delilah his blackest look, before turning away to vent his anger and frustration on the fruit machines.

Vera flicked the light switch on and off to signal last orders. Delilah felt a surge of relief. It had been one of the longest nights in history. Five hours propped on a bar stool, drinking vodka and Coke and munching her way through an assortment of crisps, salted peanuts, Scotch eggs and ham and cheese sandwiches – courtesy of Vera, who always liked to put on a bit of a spread for special occasions. Stan was completely pie-eyed, as expected, and thoroughly enjoying himself. By 9 p.m. anyone under forty had headed off into town, leaving behind the regulars – middle-aged married couples and a couple of hard and fast drinkers who stood at the same spot all night, drinking until their money ran out or the pub shut, whichever was the sooner. Stan had spent the last couple of hours treating them to his rendition of 'When the Saints Go Marching In', one of his band's particular favourites, and belting out any other requests. Shirley accompanied him on the tambourine and invited people to sing along.

Lenny had sat in the corner all evening, chatting to Gary, an old mate from work, and deliberately ignoring Delilah. He couldn't have been more pissed off about her less than favourable reaction to his wedding proposal. It wasn't as if there was anything wrong with him or anything, in fact he knew plenty of women who'd jump at the chance to say yes. He'd got a decent job, a new car, and although he said it himself, he wasn't bad looking. But it wasn't good enough for her. That was the problem with Delilah, she was never satisfied. He blamed all those fancy glossy magazines she always had her nose buried in, they'd given her ideas above her station. Why else would she have changed towards him over the past few years? He didn't understand it. She'd been so grateful, so loving when he'd first taken her away from her dad's and she'd moved into his flat, but over the years she'd become different – indifferent. They'd grown apart, he did admit that, but that was her fault, not his. And okay, they didn't even have sex very often, but again that was her, not him. There was nothing wrong with him in that department. If only she'd just put a bit more effort into things they'd be fine. After all, he was nearly thirty and she wasn't that much younger, and they should start thinking about having kids. Isn't that what all women wanted anyway – marriage and kids? She should be over the moon . . .

He looked across at Delilah, who was staring into space, sipping her drink. She was always doing that, daydreaming with that stupid dopey look on her face. Disgruntled, he turned back to Gary and continued his conversation about how Bradford City was doing in the league.

Across the room, Delilah's mind had wandered back to Charlie. She could guarantee he'd be having a much better time than she was, that was sure. As Stan launched into 'Memories', she decided it was the signal to make a move and, interrupting his crescendo momentarily, she hugged them both tightly and said her goodbyes. She'd miss them.

'Lenny, I'm going home. Do you want to share a taxi?' Delilah stuck her hands in her pockets and avoided looking at Gary, who had obviously heard what had happened and was giving her dirty looks, doing his protective friend bit. Ironic, really, seeing as last New Year's Eve he'd spent all night telling her how she'd be much better off with him and had made a pass at her by waving a withered twig of mistletoe in her face and trying to force his tongue down her throat.

Lenny bent his head over his pint glass, refusing to look up. 'No, I think I'm going to head into town with Gary.' He drained the dregs from his glass.

Delilah bit her lip. As the evening had progressed she'd started feeling a bit guilty, but now she was annoyed. This was his way of punishing her. 'Fine,' she snapped, 'have a wonderful time.'

'Oh, I'll make sure he does, don't worry about that,' sneered Gary as she walked away. Biting her lip, she pushed open the door. After the damp boozy warmth of the pub, the cold night air hit her and, sniffing, she pulled up her collar. The door swung shut behind her, muffling the sound of Uncle Stan singing and Shirley's tambourine. Stepping out into the car park, she hailed one of the waiting minicabs.

Chapter Four

Delilah pressed her nose against the glass of her bedroom window. Monday morning and it was still raining. Bloody typical. It had started yesterday, just after she'd woken up and discovered Lenny hadn't come home. He'd probably crashed out at Gary's after going to a nightclub, still sulking and wanting her to worry, to wonder where he was. She'd stared at his side of the bed, empty and neat, and realised that she didn't care where he'd stayed, or who he'd stayed with. In fact she didn't care if or when he came home. Plumping up her pillow she'd pulled the duvet close and snuggled down deep into the bed, enjoying the sense of relief she'd found from finally admitting to herself that she didn't love him anymore.

She'd spent all Sunday mulling over her decision to leave Lenny. Although she'd finally realised she didn't love him, she was still leaving behind nearly ten years of a relationship. Was she doing the right thing? Or was she stark staring mad? As she'd eaten her cornflakes in front of the telly, watching the grinning presenters on some kids' TV programme, she'd even changed her mind. But then Lenny had telephoned to say he was spending the night at a friend's and they'd ended up having another argument. There was no getting away from it, their relationship was over.

Leaving Lenny was the right thing to do, it made sense. But did it make sense to leave her home, her life, and disappear off into the 'smoke' on a romantic whim? Was it crazy? Or was it an exercise in survival? She had no job, thanks to Saturday's run-in with Pascal; the only people she really cared about, Stan and

Shirley, had buggered off to Benidorm; and, to be completely honest, if she stayed she'd die of boredom. But if she left? Who knew? It was a gamble, it was terrifying, but on the other hand it was also bloody exciting. Meeting Charlie had injected a massive rush of excitement, and she was giddy for more. If she wanted him she had to do something – and now. Delilah's mind raced as her life stood still at an imaginary set of traffic lights. They'd been red for as long as she could remember. Only she could make them change to green.

She'd made her decision, pulled her battered khaki suitcase from the top of her wardrobe and, grabbing a handful of clothes from their coathangers, squashed them inside. Piles of M&S underwear fell out of upturned drawers, shoes were stuffed into plastic bags, and with a sweep of her hand an embarrassing assortment of Boots mascaras and crumbling blushers were cleared from the bathroom cabinet. In under ten minutes, Delilah had packed her life into one suitcase, a holdall and five Tesco carriers.

She stopped, noticing her breathing was rapid, nervous, exhilarated. She laughed with relief – the hard part was over. There was just one last thing. On her hands and knees she reached under the bed and dragged out a battered leather case – her most treasured possession in the whole world – and flicked the scratched brass catches. The lid sprang open, revealing thirty-four Tom Jones records, their edges scuffed and split.

Delilah ran her hand gently over them, breathing in their familiar musky scent. If she closed her eyes she could see her mum now, ironing in front of the telly, her hair in curlers, singing along with Tom Jones, who was belting out his classic 'What's New, Pussycat?' on the radio. Delilah smiled at the memory. Her beloved mum Margaret, divorcée, legal secretary and number one Tom Jones fan, would always be singing that song. At twenty-eight she'd been walking home from work when, in less time than it takes to say Margaret Louise Holdsworth, she'd been hit by an articulated lorry and had gone for ever. It had been Delilah's ninth birthday and she'd arrived home from school full of anticipation to find a silent house, a kitchen table full of unwrapped presents and a blue E.T. birthday cake in the fridge.

In that split second her brief, idyllic childhood had been shattered, smashed into as many pieces as her mother's body, but she'd never once cried. Not even on another grey, windy Monday morning, when she'd stood in the cemetery, a small pathetic figure in a red duffle coat and long white socks, holding Uncle Stan's hand and watching a wooden box with shiny brass handles being lowered slowly into the rain-soaked grave and covered with shovels of earth. Not even when the authorities refused Stan and Shirley's pleas to adopt her and she was forced to go and live with her dad, a stranger with funny sideburns, and his new wife, domineering Sandra, a Tupperware-party organiser who didn't like kids, especially nine-year-old daughters of dead first wives. She'd spent her childhood wishing she could find a way to escape, until one day she did: under the guise of a driving instructor in a beige Mini Metro – Lenny.

For a little girl who'd always imagined (as she huddled under the duvet reading Enid Blyton by torchlight) that she'd be rescued by the proverbial knight in shining armour, it wasn't quite what she'd had in mind. But at seventeen, a twenty-something guy with his own flat (albeit rented) and a set of wheels wasn't to be passed up. So, after telling Sandra exactly where she could put her Tupperware, she left without a backward glance.

Now she was leaving again. She made a few phone calls, leaving messages on friends' answering machines: she didn't want the hassle of being told she was a deranged lunatic. In fact she felt more normal than ever before. If being infatuated with a guy you hardly know and having a half-crazy plan to track him down was normal.

As for Lenny, she decided against writing a farewell note – it was too much the stuff of cheesy B-movies and Aaron Spelling soaps. She had to say goodbye in person. She owed him that at least.

Throwing the last of her luggage under the bonnet of her rusting green Beetle, she grabbed Fatso, her spaghetti-thin whippet, and climbed into the driver's seat. Turning the ignition key, the car spluttered noisily to life, belching out large clouds of black smoke. She paused before trying to put the car into first gear – the bloody clutch was going. 'Shit,' she cursed, wishing she'd asked Lenny to fix it. Still, it was a bit late for that. She set off with a jerk, making sure not to look back. She'd learnt that lesson a long time ago.

Forty Winks looked empty as Delilah entered through the automatic doors, setting off the irritating *A Team*-theme bell that alerted Lenny to customers. There was no sign of him which was a bit strange. Lenny was never one to miss a sale – he'd live in the showroom if he thought it meant selling a few more mattresses. She climbed down the few steps which led around to the back office. Still no sign. She was about to turn back when she heard mumbled voices coming from the loading bay. 'Give it some throttle, baby.'

Delilah wrinkled her forehead. That was odd. It almost sounded as if Lenny was giving one of his occasional driving lessons. He liked to keep his hand in, said it earned him a bit of beer money.

'Mmm, yeh, give it some more, give it some more.'

She peered around the corner of the drinks machine. It wasn't quite what she'd expected. In the middle of the concrete floor, lying spreadeagled on a brand new, plastic-covered mattress, was Lenny; stark bollock naked apart from his deck shoes. Straddled across him was June, his nineteen-year-old receptionist, wearing a pink frilly suspender belt and one of those adhesive red and white L-plates stuck, like a billposter, to one of her buttocks.

'Ooh, baby, pump it, pump it.'

June let out a large grunt and became enthusiastically engaged in a series of hand signals that certainly weren't in any Highway Code book Delilah had ever seen. Her bottom wobbled as she pumped up and down with gusto, Lenny's knees wrapped around her back, his arms flailing.

'Lenny?'

He immediately stopped thrashing around: 'Delilah?'

His voice was muffled by June's double-D chest which spilled out over his face. He craned his neck to look at Delilah, who was rooted to the spot in the middle of the loading bay, taking in a full view of the gyrating couple.

'Stop, stop,' he hissed to June, who was oblivious to her audience. 'June, stop. It's Delilah.'

June came to a sudden halt. Lenny struggled to sit up and looked at Delilah, his expression similar to that of a rabbit caught in the headlights of a car. 'I can explain everything.'

Was this a set-up? Was a grinning Noel Edmonds about to jump out from behind a bedhead and cheer, 'You've been gotcha'd'? Delilah stared in disbelief at Lenny, ruddy cheeked and sweating profusely, wedged underneath June's gargantuan pink thighs. Lenny, her Lenny, was having it off with another woman. If she hadn't seen it with her own eyes she would never have believed it.

Suddenly her goodbye speech seemed rather inept. Lenny obviously wasn't going to be heartbroken – or lonely.

'I came to tell you I'm leaving—' She stopped, it was difficult to concentrate. Even though she didn't love Lenny anymore, she was still affected by the sight of him naked with another woman. She cleared her throat, determined that Lenny wasn't going to rob her of her right to do the dumping, and continued. 'I was going to say how sorry I was and how I didn't want you to be upset, but under the circumstances . . .' Delilah's voice trailed off. She'd rehearsed her speech in the car – how she'd calm him down, tell him it wasn't his fault but how they'd grown apart, how she was sorry but it was for the best – but now it all seemed a bit limp. Rather, she imagined, like Lenny's dick.

'You're leaving?' he gasped, still pinned to the mattress by June, who had been chasing her boss for months and, now she had him in her grasp, was refusing to budge. 'But why?'

Delilah couldn't believe it. Lenny had been caught cheating with his teenage receptionist, and he was the one demanding an explanation! She shook her head. He had a cheek. And bare-faced, by the look of it.

'It's not what you think. This isn't an affair, it's the first time. I was just upset about your reaction to my proposal, and the ring and everything. It doesn't mean anything to me, Dee, it was just sex,' he gabbled desperately as June glared down at him.

Delilah didn't know whether he was telling the truth or not. But did it matter? She was leaving anyway. 'It's not you, Lenny, it's me. I'm off to find a new life. Something different. Something exciting.' She started walking away. She didn't feel like arguing. Especially not when he was flat underneath his receptionist. Anyway, what was there to argue about? It was over, and long before she'd caught him with June.

'Dee . . . wait,' wailed Lenny. His thrilling affair suddenly wasn't so thrilling. 'I can be exciting, Dee. I can be something different.' Lenny felt desperate. He started to shiver, a pathetic figure underneath an indignant and unbudgeable June: a lamb to the slaughter. He suddenly felt as trapped as Delilah had.

Delilah closed the door behind her, setting off the automatic jingle again. She didn't feel hurt, or jealous. After all she'd been having imaginary sex with Charlie all weekend. It just so happened Lenny had gone one step further. In fact, she was secretly pleased. By being caught without his trousers Lenny had taken away any guilt she had for leaving, any doubts that she'd had about her decision. Ironically, Lenny had done her one big favour. His infidelity had set her free.

Chapter Five

Whoever thought to describe hell as the flame-ridden innards of the earth had obviously never been on the M1. To do this journey, alone except for a weak-bladdered whippet, in the confines of a twenty-year-old Beetle with a maximum speed of 60 mph, is the stuff horror movies are made of.

At Nottingham, Delilah's hunger pangs caused her to brave a motorway service station's 'All Day Breakfast': a plate of bullet-proof beans, soggy bread, and eggs that had been beaten to death rather than scrambled. It was a rather queasy Delilah that continued the journey. At Leicester the radio went on the blink and she was forced to block out the deafening roar of the engine by humming a Tom Jones medley while Fatso howled along as a backing singer. By the Watford Gap the skies had opened. With windscreen wipers that had trouble clearing a slight drizzle, she found herself bent double, nose squashed against the windscreen, in an attempt to see the juggernauts in front. It was a frustrated Delilah who crawled the rest of the way into London.

Once in the thick of the metropolis, Delilah decided to go with the flow of traffic. Directions had never been her strong point and she gave up trying to find the address on Charlie's business card, happily dispensing with futile map reading and choosing to cruise along, occasionally taking the odd right turn (due to having only one indicator that worked). It wasn't long before it became apparent that she was entering a 'des res' neighbourhood. Lanky white buildings with fancy iron railings lined the roadside. Delilah turned the corner and parked behind a huge Jeep with four-foot-high tractor tyres and vicious-looking bars wrapped around the headlights. So this was how to deal with all that traffic, she thought: an armoured tank.

The Beetle shuddered to a halt and she sat still for a moment, staring out of her side window, watching people walking down the street – couples linking arms, gangs of teenagers in denim jackets and tracksuits, men with briefcases and umbrellas. She caught sight of the white and black street-name, nailed high up on the house on the corner: Pembridge Road W11. It was the same postcode that was printed on Charlie's business card. She looked at her reflection in her rear-view mirror and smiled to herself. It was too much of a coincidence – it had to be fate. Buoyed with feelings of destiny and anticipation she looked across at Fatso, snoring faintly on the floor of the passenger seat.

'Come on, let's go and get some coffee.'

Picking him up, she hid him under her jacket and set off in no particular direction through a maze of tiny streets. Intrigued, she walked past glass-fronted restaurants full of middle-aged people, kinky food-voyeurs who seemed only too delighted to pay vast amounts for the privilege of being able to eat while being gawped at by passers-by. Delilah smiled, amused at the idea of her neighbours back in Bradford pulling back their net curtains so the whole street could watch as they tucked into their dinner.

Marvelling at the huge five-storey houses, she listened to the different music that wafted from individual flats, Frank Sinatra intermingling with Elvis, acid jazz with reggae. There was a gust of cold wind and Delilah shivered, pulling her jacket closer around her. Turning the corner she found herself in a larger main road and walked towards a cluster of shops. In the middle was a small café, its windows steamed up and white paint peeling off the door frame, above which the words 'Café Prima Donna' were painted. The door jangled as she pushed it open. Inside was tiny, filled with white plastic chairs and tables and a long counter that ran along the right-hand side. There was a strong smell of coffee and cigarette smoke. In one corner, a group of Rastafarians with waist-length dreadlocks played cards, in the other, a group of girls with bleached blonde hair sipped milky coffee from tall glasses and dragged heavily on cigarettes.

'What would you like?'

Delilah turned to see a shaven-headed, twenty-something guy behind the counter. He was smiling broadly at her and wiping a large battle-scarred chopping board. She smiled back. It was difficult not to.

'Oh, just a coffee.'

'Cappuccino . . . ?'

'Er, no, just a plain coffee, you know, black, without milk.' Cappuccinos were such a con. They used to serve them at L'Escargot: cups full of froth with a bit of chocolate sprinkled on top. What was the point? Delilah ran on caffeine like a car runs on petrol. She needed at least six big cups of strong black coffee a day, preferably instant. Pascal used to call her a philistine, but she didn't care. As far as she was concerned there was nothing quite like breaking the gold seal on a new jar of coffee, inhaling the smell and digging a teaspoon into the millions of freeze-dried granules.

Shaved Head grinned even wider. 'Anything to eat?'

Delilah looked at the large chalkboard behind his head: sundried this, sun-ripened that – they obviously had better summers in London than they did in Yorkshire.

'Can you do just a cheese roll?'

Shaved Head laughed. 'Yeh, sure, Italian mozzarella, Greek haloumi or Swiss Emmental?'

'How about English cheddar?' she said, slightly irritated. What was this? Name the cheeses of the world?

He began energetically buttering a baguette and Delilah noticed he had very freckly forearms that flexed with each sweep of his knife. He was wearing an oversized diving watch and a thick silver bangle that rattled rhythmically against the counter. She looked at his face. His tongue rested between his teeth as he concentrated on peeling off thin slices of cheese. He had a nice face. You could almost say he was good-looking in a funny, freckly kind of way.

'Anything for your friend?' He was staring at her chest.

Delilah jumped. She followed his gaze. Fatso was peeping from beneath her jacket. Out of the corner of her eye she could see the red and white NO PETS sign glowering on the door. She made an attempt at bravado, 'No thanks, we can share.'

Shaved Head winked and lowered his voice. 'It's okay. I'm a dog lover.'

She smiled. Maybe this guy wasn't so bad.

'Take a seat. I'll bring your food over.'

Delilah grabbed her coffee, a fistful of sugar sachets and plonked herself next to the curved fifties Coca-Cola machine.

The fluorescent light flickered above her. She stared at it, reminded of the time Tupperware Sandra warned her of the dangers of strobe lights at discos. What was it she had said? They made you blind, faint or throw up. Delilah tutted. Stupid cow.

'Here's your sandwich.'

Delilah took her eyes off the ceiling to see Shaved Head putting a plate on the table and pulling up a chair. 'Thanks.' She took a bite and chewed, trying to focus. The room was doing a great impression of being pissed and had started to slowly swirl.

'Are you okay?'

'Yeh, fine.' She clutched the table. She did feel a bit queasy actually.

'I'll get you some water.' He stood up.

Delilah tried to smile, but couldn't make out his face. His eyes had shifted, Picasso-style, into an abstract mixture of mouth and nose, a huge face of blurred proportions. She stood up but felt herself lurching forward, banging Fatso, who wriggled free from her jacket, yelping. Lashing out her arms she tried, and failed, to keep her balance and crashed into the Coke dispenser, sliding with comic grace down the plastic chair and disappearing under the table.

A tongue was licking her lips. Rapid, darting licks, moving over her eyelids, her cheekbones, tickling her ear. Delilah let out a slight moan. 'Mmmmm.' She wriggled. The tongue was moving playfully down to her neck.

'Charlie?' she murmured, holding out her hand, expecting to feel the brush of stubble against her fingers. Instead she felt a very wet, very long nose.

She opened her eyes. 'Fatso!'

Fatso's stringy body wiggled excitedly, his tail whipping back and forth against her legs.

'He looks pleased to see you.' A voice came from across the room.

Delilah wiped her saliva-soaked face with the back of her sleeve and propped herself up on her elbows. She was lying on a sheepskin rug on the floor of a small kitchen and could see out into the café. It was empty.

Shaved Head stood in the doorway looking concerned.

'What happened?' she asked.

'You fainted . . . it must have been the food.' He laughed nervously.

Delilah shakily tried to stand up.

'Hey, take it easy.' Stepping forward, he grabbed her. 'You've had a nasty fall. Don't rush things.'

'God, I'm so sorry – how embarrassing.' Delilah held onto his bare forearm and gingerly eased herself onto a faded velvet armchair.

'Hey, it's no problem. Look, stay here and I'll get you a hot drink. Do you fancy a cup of tea?'

She rubbed the large lump that had erupted on the back of her head. 'As long as it's PG Tips.'

'My name's Sam, by the way.' He smiled kindly and handed her a large mug of tea.

'Mine's Delilah.' She sipped her tea and eyed him cautiously. He was wearing an old surfing T-shirt with some kind of Day-Glo logo that had started peeling off, a pair of holey old Levi's and a stripy pinny. He seemed nice but you could never tell. After all, he was a complete stranger – and she was sat by herself with him in the kitchen. How many sex maniacs have you seen in the paper and thought were good looking?

'Groovy name. Good job I don't have any hair.' He rubbed his Number 1-razor cut and leaned against the stainless steel sink.

Delilah ignored the pun – how many times had she heard *that* line.

'So you live around here?'

She stirred her tea, concentrating on crushing sugar cubes with her teaspoon. 'No, I've just moved down from Yorkshire.'

'Oh, how long ago?'

Delilah watched the last of the sugar dissolve. 'Tonight.'

'Tonight?' Sam's voice lurched upwards.

'Yep.' She took a large slurp of tea. 'I didn't exactly get off to a good start, did I?'

Sam rubbed his chin, which sprouted a smattering of blonde fuzz, and creased his forehead.

'Dare I ask where you're staying?'

'You can ask, but I can't answer.'

'You mean you haven't fixed up anywhere?'

'Well . . .' Delilah's voice trailed off as she pictured Charlie's imaginary penthouse loft. '. . . Not exactly.'

Sam dug his hands deep into the apron slung low around his hips. 'So you've got nowhere to kip tonight?'

Delilah contemplated lying. She didn't want this guy to get the wrong idea. After all, she'd heard all about what blokes from down south thought about girls from up north. And she had just fallen at his feet, so to speak. She glanced at his feet. He was wearing sandals. Brown leather sandals *with buckles*. Somehow he didn't seem like a sex maniac. How many sex maniacs wore sandals? She decided to come clean.

'Nope, I don't know where I'm staying. I guess I'll find myself a B&B or something until I sort a few things out.' In other words, until she tracked down Charlie.

He laughed. 'This isn't Blackpool, you know. There aren't any guesthouses in Notting Hill.'

Delilah bristled. Sam obviously thought she was of the cloth cap and clogs stereotype from 'oop north' who had never been further south than Sheffield. She clenched her teeth. 'Yeh, I know, I meant a hotel.'

Sam realised he'd touched a nerve. He watched as Delilah fiddled with her hair like a stroppy teenager. 'I'm sorry, I didn't mean to offend you or anything.'

She smiled forgivingly. He was okay, in fact he seemed rather sweet.

He bent down and stroked Fatso. 'Look, I've got a friend you can stay with. Her name's Vivienne and she's pretty mad, but she's got a good heart and a spare room. You can stay there for a few days, just until you sort yourself out.'

Delilah wasn't sure. She'd imagined herself arriving in London, checking into a hotel and abusing the minibar before calling a delighted-to-hear-from-you-I-must-take-you-to-dinner-at-my-place-immediately Charlie. She didn't want to be staying in some mad woman's spare room. She rubbed the back of her head, which had begun to throb. There was no doubt about it, she had, quite literally, come down to earth with a bump.

But perhaps this was fate. The proposal. The ring. June. The address. Even that bloody strobe light. She'd got this far by taking a risk, why not take another one? After all, a hotel would make a large hole in her savings, and, mad or not, if this friend of Sam's had a spare room it would be a free place for her to stay for a couple of nights – just until she got in touch with Charlie.

'If she doesn't mind, that would be great. I'm sure I'll get things sorted in no time and then I'll be out of your hair.'

Sam smiled. 'If I had any.'

It was a corny joke, but Delilah laughed. And once she'd started she couldn't stop. She lay back in the armchair and felt the tension release, like steam from a pressure cooker, in long, loud, gurgling belly laughs – the kind of laughs that leave you with a nagging stitch and smudged eyeliner.

Sam watched, grinning, as Delilah threw back her head and giggled loudly, wiping her watering eyes with the cuff of her sleeve. Who was this crazy, fainting Yorkshirewoman? Why had she suddenly descended on Notting Hill with a scrawny looking dog? And who the hell was Charlie? He watched her until she eventually stopped laughing and looked up at him, smiling broadly, her eyes creasing up at the sides and a small dimple appearing in the side of her cheek, and decided to leave his questions for later. There was something that told him he'd be seeing a lot more of Delilah, something that told him this was only the beginning.

Chapter Six

'I have two lovers – Harold, a sixty-two-year-old ex-brigadier general, and Dwayne, a teenage bricklayer from Shepherd's Bush, who's six feet of biceps and Arsenal tattoos.'

Vivienne paused and took a long drag from her cigarette.

'But now that Harold's discovered Viagra, the bugger has become incredibly demanding. And quite frankly I'm completely exhausted by the time I see Dwayne.'

Delilah nodded politely. She was sitting in Vivienne's kitchen drinking some disgusting-tasting herbal tea while her hostess merrily divulged the gory details of her weekly shagging rota. Sam hadn't been exaggerating when he'd said that Vivienne was slightly eccentric, but what he'd failed to mention was that she wasn't just mad, she was sex mad.

They'd met half an hour ago when Sam, not wanting to waste any time, had made a quick phone call and then escorted Delilah to a large end-of-terrace house not far from Café Prima Donna. Pretty impressive, she thought as Sam lifted open the gate, which had fallen off its hinges, and she followed him up the pathway, made of thousands of tiny black and white marble squares. Two large pillars shouldered the imposing front door. It reminded her of the White House. She started to feel slightly nervous. What was Vivienne going to be like? Visions of a Hillary Clinton lookalike came to mind. To calm her nerves she counted the number of doorbells arranged in a neat line: eight.

After a moment's deliberation, Sam pushed one of the bells, setting off a series of lights and twitching curtains. Loud footsteps could be heard from inside, and after the sound of a dozen locks being turned and bolts being pulled back the door opened and an attractive blonde in her early thirties appeared. She was clad in a full-length quilted coat, Rupert-the-Bear yellow and black scarf and huge pre-1980 yeti boots. Delilah was surprised – Vivienne wasn't anything like she'd expected. She suddenly realised she was staring.

Noisily, Vivienne air-kissed Sam on each cheek, while eyeing Delilah suspiciously. 'The central heating has decided to commit suicide,' she drawled in a rasping baritone, 'hence the attire.' Then, with a theatrical sweep of her hand, she stood to one side. 'You must be the homeless northerner – please enter my humble abode.'

Sam quickly made his excuses and, after promising to call, disappeared, leaving Delilah clutching Fatso and feeling like a five-year-old on her first day at school. Nervously she followed Vivienne down a long narrow hallway painted a vicious lime green, stepping over an assault course of newspapers and magazines, until they entered her flat, and came into the kitchen. 'Excuse the mess,' boomed Vivienne, moving half-filled glasses and overflowing ashtrays to clear a space on the table. 'I had a small gathering here last night.' She paused to remove an empty condom packet that had been speared onto a corkscrew. 'Unfortunately the cleaner doesn't come until Friday.'

Determined not to appear as nervous as she felt, Delilah plonked herself down on a particularly itchy hessian-covered bar stool, ignoring Fatso, who sniffed the skirting boards whimpering, until he fell into a greedy silence at the discovery of remnants of a wild-mushroom risotto under the table. Meanwhile, Vivienne quickly brewed some kind of piss-weak herbal tea and without any introduction immediately launched into a monologue that moved swiftly from biscuits – 'Try one. They're wheat-free, gluten-free, dairy-free and sugar-free – but unfortunately not calorie-free' – to the merits of having sex with a geriatric: 'His gratitude is so touching.' It was a good twenty minutes before she eventually paused for breath.

'So are you Sam's bit on the side?'

Delilah choked on her ingredient-free cookie.

'Not that it's any of my business . . .' Vivienne's voice trailed off in an attempt at indifference, but her body gave her away. She was perched like a cat on the edge of her stool, waiting to catch any juicy titbits of gossip.

'No, of course not,' protested Delilah, feeling slightly affronted. 'I only met Sam a couple of hours ago when I fainted in his café.'

Vivienne nodded, raising her eyebrows in a I-don't-believe-a-word-of-it expression.

Despite only just meeting her, Delilah felt the need to justify herself to Vivienne. 'I'm actually in London to meet someone.'

Vivienne's eyebrows shot up two inches further, disappearing under her fringe.

'His name's Charlie.'

Vivienne fixed her with a stare and pursed her lips. Delilah felt like an orange being squeezed for every drop of information.

'And he's a TV producer.'

She felt strange talking about Charlie. It was the first time she'd told someone he existed. Until that moment Charlie had been her secret. Now she was sharing him with Vivienne. Still, it wasn't as if Vivienne knew her, or she knew Vivienne. Telling her was like telling a stranger – it didn't really count.

But Vivienne did react. She gripped the table in a sudden flurry of excitement, her bony knuckles stretched white. 'A TV producer! Good grief, girl. A media male is *the* accessory. Where on earth did you find him?'

'Bradford.'

'Bradford?'

'In a hospital.'

'A hospital?' Vivienne seemed to have lost her own vocabulary, and resorted to using Delilah's.

'We met in Casualty.'

Vivienne banged her fist on the table. 'I knew it. You're an actress.'

'An actress?' Now it was Delilah's turn to echo in disbelief. (The idea that someone thought she was an actress was akin to being mistaken for a member of All Saints.)

'Didn't you just say you met on that ghastly hospital drama on television?'

Vivienne was a snob, but Delilah couldn't help being amused by her assumption. 'No, I said *in* Casualty, not on it. I'm talking about Bradford General, not *Casualty* the TV programme.'

Vivienne looked disappointed. Leaning forward across the table she narrowed her eyes and peered closely at Delilah. 'So what are you, then?'

Delilah felt as if she was some kind of unnamed species, never before witnessed by the double-duvet-clad Vivienne. She briefly entertained the idea of making up some exotic occupation before her stubborn streak rose to the surface. Why tell lies? There was no need to feel ashamed. What was wrong with being an out-of-work waitress?

She leaned towards Vivienne, until she was an inch away from her nose. 'Unemployed.'

For the first time, Vivienne unpursed her bright ketchup-red lips and flashed a wicked smile. 'Join the club, girl. We're all unemployed. Except us Notting Hill residents like to describe ourselves as being freelance.'

Delilah leaned back, surprised by Vivienne's reaction. 'Why?'

'*Why?*' Vivienne stubbed out her cigarette in her teacup and swiftly lit up another. 'Darling, saying you're unemployed sounds boring and is boring. Being freelance, however, is all to do with anticipation. It's rather like being at an airport terminal. You do a lot of sitting around and drinking cappuccinos. But instead of waiting for your flight to be called you're waiting for your mobile to ring.' To add emphasis, Vivienne theatrically waved her arms around in the air, scattering her ash into Delilah's herbal tea. 'And of course it does ring. But it's always one of your friends – another freelancer. Which is a bloody relief, as nobody actually wants to do any work. In fact, the thought of a real job is highly alarming.'

Delilah picked the ash out of her tea. Vivienne's flamboyant energy was draining. She sneaked a look at her watch. Less than five minutes had passed since the last time she looked. She was tired. Concentrating on what Vivienne was saying was difficult when her mind was a whirling collage of images: June in her frilly suspenders, Lenny's frightened expression, Sam grinning in his sandals . . . Could it really all have happened in one day? The last twenty-four hours felt like twenty-four years. She tried, unsuccessfully, to stifle a yawn.

'I'll show you to your room. You must be tired.'

'No, I'm fine,' Delilah half-heartedly protested, but her bleary eyes gave her away.

'You poor darling,' tutted Vivienne, 'I only have to take a five-minute tube ride and I'm simply dying with fatigue. Still, you northerners are renowned for your hardy constitutions. Just look at Cathy and Heathcliff – all that running around on the moors.'

Delilah smiled. For some reason it was impossible to feel annoyed with her new lunatic landlady. Despite her nosiness, her rudeness and blatant snobbery, she rather liked Vivienne with her weird clothes and weird relationships. After a lifetime of normality, weird felt good. It felt unpredictable. And it definitely wasn't boring. Vivienne stood up, balancing her cigarette precariously at the corner of her mouth, and tightened her scarf. 'Follow me,' she barked in brigadier tones.

Delilah's room was at the back of the flat. It was tiny, and most of the space was filled with an impressive four-poster bed. Heavy brocade curtains were juxtaposed with a large black record player which stood next to the window, encased in fake-wood-panelled units. It was a peculiar mix of antique and late-seventies flat-pack furniture.

Delilah put down her carrier bags and went to look out of a sash window. It had started to spit with rain. The street below was busy with people, umbrellas and black cabs and she was comforted to see her Beetle tucked away in Vivienne's drive. Being unusually intuitive, Vivienne realised that Delilah wanted to be alone. Saying goodnight, she was just about to leave when she stopped in the doorway. 'There's just one question I must ask.' Delilah stopped looking out onto the street and turned to face Vivienne. 'Yes?'

'When am I going to have the pleasure of meeting this Charlie?'

Delilah felt her nerve-endings tingle at the sound of his name. She paused to push back a piece of stray hair that had fallen in front of her eyes. 'I've got to meet him first.'

'What? He's not expecting you?' Vivienne's eyes flashed, intrigued.

'Well, not exactly.' Delilah cast her mind back to Charlie's invitation to finish their chat. 'I need to call him.'

Vivienne rummaged inside her duvet coat and pulled out a mobile phone. 'Here.'

Delilah stared at the small black Nokia in Vivienne's palm. She suddenly felt nervous. This was the reason she was in London. This phone call was something she'd rehearsed a hundred times in her head. Now it was going to happen for real she hesitated, then chickened out. 'It's late, I'll call tomorrow.'

'Suit yourself.' Vivienne put her phone back in her pocket. 'But don't leave it too late, the good ones always get snapped up.' She raised her eyebrows knowingly and closed the door behind her, leaving Delilah alone with Fatso.

Delilah chewed her lip. Why hadn't she taken the opportunity to call him? Why hadn't she just dialled the number and said hello? She realised that she felt more nervous than she liked to admit. Pulling Charlie's card out from her wallet she ran her finger over the lettering. 'I'll call tomorrow,' she repeated, trying to convince herself that it was no big deal. But it was. Tomorrow was the your-life-is-going-to-change-for-ever day. She lay on the bed and snuggled up to Fatso, who lay curled tightly next to her. 'Tomorrow,' she murmured, and fell asleep to the sound of Fatso's rhythmical snoring.

Chapter Seven

Delilah opened her eyes. For a moment she thought she was dreaming. The room was both strange and yet pleasantly familiar – and wasn't that Tom Jones's voice she could faintly hear singing 'What's New, Pussycat?'? Suddenly her memory kicked in. Of course, she was in Vivienne's spare room, but where was the music coming from? She stumbled out of bed, treading on Fatso, who gave a disgruntled growl. 'Sorry.' Delilah bent down and kissed his wet, navy-black nose. He licked her cheek to show her that he accepted her apology. 'It's just you and me, boy, isn't it?' she whispered, gently stroking his soft, floppy ears. Somehow he made everything seem less strange, less frightening. She stood up, catching her reflection in the full-length mirror attached to the back of the door. It wasn't pleasant.

She needed a shower and she needed some fresh clothes. She'd slept in yesterday's outfit. She peeped her head around into the hall. There were three doors. Each one could be concealing the bathroom. But which one? Delilah shuddered. She didn't fancy taking pot luck. There was the possibility she might happen upon Vivienne, head-to-toe in a nurse's uniform.

She decided not to risk it. 'Sod it,' she thought, rummaging through her holdall. She quickly changed into her favourite pair of faded jeans that had started to go threadbare on the knees, and an old V-necked jumper that was two sizes too small. She looked at her reflection. She looked about eight years old. It wasn't exactly the look she'd had in mind for her first day in the fashion capital of the world.

She grabbed her make-up bag. 'You need a bit of slap, girl,' she muttered, squeezing a liberal amount of tinted moisturiser onto her fingertips. She rubbed it vigorously into her cheeks, making sure to avoid the orange tide-mark jaw and white neck favoured by women working in the make-up section of department stores. She wanted to look as if she'd got her fabulous suntan from two weeks in the South of France, not from the Boots counter in Bradford. Next, she used a very blunt and scratchy lipliner to create her best pout, and finally, three generous coats of mascara to construct lashes worthy of Barbara Cartland. Leaning closer to the mirror she blew herself a kiss, inspecting the final result. She grimaced. The effect was more Jerry Springer than Jerry Hall. She looked like a man in drag. Despite years of painstakingly following magazine tips on how to apply the perfect face she'd never quite got the hang of it. Bloody make-up, she thought as she reached for a tissue. There was nothing else for it. She was going to have to settle for barefaced cheek this morning. She squirted the tissue with baby oil and wiped the whole lot off in smeary stripes.

Tom Jones was still belting out the track at ghetto-blaster volume. Delilah stood in the hallway, her head cocked to one side and her nose in the air, doing her best Bisto-kid impression. It sounded as if the music was coming from the kitchen. She padded on tiptoe towards the door and pushed it open.

Delilah stared. Vivienne, dressed in a canary-yellow kimono, her hair piled high in fluorescent bendy rods, was screeching along to Tom Jones. In one hand she held a milk carton as if it was a microphone and in the other a bowl of cereal. She stopped when she saw Delilah and waved, spilling milk onto the wooden floorboards.

'Delilah, darling!' She rushed towards her, skidding slightly on the large white milky puddle, and kissed her on each cheek, leaving behind soggy Rice Krispies and a whiff of perfume. 'I hope you don't mind. I found your record collection and I do so love this sexy little Welshman.'

Delilah went white as she caught sight of her Tom Jones collection. Empty album sleeves lay scattered over the sofa and records were piled high on the cushions. The stereo was open: Tom Jones was spinning at 33 rpm. Her precious, irreplaceable record collection . . .

'Jesus Christ, Vivienne!' Delilah rushed over to the stereo and quickly lifted the needle from the record. The room suddenly fell silent. She delicately removed the shiny black vinyl and blew the dust away from the tracks. Her heart thudded in her ears. She'd never forgive herself if anything happened to these records. They had been her mum's pride and joy and apart from a few photos and a couple of bits of jewellery, they were all she had left to remember her by. When she played the records, every lyric, every crackle, every scratch brought memories of her mum flooding back, turned everything back to the 1970s. She could be feeling sad, or pissed off, or completely depressed, but as soon as she took out one of the records, eased it out of its sleeve, placed it on the turntable and turned up the volume, everything was all right again.

After inspecting the record for any new scratches, Delilah was relieved to see that no harm had been done. But now the crisis was over, her feelings of panic were replaced with ones of anger. Looking up, she glared at Vivienne. 'Don't ever touch these again. Do you understand?' Her voice was shaking and Vivienne looked startled. 'They were given to me by someone special and I don't know what I'd do if anything happened to them.'

Vivienne was in shock. Trembling, she wiped her eyes delicately with the edge of her kimono. Nobody ever shouted at her. Especially not strangers she'd given a spare room to out of the goodness of her heart. She sniffed vulnerably.

Immediately, Delilah regretted losing her temper. She didn't lose it often, but when she did it could be pretty fierce. She was angry with Vivienne, but she didn't want to upset her. After all, how was she to know how important the records were to her, what value she attached to them? 'Look, I'm sorry, I didn't mean to shout like that . . .' Delilah tried to smile. 'It was just a bit of a shock.' Carefully she sat on the sofa and started putting the records away, lovingly wiping each one with the sleeve of her jumper and replacing them in the battered leather case. Clicking the catches shut, a surge of calm washed over her. The kind of calm that can only be experienced when a major disaster has just been averted.

Vivienne slumped down next to her on the sofa, looking like a petulant child that had been caught stealing sweets and had her wrists slapped. She stuck out her bottom lip, not wanting to look Delilah in the eye, and stirred the cereal in her bowl. All the energy had drained from her. She affected a tiny, meek voice. 'I didn't realise. Am I forgiven?'

Any traces of anger that Delilah had left dissolved as quickly as they had appeared. How could you stay angry with Vivienne? 'Of course you are. It was a mistake, that's all.'

Like an elastic band, Vivienne snapped back into shape and jumped up from the sofa. 'Fabulous! So shall we go shopping?'

'Shopping? For what?' Delilah wrinkled her forehead. Perhaps she was expected to provide the food in exchange for a bed. Her heart sank. The thought of trailing up and down supermarket aisles wasn't high on her list of priorities for the day. And then there was the slight problem of cash. She had £500 in her wallet and that was supposed to last until . . . well, until she'd met Charlie. After that, she wasn't sure what she would do. She'd given up trying to imagine what life would be like with Charlie in it, it was like trying to imagine winning the lottery.

Vivienne was impatiently trying to untangle her bendy-rod curlers. She pulled the last one out and threw back her pre-Raphaelite curls. 'For clothes, darling. What else? Haven't you got a very important date this evening?'

Delilah's stomach flipped. The phone call. She had to call Charlie. 'Er, yes.' She stumbled over the words. 'But I thought I'd give him a ring this afternoon, you know, when he's less busy,' she fibbed.

'Don't be so silly. You just have first-night nerves. Stop making excuses.'

Delilah blushed. Was it that obvious? She gave up the pretence. 'I can't. I need a drink before I can summon up the courage to call.'

Vivienne clasped her hands together in gleeful excitement. 'Fabulous! An afternoon's shopping followed by relaxing in a bar. My kind of day!'

'But—' Delilah attempted to protest but she already knew it would be useless. She'd only known Vivienne for five minutes but she felt as if she'd known her for ages. She could already feel herself being carried away on her wave – like a surfer being taken by the swell. 'Snap, snap,' Vivienne demanded, pulling Delilah up from the sofa and pushing her down the hallway to the front door. 'You go and start up the engine, I'll be two secs.' And with that she disappeared into her bedroom in a flurry of excitement and Chanel No. 5.

Chapter Eight

They pulled up outside Adventure, a small shop painted lilac and silver not far from Café Prima Donna. Delilah hastily got out of the Beetle. Inside, the car was filled with thick, grey cigarette smoke, courtesy of Vivienne, who, despite spending the entire ten-minute journey with her mobile attached to one ear, had still managed to work her way through half a packet of Marlboro Lights. Delilah took a deep breath of inner-city air, exhaust fumes mingled with restaurant kitchen smells. It reminded her of Bradford. Some things weren't that different after all.

'Ciao, ciao.' Vivienne threw her phone into her large ethnic bag and clambered out of the car. She perched her sunglasses on her carefully-arranged-to-look-dishevelled curls. 'Okay, here we are . . .' Her attention was caught by the shop window '. . . Just look at that dress, it looks divine . . .' She rushed past Delilah and dived into the shop. Delilah hesitated for a moment to look at the window display: a tie-dye smock stitched together with bits of string and edged with velvet trim was draped across the branches of a tree. It didn't look very flattering. More like something Tupperware Sandra used to run up on her Singer sewing machine.

Delilah was curious. After all, if she did arrange to meet Charlie, she had absolutely nothing to wear . . . and looking didn't cost anything. She went to step inside, but suddenly found herself face-to-face with a deeply suntanned man, dressed in bounceresque attire: black polo-neck, shiny nylon trousers and patent leather lace-ups. He blocked her way with his arm. 'Excuse me, Madam, but can I see your business card?' He spoke in a high-pitched mid-Atlantic nasal twang.

Delilah felt confused. Why on earth did she need a business card to look at a few clothes? She stepped back off the doorstep. 'But isn't this just a clothes shop?'

The doorman brushed back his oily black hair with a flick of his wrist. 'This is an exclusive showroom for the viewing of one-off quality garments.' He put his face too close to hers and scowled. 'It is not just a clothes shop.'

Delilah went bright red. Her original confusion had turned into intense irritation. This smart-arse was starting to piss her off. Out of the corner of her eye she noticed that inside the shop a couple of assistants were staring at her. That did it. There was no way she was going to retreat back to her car with her tail between her legs.

She forced a smile. 'Silly me, I completely forgot. My card's in my bag.' She put her khaki, ex-army rucksack on the doorstep. 'Dickhead,' she muttered, bending down and slowly starting to empty her belongings around Mr Bouncer's lace-ups. Fatso's doggy biscuits, stray Tampax, a half-eaten Twix. He shuffled uncomfortably. Delilah felt a twinge of satisfaction. Finally, when the doorstep was full of enough sanitary products to stock a small chemist, she produced her wallet and casually began sorting through a wad of receipts, pretending to look for her business card. Of course she didn't have one – waitresses normally don't.

'Good grief, whatever are you doing?'

Vivienne had materialised on the doorstep, squeezed into what appeared to be a life-size fishnet stocking.

Before Delilah had a chance to speak, Mr Bouncer butted in sarcastically. 'She's trying to find her card.' Delilah gritted her teeth. His voice grated on her nerves like fingernails down a blackboard.

'Oh, she doesn't need one, silly.' Vivienne pushed Mr Bouncer in a playful gesture. 'Delilah's with me.'

Mr Bouncer reddened and started to pant. 'Miss Pendlebury, I do apologise.' He fell to his knees and began hurriedly picking up the contents of Delilah's rucksack. 'It was a slight misunderstanding.' He handed Delilah a fistful of pantyliners. She glanced in astonishment at Vivienne, who winked knowingly. Never before had she seen anyone's attitude change so rapidly and so remarkably. Mr Bouncer had metamorphosed from a cocky little git into a grovelling wimp. Delilah was very impressed.

'Come and feast your eyes on some of these outfits.' Vivienne tugged on her sleeve like an excited child.

The tiny shop was full of incredibly thin women with varying shades of honey-blonde highlighted hair, lipgloss and Klosters tans, wafting around in stages of undress. Their chattering provided a high-pitched buzz as they worked with single-minded efficiency through piles of clothes, trying on each garment and admiring themselves in the floor-length, gilt-framed mirrors before asking the staff for their opinions. The assistants were only too happy to oblige. They hovered, tweaking shoulder-straps and letting loose torrents of flattery. 'Stunning, simply stunning,' they squealed – their opinions being totally unbiased and in no way affected by their fifty per cent commission.

Delilah put her rucksack on the floor and looked through shelves of patchwork velvet cardigans that appeared to have been boil-washed and then pulled out of shape. So this is what all the fuss was about? She held a cardigan up against herself and looked in the mirror. It barely covered her nipples. Talk about scrimping on material, the tight sods, she thought, putting it back on the shelf in a crumpled heap. An assistant immediately pounced on it and painstakingly began folding it as if it were a napkin. Delilah watched in fascination to see if she shaped it into a fan.

'How do I look?'

Vivienne flung back the cubicle curtain. Delilah cringed. The fishnet-stocking dress had been replaced by a tightly laced corset and flared knee-length skirt made of quilted fuchsia velvet. She was bulging in all the wrong places.

'Well?'

Delilah desperately tried to find the right words. She'd only known Vivienne for a few hours and she probably wouldn't take too kindly to being told she looked like a pantomime dame. 'It's very . . . different.' She tried to sound enthusiastic. It fell flat.

'Different?' snorted Vivienne, twirling in front of a gaggle of drooling assistants. 'I think it's more gypsy meets Vivienne Westwood – don't you?'

The assistants cooed and nodded vigorously, their pearl chokers rattling against their scrawny vulture necks. Delilah gave them a dirty look. She didn't want Vivienne walking out of the shop looking like an extra from *Carry On Dick Whittington*. She grabbed the embroidered silk coathanger, looking for a price tag. There wasn't one. Adventure worked on the principle that if you had to ask how much something cost, you couldn't afford it. 'How much is it?'

There was an en-masse intake of breath. The shop fell into a horrified hush. Delilah refused to be intimidated. Ignoring the eyes focused accusingly upon her she repeated the question, deliberately adopting a very broad Yorkshire accent. If the knife was in, she might as well turn it. 'I said, how much brass for t'dress, like.'

Coughing authoritatively, one of the senior shop assistants stepped forward. She was wearing a pair of thick, black-framed glasses and bore an uncanny resemblance to Elvis Costello. 'The exquisite bordello skirt and hand-embroidered corsetière come to a total of £3,000 . . . Madam.' The words stuck in her throat.

Delilah let out a snort. Three grand! Who did they think they were kidding? Who the hell was going to pay the equivalent of an all-expenses fortnight in the Caribbean to look like Widow Twankey?

'I think I'll take it,' announced Vivienne.

There was a small ripple of applause from the circling vultures.

'Are you sure? I mean, there's lots of other stuff here that's much nicer . . .' Delilah cased the room, frantically trying to spot something she liked. She felt as if she was an accomplice in some big con, rather like a modern-day version of the emperor's new clothes. Elvis Costello's double tapped her on the shoulder as she rifled through a rack of Holly Hobbie dresses.

'Are you the owner of the green Volkswagen parked outside?'

Delilah swung round. 'Yes,' she snapped defensively. Perhaps this was a tactic they learnt in shop school: distract the enemy so that you can rip off the gullible friend.

The lookalike sneered. 'Well, it looks as if you're about to get a ticket.'

Delilah looked across the road to see a traffic warden zealously taking down her number plate. 'Shit, shit, shit.' She ran outside, leaving Vivienne with the commission-hungry staff, who immediately seized their opportunity and led her, like a victim to the gallows, towards the cash register.

'Wait, wait . . .' Never one to play it cool, Delilah flung herself across the bonnet of her car. 'You can't give me a ticket. I'm not parked on any yellow lines. I'm not doing anything illegal!'

The traffic warden ignored her and continued to punch the details into his hand-held computer.

'I said, I'm not parked illegally. You can't give me a ticket!' Delilah raised her voice, until she was almost shouting.

There was no reaction. Without looking up the traffic warden casually tore off the piece of paper that he'd just printed, popped it in a plastic folder, leaned over the prostrate Delilah and lifted up one of her defunct wipers. Smugly, he placed the ticket on the windscreen before strolling onto the next car.

'Fascist,' muttered Delilah, snatching the ticket and tearing it out of its yellow and black chequered wrapper. 'Bloody fascist!' she hollered louder when she saw the size of the fine. How the hell could she be fined forty lousy quid for simply parking on the street? She scanned the small print – 'vehicle parked in a resident area without a permit'. Delilah felt like screaming. What was going on in this city? Business cards to get into shops, permits to park on the streets. It was like being in some Orwellian nightmare.

She ripped up the ticket and threw it into the gutter. A passer-by tutted. Delilah glared. Today was not going well. She closed her eyes, leaned against the car and waited for Vivienne, who was happily exercising her Amex. At least things can't get any worse, she thought, turning her face towards the weak March sun.

Vivienne skipped out of the shop and towards the car, triumphantly swinging her billboard-sized cardboard bag. 'So, is it time for drinks?' she chirped happily.

'God, yes.' Delilah opened her eyes and stood up. If there was one thing she needed right now it was alcohol, and lots of it. She felt in her jeans pocket for her car keys. They weren't there. Of course, they were in her rucksack. In all the confusion over the parking ticket she'd forgotten she'd left it inside the shop. 'Didn't you pick up my rucksack?' She squinted in the sun at Vivienne who was rummaging for her mobile, which was making a muffled ringing noise at the bottom of her bag.

Vivienne looked blank. 'What?' A last stab into her bag produced the phone. She switched her attention to the caller. 'Hello, Hilary?'

Delilah sighed, realising she was going to have to return to the fray. Bypassing Mr Bouncer, she quickly ran indoors. The floor was empty. She felt a flutter of slight panic. 'Excuse me, have you seen my rucksack?'

Delilah grabbed hold of one of the assistants who was robotically folding scarves. 'I'm afraid not.' She shook her head, peering haughtily at Delilah.

Delilah's stomach lurched. Frantically she rushed around the shop, asking the same question, getting the same answer. It couldn't be happening, this couldn't be happening. She could feel the tears welling up. No rucksack, no wallet. No wallet, no business card. No business card, no telephone number. No telephone number, no Charlie. Defeated, she stumbled outside, ignoring Vivienne who was chatting into her phone, and slumped onto the pavement. The consequences of what had just happened started to appear like a rash. Not only had she lost Charlie's telephone number, but her wallet had contained all her money. It was a double-whammy. She wiped her eyes, trying to stem the tears that had started to run in trickles down her cheeks. She was now penniless. And she was in London. What the hell was she going to do?

Chapter Nine

'Don't worry, Delilah, everything will be okay.' Sam leaned over and put his arm reassuringly around her shoulder. 'We'll be able to sort things out.'

Delilah smiled weakly, wiping her red and puffy eyes with a screwed-up, gin-soaked serviette. Her face was a blotchy mess. She'd been crying for over an hour, the first twenty minutes of which had been outside Adventure, which is where she'd have remained if Vivienne hadn't decided that a hysterical wailing friend was not a good look, and taken charge. Without removing the cigarette that was welded to her bottom lip, she'd scooped Delilah up from the pavement and frog-marched her to the Pantry, a restaurant-cum-bar with wall-to-wall shelves of tins of baked beans, bottles of HP and packets of dried custard, pausing briefly to call Sam for his advice on what to do with a hysterical, sobbing northerner. Sam had been happy to oblige. He was the fourth emergency service – a genuine Mr Fix-it. Whatever the crisis, whether it was being dumped by one of her many lovers or the time she caught sight of her cellulite in the bathroom mirror, all Vivienne had to do was pick up the phone and she could rely on Sam to sort things out. Now it was Delilah who needed his help. True to form, he'd closed the café early and met them at the bar, armed with a stiff gin and tonic and wearing his best Samaritan smile.

'I know it's upsetting to have things stolen, but it's not the end of the world.' Sam stroked her hair. Delilah nodded dumbly while shredding her beer mat into a hundred pieces. She'd even lost the ability to speak. Instead she was concentrating on trying to stop snivelling, but failing miserably – every time she thought about her predicament her eyes would automatically water and her nose would run. It still hadn't sunk in that her entire month's wages had gone, vanished, legged it. She sniffed noisily and blew her nose, trying not to dwell upon the terrifying thought that without any funds, and minus Charlie's business card, she might have to get back on the M1 and go back to her old life. She felt her eyes well up again at the thought.

'After all, it's only money, isn't it?'

Delilah chewed her bottom lip. Sam was under the mistaken impression that this was just a cashflow problem. She hadn't told him about Charlie or the missing telephone number. Somehow it didn't feel right.

'Thanks, Sam.' Delilah lifted her head and forced a smile.

'For what?'

'For listening. For not telling me to pull myself together. For being here.' Delilah smiled. Kind, understanding Sam. He'd spent the last two days sorting out her life. Thank God she'd met him when she'd first arrived. Without him she didn't know what she'd have done. It was like having her very own guardian angel.

Sam put his hand on hers and grinned, showing two very neat rows of small white teeth. He really liked Delilah. She'd looked so endearing when he'd seen Vivienne leading her towards him, her freckled face swollen from crying and her clothes creased and covered in a fine layer of dog hairs. She was so unlike the high-maintenance women that hung around in Notting Hill in their kitten heels and designer clothes, trying to give the impression that they led designer lives. Delilah didn't seem to be trying to be anything. Or if she did, she wasn't pulling it off very successfully.

'Have you thought about ringing Charlie?'

'What?' Delilah cracked an ice cube between her molars.

'It was just a suggestion. Perhaps he can help.'

'How do you know about Charlie? Has Vivienne said

something?' Delilah could just imagine Vivienne gossiping to Sam. Vivienne thought a one-to-one conversation meant blabbing to anyone that would listen on her mobile.

'No. You mentioned him yesterday, just after you fainted.'

'What did I say about him?' She was on the defensive.

'Nothing, just his name. Look, I didn't mean to say the wrong thing. I just thought that if you were in a bit of mess with money and stuff, maybe he'd help you out.' Sam put his hand on her knee, regretting he'd ever brought up the subject. Talk about a sore point.

Delilah felt uncomfortable. Just the mention of Charlie's name made her jittery. 'Maybe he would, but I can't get in touch with him. His business card was in my rucksack,' she muttered glumly.

His business card? Sam was surprised. So Charlie was just a business acquaintance? He tried not to look as pleased as he felt. He'd had a nagging suspicion that Charlie was Delilah's boyfriend and, if he was honest with himself, he was rather hoping that he wasn't. 'Why don't you get his number from Directory Enquiries?'

Delilah experienced a sudden feeling of hope. Of course! Why hadn't she thought of that? She'd been so busy panicking she'd forgotten all about ringing 192. All she needed was the name of the production company and she was sorted. Except there was one slight hiccup. She couldn't remember the name of the production company, or the address. And talking of names, what the hell was his surname? She tried to visualise the card using a Uri Geller-type memory trick she'd once seen on TV. It didn't work. Her mind had gone AWOL.

'I can't. I've forgotten the name of the company he works for.' Delilah sighed miserably, fiddling with the strands of fraying denim on her jacket sleeve. Sam must think she was useless. Not only was she homeless and penniless, she'd also caught a bout of amnesia.

'Look, I've already told you not to worry. You're still suffering from shock, you're bound to forget things, it's only natural.

You'll remember them in time.' Sam gently lifted up her chin. 'Just chill out.'

Delilah looked into his eyes. They were like her own, brown with pale green flecks. He was right, she needed to calm down. She'd faced tougher times than this and got through them. She took a lungful of cigarette smoke and alcohol fumes. That's what she needed: alcohol. 'It's my round. Let me buy you a drink.' Delilah stood up, steadying herself on the back of Sam's chair. She felt slightly wobbly after two gin and tonics and a double brandy. 'It's the least I can do.'

Sam leaned back in his aesthetically-impressive-but-buttock-numbing curved perspex chair and started laughing. 'But you've got no cash.'

Delilah smiled. Her money might have disappeared, but her sense of humour had returned.

'You'll have to lend me a tenner, then.' She held out her hand, waiting, as Sam reached into his pocket. Normally she hated borrowing money, but she knew that Sam wouldn't mind. Generosity was his middle name – unlike most of the blokes she knew. For the first time in two days she thought of Lenny and how he used to drive ten miles to save a penny on his petrol. Or how he'd always go to the loo when it was his round in the pub. She shook her head. She hadn't left a moment too early. 'What are you drinking?'

'I'll have a beer, thanks.'

'What about Vivienne?'

Sam pointed to the bar. 'I think she's taken care of, don't you?' Delilah looked across to see Vivienne surrounded by a pack of sweaty-faced, slavering solicitors. She'd hitched her skirt up to her waist and was gleefully showing them the Japanese tattoo on her inner thigh. Her captive audience panted heavily, their bloated bellies straining against their tourniquet belts, their eyes bulging as she teasingly invited them to take a closer look. Never the shrinking violet, Vivienne was thoroughly enjoying herself. Next to sex, being the centre of attention was her favourite position.

Delilah swayed towards the bar and hauled herself onto a bar stool. She waited to be served. And she waited. Fifteen minutes passed and she was starting to feel annoyed. Eventually, just as she was about to give up, a tall, staggeringly handsome barman appeared. He seemed to glide, rather than walk, towards her.

'What can I do for you?' Furrowing his brow he attempted his best James Dean expression.

Delilah sighed inwardly. Not another prat. First Mr Poloneck and now some idiot who thought he was a rebel without a cause. 'Erm, a beer and a vodka and Coke.'

'Did you say *Courke*?' He mimicked her Yorkshire accent and winked.

Delilah fumed. Was that supposed to be humorous? Or was it a terribly miscalculated attempt at flirting? She had an urge to tell him to sod off. Instead she winked back. He leered, smarmily. This chick was in the bag. Delilah pouted and narrowed her eyes. 'Can I tell you something?' She gave her best breathlessly seductive whisper.

'Sure.' Cockily, he pushed his fringe back from his eyes and leaned across the bar. A strong stench of aftershave wafted towards her. Delilah licked her lips and put her mouth close to his ear.

'Has anyone told you . . .' she paused, allowing his ego to swell, before hissing loudly '. . . that your flies are undone?'

It was a clichéd line but it still worked. He jumped back from the bar like a jack-in-a-box and looked down at his slightly-too-snug black leather trousers. Delilah laughed throatily. Game, set and match to her. The flustered barman made no attempt at verbal retaliation. Instead he tried pathetically to regain his last vestiges of cool by juggling the beer and vodka bottles and doing some fancy footwork around the ice and sliced lemon. Delilah watched, amused as he did his peacock strut with a container of straws. It was like watching a David Attenborough documentary on the habits of the lesser brooding barman.

'Excuse me, are you waiting to be served?' A short, swarthy man in his forties had sidled up beside her. He spoke with a thick Italian accent.

'No.' She forced a tight smile.

'Excellent.' He parted his huge fleshy lips, baring several gold teeth, and edged closer. Delilah stared determinedly ahead at the barman, telekinetically willing him to get a move on with the drinks.

'Let me introduce myself. My name's Vince and, and this—' he paused for effect '—is my place.' Out of the corner of her eye, Delilah saw he was holding out his large hand, which was covered in several large gold sovereign rings and a dodgy assortment of bracelets. He had the kind of hands that have coarse tufts of black hair growing on each segment of his fingers, like a human tarantula. Her heart sank into her Nikes. There was no way out. Polite chit-chat with an ageing Latin Lothario wasn't exactly high on her list of 'things to do', but ignoring him was impossible. She'd met his type before, the type that sticks to your side like chewing gum, refusing to budge unless you agree to go out with him for dinner or manage to somehow steer the conversation around to your recurring thrush problem. Yep, she was well and truly cornered.

'I'm Delilah.' She held out her hand. Vince shook it energetically, keeping hold of it for longer than was necessary.

'So, what do you think of my bar?' He puffed up his chest. Delilah noticed the thick curls of black hair climbing up and around the collar of his shiny, satin shirt.

'It's very nice.' She smiled, nodding.

'Do you know I also have a restaurant downstairs?'

'Er, no.' Oh God, please don't let him be going to ask her on a dinner date. She hated this bit, when the man asks you out and you turn him down. However hard you try to be nice about it, they always get so rattled – the charm disappears immediately and they try and salvage their male pride by being all huffy. She glanced at Vince, waiting for the inevitable question. If only she found him the tiniest bit attractive she wouldn't mind going out to dinner. With no money, having dinner bought for her would be pretty handy.

Suddenly her brain kicked in. Of course! The answer to her money worries was staring her in the face. Okay, so it was the last thing she wanted to do in London, but it was something she knew she could do, and she'd only have to do it for a couple of weeks, just until she'd found Charlie and begun her new life. She changed her expression from frosty to one of utter rapture, smiling brightly at him and shaking her hair free from its make-shift plait.

'Do you need any waitresses?'

'You would like a job in my restaurant?' He sounded incredulous. This was too good to be true.

'If you've got one, yeh. I'd love to.' She tried to sound as enthusiastic as she could about the thought of being a waitress. Just think of the money, she thought to herself as she fixed on her Miss World grin, an expression she reserved for job interviews, first dates and doctor's appointments. A kind of I-might-look-really-enthusiastic-but-really-I'm-not smile that hung rigidly from her cheekbones.

'Have you been a waitress before?' He still wasn't sure if this was a wind-up.

'Yep, lots of times. I love waitressing.' Bloody hell, if Pascal could hear her now he'd be turning on his built-up heels.

Vince was satisfied. 'Well, I think we might have a vacancy.' He beamed and lit up a fat, twelve-inch-long cigar. Sucking hard, he blew out a large grey cloud of scented smoke. 'Be here tomorrow at seven.' He licked his lips and attempted to chew seductively on the moist tip of his Monte Cristo. Thankfully, the drinks arrived and, grabbing her vodka and Coke, Delilah took a large gulp to drown her second thoughts.

'Okay, I'll see you at seven,' she gasped quickly, about to make her escape. But she wasn't quick enough. Vince lurched forward and planted a slobbery kiss on each cheek. Delilah tried not to recoil as he left two damp patches of saliva on her face.

'I look forward to it . . . *bella.*' He beamed victoriously, as Delilah, deciding it was now or never, made a dash for freedom and sprinted across the crowded bar area. What a creep, she thought, pushing past a large group of suits and spilling Sam's beer. Still, it meant she now had a job, and, more importantly, some cash. She smiled as she reached Sam.

'I got a job.'

'Where?'

'Here. I start tomorrow.'

'Congratulations.' Jumping up from his seat, Sam grabbed her by the waist and gave her a hug, his large frame bent double to accommodate Delilah's tiny five-foot-four figure. He held her tightly as she shrieked with laughter, holding the drinks high above her head.

'Sam, stop. I'm going to spill what's left of this beer all over you.' Immediately he loosened his grip and pulled away awkwardly.

'Sorry, I got a bit carried away.' Two spots of colour burned on his cheeks.

Delilah put the drinks down on the table. 'Don't be daft. It's just the booze.' In her relief at finding a way to replace the cash she'd had stolen, she didn't notice Sam's acute embarrassment, or the way he was staring at her.

True, he'd had a few beers, but his reaction wasn't anything to do with the San Miguel. It was how he'd felt as he'd held her close. The way it had made his legs turn to jelly and his palms start to sweat. There was no mistaking those signs. He fancied Delilah big time. In fact it was more than that, more than just thinking she was beautiful and sexy and so bloody lovely he wanted to grab hold of her and kiss her there and then. He was besotted. He wanted to talk to her, find out everything about her, watch old movies with her, cook his favourite meal for her, lie in bed and eat takeout pizza with her. He wanted to be with her. Full stop.

He smiled across at her. She was jigging around the table, a grin plastered all over her face. She looked so happy, so carefree. He didn't want to spoil the moment by getting all heavy. He held up his bottle. 'Here's to your new job. Cheers!'

'Cheers!' grinned Delilah, happily clinking her glass. Sam had been right. Everything was going to be okay, everything was back on track.

Chapter Ten

'Shit.' Delilah cursed as she snagged yet another pair of tights. That was the third and final pair from the 40-denier value pack she'd bought at the chemist's. She looked at her watch: 6.30 p.m., only thirty minutes before she had to be at the Pantry. 'Vivienne,' she yelled, rushing into the hallway and knocking on her bedroom door. 'Vivienne, have you got any tights I can borrow?'

The door flew open. Vivienne was wearing a knee-length overall, press-studded all the way up the front, and a white elasticated shower cap. In her left hand she was holding a rolling pin. 'What do you think?' She did a small twirl. 'I'm expecting Dwayne in half an hour.'

Delilah tried not to smile. 'What are you supposed to be?'

'A dirty dinner lady.'

Delilah couldn't help herself. In disbelief she started laughing. It was like something out of the *News of the World*. 'Are you sure Dwayne's into dinner ladies?'

'Of course! All men love a bit of dressing up.'

Delilah thought about Lenny. Maybe that's where she'd being going wrong all those years. Perhaps a few costumes could have spiced up their boring sex life. She dismissed the idea. No amount of fancy dress could have transformed Lenny into a sexual gymnast. Quite the opposite. Anything deviating from the sexual norm would have brought on an attack of brewer's droop. No, Lenny's idea of dressing up was rather more clichéd: red and black lacy push-up bras and satin G-strings were more in his line – throw in a garter and he'd have thought Christmas had come early.

'Do you mind me asking what you're going to do with the rolling pin?' Delilah was intrigued.

Vivienne was twirling it around in her hand like a majorette. 'It's for when he's being naughty and doesn't eat up dindins. A quick slap on the bottom and he's gagging for pudding.'

Delilah wanted to stay and find out more about Dwayne and his dinner lady fantasies, but she was running late. 'Before I got sidetracked, I was going to ask you if I could borrow a pair of tights. I've got holes in every single pair and I don't have the time to go and buy some more.'

Vivienne adjusted her shower cap. 'Of course, darling, but I don't wear tights. They're too secretarial for me. But if you wait one moment . . .' Striding over to her antique dressing table, she pulled out the top drawer '. . . you're welcome to borrow any of these.' She began rummaging through an alarming assortment of PVC knickers and nippleless bras. Vivienne was not part of the eighty per cent of the female population who bought their underwear in multi-packs from M&S. She was the kind to blow a week's trust fund on a rubber basque from Agent Provocateur.

'Goodness, that's where you've been hiding,' she squealed, tugging at something and throwing it on the bed. It looked like a girdle. It *was* a girdle, except it wasn't the kind your granny would wear. This one was leather . . . and studded. 'Aaah, this is what I'm looking for.' Vivienne beamed, holding out several packets of fishnet stockings. 'I've got a spare suspender belt if you need one.'

Delilah groaned. She was going to look like something out of the *Folies Bergère*. Still, she didn't have much choice. She looked at her watch: 6.42. It was fishnets or nothing. She grabbed the fishnets. 'Have a good evening,' she yelled, rushing back down the hallway and into her bedroom.

'Oh, I thoroughly intend to,' boomed Vivienne, slamming her door with her rolling pin.

Delilah hurriedly strapped herself into the suspender contraption and fidgeted uncomfortably. How could men find these sexy? It was like wearing some kind of torture device – a modern-day chastity belt. Brushing off the dust from her black waitress skirt, she took a final look in the mirror. She'd do. Kissing Fatso, who was curled on the bed, she grabbed her car keys (thankfully she'd found her spare set before Vivienne could try out the hotwiring skills she'd learnt from Dwayne) and clattered down the hallway in her only pair of stilettos. This might be a crummy waitressing job, but it was her only job, and she didn't want to be late.

The Pantry was heaving by the time she arrived. At the bar, a group of silicon-enhanced models were being plied with Del-boy cocktails from the George Hamilton lookalikes doused in Cacherel and Grecian 2000, while huddled around the edges budding rockstars wearing mirrored shades and velvet suits were chatting up wannabe actresses, who were too busy pouting and smoking cigarettes to realise they were talking bollocks.

Delilah felt very uncomfortable. Her clothes were less actress-cum-model, more mother-cum-typist. She was actually relieved to catch sight of a cigar-wielding Vince, licking his lips and pushing through the crowd towards her.

'*Bella, bella,*' he cooed. A cloud of cigar smoke engulfed her. 'Follow me and you can meet the others.' He squashed his clammy hand into hers and with a vice-like grip led her around the back of the bar and down the large flight of stairs to the empty restaurant. 'We don't begin dining until seven-thirty, just enough time for you to change into your costume.'

'Costume?' Delilah looked at her reflection in the wall-to-wall mirrors. Black skirt, white blouse – the usual waitress garb. What was wrong with that? Suddenly she saw a girl walking towards them; no, hang on a minute, that was her reflection. She was actually behind them. Delilah turned round. As she did, Vince placed a chubby hand on her arm.

'Delilah, I want you to meet Fifi. You'll be working together.'

Platinum-blonde Fifi was shoehorned into a skintight black satin minidress, her 38DD chest looking as if it would escape at any moment from her plunging neckline. Delilah winced. Please don't let this be *the* costume. She crossed her fingers tightly. If she'd been religious, she'd have got down on her knees and prayed.

'Great to meet you!' Fifi flashed Delilah a Hollywood smile while rapidly chewing gum. 'Are you the new cigarette girl?'

Delilah turned to Vince. 'Am I?'

Vince sucked on his cigar. 'Why, of course. Only the prettiest girls get the best jobs. And being one of my *sigaretta* girls is the best job in the world!' He clapped his sweaty palms together and chewed the end of the cigar vigorously.

Delilah stared at him. Since when did flogging cigarettes in a poncy restaurant become the best job in the world? She looked at Fifi who was buffing her two-inch talons on her chest. Hardly the best advertisement for this so-called promising career.

'But I thought you said I was going to be a waitress?' Delilah was desperate. Waitressing suddenly seemed to take on a much more favourable light when compared to being a cigarette girl. Serving up meat and two veg she could handle, prancing around like Fag Ash Lil in a minidress she could not.

'No, no, no.' Vince clutched her hand in his and flashed his gold teeth. 'You are *bellissima*, too beautiful to hide away in the kitchen, worrying about knives and forks, starters and main courses.' He flung out his arms. 'You need to be out here, with all my guests.'

Fifi butted in. 'Hey, this is a much better gig than waitressing. The tips are much bigger and we can have a bit of a laugh.' She winked mischievously. 'Stick with me, honey, and it will be a breeze.'

Delilah surrendered. What was the point in arguing? A job was a job after all. And if it meant earning more money, she could put up with a shorter hem than usual.

'Okay, where shall I change?'

'Over here,' said Fifi, pulling out her gum from between her teeth then sucking it back in. She set off wiggling towards the toilets in her three-inch stilettos. Delilah followed, ignoring Vince, who smiled triumphantly to himself. 'See you later, my *bellas*.'

'I can't go out there wearing this!' Delilah put her head in her hands. The costume was much, much worse than she could have ever imagined.

Fifi, who had dropped her squeaky baby-doll twang and adopted a normal adult voice since moving out of earshot of Vince, was sympathetic. 'Don't be silly, you look great. Just think of all those tips.'

Delilah peered at her reflection through her fingers. Her dress consisted of one tiny piece of tubular Lycra which gripped like a surgical stocking, making it difficult to breathe. Not only that, but it was silver! Not gun-metal-grey silver, but shiny, tin-foil silver. She looked and felt like a right turkey. Perhaps Vince had got confused and was thinking of serving her up with a few roast potatoes and some gravy.

'You look a knockout.'

'You mean I look like something that should be on *It's a Knockout*.'

'No, you look great, trust me.' Fifi stood behind her, pulling Delilah's hair back into a high ponytail. 'I know what you're thinking. How can I trust a dumb blonde?' Delilah tried to protest but Fifi continued. 'I don't blame you. Everyone here thinks that too, but the whole blonde thing is just an act. My name's actually Lisa and I'm studying for a PhD in Victorian Literature.' She paused as Delilah's eyes widened. 'Shocked? Most people are when I tell them. Not that I tell any of the punters here. I just sell them their cigarettes and smile. They like to think you're some pretty little thing without a brain. It makes them feel good. And if they feel good, you get a nice big juicy tip. Which is why we're both here, isn't it?' She smiled wryly at Delilah. 'I need the money to finish my doctorate and you need the money to . . . ?' Her voice tailed off.

Delilah looked in the mirror. '. . . To start a new life.'

'Which is why wearing these stupid dresses and flogging fags of an evening isn't so bad after all!'

Delilah looked at her reflection. She was unrecognisable. She wanted to be unrecognisable. Lisa was right. This job was a means to an end. A few days – a week at the most – and she'd be out of there. Just as soon as she found Charlie.

'Okay, time to make a move.' Lisa blotted her lips with a piece of tissue paper.

Delilah nodded, trying to adjust her stockings. For the millionth time that evening she deeply regretted her decision to wear a suspender belt. The fasteners were digging into the tops of her thighs, creating unsightly bumps underneath the silver Lycra. It looked as if she was suffering from acute cellulite.

Lisa fluffed up her candyfloss curls. 'Oh, shit,' she tutted, 'nearly forgot the smokes.' Fishing a key from out of her cleavage she unlocked the cupboard in the far corner and pulled out two huge trays, stacked high with various brands of cigarettes. She handed one to Delilah. 'Don't worry, it's pretty light.'

Delilah hung it around her neck. She felt like one of those usherettes she used to see during the interval at the cinema, the ones who used to shout 'ice cream, popcorn,' and look totally pissed off. Still, at least it was something to hide behind – and it covered most of the dress. She looked across at Lisa, who was adjusting the straps of her tray so that her breasts balanced precariously on the edge of the Benson & Hedges. Switching back into bimbo mode Lisa became Fifi again. 'Ready?' she squeaked in her baby-doll voice, pushing out her boobs and her bum.

Delilah took a deep breath and grabbed onto her tray for support. 'As ready as I'll ever be.'

Chapter Eleven

A chink of sunlight squeezed its way through a gap in the curtains and focused brightly on Delilah's forehead, which peeped out from underneath the heavy goose-feather eider-down. Instinctively she wriggled her head into the comparative darkness of the side of her pillow, but it was too late, she'd woken up. Groaning, she pulled the covers down from her face and eased open her eyelids. Her vision was still blurry from sleep, but as the images sharpened she found herself staring at the silver dress, rolled up and knotted with the suspender belt and fishnets, hanging limply over the back of the chair.

It triggered off memories of last night, which had – to put it mildly – been an experience. The first hour had been the worst. If you've ever seen a nervous contestant at a local beauty pageant walking unsurely up and down in a swimming costume on a makeshift catwalk, then you've got a pretty good idea of how Delilah looked – and felt: first-night nerves mixed with utter disbelief at her situation. What the hell am I doing? she'd thought as she'd tottered up and down the restaurant floor, trying not to catch anyone's eye. It was tricky. For someone who'd always blatantly ignored dodgy men and their dodgy chat-up lines, she was now forced to stop, smile and listen will-ingly. If she didn't she might miss a sale: miss a sale and she'd miss out on the tip. Delilah had watched Fifi for inspiration. She worked the room like a pro, chatting to the suits and out-of-town businessmen – the big spenders with platinum cards behind the bar – and whizzing past the wannabe crowds: the men and women who hadn't yet made it, and counted their change like professional Fagins.

Delilah had tried her best to mimic Fifi's slick routine, she'd made it seem so easy. In reality it was a lot harder than it looked. As a cigarette girl you were supposed to split your time between mingling in the bar and doing laps up and down the dining area, but Delilah had realised very early on in the evening that walking up and down between the restaurant tables made her feel as if she was there solely to entertain the customers in between courses, and that she much preferred the sanctuary of the bar – it was a lot darker and she felt a lot less conspicuous. The downside was that in the bar you were more likely to get hit on. And she had been, but thankfully only twice. The first time by a French bloke who'd said he was a clothes designer specialising in suits, and had offered to make her one 'if he could 'ave 'er measurements' and the second by a very drunk Irish guy who was actually rather sweet and kept buying cigarettes as an excuse to chat her up. By the time he disappeared off to his dinner table he must have bought about ten packets.

But the hours had still ticked slowly, painfully by, until at around midnight Fifi had noticed Delilah was on her last legs and offered to hang around for the stragglers, letting her finish a bit early. And she'd needed to. Her feet were bloody killing her and the sides of her cheeks ached from the phoney smile she'd had to have plastered on her face all evening. Still, things had felt a lot better when she'd counted up her tips – £35 – plus her wages. Not bad for her first night. In a couple of weeks she'd have made back all the money she'd lost.

There was a brisk rap at the bedroom door and Vivienne popped her head round. 'Good, you're awake. Would you like to go and have lunch?' Removing the fag from her lips she breathed out a cloud of blue-grey smoke. Delilah wrinkled her nose. Cigarette smoke. She never wanted to smell bloody cigarette smoke again. Rubbing her eyes, she propped herself up on her elbow.

'What time is it?'

'Two-thirty.'

'God, is it that late? I must have been really knackered after last night.'

'How was it?'

'Oh, okay.' Delilah suddenly felt a bit embarrassed. She wasn't sure if she should tell Vivienne that she'd actually ended up being a cigarette girl. It wasn't exactly a job you wanted to boast about. She deliberated for a moment but it was too late; Vivienne had already spied the silver dress.

'Oooh, is that what you have to wear?' Striding across the room she picked it up, unravelling it from its suspender belt and stockings, and held it in front of her, stretching it against her body as she looked in the mirror. It came down to her pelvis. 'Goodness, it's a bit risqué for waitressing, isn't it?'

Delilah nodded resignedly. 'That's just it. When I got there I found out there wasn't a waitressing job. I had to sell cigarettes.'

'You're a cigarette girl?' Vivienne raised her eyebrow, intrigued. 'How glamorous.'

Not quite the reaction Delilah had been expecting. She smiled wearily. 'It wasn't, believe me.'

'Yes, but surely you must get lots of male attention.'

'Oh, you get plenty of that all right.'

'Really?' Vivienne perched on the end of the bed and crossed her legs. This was getting more and more interesting. Perhaps she should consider getting a job herself. Unfortunately there was actual work involved. She dismissed the idea. Working was not on her list of things to do in life. Shopping, trips to the gym, massages, holidays abroad and sex. They were on her list.

'So, do you fancy lunch? I thought we could go to one of my favourite little haunts if you like, and then maybe we can take a walk down Portobello and I'll show you around. Although after that bloody *Notting Hill* film, the place is always overrun with tourists looking for Hugh Grant's bookshop, or where Julia Roberts spilled her orange juice. I mean, really. Haven't these people got anything better to do than take pictures of every blue door they see, hoping it's the one in the movie? I mean, don't they have jobs to go to?' She tutted loudly, examining her chipped nail polish. 'Which reminds me, I really must book an appointment with my manicurist. Maybe I'll do that after we've had lunch.'

Delilah smiled, amused by Vivienne's rambling. 'Sure, whatever. I'll throw on some clothes and meet you downstairs in five minutes.'

'Great,' boomed Vivienne, padding downstairs. Within minutes Delilah could hear her on the phone booking a French manicure.

At Connor's they had to stand in a queue waiting for a table. Vivienne wasn't pleased. She kept tutting and impatiently asking the waiter when they'd be seated, and he just kept shrugging his shoulders and looking woeful. Delilah smiled apologetically for her friend. Too many times she'd been that waiter, trying to calm down irate customers, being polite when they were just being bloody rude.

'I'm sure it'll only be another few minutes,' comforted Delilah, who was actually enjoying standing in the deli part of the café, gazing at the cabinets full of stodgy-looking cakes and glossy, glazed fruit tarts, watching people pop in to buy the large sandwiches with exotic-sounding fillings piled high in straw baskets near the door. It was amazing how busy it was, even in the middle of the afternoon. Why wasn't anyone at work? Maybe Vivienne was right. Maybe nobody did work. Maybe they just flitted around with their mobile phones, looking nice in their designer clothes and drinking cappuccinos. Even the women with toddlers looked glamorous, with their tawny limbs and tawny hair, pedicured feet slipped into impossibly high heels. These women obviously didn't have to catch buses laden down with double buggies and bulging supermarket bags. Which probably explained why they looked so unharassed and happy as they casually selected a tub of olives, a French stick and a jar of horrendously expensive vegetables marinated in extra virgin olive oil.

Finally they got a table and were able to eat lunch. Not that Vivienne ate much of her salad. Instead she picked at a few lettuce leaves in between smoking her way through a packet of fags.

'So, how long have you lived in London?' asked Delilah, tucking into her plate of poached eggs.

'All my life,' exhaled Vivienne, sending smoke all over Delilah's food. 'I was born in Hampstead and lived there until I was about seventeen, when my parents decided I would benefit from a couple of years at finishing school.'

'Finishing school?' It sounded like somewhere only the members of the royal family went. 'Why did they want to send you there?'

Vivienne smiled ruefully as the memories came back. 'I was a bit of a wild child. Even as a toddler I was always being naughty. Mother says that's why I'm an only child, they dared not have any more after me.' She rolled her eyes sardonically. 'Father was away an awful lot, I didn't see much of him and I guess I just went a bit off the rails. It was all attention-seeking stuff really. Boys, drugs, alcohol. I discovered them all when I was at boarding school and couldn't get enough. I think it's keeping you cooped up with a bunch of nuns that does it. I can't even begin to tell you the things I used to get up to.' She paused, smiling to herself. Glancing up she caught Delilah's expression.

'You don't have to look so worried. I've calmed down a lot since then. It was the drink that sent me bonkers, and I gave that up ten years ago, along with all those ghastly joints I used to smoke. I'm now what they call a recovering alcoholic. I've given up drugs, drink, gluten, wheat, caffeine. The only thing left to give up is sex!' She snorted loudly at the ludicrousness of the idea, flicking ash all over the table next to her.

'There's always the fags,' suggested Delilah, turning her head away from the people on the next table who were staring furiously.

'Nonsense,' barked Vivienne gaily. 'I've got to pollute my body with something!'

'Well, that's all very well,' interrupted one of the men sitting
on the next table, 'but we'd rather not have our bodies polluted,
thank you very much.' He swallowed rapidly, pushing back a
lock of Brylcreemed hair that had fallen forward and swung
across his forehead like a pendulum.

Vivienne pulled a face. 'Oh God, it's the clean air brigade,'
she retorted loudly.

Delilah sank into her seat with embarrassment as an argument started between Vivienne and the next table. Going out
with Vivienne was a liability.

'The impudent oaf, did you hear him! "A menace to society"!
Who does he think he is calling me a menace to society with
that ridiculous haircut and those clothes? Did you see them? If
anyone's a menace he is, with that offensive jacket.'

They were walking down towards Portobello Market.
Vivienne was fuming. She'd still have been there arguing if she
hadn't been dragged away by Delilah, who wouldn't have put it
past Vivienne to start slinging a few punches.

'Is that Hugh Grant's bookshop?' Delilah interrupted
Vivienne's ramblings to point to a pretty wooden-fronted shop.
A crowd of tourists jostled outside, taking it in turns to have
their photos taken.

'Oh, yes,' grumbled Vivienne, who'd plunged headfirst into a
foul mood. 'Blasted tourists, cluttering up the streets. I mean,
who on earth wants their picture taken in front of that?' She
looked incredulously at Delilah.

Delilah didn't answer. She'd never admit it to Vivienne, but
she wouldn't mind a photo herself. She'd never seen a real-life
film location before and she could send the picture to Auntie
Shirley, she'd love that. Hugh Grant was one of her favourites.
'Yeh,' she nodded in agreement, trying to act like a cool resident
when in fact she felt more like one of the totally uncool tourists
with their maps and cameras.

They passed lots of musty old antique galleries, wedged in
between shops selling discount shoes and electrical goods and

hidden by the fruit and veg stalls that spilled out across the pavements and into the road. There was a nip in the air and the stallholders bundled themselves up in layers of cardigans and fingerless gloves, their cracked, red fingers poking out of the ends, twirling paper bags full of runner beans and carrots, weighing out pounds of King Edwards and Granny Smiths. Vivienne told her the place was manic at the weekends. Delilah couldn't imagine it being any busier than it already was. People milled around in the street with bicycles, skateboards, roller-blades, bags full of food and sprawling bunches of flowers. Outside the pub on the corner, hardy groups sat on the wooden benches, drinking pints of lager and eating jacket potatoes from a mobile van.

Delilah loved it. She'd never been anywhere quite like it before. It was so vibrant, so different, so interesting. She walked about with a daft grin on her face, listening to Vivienne's running commentary, her eyes darting around her trying to take everything in.

'Oh, look, there's Sam!'

Delilah turned to where Vivienne was pointing and caught sight of Sam heading towards them. He was carrying a large crate stacked high with cartons of milk, his forehead wrinkled with concentration as he manoeuvred his way between stall-holders and crowds of shoppers. His face relaxed into a huge smile when he saw Vivienne and Delilah.

'Hey, what are you guys up to?' He ducked his head and gave Vivienne a kiss on each cheek. Delilah felt herself blush awkwardly, knowing it would be her turn next. She wasn't used to this kissing habit everyone seemed to have – kissing when you say hello, kissing when you say goodbye. She stood stiffly as he leaned over to kiss her. Feeling her embarrassment, Sam reddened. He felt self-conscious as well, but for a different reason. Since that night at the Pantry he hadn't been able to get Delilah off his mind. In fact he'd thought of nothing else. Seeing her again reinforced how he felt: smitten.

'We've just had lunch at Connor's, and there was this real

pain-in-the-arse on the next table . . .' Without pausing for pleasantries, Vivienne launched into a whinge, oblivious to the fact that Sam wasn't listening. Instead he was smiling distract-edly at Delilah, wanting to speak to her. Luckily for him Vivienne was interrupted by the sharp trill of her mobile phone, and began scrambling about in her bag.

'How did it go last night?' He was surprised by how nervous he suddenly felt.

'Oh, fine,' breezed Delilah, not wanting to go into details. She changed the subject. 'How come you're not at the café?'

'The milk delivery never turned up.' He shrugged his shoulders, still holding the crate. 'Which is why I had to come out and get some more supplies before we ran clean out. It wouldn't be much good for business, would it? A café without cappuccinos.'

Delilah smiled. 'So who runs it when you're not there? Have you got lots of staff?'

Sam snorted. 'You're joking, aren't you? I can hardly afford to pay my own wages let alone anyone else's, not with the bloody rent I have to pay. I've got a landlord who likes squeez-ing me dry of any profit I make.' Realising he was getting wound up, he made himself relax. 'No, a friend of mine, Patrick, is holding the fort. I think you probably saw him the other night when you came in. Jamaican guy, dreads down to his shoul-ders.' He looked at her for recognition – there wasn't any. 'Maybe not. You were too busy fainting to notice anybody.' He smiled cheekily.

Delilah groaned. 'Don't mention that, I feel such a prat. You must have thought I was some kind of loony.'

'Nah, you were sweet.'

Their eyes locked for a moment before Vivienne broke in.

'Guys, guys, I've got to dash. That was Christina at Nails to Go. They can fit me in for an earlier appointment if I get there in five minutes.' She kissed the tips of her fingers and waggled them in the air. 'Bye, sweeties. See you later, Sam, and Delilah, darling I'll see you back at the house.' She started trotting away, clattering across the road in Gucci slingbacks. Delilah looked at Sam and burst out laughing. 'She's completely mad. I don't think I've ever met anyone quite like her.'

'You won't have. She's a one-off.' He shook his head, watching Vivienne disappear down the street, exaggerating the swing of her hips as she strutted past a group of workmen, who stopped working to stare and whistle appreciatively. 'But she's got a heart of gold, you know.'

'I know,' nodded Delilah, thinking how grateful she was that Vivienne was giving her a roof over her head.

'Look, I'd better be getting back.' He gestured with the crate, which was beginning to make his arms ache. 'Patrick will think I've done a runner.' He paused, not wanting to leave her. 'Fancy coming along for a coffee?' He desperately wanted to chat to her, to get to know her better. There were a thousand questions he wanted to ask her.

'I'd love to, but I'd better go back and take Fatso for a walk. The poor thing's been cooped up all day.' She smiled apologetically.

'Oh, okay.' He tried to hide his disappointment. 'Well, erm, I'm sure we'll see each other around. Pop into the café any time.'

Delilah nodded. 'Thanks, I will.' She turned her head at the wrong time and they banged noses as Sam kissed her goodbye on the cheek. Giggling shyly, she began walking away and then turned, as did Sam, at exactly the same moment. Balancing the crate on one hand, he waved.

'Coffee's on the house,' he yelled down the street. Delilah waved back, grinning happily. Yep, she'd definitely made the right decision coming to London. She'd met Sam, who was lovely, and Vivienne, who was mad, and she'd even found a job – okay, so it was pretty crap, but it was still a job. All she had to do now was find Charlie and everything would be perfect.

Taking a deep breath she set off back to the house, arms swinging and a spring in her step, unaware that back along the street stood Sam, watching her work her way through the crowd, her wavy hair bobbing up and down with each stride. He waited until her tiny figure got lost in the crowd before trudging back to the café, the crate on his shoulder and Delilah on his mind.

Chapter Twelve

Walking to work a week later, she was beginning to have serious doubts – doubts that caused the spring to disappear from her step. There'd been no sign of Charlie, and she hadn't got any closer to contacting him. In fact a whole week had passed and she'd done nothing but work every night at the Pantry, collapsing into bed afterwards, constantly knackered and stinking of cigarette smoke. This wasn't what she'd had in mind – sleeping in until the afternoon, staggering out of bed before getting ready to go back to work again – and she was growing despondent and disillusioned.

Turning into Ledbury Road, she climbed the steps, wearily pushed open the door of the Pantry and, taking a deep breath, scanned the customers for any sign of Charlie. Not that she really expected to see him. After all, if this was one of his haunts she'd surely have seen him by now. Catching the eye of Vince, who was propping up the bar, she forced a smile. She'd do it for a couple more nights and that was it, she promised herself.

'Excuse me, do you have any Silk Cut?' An attractive twenty-something female in a cut-off T-shirt waved a fiver in front of her nose.

Delilah peered over her tray. Marlboros, Marlboro Lights, B&H, Camel . . . but no Silk Cut. 'If you can hang on a minute, I'll see if my friend has any.'

Ms Cut-Off T-Shirt tutted in exasperation. 'Well, okay, but you'll have to bring them over. I'm sitting on the table by the far window with a group of friends.'

'Sure.' Delilah smiled. Rude bitch. She'd met her type before, looking down their noses at waitresses, shop assistants and girls who happened to sell cigarettes. 'I'll come and find you.'

'Try not to be ages, will you?' The girl flounced off across the room.

Delilah bit her tongue and made her way towards Fifi, who was flirting like crazy with two merchant bankers.

Fifi waved as she approached. 'This is my friend Delilah, Delilah meet Bob and Brian, the guys from Shelling, Telling and Anderson.' Delilah put on her well-rehearsed smile and shook hands with the Brothers Grim. Two fifty-year-old Yanks in expensive Italian suits and Mickey Mouse ties. She couldn't believe it. How could anyone still be wearing those things? Hadn't they been laid to rest along with the other fashion disasters from the eighties: puffball skirts, 'Frankie Says Relax' singlets, cowboy boots. She looked down. They were wearing cowboy boots.

'Nice tie.' Delilah spoke to Bob.

'Gee, thanks, I thought it was kind of wacky.' Bob beamed with pride. 'It kinda matches my socks, doesn't it?' He pulled up his trouser leg to reveal a thick, hairy shin protruding from his boot, and a sock printed with miniature Daffy Ducks.

Delilah tried not to laugh. If only Sam were here. Or Vivienne. She suddenly felt a twinge of homesickness. Imagine what her friends back in Bradford would think if they met Bob. She tried to picture him in the Dog and Duck. He wouldn't stand a chance in his Daffy Duck socks and Mickey Mouse tie. If Vera didn't eat him alive with her withering sarcasm, Uncle Stan and the other regulars would spend the evening mercilessly *taking* the mickey.

'So, do you like working here?' smoothed Brian, taking a sip from his martini.

'Yeh, it's great. You get to meet all kinds of interesting people.' Dear God, what was she saying? Any minute now and she'd start telling everyone about her ambitions to work with children and sick animals.

Delilah turned to Fifi. 'Before I forget, I came to ask if you had any Silk Cut.' She couldn't take any more chit-chat. Soon she'd be asking Brian if he came here often. 'I don't seem to have any. Do we sell them?'

Fifi rolled her eyes and, leaning forward, whispered in her ear, 'Yeh, we do, but we try not to. The Silk Cut brigade are the tight-arse smokers. They think a tip's a bit of advice.' She leaned back. 'I don't normally carry them, but I've got a couple of packets under here.' She picked up her pile of matches. 'Take as many as you like. I prefer to stick with the Marlboro men.' She winked knowingly.

Delilah quickly made her excuses and started weaving her way towards Table Six, concentrating hard on not tripping over anything. Delilah was no stranger to accidents. As a child she'd been in and out of hospital with so many broken limbs her mum had threatened to make her live there. Of course she'd only been joking, but it had made Delilah a lot more careful. If only the same could have been said for her mum.

The table at the far window was large and rectangular. Around it eight people – four men and four women in their late twenties, early thirties – all jostled for space. They were on the dessert course of jelly and ice cream, apple pie and custard, bread and butter pudding – Pantry-style fodder – which lay half-eaten in bowls around the table. The men had moved on to flaming Sambucas, while the women were mixing champagne and espresso and nibbling on the pieces of dark chocolate that had arrived with their coffee, trying to satisfy their cocoa craving.

'Hi, I've got those Silk Cut if you still want them.' Delilah boldly addressed the table, trying to look confident, but feeling as nervous as hell. She hated addressing big parties of people, especially when they were all pretty drunk.

'Over here.' The girl in the cut-off T-shirt was sitting at the end of the table, waving her arm in the air, jangling her cheap plastic bracelets against her Cartier watch. She was leaning against a dark-haired guy who was concentrating on trying to set fire to a new round of Sambucas.

Holding out the cigarettes, Delilah squeezed between the chairs, not an easy task wearing a tray on your belly. This is what it must be like to be pregnant, she thought as she apologised for bumping someone on the head for the hundredth time. The girl grabbed the packet greedily and gave her the fiver. Fifi was right. No tip. She was about to head back into the main area of the restaurant when the dark-haired guy spoke.

'Excuse me, do you have any matches? I can't seem to light these drinks.'

He looked up at Delilah. She dropped the matches into his Sambucas. It was Charlie. Charlie Mendes of LLB Productions. Charlie whose surname she'd forgotten but which now came flooding back – along with a cartwheeling stomach and racing pulse. Charlie, who she'd almost given up hope of ever seeing again . . .

Delilah realised she was staring, open-mouthed. 'Charlie?'

He stared back. 'Don't I know you from somewhere?' He wrinkled his brow. Delilah's legs were starting to buckle. She'd pictured that brow a thousand times.

'Bradford General. You were filming.' She was having trouble getting past the monosyllabic stage.

'Jesus, Delilah, *is that you*?' He pushed the strands of hair back from his eyes. 'What on earth are you doing here . . .' He looked closer at the silver costume and piles of fags. '. . . And what are you doing with those cigarettes?'

'I work here.'

'But I thought you lived in Yorkshire.'

'I moved to London.'

Charlie fell back against his seat, grinning. 'And I thought I was the dark horse.' He was surprised at how pleased he was to see her again. When he'd first met her that night in the hospital he'd fancied her immediately. Not that that was anything new, he fancied plenty of girls, but it was why he fancied her that was different. Normally he went strictly for looks – long legs, cheek-bones, that kind of thing – but Delilah didn't have any of that. She was pretty, but it wasn't as if she was stunning or anything; in fact, to be honest, that night she'd looked a bit of a mess. No, it was something else about her that had been very appealing. That's what made him give her his card. He'd never really thought he'd see her again, but he wanted to make sure there was a chance that he might. And now, out of the blue, he had.

He looked around the table that had suddenly gone very quiet. His friends were staring in bemused interest at Delilah. 'Guys and gals, I want you to meet a friend of mine – Delilah.' He stood up and softly pressed his lips against her cheek. Delilah felt light-headed. It was finally happening.

Feeling slightly dazed, she started to shake hands with a few people at the table. Everybody was in soft-focus. Which was just as well, otherwise she'd have noticed Ms Cut-Off T-Shirt blowing smoke rings and giving her looks that could freeze the steam off a cappuccino.

'So, when are we going to finish our conversation?' Charlie whispered in her ear.

He'd remembered. Delilah smiled in delight. 'Erm . . . how about tomorrow evening?' she stammered, suddenly hit by the reality of what was happening. She was fixing a date with Charlie. Gorgeous, sexy Charlie with his job in TV and his exciting life in London. Her heart started beating like a jackhammer.

'How about eight?' He smiled that deliciously crooked smile.

She swallowed. Her mouth had gone as dry as the Sahara. 'Yeh, okay.'

'Give me your address and I'll pick you up.' He gave her a long, lingering look. 'By the way, the dress code is pretty relaxed.' Delilah followed his gaze – he was staring at her silver costume. She groaned inwardly. First the Alice Cooper impression at the hospital and now Ziggy Stardust. He must think she was some kind of Glam Rock freak.

She scribbled down her address on the back of some matches. 'I hope you can read it.' Delilah's usually steady hand had started to shake with a cocktail of nerves and excitement, transforming her handwriting into unreadable hieroglyphics.

'I'm sure I will.' He ran his finger over the squiggles of biro. 'I guess this is goodbye until tomorrow.' Sexily, he stared into her eyes.

'Yeh . . . until tomorrow.' Delilah smiled and without another word walked away. She knew he'd be watching her and so she tried her hardest to do her best wiggle across the restaurant, ignoring cries from customers for packets of B&H and groups of guys offering her flutes of champagne. She wasn't interested. Who needed cigarettes and alcohol when she could have Charlie?

Chapter Thirteen

'Dwayne's left me.' Vivienne lit up a cigarette and inhaled deeply.

'Left you?' Sam ripped off the side of a sugar packet and let the brown granules trickle into his coffee. 'What do you mean, he's left you? I never thought you two were really together.'

Vivienne flicked her ash onto the floor. 'We were very close. We understood each other but now . . .' She took a deep breath as if she was summoning all her courage to finish her sentence. '. . . He's dumped me, like a binliner, in the dustbin of life.'

It was 10 a.m. and Café Prima Donna was finally empty after the early morning commuter rush. Sam was knackered. For the last four hours he'd made coffee and toasted sandwiches for grumpy City suits, and when finally he'd found a moment to grab a croissant and read the paper, Vivienne had marched in wearing a shocking-pink silk sari and designer duffle coat. Scowling, she'd ordered a fry-up – 'I need nourishment' – and thrown herself, like an exhausted traveller, into a chair. Sam hadn't said a word, not even to remind her of her self-diagnosed wheat and dairy allergy. Trying to speak to Vivienne when she was in one of her moods was at best unpleasant, at worst dangerous. Instead he simply folded his paper, got up from his seat, and poured some oil into a large frying pan. Five minutes later he put a full English breakfast in front of her and pulled up a chair.

'I've been cast aside, abandoned, rejected . . .' Vivienne stuck her fork like a dagger into her fried egg, bursting the yolk. It oozed over the rashers, coagulating in a yellow pool around the dollop of baked beans.

'When did this happen?'

'Last night. The swine telephoned and said he was leaving me for some trollop called Trisha from the pick'n'mix sweet counter in his local shopping mall. Can you believe it?'

'Did he say why?'

Vivienne ripped apart a piece of bacon and chewed vigorously. 'He said he wants a relationship with somebody normal. What's he talking about? I'm normal, aren't I?'

Sam pressed his lips together to stop himself from smiling. Vivienne had been called many things, but normal wasn't one of them.

'I mean, what's normal, for heaven's sake? Someone who spends their days worrying about wine gums and sherbet pips? Is that what you call *normal*?' Her voice had climbed an octave and was getting louder. She screwed up her forehead, dislodging her bindi, which fell onto her plate. 'Christ,' she muttered, licking off the ketchup and squashing it back, upside down, between her eyes.

'Of course not, but who is—' Sam began but was interrupted.

'Exactly. He's just talking utter rubbish. It's quite obviously an age issue.'

Sam gave up trying to argue. He rested his chin in his hands and leaned on the table. 'Why, how old's Dwayne?'

She gasped in frustration. 'Nineteen. But I'm not talking about Dwayne. I'm talking about Miss Pick'n'Mix.'

'Well, how old is she?'

Vivienne narrowed her eyes and speared a mushroom. 'Sixteen. Sweet sixteen.' Waving it in front of his nose, she grinned maliciously. 'Which I suppose is quite appropriate. For someone whose occupation is selling sweets.'

Sam smirked. Vivienne was very entertaining when she was annoyed. 'Look, I know you're not going to want to hear this . . .' He held her wrist and slowly lowered the offending mushroom to the table. '. . . But she is nearer his age.'

'And I suppose I'm old enough to be his mother?' she snapped.

'I'm not saying that. But he's only a teenager, Vivienne, and so is she. And if you're honest, you were just in it for the sex, you've said so yourself.'

She dropped the fork dismally. 'I know, I just can't bear to think I've been shelved for some pert-nippled, stretchmark-free filly. I mean, sixteen! What can she offer? She's practically a foetus!'

Sam could see Vivienne was revving up to launch into her favourite topic, 'Men and Younger Women'. He tried to change the subject. 'Aren't you still involved with that army bloke?'

'Ex-brigadier,' she corrected, rather irritated. *Army bloke!* Sam made him sound like some snotty-nosed squaddie. 'Yes, I suppose I've still got Harold, which is some consolation. At his age he's just grateful to have a woman that's still breathing.'

Thankful that he'd averted a full-scale tantrum, Sam stood up. 'Do you fancy a cuppa? I've got some camomile.'

Vivienne's face softened. 'Yes, thank you, sweetie. And thank you for listening to my little outburst. I just had to tell somebody about it.'

'No problem.' He flicked a tap on the hot-water boiler, allowing the steam to escape. 'But why didn't you talk to Delilah? You two seem to be getting on really well.'

'We are, but she was still in bed when I received the crisis phone call. I think she got in rather late.' Vivienne stopped mid-sentence, distracted by a muscular guy, wearing wrap-around shades and a sarong, leaning his mountain bike against the railings outside. Jumping up from her chair, she rushed over to hold open the door for him, smiling vampishly.

'Cheers,' he nodded, sliding his shades up and over his fringe. He smiled, slightly embarrassed, before turning to Sam and ordering a sandwich in a strong Australian accent. An Antipodean! Vivienne switched her expression to 'coy', always a winner with the more macho surfer-types, and leaned against the large, American-style fridge.

'Whereabouts in Australia are you from?' she asked in her best tourist information voice.

The surfer-type fiddled with his woven bracelets. 'Er, Sydney. Manly Beach.'

'Really?' she rasped, before lowering her voice and muttering, 'How apt,' as she checked out his pecs with approval. Vivienne was like a bloodhound, one whiff of a man and she was on the hunt. And an out-of-town foreigner was easy meat.

Sam butted in. He wanted to know more about Delilah. 'So how's she been getting on at the Pantry? I haven't seen her since I bumped into you in Portobello last week.' Grabbing a knife, he sliced a ciabatta roll in two.

Vivienne dragged her attention away from the Australian's pecs. 'The poor thing's been working every night, she's completely shattered.'

'I hope she's okay. You can get some dodgy blokes in there.' Deftly he started chopping thick wedges of mozzarella.

'Oh, I'm sure Delilah can handle herself,' she said, before giggling teasingly. 'Do I suspect a soft spot?'

'Shit!' Sam cut his finger. A small trickle of blood appeared. 'Are you okay?'

'Yeh, it's nothing, just a nick.' Annoyed, he threw the tomato in the bin and turned on the tap, holding his finger under the jet of cold water.

Vivienne studied him for a moment. Normally placid, Sam suddenly seemed agitated. Was it Delilah? Had she touched a bit of a nerve without realising it? After all, she'd only been joking when she'd mentioned his soft spot. Vivienne watched the muscle in his jaw twitching. Sam was definitely hiding something, but getting him to admit it wouldn't be easy. He always played his cards very close to his chest. Unlike herself. She was quite happy to let everyone look at her cards and her chest. No, with Sam she'd have to try the softly, softly approach.

'You've fallen for Delilah, haven't you?' Vivienne wasn't much good at softly, softly.

Sam blushed. 'No, I just like her, that's all. I wouldn't want to see her being taken advantage of.' He unpeeled the sides of a bright blue plaster and stuck it carefully around his finger, smoothing down the wrinkled edges.

Vivienne nodded, not believing a word. 'Except by you, of course.'

Wiping his hands on his apron, his face clouded over. Although he and Vivienne had been friends for years, the last thing he wanted was her knowing his true feelings. He wanted to bide his time, to wait until the right moment before he told Delilah how he felt about her. He didn't want her finding out through blabbermouth Vivienne. 'It's not what you're thinking. Some people aren't obsessed by shagging, you know.'

The Australian coughed and scratched the back of his neck. Vivienne folded her arms defensively. 'And what's that supposed to mean.'

'You know what I mean, Vivienne, don't go all innocent on me.'

Peeved, Vivienne lifted her chin and checked her lipstick in the stainless-steel fridge door. 'Well, I wouldn't bother anyway. She's into some guy called Charlie.'

Moving her out of the way and pulling open the fridge, Sam grabbed a large handful of basil and began shredding it over the ciabatta. 'No, she's not. He's just some business acquaintance.'

'How do you know?' said Vivienne, rattled that Sam seemed to know more than she did.

'She told me a couple of weeks ago in the Pantry . . .' He wrapped the sandwich in a paper bag. '. . . While you were giving those guys a peep show.'

Vivienne glanced at the Australian, who was reading flyers on the counter, pretending not to listen. He was fooling no one. Ignoring his presence, she continued. 'So why was she so desperate to call him?'

Sam handed over the sandwich. 'I don't know. Maybe it was

about a job or something. That's probably the reason she came to London in the first place.'

'Maybe.' Vivienne wasn't entirely convinced. She'd seen the way Delilah's eyes had lit up when she'd mentioned Charlie's name. Nobody's eyes did that about a job. Jobs were to be endured, like small penises and hairy backs. You put up with them to get the end result, be it a wage or an orgasm. An image of Harold's 'little gunner' flashed before her eyes. Well, maybe not, she thought, changing her mind as she caught sight of the outline of the Australian's crotch underneath his Thai-silk sarong.

Putting his shades back on, the Australian held out a tenner. Sam smiled, shaking his head.

'It's on the house. Sorry about the wait.'

The Australian grinned. 'Hey, cheers mate.' He looked across at Vivienne, his testosterone levels surging as a result of the what-have-I-got-to-lose mechanism that had just kicked in: a characteristic unique to men which forces them to have a go at chatting up strangers as they're about to leave the pub/shop/cashpoint queue. Probably one of those quirky throw-backs of nature, originally intended to give Stone Age man a last chance to sow his sperm before he risked his life mammoth-hunting.

'See you around, maybe,' he smiled hopefully.

Vivienne fluttered her eyelashes. 'Yeh, maybe.'

Grinning cockily, he swaggered out of the café.

Sam shook his head. 'You shouldn't tease poor blokes like that. He must have only been about twenty-one. You'd eat him alive.'

'Exactly what I had in mind,' she laughed throatily, fluffing up her hair while looking at her reflection in the fridge door. To her it was all a game, and, winning or losing, she loved playing it. Out of the corner of her eye she watched as Sam moved over to the window and stared outside, deep in thought. 'You're thinking about Delilah, aren't you?'

He flinched. 'No.'

Vivienne lowered her voice and continued messing with her hair. 'Suit yourself. But if I'm right about what you feel, you should say something. Girls like Delilah don't come along every day.'

He didn't answer. Out of the window he'd seen something that might just prove Vivienne wrong.

Chapter Fourteen

They were instantly recognisable amidst a sea of designer shades and black and grey winter clothes slouching and strutting along Westbourne Grove. Dressed in an oversized faded-red tracksuit which gathered in floppy pleats around her ankles, Delilah jogged along the street. She was whistling to Fatso, who kept lagging behind, stopping outside the cluster of antique shops and peeing on the Louis XIV dressing tables and grandfather clocks that were being displayed on the pavement. Sam watched them both weaving their way in and out of the traffic. It looked as if they were heading towards the café.

They were. The door flew open. 'Hi, Sam.' Delilah burst in, panting heavily. 'Good morning Vivienne.' Bending over she put her hands on her knees and took a few deep breaths. 'I thought I'd run over here and give Fatso some exercise. We don't want you getting a spare tyre, now do we, boy?' Fatso let out a small bark in disagreement, his skin stretched tight over his ribcage.

'So, how was last night?' Vivienne's curiosity was bubbling over.

'Brilliant,' gushed Delilah, standing up and stretching. She'd woken up still heady from the night before, and had hammered on Vivienne's bedroom door. Except she wasn't there. Which was a bit of a let-down as Delilah was desperate to tell somebody about Charlie. Which explains why she'd decided to go and bore Sam with the good news. Being a bloke, he probably wouldn't be that interested in hearing how sexy Charlie looked, or want to join in a detailed analysis of what he said and how he said it. But she still wanted to tell him. After all, isn't that what you do with good news? Broadcast it. Even if no one really understands what the big deal is.

'Meet any unsavoury characters?' Vivienne smirked. Sam scowled and kicked her underneath the table. Vivienne kicked him back and missed. Fatso yelped loudly.

'A few. But listen, guess who I bumped into?' Delilah collapsed onto a chair opposite them, trying to contain her excitement.

'Who?' asked Sam.

'Charlie?' said Vivienne.

'How did you guess?' Delilah was slightly disappointed. She'd wanted to surprise them both.

'I'm a good guesser.' Vivienne smiled smugly, not daring to look at Sam. You didn't have to be the Brain of Britain to guess a guy was involved. Delilah was glowing. And she had that same bright-eyed look she had whenever Charlie cropped up in conversation. Vivienne suddenly felt jealous. Delilah was in lurve.

'I thought you'd lost his number?' asked Sam, feeling slightly miffed.

'I did, but he was at the restaurant last night with a group of friends. Isn't that amazing? Talk about a small world.' She smiled, looking very pleased with herself.

'And?' prompted Vivienne.

Delilah couldn't hold off any longer. 'He asked me out,' she announced triumphantly. 'We've got a date this evening!' There, she'd said it out loud. *Charlie* had asked *her* out. She still couldn't believe it was true.

'But I thought he was just a business acquaintance?'

Delilah wrinkled her nose. 'A *business* acquaintance? Where did you get that daft idea?'

She looked at Sam in bemusement. So did Vivienne, who raised her eyebrows in a told-you-so expression.

Sam felt crushed. He realised he'd jumped to conclusions, and unfortunately for him they'd been the wrong ones. He felt like an idiot. There he'd been, biding his time and waiting for the right moment to pluck up his courage to ask her out on a date, to confess how he felt about her, when all along she'd been interested in some other bloke. Some other bloke who had suddenly appeared from nowhere and wrecked any hopes he'd had of getting things together with Delilah. He glanced across at her. She was listening in amusement to Vivienne, who appeared to have recovered remarkably from her heartbreak over Dwayne and was telling her about the Australian surfer-dude. She looked gorgeous. Sighing, he turned away. Why is it that when you discover you can't have something, you want it even more?

'. . . And you should have seen the size of his didgeridoo!' exclaimed Vivienne, banging her fist on the table. Delilah threw her head back, laughing. God, she couldn't remember ever feeling this great – in fact, she had no idea you *could* feel this great. For a long time she'd suspected there was more to life, but she'd never imagined how much more. It was like flying economy all your life and then discovering the existence of first class.

Wiping her eyes, she noticed Sam was staring into space.

'What's up, Sam? You've gone very quiet.'

Sam and Vivienne looked at each other. If Vivienne had been about to say something she soon had second thoughts. His look was withering.

'Oh, nothing, just a bit knackered. I've been here since six. Isn't that right, Vivienne?'

Taking the hint by its horns, Vivienne shook her head rapidly. 'Oh yes. Sam's exhausted, utterly exhausted. In fact I'm surprised he can still keep his eyes open he's so exhausted.'

Delilah was sympathetic. 'I know what it's like, being on your feet all the time.' She wiggled her ankles; her feet were still recovering from last night's death-by-stiletto ordeal. 'Last night was a killer.'

Vivienne was still preoccupied by the Charlie revelation. 'So where's Charlie taking you?'

'I don't know. He just said he'd pick me up at eight.'

'What? He's coming round to the house?' Now it was Vivienne's turn to get excited. The thought of catching a glimpse of one of London's endangered species, an SSMM – straight single media male – was worth staying in for. She made a mental note to cancel Harold.

'Yeh, I mean, I'm pretty sure that's what he said. To be honest. I couldn't take it all in. I was so chuffed to see him.' Delilah grinned.

Chuffed! Sam fiddled with his teaspoon, slowly bending its neck until it was at a right angle. Since when did she become so chuffed about seeing this Charlie bloke? Before, he'd barely merited a mention and now she couldn't stop bloody going on about him. The head of the spoon snapped off in his hand. Obviously he was missing something here. Rather like watching the beginning of a movie and then fast-forwarding to the end.

'Are you sure everything's okay?' Delilah was puzzled. Sam was acting really strangely.

'No, I mean yes, I'm fine.' He smiled, but it fell short before reaching his eyes.

Delilah wasn't so sure. She couldn't put her finger on it, but there was something suspicious going on. Maybe he'd had an argument with Vivienne: there had been a lot of under-the-table kicking going on when she'd first arrived. And Vivienne wasn't exactly acting normal, but then when did she? She looked at her watch. It was nearly 11.30 – eight and a half hours to go. Her stomach churned. It reminded her of the feeling she'd had as a kid on Christmas Eve, wondering what presents Santa would bring. With any luck, tonight she was going to get a six-foot-two action man.

'Well, I'd better make a move.' Bending down, she put Fatso on the lead. 'I've got to start getting myself ready for tonight.' She widened her eyes in excitement. 'But I just wanted to come and tell you the good news.'

'Yeh. That's brilliant news.' Standing up, Sam awkwardly gave her a kiss on the cheek. 'Have a good time tonight, yeh?'

'You bet I will.' Opening the door, Delilah ducked past a group of Japanese tourists huddled under the awning having their photograph taken. 'And you get some rest.'

Sam smiled as Vivienne waved her cigarette in the air, booming, 'I'll see you back at the humble abode.' The door chimed as it swung shut.

Sam faced Vivienne. 'Before you say it, don't.'

'Don't what?'

'Tell me you were right. Right about that Charlie bloke. Right about me. Right about everything.'

'My lips are sealed.'

'Well, keep them that way.' Walking behind the counter, Sam emptied his cup in the sink and watched the dregs swirl down the plug hole. Feeling as he did that moment, it might as well have been his life.

Chapter Fifteen

'For that special evening glamour, team a chic black trousersuit with a pair of have-to-have diamanté mules and the essential pashmina.' Delilah was steadfastly working her way through Vivienne's back issues of *Vogue*. Have-to-have diamanté mules? Essential pashmina? She sighed. Hardly the kind of outfit she could rustle up with £50.

It was six o'clock and she'd spent all day trying to decide what to wear: should it be her black A-line skirt and black fitted shirt? Or what about her black flat-front flares and a black T-shirt? Realising there seemed to be a recurring theme here, she'd resorted to *Vogue* for advice. Unfortunately the only advice she could find seemed to be a) slim down to within an inch of your life, and b) spend vast amounts of money at Harvey Nichols. Exasperated, she flicked to the back of the magazine and scanned the beauty pages. A feature explaining how to achieve 'toned thighs and a flat stomach in ten easy steps' sat opposite a photo of Naomi Campbell. Delilah was unconvinced. Somehow it was going to take more than a few lunges holding a couple of baked bean cans to make her legs look like an airbrushed supermodel's. Heinz might boast fifty-seven varieties, but unless one of those was 'limb lengthening' it was a bit of a non-starter.

Delilah threw the magazine back on the pile in disgust. Those things should carry a health warning: 'Reading this load of bullshit could seriously damage your mind/bank balance/ self-esteem.'

*　*　*

'Delilah, darling, where are you?' Vivienne's voice echoed down the hallway.

'In here.' Delilah heard the front door slam and the thud of Vivienne's feet as she scrambled across the assault course in the hall. She barged into the living room.

'So, tonight's the night!' Vivienne whooped, accidentally standing on the hem of her sari and falling, hands outstretched, towards the Balinese coffee table. Delilah caught her before she hit the coasters. 'Blasted sari!' she cursed, staggering upright. 'This East meets West look might seem a doddle – I mean, Jemima Khan seems to be coping – but I simply can't get the hang of all this swaddling.' Vivienne held up the swathes of silk, looking bewildered. 'I must get a few tips from Fatima at the yoga centre. It must have something to do with my karma. Or lack of it.' She looked at Delilah and remembered her earlier train of thought. 'Ah yes, tonight. What are you going to wear?' Vivienne had severe doubts about Delilah's wardrobe, which seemed to consist entirely of jeans and T-shirts.

Delilah twiddled a strand of hair between her thumb and forefinger. 'Well, I think I'm going to wear my black flared trousers and a little vest top I bought a couple of weeks ago from the catalogue.'

Vivienne's mouth went dry. *The catalogue?* The nearest she'd ever come to one of those mail-order monsters was the time she'd had the misfortune to look through one of those irritating pamphlets that had fallen out of her Sunday newspaper. It had featured appalling photographs of women in flowery house-coats and belted dresses. It had not been a pleasant experience. She tried to appear casual. 'Why don't you borrow something of mine?'

Delilah felt slightly miffed. 'Why, what's wrong with my own clothes?' she asked. Just because she didn't blow three grand on an outfit didn't mean she was on a fashion blacklist.

Vivienne looked flustered. 'Why, nothing, nothing. I was just thinking that I have the perfect thing for you.' Hastily she tripped out of the room – 'Blasted hem!' – leaving Delilah crosslegged on the floor, still affronted by Vivienne's insistence on dressing her. Did she really think her clothes were that awful? And what the hell was she going to give her to wear? Delilah pictured the Adventure ensemble and groaned – dear Lord, don't let her suggest that. After the silver dress, Charlie would think she had some weird kind of cabaret fetish.

'If seduction is your aim, you can't fail with this.' Vivienne returned, brandishing a scrap of black material. 'I call it my secret weapon.' Delilah felt her anger trickling away like sand in an egg-timer. Vivienne was clutching something that looked suspiciously gorgeous. Taking the garment, Delilah held it up to the window. It was a dress – great. It was a black dress – even better. The only snag was the size. It looked *tiny*. Pulling off her jeans, she tried it on. It *was* tiny. This wasn't the kind of dress you'd choose when you were suffering from PMT and a bad case of water retention. This was a knock 'em dead, Liz Hurley number. A man-magnet held together by two shoestring straps and an awful lot of willpower.

'Do you think it suits me?' Delilah stood on tiptoe, inspecting herself from every angle in the mirror which hung over the fireplace. She wasn't sure if it was a bit OTT.

Vivienne balked. 'What do you mean, suits you? That dress doesn't suit you, it transforms you.' Even with no make-up and her hair twisted into two unwashed bunches, Delilah looked sensational. 'But how does it feel?'

'I feel like a million dollars,' murmured Delilah, amazed by her reflection. The dress pulled in her waist and pushed together her boobs, creating a pretty impressive cleavage. Well, impressive for someone who owed what little she did have to Gossard.

'Good. Seeing that it nearly cost that much,' cooed Vivienne, before laughing heartily at Delilah's shocked expression. 'Only teasing. It was a gift from friends at Dolce & Gabbana.'

Dolce & Gabbana! Delilah did a double-take. The nearest she'd ever come to a designer dress was at L'Escargot when she spent her teabreaks with Jean-Claude, the gay sous-chef, and his weekly copy of *Hello!*, taking the piss out of the honourable

Arabellas and horsey Pippas in their gold-but-toned Jackie O. Chanel suits and Regency-striped drawing rooms.

'But are you sure it's not too revealing?' Delilah was standing with her hands on her hips, looking worried.

'It's sexy!' protested Vivienne, losing patience. What did the girl want to wear on a romantic dinner date, dungarees?

Delilah felt unsure. There was a fine line between the very desirable can-I-buy-you-a-drink sexy and the not so desirable are-you-the-stripogram sexy. 'I just don't want to look as if I'm trying to be something I'm not.'

Vivienne was confused. 'Why? Everybody else does.'

Sighing, Delilah took a last look at her reflection. It was a toss-up between the dress or the black flares and catalogue top. She dug out a pound coin from her jeans pocket. Heads: her tried-and-tested Friday-night pub-crawl outfit; tails: Vivienne's secret weapon of seduction. She flipped the coin. It was tails. Although she didn't want to admit it, she was secretly pleased. She'd always dreamed of wearing a dress like this, and now she had the perfect opportunity. 'Are you sure you don't mind me borrowing this?'

'Of course. I haven't worn it for ages. I don't seem to get much opportunity for seduction these days.' Vivienne stuck out her bottom lip and flopped onto the sofa looking miserable.

Delilah ignored her. 'Great! I'll just go upstairs and pop in the bath if that's okay. Start getting myself ready for tonight.' She picked up her jeans and opened the door into the hallway.

Vivienne nodded miserably. 'Of course you must.' She lay slumped on the cushions, forlornly fingering the ripped sari material. 'Oh, to be young and in love. The rush of emotions, the pounding of the heart, the coming together of two souls.'

Without saying a word, Delilah left Vivienne wallowing in melodrama, and sidled out of the living room.

After an hour locked in the bathroom with a pumice stone, a loofah and some expensive exfoliating cream, which appeared to be made of crushed-up nuts and bits of muesli, a flushed but much smoother Delilah reappeared. She felt excited and nervous, a heady combination on an empty stomach. She heard the phone ringing downstairs and Vivienne talking hurriedly, her voice going up and down like an ambulance siren.

'Delilah, darling, it's for you-ooooo.'

Wrapping her towel tightly around her, she padded down the stairs. Only Sam, Vince and Charlie knew her number, so it had to be one of them. Crossing her fingers she hoped it wasn't Charlie ringing to cancel. At the end of the hallway she saw Vivienne clutching the receiver and frantically mouthing something. Delilah grabbed it from her.

'Hello?' She tried to sound calm and sophisticated. Not an easy task when Vivienne was buzzing around her like a bluebottle, earwigging on the conversation and gesticulating wildly.

'Hi, Delilah, it's Charlie.' His voice oozed down the line. 'I'm just calling to let you know I've made dinner reservations at General Practice, a restaurant in Soho, for eight o'clock . . .' He paused, waiting for Delilah to speak. She didn't. '. . . But I'm afraid I'm going to be caught up at work a little later than I'd expected and so it's going to be impossible to pick you up. I was wondering if we could meet there.'

'Yeh, of course. That sounds great.' Delilah turned her back on Vivienne, who was nodding her head like one of those plastic dogs you see in the back of minicabs.

'Are you sure? I feel kind of rude not coming over to yours, but you know what it's like when you're editing.'

'Yeh, I bet.' Delilah lied.

'Okay . . . look there's someone on the other line. I'll catch you later.'

'Yeh, bye.' She put down the receiver, kicking herself. What had happened to her vocabulary? He must think he was going out to dinner with someone whose conversational skills consisted of monosyllables and the word 'yeh'. She looked at Vivienne glumly. 'Did I sound like a moron?'

Vivienne wasn't listening. 'You're having dinner at General

Practice. How fabulous! How simply fabulous.' She rubbed her hands together gleefully. 'And he sounds utterly divine.'

Delilah stared at the telephone as if it were her enemy. 'Bloody thing.'

'Now, don't start being silly. Hurry up, you've got less than an hour. I'll call you a cab.'

'I'll catch the tube.'

Vivienne froze. 'In that dress?'

'I'll be fine, I'm a big girl you know.'

'Exactly. One glimpse of that cleavage and you'll be devoured.' Vivienne shuddered. 'Have you ever taken the tube?'

'Of course!' protested Delilah, lying through her teeth. She'd never even seen a map of the Underground, let alone got on a train, but she wasn't going to admit it. The sad fact was she had less than a tenner and it was either the tube, the bus, or walking. She chose the lesser of the three evils, or so she thought.

'I hope you realise there are no first-class carriages. You can end up rubbing shoulders with thieves and vagabonds . . .' Vivienne's voice boomed behind her as she ran up the stairs. 'Well, don't say I didn't warn you!' Delilah shut her bedroom door. She had less than fifteen minutes to transform herself into a blow-dried, nail-polished, lipglossed femme fatale. But there was no need to panic. Everything was under control. Or so she thought until she caught sight of her wet-haired, nail-bitten, freckled-face reflection. And panicked.

Chapter Sixteen

After a quick makeover: mascara, lippy, concealer, concealer, concealer (she'd broken out in a nervous rash), Delilah grabbed her denim jacket ('Very CK,' nodded Vivienne approvingly), a tube map ('disembark at Tottenham Court, darling, and not a moment later') and staggered to the station (after spending every evening for the last week in high heels, her feet had had to be forcibly coerced into her stilettos). Fifteen minutes later and she was still in the ticket queue, waiting behind the family of four tourists who seemed to be trying to buy a year's worth of zone 1, 2, 3 and 4 travelcards, using a mixture of French and German and air-traffic-control hand signals. When eventually it was her turn, the man behind the counter, who had exhausted all his patience, briskly pulled down his grubby little cream blind, making no attempt to try and hide his sneer.

Stifling the urge to scream obscenities, Delilah attempted the computerised ticket machines. Another five minutes were wasted pushing a sequence of buttons within a set time limit and feeding her £5 note into the machine several times in every way possible, until it finally disappeared and the EXACT MONEY ONLY sign flashed up. By now, Delilah was nearly in tears and had to seek help from the lecherous attendant in a Day-Glo pinny and peaked cap, who slavered at her cleavage while retrieving her fiver and giving her a ticket.

Clutching it thankfully, and with Vivienne's warning ringing in her ears, she charged onto the escalator and immediately wedged her stiletto heel between the metal grooves. 'Shit,' she muttered, wiggling her ankle furiously. Unfortunately for Delilah, as an Underground novice, she was oblivious to the fact that she was breaking one of the unspoken rules of the tube by standing on the wrong side on the escalators. She soon found out. While balancing unsteadily on one foot, she was nearly sent flying by 'a yoof', who barged past her shouting, 'Move out of the way, you silly cow.' Luckily, his shove freed her shoe and she was able to disembark safely. Limping miserably onto the platform, she sought refuge by the chocolate machine.

'Epping . . . 2 minutes.' The orange computerised writing flashed on the hoarding. She looked at her watch: 7.45. A businessman in a macintosh edged closer, as if there was no more room on the platform, and pretended to read the *Financial Times* while peering sideways at her over his half-moon spectacles.

There was a rush of wind and the train thundered into the station. Delilah cheered up, remembering *Sliding Doors* and imagining a carriage full of horny John Hannahs and wistful Gwyneth Paltrows. But this wasn't the movies. It was the 7.50 Central Line from Ealing Broadway, stopping at every station to Epping, and Delilah found herself squashed into a corner, trying to keep her balance by grabbing wildly onto whatever was screwed down. Easier said than done. She lurched intermittently into the busker playing a rendition of Simon and Garfunkel songs on his accordion, and the twenty-five rowdy teenage Italian students with their twenty-five multicoloured Benetton backpacks. By the time she reached Tottenham Court Road she was bruised and battered, not least because of an umbrella she could feel wedged into the small of her back.

Like the biblical parting of the seas, the doors slid open and Delilah stumbled onto the platform, feeling a sense of relief and shock. She turned, determined to give the umbrella-holder a dirty look, but stopped dead in her tracks. The accused was a balding forty-something man bursting out of a zip-up bomber jacket and a pair of suspiciously bulging marble-wash jeans. Suddenly she felt rather queasy. He didn't have an umbrella. Just a leery grin on his face.

Feeling slightly shaken from her ordeal, Delilah emerged thankfully from the station and made her way into Soho, where she saw General Practice, a large white monolith of a building, lit up by blue strobe lights. Gratefully she whirled through the revolving doors into the safe haven of the foyer, where a six-foot redhead wearing a skimpy A-line white tunic slouched behind the reception desk.

'Excuse me, I'm here to meet Charlie Mendes.' Delilah's voice echoed loudly around the room. She was still slightly deaf from the accordion player.

The redhead dragged a deep purple fingernail down her clipboard. Even with an unforgiving 100-watt spotlight directly above her, she looked immaculate. Delilah tried not to think about the cover-up on her chin which was slowly forming an American Tan crust.

'Yes, we have the booking.' She looked Delilah up and down, noting the Dolce & Gabbana dress, before flashing a set of very white teeth. 'Please go through to the bar.'

Trying to act cool and sophisticated, Delilah strode rigidly across the shiny parquet floor to the stainless-steel bar that ran along the far side. She felt nervous and unsure of herself. She'd never been to a restaurant like this before, the poshest one she'd ever been to was the Italian in Bradford, and that just didn't come close. This was the kind of place you felt you should talk in whispers. A steady hum of conversation buzzed from a party of glossy blondes wearing Joseph and five-star Caribbean suntans, poised on black leather chairs in the corner. Taking off her coat, Delilah wriggled onto the bar stool and scanned the drinks list. It wasn't cheap. The only thing under a fiver was tap water. She ordered a gin and tonic – remembering the vodka and Coke fiasco – and tried to avoid all eye contact with the boisterous Ralph Lauren brigade to her left. She felt very self-conscious. It was as if she was eight years old again, playing grown-up in one of her mum's evening dresses. Desperately, she sucked the gin through her straw and fiddled with her hair. At times like these she regretted never having taken up smoking. It was 8.20. Where the bloody hell was Charlie?

★ ★ ★

'Delilah, you look terrific!'

She looked up from her drink to see Charlie in a white linen shirt, half unbuttoned, with the collars hanging wide open revealing his smooth, nut-brown chest. He dripped sex appeal.

'Hi!' she squeaked, experiencing a sudden rush of hormones and gin.

Charlie bent down and gave her a kiss on each cheek, his stubble tickling her face. He smelled faintly of whisky. 'Sorry about the delay, I had to stay back for a quick drink with the team.'

'But I thought you were editing?'

'I was, but you know how it is at the post-production stage. Everyone kicks back and has a few bevvys when it's wrapped.'

Delilah nodded wisely. She didn't have a clue.

'Anyway, let me introduce you to some of the team. They thought they'd tag along and have dinner with us. That's if you don't mind, of course.'

Mind? She was gutted. Her much-dreamed-about romantic dinner for two had suddenly turned into a free-for-all. Hiding her disappointment, she shook hands politely with 'the team': Wendy, Nickii, Mandy, Andy, Jamie and Johnny, a six-strong posse of leather jackets and mobile phones who were seemingly unaware that collectively they sounded like the characters from a children's TV programme. She smiled, saying hello and forgetting names as soon as they were spoken. She was a bag of nerves. She wanted to make a good impression, for his friends to like her, so that Charlie would like her even more. Getting the bloke's friends to like you is crucial. Especially in the beginning. *And hopefully this was only the beginning . . .*

Nickii (with two 'i's and pronounced 'Nick-ee') was Ms Cut-Off T-Shirt from the night before. She smiled falsely. 'Delilah, it's so nice to meet you again. I hardly recognised you without your cigarette tray.' Tittering loudly, she looked around at the rest of the team like a comedienne waiting for applause. Delilah smiled unsurely. Was that supposed to be a dig? She wasn't certain, but it felt like one. She brushed it off – they'd only just met – and tried to ignore her gut instincts which told her she and Nickii weren't going to be friends. These feelings weren't helped by her first impressions. Nickii was wearing a ridiculously large white fur hat, which she obviously thought made her look like Julie Christie from *Dr Zhivago*. She was sadly mistaken. Delilah thought she looked like a rabbit.

'Where are you from?' cooed Wendy, cocking her head on one side and widening her baby-blue eyes. She harboured ambitions to be a TV presenter and greeted every new person with an eager interest, practising her technique for when she got That Break and could ask her guests the same question.

Delilah smiled. Since arriving in London she'd been asked that a hundred times. As soon as she opened her mouth, everybody said the same thing. She tried to look delighted, to pretend it was the first time anyone had asked her that interesting question. But it was difficult. Difficult to try and inject a note of enthusiasm into her well-rehearsed answer: 'Bradford'.

Wendy screwed up her button nose, looking nonplussed. 'Is that near Scotland?'

'Sort of,' Delilah nodded kindly. Now wasn't the time for a geography lesson.

'I thought so. I seem to have a real gift for recognising accents. I knew yours was Scottish immediately.' Wendy beamed, looking really pleased with herself. Delilah didn't have the heart to correct her.

'Are you from London?' Delilah tried to resuscitate the flagging conversation.

'Me? No, I'm from Tunbridge Wells,' she giggled self-consciously. Wendy's gift for accents obviously included dropping her cut-glass one and replacing it with one from Sarf London.

Charlie ordered two bottles of champagne. 'So, Delilah, how do you like the restaurant? A friend of mine designed it.' He brushed his hand against her knee.

'It's very . . . unusual.' Delilah's mind went blank. Making

intelligent comments on the decor wasn't easy when all she
could think about were his fingers gently rubbing her kneecap.
'I mean, I've never seen a restaurant like this before.' She
cringed. Jeez, she sounded like a complete idiot.

'It's modelled on a doctor's examination room.'

'Hmmm, lovely,' she nodded, chewing on her straw.

His fingers slipped underneath the hem of her dress and
started slowly moving up her thigh. Leaning closer he whispered in her ear, 'And I wouldn't mind examining you.' Delilah
made a loud gurgling noise as she hoovered up the last of her
gin from around the ice cubes. Things were moving a little
faster than she'd expected.

'I love all those little glass bottles of pills and things.' Playing
for time, she changed the subject and waved her hand arbitrar-
ily around, nervously uncrossing and crossing her legs, releasing
Charlie's hand. 'Are they real?'

'Probably,' he smirked, amused by how flustered she seemed.
'Here, let me get you another drink.' He leaned closer, removing her glass, and the straw which she was absentmindedly
chewing on, like a cow chewing cud. 'Would you like some
champagne?'

Delilah smiled, a trickle of excitement dripping down her
spine. *Champagne.* Just the word conjured up a feeling of excitement and anticipation. Of a special occasion. Of celebration. Of
romance. She nodded eagerly. 'Yes, please.'

Beckoning to the barman who was filling up the champagne
flutes at the side of bar, he asked him to pass him one and then
gave it to Delilah. Allowing his fingers to linger over hers he
winked smoulderingly.

'Can't we eat, I'm starving!' Nickii glared at Charlie, flicking
her ash on the floor. The posse murmured in agreement.

Smiling lazily, Charlie turned his face away from Delilah and
swivelled round on the bar stool. 'In a minute. First you've got
to whet your appetite.' He started passing round the flutes of
champagne that had been lined up on the bar. 'Here's to a great

show.' He raised his glass and then turned to Delilah. '. . . And
to our honorary team member, Delilah.' Everyone chinked
their glasses, eagerly slurping down the honey-coloured
bubbles. Nickii necked hers in one, glowering at Charlie, who
was grinning, champagne in one hand, Delilah eating out of the
other.

Covered in burgundy leather, the polished oak dinner table
resembled a huge desk. Charlie ushered Delilah into the seat
next to his as 'the team' clambered into their seats, hungrily
grabbing the menus that had been designed to look like oversized cardboard medical prescriptions.

'So, how long are you thinking of being in London?' Charlie
took a mouthful of Dom Perignon and stared deeply into
Delilah's eyes.

She held his gaze. 'Indefinitely.'

He smirked. 'You certainly are full of surprises, aren't
you?'

'Well, everyone loves surprises, don't they?' Sipping her
second glass of champagne, she tried not to laugh. She couldn't
believe what she'd just said. The dangerous combination of
Dom Perignon and lust was turning her into an outrageous
flirt. She looked at Charlie's mouth longingly. The last time
she'd felt this horny was when a Ewan McGregor lookalike had
come round to fix the central heating.

'And are you enjoying London so far?' He drained the last of
his champagne and poured himself another, giving Delilah a
top-up.

She watched the bubbles fizz to the surface. 'Yep, especially
tonight.' She grinned happily. Oh, what the hell, she thought,
taking a gulp of her drink, any ideas of playing hard to get
disappearing as fast as her champagne.

'Well, we'll have to make sure we have a lot more tonights,
won't we?' He smiled and clinked her glass with his.

Delilah nodded dreamily. The flirting was so highly charged,
she felt as if she had enough electricity running through her to

power bloody Blackpool Illuminations. She took a deep breath. 'That would be great.'

'Great,' murmured Charlie, lifting her fingers to his mouth and rubbing them against his lips.

She swallowed, clamping her mouth shut in case she let out a sigh, or even worse, a groan. God, this was more of a turn-on than any sex she'd ever had. She could hear the sound of her own heart thudding in her ears – loudly, rapidly. It was as if the posse and the restaurant had faded into the background and all she was aware of was her body and Charlie still holding her fingers. Feeling the tip of his wet tongue against them. She felt herself blush with lust and alcohol. It was like something out of one of those slushy women's novels, the ones you read, cringing at the corny sex scenes and thinking, 'yeh, right', as if you could ever feel like that. But she did, and she vowed never to take the piss again. Corny or not, it was like that and it felt fantastic.

'Would you like to order?' The waiter materialised wearing a hospital-blue tunic and trousers and carrying a clipboard. He looked as if he was just about to audition for *ER*.

His appearance brought Delilah back from her orgasmic trance, sobering her up slightly. He also had an immediate effect on the posse. All mobiles were switched off as they squabbled over the menu. Wendy and Mandy did a lot of oohhing and aahhing over the 'shallow-fried shitakes flambéed in port' while Jamie and Johnny chanted a mantra of 'order asparagus mash' to anybody that would listen. Delilah ordered chicken.

'Ugghh, how disgusting, aren't you a vegetarian?' crowed Nickii, blowing out a cloud of cigarette smoke.

Delilah was too pissed and loved-up to get annoyed. 'No, why, are you?'

'Of course. Eating dead animals is just revolting, isn't it, Charlie?' pouted Nickii, determined to grab his attention away from Delilah.

'Actually, I'm having steak.' Charlie licked his lips slowly, 'Medium rare.'

Smarting, Nickii sunk back into her chair, stubbing out her cigarette sulkily.

The food arrived, as did the glasses of chardonnay, merlot, whisky and Sambuca, until the conversation had deteriorated into slurring strings of non-related sentences. Andy and Wendy were snogging across the table, Jamie and Johnny had turned asparagus green as a result of stuffing their faces with eight side-orders of mash and Mandy was crying hysterically and telling Nickii all about her weight problem/cheating boyfriend/overdraft. Which left Delilah and Charlie. Without looking at the bill he paid for dinner, and placing his hand on Delilah's waist, he led her unsteadily outside. It was raining.

'Do you want to come back to my place?' Charlie put his arms around her, pulling her towards him.

Delilah closed her eyes. She could feel his warm body through her flimsy dress. It felt bloody marvellous.

'Well?' Charlie put his hand under her chin. Tilting her head he kissed her, parting her lips with his tongue. Delilah thought she'd died and gone to heaven. And she wanted to stay there, but she couldn't, not tonight. Despite a blood-to-alcohol ratio of 1:3 she knew that if she wanted to see Charlie again she had to go home alone. Uncle Stan had always said that courting a fella was like fishing: hooking them was easy; it was reeling them in that was the difficult part.

Charlie groaned sexily and kissed her, deeper and deeper.

'Charlie, I'd better go home.' She pulled away reluctantly. It was like putting the lid back on a half-eaten tub of Häagen-Dazs.

'Why?' mumbled Charlie, his blue eyes looking double-glazed. He wasn't used to being turned down. 'I really want us to spend the night together.'

God, this is tough, thought Delilah. Resisting temptation wasn't easy when you'd drunk the best part of two bottles of

Dom Perignon and enough spirits to fill a minibar. 'So do I, but not tonight.'

Charlie kissed her neck slowly. Even though he wanted her, he was too pissed to start trying to make her change her mind. 'Can I see you tomorrow?'

Her prayers had been answered. Delilah felt a surge of relief, she wouldn't have been able to hold out for much longer. 'Yeh, I'd love to see you.' She waved to a black cab which did a U-turn and pulled up alongside the kerb.

Charlie sighed, letting her go reluctantly. 'I'll call.'

Without answering, she opened the cab door and snuggled down into the black vinyl seats. Silently she thanked Uncle Stan. It looked as if Charlie was hooked. Now all she had to do was start trying to reel him in. Drunkenly, she smiled to herself. She couldn't wait.

Chapter Seventeen

'God, I feel terrible.' Delilah put her head in her hands and groaned loudly.

'You shouldn't have drunk so much champagne,' barked Vivienne, sweating profusely. 'It's meant to be sipped delicately, darling, not poured down one's throat like cheap house wine.'

Delilah couldn't speak. She was slouched on the rowing machine in Vivienne's private-members gym, feeling decidedly nauseous. What on earth possessed her to drink so much? And why oh why did she have that final, fatal Sambuca?

Vivienne tutted loudly, pedalling furiously on the bicycle machine. 'Come on, girl, show some spirit!'

Delilah tried to stop the bile from rising up her throat. If Vivienne wasn't careful she was going to be seeing more spirit than she bargained for. In fact a whole cocktail of spirits all over her Adidas trainers. 'I can't. I don't feel well.'

Vivienne stopped pedalling and adjusted her Olivia Newton-John sweatbands. 'If you can't handle your alcohol, you shouldn't drink,' she crowed piously.

Delilah ignored her. Vivienne was being a right pain in the neck. As someone who had been teetotal for ten years, she was taking great pleasure in chirping on about the evils of drinking. Which seemed slightly unfair. Especially as she'd enjoyed twelve fabulously debauched years of sex, drugs and alcohol, before finally collapsing in an alcoholic haze on the proverbial wagon.

It was 9 a.m., only seven hours since she'd been swapping saliva with Charlie. Delilah licked her lips. She could still taste him – or was it the Dom Perignon? She groaned, feeling her head thump in time to Fatboy Slim, which was pumping loudly from MTV on the monitors: all twenty-bloody-one of them. What had possessed her to let Vivienne drag her to the gym and inflict a tortuous regime of push-ups and sit-ups? All she wanted to do was some lie-downs, preferably next to Fatso under her duvet.

'So, come on, spill the beans,' demanded Vivienne. 'You haven't told me what that sexy little producer said when you left the restaurant.'

'He asked me to go back to his.'

'He *what*! Why the hell didn't you?'

'Because I thought that if I slept with him on the first night he wouldn't respect me.' Delilah's voice was muffled behind her hands.

Vivienne practically choked. 'Are you completely bonkers?'

'No,' said Delilah defensively, delicately lifting her head up and squinting at the harsh lights.

'Are you a virgin?'

'God, no.'

'Well then! What on earth are you doing?'

'I don't know,' mumbled Delilah feebly. She'd asked herself that same question when she'd woken up – alone – this morning. Last night, in her drunken bravado, she'd been certain she was doing the right thing, but now she was beginning to have second thoughts. What if he thought she was frigid? Or celibate? Or a dead loss? It was all right Uncle Stan spouting on about fishing, but what if Charlie was one catch that got away? She sighed miserably. 'I guess when it came to the crunch I wanted to wait.'

'*Wait!*' shrieked Vivienne, gripping the handlebars and flinging herself across the digital control panel. 'You don't start waiting when a highly desirable media male is offering you a fuck!'

'Vivienne!' hissed Delilah, looking over her shoulder in embarrassment. A pregnant woman with a shiny bob and ruddy cheeks glared, patting her bulge protectively.

'Well, a good piece of rump is an endangered species. They don't come along every day, you know.' Vivienne wriggled her shoulders and twanged her sports bra. 'You're lucky. Now that Dwayne's abandoned me, I'm having to make do with Harold three times a week.' Pressing her temples, she took a deep breath. 'And I can assure you that quantity does not make up for quality.'

Delilah watched Vivienne, eyes closed, nostrils flaring. It was truly amazing how she always managed to bring the topic of conversation back around to herself. 'Why, what's wrong with Harold?'

'What isn't?'

'But I thought you liked him?'

'I do, but not only is his Viagra costing a fortune on the Internet, he's still not . . .' Vivienne lowered her voice '. . . how shall I put it . . .'

Delilah leaned closer – as did the pregnant woman.

'. . . Fully erect.'

'Uggghhh, Vivienne.'

She looked affronted. 'Well, if you're going to be childish . . .'

'No, go on. I'm sorry.' Delilah sat up straight, trying to look sensible.

'Well, it's rather like a Tampax. Once he's inserted it, he plunges away for hours as if he's unblocking the sink, until finally it's expanded to fit. By which time I'm bored beyond belief. In fact last night he was so tiresome, I was tempted to start French polishing my nails.'

'But I thought you did all that, you know, kinky stuff?'

'Oh, we do, but Harold suffers from heart trouble. We can't get him too excited. There's only so much whipping the old boy can take.'

Coughing loudly, the pregnant woman prissily pulled down her 'Baby On Board' T-shirt.

Vivienne waved across at her cheerily and hollered. 'Not that you have to worry about that, sweetie. We already know what you've been up to with your chap.' The baby-carrier hotly heaved herself up from the exercise mat and scurried towards the exit, scowling.

Delilah put her hand over her mouth to stop herself from laughing out loud, while Vivienne beamed in a saintly fashion. Dabbing her forehead with a tissue she climbed off the bicycle. 'That's the legs sorted. Now for some bottom control.'

'Why, hi there, guys!' Delilah jumped as a loud American drawl roared through the gym and a tall muscly jock in a navy sweat-shirt with the logo 'Linton Villas Gym. Here to Serve You', bounded towards them. Heartily he slapped Vivienne on the back. 'So, how've ya been, honey? Haven't seen ya around for a long time!' He grinned, flashing ten years and $20,000-worth of orthodontistry.

'I've been terrific.' Vivienne tried to smile politely through gritted teeth. 'And you?'

'Gee, these last few months have been amazing. I've been doing a lot of film stuff and stacks of commercials. And then of course I'm getting serious feedback on the script I'm writing . . .'

Vivienne cut in quickly. 'Let me introduce you to my friend. This is Delilah.'

Delilah nodded feebly, trying not to stare at the enormous muscles in his neck. They made his head look like a pea.

'Hi, I'm Saviour.' He held out a frying-pan-sized hand.

Delilah shook it, trying not to smirk.

'Actor, screenwriter, former Gladiator and personal trainer at your service,' he drawled, inflating his chest like an inner tube. She watched as a network of knotted veins bulged alarm-ingly. Somewhere under his vest there was probably a valve you could unscrew and all that hot air would disappear, leaving him a shrunken balloon of fake-tanned skin and perfect teeth.

'That's nice,' said Delilah wearily. She was too hungover to try and think of something witty to say.

Vivienne stood up, wincing at her tender loins. 'Well, it's a shame we can't stay and chat, but we were just about to visit the steam room.' She turned to Delilah. 'Weren't we?' she trilled brightly – too brightly.

'Er . . . yes,' said Delilah.

Saviour shrugged, setting off a shock wave of rippling muscles from his armpits to his ankles. 'Gee, another time then, guys. Hey, nice meeting you, Deirdre.'

'Delilah,' corrected Delilah under her breath, dragging herself up from the rowing machine and following Vivienne, who had suddenly found a reserve of energy and was accelerating towards the door marked STEAM.

Condensation dripped down the white tiled walls. Delilah leaned against them, feeling as if she was being slowly steamed in a pressure cooker, like a large sponge pudding. 'Bloody hell, it's hot in here.'

'Just think of all the toxins you're eliminating,' barked Vivienne, lying spreadeagled and naked on the upper bunks.

Delilah could feel the alcohol oozing out of her. Her sweat probably tasted of champagne. 'I hope Charlie calls.'

'He will. Men are hunters, they don't like to go home empty-handed.'

'I don't want him to ring just because he wants to shag me.'

'Really?' This was a new concept to Vivienne.

'No, I want him to call because he wants to get to know me as a person.'

'Oh,' said Vivienne, slightly taken aback. Her idea of getting to know somebody meant discovering if they wanted to spank or *be* spanked. 'You did make sure the answering machine was turned on, didn't you?'

'Of course,' said Delilah. She'd checked the on/off switch about ten times.

'Super. There should be a juicy message waiting for us . . . I mean you, when we get back!'

'I hope so.' She closed her eyes, rerunning the moment when he'd kissed her for the hundredth time. Most of the night was a blurry haze, but she could pause those few minutes, frame by frame, in her head. His alcohol-tinged mouth, his tongue slowly parting her lips, the firm softness of his body through his linen shirt. She breathed deeply, feeling the condensation trickling down between her legs. God, she felt horny.

'So, what did you think of Saviour?' barked Vivienne. Her voice was like a bucket of cold water.

Delilah opened her eyes lazily. 'He was an arsehole,' she giggled faintly, wiping her neck with the white fluffy gym towels. 'And he thinks he's gorgeous.'

'I quite agree,' sighed Vivienne, extending her arms above her head and stretching like a cat. 'I can't think what possessed me to sleep with him.'

'My God, Vivienne, you didn't!'

'I'm afraid I did.'

'What was it like?' After ten monogamous years with Lenny, Delilah was very curious about the sexual performances of random blokes.

'Very disappointing. Not only had he given himself a full body wax, but he was slathered in baby oil, making him impossible to grab hold of.'

Delilah started laughing, imagining Saviour, plucked and greased like a oven-ready chicken.

'I tried everything – rubber gloves, talcum powder – but it was no good, he kept slipping through my fingers and sliding all over my satin sheets like an engorged goldfish, covering them in streaks of fake tan. I must have had those sheets dry-cleaned ten times, but you could still see the orange marks. In the end I had to donate them to Oxfam.'

The door wafted open and two middle-aged women came in, their diamonds glinting through the steam, and flopped their Swiss-masseured bodies onto the benches. They started twittering about Felix and Freddy's boarding school fees and some 'super new curtain fabric' from John Lewis.

Vivienne stood up. 'Time to go,' she trilled. 'We don't want to overcook and turn into wrinkled old hags, now, do we?'

Wrapping her towel around her head like a turban she disappeared in a cloud of steam through the swing door, leaving Delilah's toes curling with embarrassment. Vivienne's inability to mince words had her in a constant state of mortification. Keeping her head down she wrapped her towel tightly around her and made a break for the door, relieved that the curtain fabric wrinklies couldn't make eye contact through the condensation.

Hanging her towel over the metal hook, she stepped into the shower and pulled on the pink, plastic curtain. She felt slightly nervous. It was nearly time to go back to the house and see if Charlie had called. To find out if she hadn't blown it by being such a prude. Please let there be a message, she prayed. Please let the little red light be flashing on the answering machine as she walked through the door. Turning the silver dial to COLD she stood, fingers crossed, relishing the icy water as it sprayed onto her face.

Chapter Eighteen

It had been two days and there had been no phone call. Delilah was depressed. In the last forty-eight hours she'd skimmed like a big fat pebble over a huge lake of emotions. Each time she'd bounced on the surface she'd felt different: hopeful, frantic, upset, pissed off, disappointed, frustrated, angry – before finally hitting the water and sinking, with a resounding plop, into depression.

Had she really thought it would be so easy? That she could just jump ship in Bradford and come to London, find Prince Charlie and live happily ever after in a whirl of champagne and flaming Sambucas? Well, yes, she had. She'd never stopped to think about what would happen if it didn't work out. Simply because she'd never allowed herself to.

Delilah was determined that it would work out. One of the few pieces of advice her mum had given her as a seven-year-old, torn between wanting to be a ballerina and building a tree house, was that you can have anything you want, but first you have to decide what you want. And she'd been right. When she'd finally decided that she'd much rather be climbing trees than prancing around in a tutu, she'd built the tree house in two weeks, with the help of ginger-haired Gary from across the street.

When it was finished, her mum had brought her a packed lunch and she'd eaten cheese and piccalilli sandwiches while looking out onto the roof of next door's garden shed. She'd never forgotten that sense of power, and the realisation that once you make up your mind, you can achieve anything. Unfortunately, once she'd passed the age of seven, trying to

decide what she wanted in life became more difficult and
required a lot more courage: throwing away a leotard and a pair
of ballet pumps was slightly easier than throwing away a
boyfriend, a home, a job and a life. Which is why she'd stayed
with the same boyfriend, in the same town, in the same job, in
the same life, for so long. But seeing Charlie had made her realise what she wanted. And that evening at General Practice she'd
clung on to the hope that with a bit of determination and a
Dolce & Gabbana dress, he would want it too.

Except that now it didn't seem so certain. She'd spent the
last two nights working at the Pantry, hoping that Charlie
would show up, but there was no sign. Unfortunately the same
couldn't be said for Vince, who'd stalked her both evenings,
crooning *bellissima* in her ear and trying to persuade her to
come back to his 'pent'ouse' for coffee and tiramisu. Not
wanting to lose her job (and therefore putting paid to the
option of telling him to stick his tiramisu where the sun don't
shine) she'd made up a dozen excuses, ranging from being on
a diet to having to rush home to tackle piles of ironing that
simply couldn't wait. Delilah could be naive sometimes but
she wasn't that naive. She knew full well that there was a lot
more than just a bowl of sponge fingers in store for her if she
went back to his 'pent'ouse'.

On Sunday morning the phone finally shrilled. Sweaty-
palmed she army-dived for the receiver, but delight swiftly
turned to defeat. It was Sam, not Charlie, asking her if she
wanted to go to Brighton, seeing as it was the bank holiday
weekend. Hiding her gnawing disappointment she said yes – a
day at the seaside had to be better than moping around the
house watching Vivienne chainsmoke herself to death. There
was just one snag. His car was in the garage being welded back
together after it had been smashed into smithereens by the No.
27 bus. Could she drive?

Delilah gave up trying to overtake the National Express coach
and moved back into the slow lane. Ahead was an old Datsun

Bluebird crammed with two adults, two kids and what looked like the entire contents of their house. One of the kids, a little girl of about eight, was hitting her brother over the head with a green plastic spade. A family on their way to the seaside. She felt a sudden pang of sadness. Missing what she'd never had. Her mum had taken her to Scarborough once, but she could only remember it by the photos. A chubby toddler sat on a donkey, an attractive brunette wearing a 'Kiss Me Quick' hat holding her so she didn't fall. Her mum must have loved that hat, she was wearing it in every picture . . .

'So, what happened with your date the other evening?' asked Sam oh-so-casually while pretending to look at the road atlas.

'It went okay.'

'Just okay?' He ran his finger down a red wiggly A-road in an attempt to give the impression he was planning a route.

'Well, no, actually it was fantastic, but the real bummer is that he hasn't called me since.'

'Oh.' Sam didn't know whether he should be pleased or not.

'So, I s'pose he wasn't really that interested.'

'I s'pose so . . .'

Delilah looked across at him and glared. 'You're not supposed to agree with me, Sam. You're meant to say that of course he's interested in me and that there'll be a bloody good reason why he hasn't called.'

'Oh, yeh, that's what I meant. Of course he'll call you. If that's what you want . . .' His voice tailed off.

Delilah sighed and looked out of the windscreen. 'I really liked him. Well, I still do. He's so gorgeous. I just wish he'd called.'

Sam leaned forward and stroked Fatso, who was curled tightly at his feet. When he'd suggested a trip down to Brighton he hadn't intended for Charlie to hitch a ride. But here he was, slap-bang in between them. And he was the odd one out. He looked into Fatso's inky black eyes and rubbed his velvet-soft ears. 'It looks like it's just mates, then,' he whispered, his voice drowned out by the Fly-mo whirr of the 1100cc engine. Since that day at the café he'd been harbouring a smidgen of hope that she might have changed her mind about Charlie, that there might be a chance to be more than just good friends.

'So, what's Brighton like?' Delilah flicked on the radio cassette. It crackled loudly.

'It's fun. I think you'll like it.'

'Do you go there a lot?'

'It's where I grew up. My mum still lives there.'

'What? So we can visit her?'

'Well, yeh, I was going to suggest it, but only if you don't mind.'

'No. I'd really like to meet your mum.' Delilah fiddled with the dials, whining backwards and forwards through the radio stations. Frustrated, she pushed the cassette into the tape deck and turned up the volume. Tom Jones' 'Delilah' belted out of the speakers.

Sam looked across at Delilah, swaying her head from side to side as she sang along. She knew all the words off by heart.

He watched as she jabbed her hand in the air in time with the blasting chorus of trumpets.

The song finished, as did the tape. She pushed the rewind button.

'So you're a bit of a Tom Jones fan?'

'You could say that.' She spoke quietly, slightly out of breath from her duet with Tom, before pausing to think for a moment. 'I'm glad you asked me to come with you today.' She brushed the hair out of her eyes.

'I'm glad you came.' He looked down, fingering the pages of the road atlas.

'But there's just one thing I have to ask.' Delilah stared ahead, a faint smile playing in the corners of her mouth.

'What?'

'Why are you looking at a map of Wales?'

Sam started laughing. His cover had been blown. 'I guess you could say I'm a useless map reader.'

'Me too.' Her mouth broke into a wide smile and she turned to face him. It was only then that he noticed the tears on her cheeks. And he suddenly realised she'd been crying.

Chapter Nineteen

Brighton was chock-a-block. It was Easter weekend, and despite an icy wind the beach was full of hardy Brits, doggedly determined that nothing would spoil their annual trip to the seaside. Pensioners lined the seafront in deckchairs: a regiment of see-through plastic hoods and tweed flat caps, while families gathered in small windswept clusters on the pebbles. Mums with perms doled out ham and cheese butties to puppy-fat teenage daughters who listened to B*witched on their headphones and whinged about being cold and bored, and beer-bellied dads read the *Sun*, keeping one eye on the topless titbit on page three and the other on their kids dipping frozen pink toes into the water. Delilah watched a group of children trying futilely to build sandcastles out of stones and sludge. Idly, she wondered if one of them was the little girl from the Datsun Bluebird.

'My dad used to bring me down here at weekends. He'd buy me an ice cream, the kind with a flake in the top, and then tell me stories about shipwrecks and pirates.' Sam grabbed a plastic stirrer from the hot dog stall and stuck it into his polystyrene cup, trying to crush the sugar cube at the bottom. 'And I used to believe him, until I was about ten and I realised that this was Brighton beach we're talking about, not Cornwall.'

'Are your mum and dad still together?' Delilah took a large gulp of instant coffee and burned her tongue.

'No, Dad ran off with his secretary. It was a classic case of middle-aged bloke falls for twenty-five-year-old blonde. It'd be funny if it wasn't so pathetic.'

'Trust me to put my foot in it.'

'It's okay, it was over ten years ago now. I've got over it.'

'Do you still see him?'

'Not really. We never got on. At the time I hated him for leaving, 'cos of what he was doing to Mum, but there was a part of me that was relieved. No more arguments.' Sam sat down at one of the green fold-up tables. 'God, this is all a bit heavy, isn't it?'

'Don't be daft,' Delilah said, fiddling with the squeezy bottles on the plastic checked tablecloth. Red for ketchup; brown for HP Sauce; yellow for Colman's. Absentmindedly she started peeling off the drips of mustard that had congealed around the spout. 'So, does your mum still live in the same house?' Realising what she was doing she stopped. It was a disgusting habit.

'No. Dad remortgaged it against his business. When he left Mum he went off to live in Spain with Jackie, the secretary, and his business went bankrupt. The house was repossessed and Mum ended up renting. The bastard didn't leave her with anything. Twenty-two years of marriage and she got nothing.' He crushed his polystyrene cup bitterly. 'But what about your mum and dad. Do they live in Bradford?'

'Dad does, with his second wife.'

'What about your mum?'

Delilah paused. 'She's dead.'

Sam was shocked. 'Your mum's dead?'

She nodded, not looking up. 'Tuesday, 13 September 1981 at two forty-five. She usually finished work at five o'clock, but that day she left early to get things ready for the party. My ninth birthday party. If she'd left the office at the usual time she'd still be alive.'

'Why, what happened?' His voice was quiet.

'A lorry driver who'd had one too many beers. He took the corner too quickly and mounted the kerb. He couldn't stop. Mum was walking along the pavement. She didn't stand a chance. Eight and a half stone compared to two tonnes. Not much of a competition really.'

Sam put his hand on hers. It felt warm against her frozen fingers. 'I'm sorry, Delilah. You should have said something. God, you must think I'm a right prat going on about my dad.'

'No, I don't. I know what it's like to lose a parent, whether they die or walk out. You still feel abandoned.' She squeezed his hand reassuringly.

'Is that why you were upset in the car?'

'Yeh. It was the song. Mum loved that song. It was playing on the radio the day I was born. Hence my name.' She smiled wryly and looked out across the beach. 'Her and Dad split up while I was still a baby, and when I was little I'd listen to Mum's Tom Jones records and pretend he was my dad.' She broke off, feeling self-conscious, and fiddled with the cuff of her denim jacket. 'Kid's stuff, you know.'

As if on cue, Fatso changed the subject by letting out a long whimper. He'd caught a whiff of hot dogs from the nearby stand. 'I think greedy-guts Fatso wants feeding.'

Sam grinned. 'Come on, we'll get some food at Mum's. No doubt she'll have rustled up something. You know what mums are like.' He stopped short. Now he was the one putting his foot in it.

'It's okay, you don't have to treat me with kid gloves, you know.' Putting Fatso on his lead, she started to sprint along the seafront. 'Come on, then, slow coach!'

'But you don't know the way!' Shaking his head he watched her for a moment as she ran, full pelt, zig-zagging around the bikes and pushchairs. Keeping up with Delilah wasn't easy.

'Mum, this is Delilah.'

Squeaking excitedly, Sam's mum wiped her hands on her apron and hugged her as if she was a long-lost friend. Delilah stood rigidly, inhaling a heady rush of lily of the valley and Lenor fabric conditioner. She wasn't sure what do. Bear-hugging complete strangers wasn't a Yorkshire tradition. Shows of affection were strictly reserved for babies, boyfriends and grannies. Anybody else and people would think you'd gone bonkers.

'It's lovely to meet you, my dear,' she trilled in a thick West Country accent. 'I wasn't expecting you until later, the dinner isn't ready yet and I look a terrible mess.' Flustered, she brushed her curly black fringe from out of her eyes with the back of her sleeve, trailing a white powdery stripe of self-raising flour through her hair. It made her look like a badger. A plump, rosy-cheeked, four-foot-ten badger wearing a butcher's apron.

Delilah looked at Sam. He was smiling and shaking his head in amused affection.

'And you, you are terrible, Samuel. You never come to see me, your poor mother,' she clucked, tilting her face towards him.

Sam dutifully plonked a kiss on her perspiring cheek. 'I know, I know. I've been busy at the café.'

'Oh, that café.' His mum tutted and started peeling a mountain of Brussels sprouts. 'You should be in an office, none of this terrible café business.' She twirled the knife dangerously in the air, scattering sprout leaves onto the floor. 'Did he tell you that he's a lawyer?' She peered at Delilah. 'I am sorry, dearie, I keep forgetting your name.'

'It's Delilah.'

'Ah, yes, Delilah. Did you know that my son could have been a big lawyer in the city?'

'Mum!' groaned Sam. 'I did two years of a law degree. That hardly makes me a solicitor.'

'It's still a terrible waste.' She continued chopping sprouts vigorously, her mind made up.

'What's wrong with being a chef? C'mon, Mum, you of all people, you love cooking!'

'Being a chef is wonderful. But you aren't. You're making sandwiches and scrambled eggs. It's not cooking.'

Sam leaned against the sink and started eating raw green beans out of the colander. 'For the moment, yeh, but that'll change.'

Tutting in exasperation, his mum slapped his wrist with the tea towel. 'You're always picking! Stop it.'

Laughing, Sam dropped the beans and put his hands around her middle. 'What would I do without you, eh, Mum?' He stooped down and rested his head on her shoulder.

'I have no idea!' She wriggled free, shoving her chubby hands into a pair of pink gingham oven gloves and wrenching open the oven door to check on the roast potatoes.

The kitchen sweated like an athlete. Pans of diced carrots and string beans fogged up the windows, reminding Delilah of the steam room at the gym, except this time the aroma was one of onion gravy, not Eucalyptus oil. Sam's mum was perspiring profusely, a mixture of a hot flush and an impromptu facial from the pan of Brussels. Delilah offered to help but was firmly turned down. 'Don't be silly, dearie, I've got everything under control,' she gasped, fussing and bustling at the cooker, ambidextrously stirring two pans at once, while instructing Sam to lay the table – 'No, not those plates. We've got guests, use Grandma Godfrey's china.' Her court shoes clickety-clicked on the lino, like a tap-dance routine, as she yo-yo'd from the table, piling more and more dishes of food on her white lacy tablecloth.

Delilah was mesmerised. Would her mum have turned out like Sam's? Would she have become cuddly and comfortable, a dab hand at getting the lumps out of mashed potato, a woman nearing fifty with an M&S wardrobe and colour-coordinated soft furnishings? It was hard to imagine it. Her mum was frozen in time, a skinny twenty-eight-year-old who burned fish fingers, wore bell-bottom flares and Princess Di ruffled collars and drank Cinzano and lemonade when she went dancing on a Saturday night.

'Would you carve, Samuel, you know how you always do it so beautifully!' Sam's mum handed him a large serrated knife and glowed proudly, hands on hips, as he carefully shaved perfect wafers of roast beef. Delilah felt envious. Sam was lucky to have a mum like his. She was the kind of mum that worried he wasn't eating properly and still bought him Y-fronts in three-packs from the supermarket. The kind who'd always be there for him, whatever he did, whatever happened. Delilah thought about Tupperware Sandra, uninterested and child-phobic, hardly a first choice when it came to surrogate mothers.

'There, doesn't that look wonderful!' She wafted a plate of roast beef under Delilah's nose. 'Isn't Samuel the best carver you've ever seen?'

'Mum, you're embarrassing,' groaned Sam. Maybe introducing his mum to Delilah hadn't been such a good idea. He could feel whatever street cred he'd had slowly evaporating into the steam-filled kitchen. 'I'm sure Delilah doesn't want to hear about my carving skills.'

'I'm sure she does,' she protested protectively. 'Don't you, Delilah?' Sam's mum, who had swollen up with parental loyalty under her machine-washable chenille jumper, began energetically dishing out mountains of diced carrots.

Delilah wouldn't have dared to disagree, even if she'd wanted to. 'It all looks great.' She fixed his mum with a Sunday school smile as she drowned her plate in onion gravy. 'Especially the beautifully carved roast beef.'

She winked at Sam, who pulled a face before swiftly morphing it back to normal as his mum jammed herself into the chair next to him, puffing loudly. He put his arm protectively around her shoulder. 'This is fantastic.' He raised his crystal wine glass – one of four remaining from a twentieth-wedding-anniversary present. 'Thanks, Mum.'

'Yeh, thanks Mrs Godfrey.' Delilah happily chinked her glass against his.

'Call me Gladys,' she said, sipping her Liebfraumilch and turning as pink as her rare roast beef.

Chapter Twenty

Gladys snored loudly in the armchair, head lolled back and mouth wide open. She'd been like that for over an hour, ever since she'd polished off a huge plate of seconds – 'waste not want not' – and a 'goodly dollop' of crumble and custard. It was her body's way of reserving all its energy to embark on the staggering task of digestion. Delilah grinned and carried on washing up. 'Your mum's knackered, she must have been up since the crack of dawn getting this lot ready.' She finished scrubbing the baking tray with a brillo pad, having finally got rid of the incinerated remnants of the roast potatoes, rinsed it under the tap and passed it to Sam.

'I know, but she loves making a big fuss. She always has.' He wiped the tray and balanced it on the teetering pile of crockery on the sideboard. 'I think that's what she missed most when Dad left. I was already at university and so she didn't have anyone to make a fuss of.'

'Did you like university?' For someone who'd given up halfway through her A levels due to wanting to go out with Lenny rather than stay in with Jane Austen, Delilah's idea of university was constructed from watching the Oxford and Cambridge Boat Race on the news and reruns of *Chariots of Fire*: a plethora of pasty-faced academics in Shetland jumpers and half-mast corduroys vigorously debating politics and philosophy while nerdishly trying to lose their virginity.

'Not really. The people were okay but I hated doing law. I wanted to be a chef, but Dad went on and on at me to follow in his footsteps.'

'Your dad's a lawyer?'

'A solicitor, yeh. Ironic, isn't it? Look where it got him.'

'So what happened?'

'When Dad left I thought sod it, I'm doing what I want to do. So I jacked it all in and went to catering college.'

'And what about your mum?'

'She always makes out she's really bothered, but deep down I know she's pleased. She's always loved cooking. I guess that's where I get it from.'

'Chefs can make loads of money, you know. Just look at Delia Smith and all those guys on the telly.' Delilah thought of all those evenings she'd sat on the sofa, bored out of her mind as Lenny channel-hopped with the remote control. He'd always paused at the food programmes, which was amazing considering the only food he ate came out of tinfoil trays from the Indian takeaway down the road.

Sam shrugged, wiping a large frying pan. 'But I don't want to be on TV, faffing around on lunchtime cookery programmes, showing sad housewives how to make the perfect jam sponge. Or slaving away in one of the poncy joints in town. What I really want is to turn the café into a restaurant, run it myself.'

'Wow, that'd be great.' Delilah scrabbled around in the bottom of the bowl for the last of the teaspoons. 'Do you think you will?'

'One day. The guy who owns the premises says he might be interested in selling me the lease, but he's asking a bloody fortune.' He tutted bitterly. 'He's a bloody rip-off merchant, but what can I do? If I want to buy the lease, and of course I do, then I'm going to have to come up with the cash, and we're talking lots of it.'

'So what are you going to do?' Yanking out the plug, Delilah scooped the plankton of cabbage and floating sprouts out of the sink and into the pedal bin.

Sam pushed up his shirtsleeves. 'Keep slogging my guts out and saving, I guess. Or maybe I'll win the lottery, you never know. I'm an eternal optimist, something will turn up, trust me.' He smiled and picked up a bunch of soap-sudded cutlery.

Delilah watched him drying the prongs of the forks, his silver bracelet clanking against the handles. She didn't need to be told, she already knew that she could trust him. Vivienne always said his phone number should be 999, but there was a lot more to Sam than just a bloke who sorted you out in a crisis. He had dreams and ambitions. He didn't want to spend the rest of his life making scrambled eggs and serving coffee. And he wasn't going to. One day the café would be a restaurant and he would be the renowned chef, devising wonderful menus for appreciative customers. One way or another he was going to make it happen. Delilah was sure of that.

Dipping his rangy body under the grill, he started wiping the gas rings on the cooker. She caught sight of the bottom of his back, pale and broad, as his T-shirt came untucked from his jeans. He had a pretty good figure, lean but strong, like a long-distance runner. Her eyes moved down his body, past his baggy jeans bum and his lanky, slightly bowed legs. She looked at his feet. He was still wearing those bloody sandals. She stared at them for a minute. Something rather odd was happening. They looked okay, in fact they were starting to grow on her.

Gladys snorted violently and woke herself up with a start. 'Ooh, my goodness, I must have dropped off for forty winks.' She patted her flattened curls and hauled herself up from the chair. 'Now then, my lovelies, are you two staying the night? I've made up the spare room.' She beamed hopefully.

Sam looked at Delilah, feeling suddenly shy. 'Thanks, Mum, but we're just friends.'

Gladys chuckled, her bosom heaving up and down like a haulage system. 'Dearie me. I didn't know. I never like to ask with you young ones!'

Delilah smirked. 'I think we're going to drive back tonight anyway.' She looked at Sam. 'Aren't we?'

Sam nodded. He didn't want Delilah to think he'd roped his mum in as a co-conspirator to help him have his wicked way.

Not that he would mind having his way, wicked or otherwise, with Delilah. 'Yeh, I've got to get back to open up the café.'

'But it's a bank holiday,' protested his mum, looking crestfallen.

'I know, but I can't afford not to.' Sam bent down and kissed her gently on the forehead. 'I'll try and pop down in a couple of weeks.'

Gladys sighed as if it was her last breath. 'Don't you worry about leaving me all on my lonesome.'

'I won't,' grinned Sam. Grabbing Fatso by the collar he waited for Delilah to say her goodbyes. And waited. And waited. Gladys wasn't in any rush. She billed and cooed, clinging on to Delilah like she was a life raft and smothering her in frosty pink Yardley lipstick. After five minutes Sam decided enough was enough and rescued her from eau-de-toilette and chenille suffocation by firmly ushering her into the porch.

Laughing to each other they jumped in the Beetle. Delilah stuck the key into the ignition and turned. Not a dicky bird. She flicked the key again. Silence. She was flummoxed. In all the years she'd had this car it had always started. 'Shit!' She thumped her fist in the middle of the steering wheel, hooting the horn.

'Don't worry, I'll go have a look,' said Sam, clambering out of the car. 'Mum's probably nicked a spark plug or something to make us stay.' He smiled wryly and paced around to the back, lifting up the rusting engine flap. Delilah twisted the rear-view mirror to see what he was doing. It was no good, she couldn't see anything apart from Gladys, who'd swiftly appeared on the front steps and was grinning like a quiz-show contestant, unable to hide her delight at the sudden turn of events.

They decided to wait until morning to call the AA, a decision due partly to Delilah's sneaky feeling that she hadn't renewed her membership and largely to Gladys's insistence that she put the kettle on 'and make us all a nice brew'. After two cups of tea, so strong it could take the enamel off your teeth, and half a packet of biscuits – 'anyone for another custard cream?' – Sam asked Delilah if she fancied a bit of fresh air and suggested a walk on the beach. At the mention of the word 'walk' Fatso's ears pricked up and his tail started wagging violently. Barely able to contain his excitement he stared imploringly at Delilah, who answered his canine prayers by saying that would be a great idea, put on her jacket, clipped him onto his lead and followed Sam outside into the cold April evening.

They climbed down the concrete steps and onto the pebbly beach. The light was starting to fade and the beach was pretty deserted, apart from a couple of teenagers who sat, bundled up in padded fleeces, sharing cigarettes and drinking cheap bottles of cider. Delilah let Fatso off the lead and he ran, like a bullet from a gun, down to the edge of the sea. She stopped and watched him skipping manically through the water, laughing at how his skinny legs looked even skinnier when they were wet, like soggy pipe-cleaners. Sam stood next to her, smiling at her amusement, studying the silhouette of her face, how her nose scrunched up when she laughed, how her bottom teeth were slightly crooked because she'd given up wearing her brace as a kid, how her hair fell in mad Medusa waves over her cheek-bones and down across her shoulders, flapping gently in the wind. A strand became tangled in the collar of her jacket and he had an urge to lean across, put his fingers gently down the side of her face and free it. He stopped himself.

'So what brought you down to London?' Squatting down he picked up a large handful of pebbles and let them fall through his fingers.

Delilah stuck her hands in her jeans pockets and kept watching Fatso. 'Oh, you know. I've lived in Bradford since I was born and I was bored. I wanted a change. Something new and different, something exciting . . .' She thought about Charlie. She didn't want to tell Sam about the night she'd met Charlie in the hospital, it wouldn't do her credibility much good, he'd think she was some kind of lovestruck teenager. Either that or she was completely barmy.

'What were you doing in Bradford?'

Turning, she squatted down next to him, balancing her bum on the backs of her trainers. She picked up a stone, running her fingers across its smooth surface, and threw it as hard as she could. It landed short of the water. 'Living with my boyfriend Lenny and waitressing.' She stared out at the sea. 'We were together a long time but in the end it didn't work out.' She thought about him lying naked under June. 'We grew apart.'

'And what happened to your job?'

'Oh, I jacked it in. It was crap anyway, waitressing always is.'

'So why do you do it?'

'Why do you think?' she tutted. 'To earn money, the same reason you work in the café.'

'Yeh, but I'm not going to do that for ever, it's just a starting block.' He looked at her. Her lips pressed defensively together and he realised he'd touched a spot as raw as the wind that scudded across the beach. 'You've got me wrong, I'm not getting at you, Delilah. It's just that I hate to think of you waitressing, you've got so much more going for you. You're so bright and funny and intelligent, it seems such a waste. It's okay for a time, to get you by while you get your shit together, but surely there's something you want to do, something you dream about?' He fell quiet, suddenly aware of how loud his voice was against the lapping of the water. God, he'd really gone into one, he sounded like a fucking preacher.

Delilah sat silently, hunched over, her fingers digging at the pebbles around her. Sam regretted his big mouth. He'd really offended her now. He was about to apologise when she spoke, her voice barely audible against the sound of the waves.

'There was something I used to dream about. When I was little I used to spend hours playing with pots of paint, experimenting with different colours. My uncle used to be a painter and decorator and in the school holidays I'd go with him and watch him, fascinated by how he could completely change the feel of a room, just by using different colours. I guess that's when I decided I wanted to do something like that, but I didn't know what . . .' She paused and rubbed away a dewdrop at the end of her nose with her sleeve. 'It wasn't until I was a lot older that I heard the words "interior design", and realised there was a lot more than just paint and paper, a lot more you could learn. It was as if the picture had suddenly got so much bigger, so much more exciting. I was always pretty good at art and technical drawing and a couple of teachers helped me find out about courses. I dreamed of going to college, I knew that's what I wanted to do. I had loads of ideas, some of them were totally mad, but others were simple . . . ideas for houses, shops, restaurants . . .' She looked at Sam. 'It sounds stupid, doesn't it . . .'

'No, why should it sound stupid?'

She shrugged.

'So, why didn't you follow your dream? Why didn't you go to college?'

'Life got in the way, I guess – it tends to with dreams.'

'It doesn't have to. It's not too late, you know. You could go to college, part time or night school, there's a hundred ways round it. It could happen if you wanted it to . . .'

Delilah didn't answer. Instead she stared at her trainers, fiddling with the flap of leather that had started to come away from the sole. Her head was all mixed up. Sam had reached deep inside her and plucked out feelings and ambitions that Lenny, her life, her job, everything over the past ten years, had practically extinguished. She'd never thought that anyone would take those ambitions seriously, had thought that like Lenny they'd just laugh at her and tell her she was being an idiot. But Sam didn't. He didn't think she was stupid. He actually believed that she could go to college, study interior design, build a career. It didn't have to be just a daydream.

But now she felt confused, unsure. She'd given up those dreams for dead, and now here he was trying to bring them back to life. Trying to make her believe the dream she'd given up on ten years ago was possible. Was it? Maybe it was, maybe he was right. But hang on a minute, didn't she have a different dream now, anyway? Wasn't her dream Charlie, an exciting life with Charlie? Wasn't that why she'd come to London? Wasn't that what she wanted more than anything else in the whole world?

'I'm freezing.' Unable to cope with her turgid emotions, her mind gave up and focused its attention on the icy wind, making her aware of how her body was stiff with cold. Rubbing her hands together, she cupped them around her mouth and blew hot, damp breath onto her frozen fingers.

'Give them to me. I'll warm them up for you.' Grabbing hold of them, Sam squeezed them gently. His hands were as warm as toast. 'Let's go back.'

Delilah nodded and stood up, stretching out her aching limbs and whistling for Fatso, who was far along the shore, sniffing out crabs and stray knots of seaweed. He raced towards them and, putting him back onto his lead, they began walking back to the house. As they did, Sam pulled off his old sheepskin jacket and put it round her, resting his arm on her shoulders. She smiled appreciatively, snug against the warm lining of the tufts of wool. For the first time she didn't feel awkward with his affection. A subtle change had taken place between them, as if sharing her dreams had brought them closer. Sam could feel it too and breathing in the cold air, he pulled her against him. It felt so comfortable, so natural, so right. And together they walked home like that, neither of them speaking. Two figures huddled against the wind, trudging over the pebbles on a deserted beach, a small skinny dog running alongside.

Back at the house, Delilah started to yawn. The fresh air and food had left her feeling knackered. Being a gentleman, Sam offered to sleep in the lounge, and led her and Fatso, who had to be prized away from the two-bar electric fire, upstairs to the spare room. Once outside, he hovered behind her in the stairwell as she pushed open the door, letting Fatso timidly explore first.

'Are you sure you don't mind sleeping on the sofa?' Delilah pushed her hair away from her face. Sam shook his head, noticing the fine silver chain resting in the hollow at the bottom of her throat, the shape of her neck, the small vein throbbing by the side of her ear. Of course he minded sleeping on the sofa. He wanted to sleep next to her, to kiss her throat, her neck, the side of her ear. To feel her small, delicate body next to his. She looked so gorgeous, sleepy-eyed and tousled. Sam smiled nervously. It was now or never. He looked at Delilah. She was staring at him. Waiting for him to speak.

'Well, sweet dreams.' He cringed. He couldn't believe what he'd just said. He sounded like her bloody grandad.

There was an embarrassing pause. 'Yeh, you too.' Delilah leaned against the door-frame. For a moment there she'd thought he was going to say something else, do something else. She waited for him to speak again. He didn't. Couldn't. He'd been rendered speechless by his appalling one-liner. She suddenly felt a bit awkward and fidgeted uncomfortably. They'd been so close on the beach, both mentally and physically. Earlier, Sam's arms had been wrapped around her but now she felt weird about giving him a goodnight hug. It was as if the floral wallpaper and chintzy curtains had brought them back to reality, shifted things back to how they were before and reminded them of the boundaries of their relationship.

She tried to see his expression, but the lamp in the corner cast a shadow over most of his face. 'See you tomorrow, then.' She had no choice, she had to break the silence. She couldn't just stand there all night.

'Oh, yeh . . . tomorrow.' Smiling half-heartedly he stuck his hands deep into his pockets as Delilah did a little wave and disappeared into the bedroom. The door clicked shut as his face fell. He stared at the door. Damn, damn, damn.

★　　★　　★

Inside, Delilah flopped onto the pale-blue candlewick bedspread and stared at the cream Anaglypta walls. For a few moments out there she'd thought she felt something. That Sam was going to say something. Or do something. She'd even thought for a minute that he was going to try and kiss her. Giggling, she rolled her head sideways on the pillow, smiling at the craziness of such an idea. Naaaahhhh. Sam wasn't interested in her that way at all, they were just mates, good mates, the best of mates. Weren't they? She remembered the feeling in the hallway. If he had tried to kiss her, what would she have done? Would she have pushed him away? Catching herself, she tutted. What the hell was she thinking? Jeez, she must be tired, all that sea air was beginning to make her hallucinate.

Without getting undressed she patted Fatso onto the bed and wriggled under the eiderdown, inhaling the carefully ironed sheets which smelled comfortingly of fabric conditioner and pot-pourri. Closing her eyes she snuggled next to Fatso and in her half-slumbered state started dreaming of roast beef and mashed potatoes, Gladys and her chenille jumper, Sam and . . . Her breathing changed into deep, unconscious breaths. This was the first night she had fallen asleep without thinking about Charlie.

Chapter Twenty-One

They arrived back in London at five in the afternoon. It had taken them nearly four hours crawling bumper-to-bumper on the M23, which had been reduced to one lane of cones especially for the bank holiday, listening to Tom Jones tapes and working their way through Gladys's lovingly prepared roast beef sandwiches and two flasks of tea, 'one with sugar, and one without'. Delilah was shattered. She'd been up since seven waiting for the AA man, who had taken a lot longer to arrive than on the adverts. When eventually he'd turned up, there'd been a lot of frowning, tutting and shaking his head before he'd bluntly informed her that her car was due for the knackers' yard. Well, he didn't say that exactly, but that's what he meant. Delilah was undeterred, she wasn't about to see her beloved VW being towed away to scrap-metal heaven. So, putting on her best display of flirting, she'd pouted and whimpered, teary-eyed, until he was putty in her hands and her Beetle had wheezed back to life.

Rattling down Westbourne Grove she did a handbrake turn (her brakepads had worn down to blotting-paper thinness), skidding past Mungo's Jamba Juice Bar and a row of green wheelie bins, before rumbling to a standstill outside Café Prima Donna. She left the engine running – turning it off could be fatal.

'Well, thanks for a lovely couple of days.' She smiled at Sam gratefully. She might be tired, but she was in a much better mood than she had been in ages. A day at the seaside and some home-cooking had been just what she'd needed after a couple of weeks of London living: takeouts, traffic and tourists. And it had stopped her eyeballing the telephone, waiting for Charlie to call – or not.

Sam didn't answer. Presuming it was because he couldn't hear over the drone of the engine, she shouted, 'I said, thanks for a lovely couple of days.'

Sam jumped. He'd been preoccupied, dithering about whether he should ask Delilah out for dinner. Mentally, he'd been rehearsing what to say since Elephant and Castle. After his 'sweet dreams' line the night before he no longer believed that spontaneity was the way to go. Rubbing his hand over the tufts of bristles sprouting on his chin he decided to take the plunge. 'I was wondering if you'd like to have dinner tonight. I . . . erm . . . I was going to cook us some food, check if the old chef skills are still working.' Not what you'd call slick delivery, but better than last night. He waited for her to reply. It seemed like forever.

'Of course, I'd love to,' she laughed, breezily. 'Though what with you and your mum I'm going to turn into a right fatty.'

Sam looked shell-shocked. Never expecting her to say yes, he'd geared himself up for a rejection. Now he was speechless.

'Only joking, idiot.' She punched him playfully. 'What time?'

'Er . . . about eight?'

'Great, I'll look forward to it!' She waved happily as he got out of the car and walked in a daze across the pavement. Pulling away from the kerb she glanced in her rear-view mirror, watching him grow smaller as she neared the traffic lights. Sam was a lovely bloke. She was lucky to have found such a good friend. Yanking the car into third gear she let out a giggle, remembering what she'd been thinking about last night. God knows what had got into her, imagining Sam was going to kiss her. He didn't fancy her, just like she didn't fancy him. Simply because she was female and he was male, it didn't mean there had to be any kind of sexual attraction between them, did it? Theirs was a platonic relationship. They were just friends. *Just good friends*. Revving loudly, she smiled contentedly and spluttered round the roundabout, tilting sideways on two bald tyres, and headed home.

Feeling light-headed, Sam watched the green Beetle disappear in a cloud of carbon monoxide. She'd said yes. Delilah had said yes to dinner. Closing his eyes he tilted his face to the sun and took two lungfuls of London air. It had never smelled so good.

'Hello, anyone home?' Delilah slammed the front door and hopped, skipped and jumped over the hallway assault course. She was improving. A few more weeks of practice and she'd be able to negotiate it with her eyes closed.

'In the living room, darling!' baritoned Vivienne.

Delilah appeared with a thud at the doorway. 'Hi!' She stopped short. Vivienne was reclining on a chaise-longue next to some old bloke with white wispy hair, draped in what appeared to be a dead animal. Stuck on her finger was a huge, Rubik's-cube-size diamond. Something weird was going on. Over the bank holiday Vivienne had turned into Elizabeth Taylor.

Beaming brightly, she waggled the rock on her hand. 'Delilah, meet Harold, my fiancé!' Grabbing Harold by his fleshy ears she planted a sloppy kiss on the top of his shiny pink head, before turning triumphantly to Delilah. 'Isn't it simply marvellous!'

Delilah was gobsmacked. She blinked, speechless and rooted to the spot. Fiancé! Harold looked about *ninety*. Not only did he have a brown plastic hearing aid welded to his left ear, but he had the type of skin that was transparent and mottled with age spots, the sort you get at the same time as a telegram from the Queen.

Vivienne jumped up and began twirling around the room, her pelt missing the antique bone china by a whisker. 'We're going to have a church wedding in July. Isn't it simply marvellous?' she gasped, spinning to a standstill. Delilah wished dearly that Vivienne would stop saying that word. Marvellous was not the adjective she'd choose. More like horrendous. What was he thinking of? The next time Harold went inside a church it would be in a bloody coffin, not as a groom.

'Isn't it all a bit sudden?' Delilah didn't want to spoil the party, but felt that someone needed to get a grip here. Vivienne was off in cloud-wedding land, while Harold was lolling on the chaise-longue not looking like he knew where the hell he was – or who he was. Any minute now and he'd start dribbling.

'I know, but when he popped the question I couldn't say no.'

Delilah resisted the urge to ask why not. 'And when did he *pop the question*?' What a stupid phrase. Somehow Harold didn't look as if he had enough energy to pop anything.

'At his house in the country. Just before he went hunting.'

'And is that part of the fox?' Delilah pointed to the fur coat.

'No, no, no, silly. This is mink. Harold gave it to me as part of the engagement present, as well as the ring. Have you seen the ring?' She stuck it under Delilah's nose.

'I couldn't miss it,' muttered Delilah. Vivienne was behaving very oddly. Where was the cynical, chainsmoking bitch that she knew? 'When did you go to the country?'

'Yesterday. Well, I wasn't going to stay in the house all week-end, *by myself*.' She glared pointedly at Delilah.

'Oh, so it's my fault that you're getting hitched, or should I say, *stitched up*.'

'Sssshhhh,' Vivienne hissed, putting her finger to her mouth. 'Not so loud.'

'He's hardly going to hear us, now, is he?' muttered Delilah, sulkily.

Vivienne glowered and pushed her into the kitchen, while sing-songing over her shoulder, 'Only be a second, darling, just girly gossiping!'

Harold lifted his drooping eyelids, hurrumphed, then closed them . . .

* * *

'What's going on?' Delilah came straight to the point.

'Harold and I are getting married.' Vivienne stuck out her chin defiantly and stroked her mink lovingly. 'I'm going to be a bride.'

'Since when did you want to be a bride?' Delilah was still reeling from the announcement. Vivienne talked about a lot of things – sex, men, her wheat allergy – but never had she ever mentioned wanting to be a bride.

'Every woman wants to be a bride. Why should I be different?' She looked at Delilah, her eyes beseeching. 'It's all right for you, you're still in your twenties, but I'm thirty-five. I'll be thirty-six this year and time's running out for me. Already I'm being dumped for younger models . . .' Her voice tailed off as she thought about Dwayne and Trisha, his sixteen-year-old sweet-seller. 'And if I'm not careful I'll end up on the shelf. All my friends are married, or getting engaged. It's an epidemic. Everyone's getting married. Everywhere you look there's pictures of women in big flouncy white dresses. On the front of those dreadful tabloid magazines, even in *Vogue*. It's the thing to do, and I want to do it too.'

She looked so forlorn Delilah felt slightly guilty. Who the hell was she to start judging what other people did with their lives? She didn't exactly have a brilliant track record. 'I'm sorry. I didn't mean to be so horrible about the wedding and the coat . . .' She faltered. '. . . And Harold. It's just caught me by surprise, that's all. I don't want you rushing into something and regretting it.' She winced. Talk about do as I say and not as I do.

Vivienne fluttered her eyelashes and did her little-girl-lost look. 'You *were* pretty horrid,' she whimpered, sticking out her bottom lip.

To avoid a full-scale sulk, Delilah switched tactics. 'It's a bloody fantastic ring,' she enthused. Flattery was to Vivienne what boiling water was to a Pot Noodle. One minute she was cold, hard and impossible to stomach, the next she was transformed into something warm, soft and oddly appealing.

'Isn't it?' shrieked Vivienne, immediately springing to life. 'It was Harold's mother's: an eighteen-carat-gold, princess-cut, five-carat diamond ring. Damn marvellous, don't you think?'

Delilah nodded vigorously, throwing in a few oohs and ahhs for good measure. 'But . . .' – she had to choose her words very carefully here – '. . . are you sure Harold's not a little . . .' She grasped for the right word. '. . . Mature?'

Vivienne breathed on her ring and rubbed it with the edge of an oven glove. 'I know he's not exactly what you'd call An Ideal Husband, but he is terribly sweet, and he does love me.' Holding her ring finger up to the light she wiggled it approvingly.

'But do you love him?'

Frowning, Vivienne stopped admiring the rock and looked at Delilah. 'I'm very fond of him.'

'But are you in love?'

'How can you tell? What does *being in love* feel like?'

Delilah sighed. 'It can feel great, or it can feel bloody awful. But either way, you know if you are.' She thought of Charlie.

Vivienne snuggled into her mink. 'Oh well, you can't have everything.'

'Why not?'

'Because this is real life. Not a Barbara Cartland novel.'

Delilah felt suddenly deflated. Did real life mean having to settle for a comatose geriatric with a shiny bald head and a plastic hearing aid? What was wrong with dreaming about romance, true love and being whisked away by a dark hand-some stranger, preferably called Charlie? Sighing, she leaned against the cooker. 'Oh well, at least one of us got our man.'

'Why, what happened to you and Charlie?'

'Nothing. He never rang.'

Vivienne howled and clamped her hand to her mouth, nearly breaking one of her veneers on the diamond. 'Darling, I completely forgot.'

'What?'

'Charlie left a message.'

'A message? When?' Delilah couldn't believe what she was hearing.

Vivienne swallowed nervously. 'Yesterday.'

'Yesterday!'

Vivienne nodded dumbly.

'What did he say?'

Fearing that she was going to be chastised, Vivienne started wittering. 'He was in Scotland. Apparently he's been filming in the Outer Hebrides or some other godforsaken place and wasn't able to call. No phones or something terribly uncivilised. I mean, how these people can live without mobile phones is simply beyond me – they're obviously heathens or—'

Delilah swore. 'For God's sake, Vivienne, just tell me what he said.'

Vivienne stopped in full flow. 'He's picking you up at eight.'

'Tonight?'

'Yes, at eight.' Now it was Vivienne's turn to look exasperated.

Delilah was silent. Turning white, then pink, then red – like one of those seventies lava lamps – she started grinning. 'I knew there had to be a good reason why he hadn't called. I could tell Charlie wasn't the kind of man to tell a girl lies.'

Vivienne didn't like to point out that this was a slightly different view to the one Delilah had held two nights ago when she'd arrived home from the Pantry, worse for wear on Red Bull and vodka, yelling 'Lying bastard' at the top of her voice while trying to use the phone as a football.

'So are you going to go out with him?'

'Of course I am!' gasped Delilah, incredulous that Vivienne should be in any doubt. 'With any luck, you and I will be having a double wedding.' She giggled, flushed and excited, at Vivienne's expression, and darted for the door. 'Better take a quick shower. Could you babysit Fatso?' Bounding up the stairs, two at a time, she started laughing. For once, Uncle Stan had got it wrong. Reeling in a bloke hadn't been that difficult. It had just meant having to wait. And knowing Charlie, he'd definitely be worth waiting for.

Chapter Twenty-Two

Sam unwrapped the layers of newspaper and took a deep breath. There weren't many things in life as wonderful as the smell of fresh salmon. Add some coriander and lime juice, sear slightly, and serve on a bed of rocket with a drizzle of sage butter. Perfect.

It was 6.30 p.m. The café was silent. Empty. Closed. As soon as Delilah had agreed to have dinner, he'd decided against opening up and instead had rushed down to Portobello to buy the ingredients for tonight's gourmet meal. With great enthusiasm he'd carefully selected the freshest fish, squeezed, prodded and sniffed each and every fruit and vegetable – much to the dislike of the stallholders – until he'd found the ripest, and picked the brains of the local purple-nosed wine merchant to find the best grape and vintage to accompany each dish. Sam was determined to create a menu and an ambience for Delilah that would surpass that of any top London restaurant.

Tying his apron in a double knot he started assembling the ingredients: bunches of fresh herbs, handfuls of sugar snaps, baby courgettes and vine-ripened plum tomatoes, bags of oyster mushrooms, a bulb of elephant garlic, and a hunk of deliciously crumbly and deliciously pungent parmesan. He was excited. That evening he planned to tell Delilah how he felt. To throw caution to the wind and see if she felt the same way. There had been something between them that night on the beach. Maybe only a glimmer. But it was a glimmer of something.

He opened a punnet of raspberries and let them tumble into a bowl of icing sugar – they were part of a summer pudding recipe. His mouth watered as he ate one. With any luck, if he and Delilah got it together tonight, there would be dessert of a different kind on the menu. For the next hour and a half he worked non-stop to make everything look, smell and taste wonderful. He chopped herbs, sautéed mushrooms, shaved parmesan and whipped crème fraîche – and himself – into a frenzy. Sauces were whisked and sieved through muslin, asparagus spears were arranged with a surgeon's precision on large white plates and a bottle of red wine was uncorked and left to breathe. The shutters were pulled down, benches cleared back and one trestle table placed in the middle of the floor. A scattering of tealights twinkled softly around the café and a steel dustbin was turned into a make-shift vase and filled with a bunch of large white lilies. At five to eight Sam pulled off his pinny, ran his fingers over his half-a-centimetre-long hair and leaned back against the Coca-Cola machine. 'Perfect,' he whispered, looking around at all his hard work. The café had been transformed into a beautifully romantic grotto, even if he did say it himself.

Pouring himself a glass of wine, he changed into the shirt he'd just picked up from the dry-cleaner's and sat at the table, shining the knives and forks with a napkin. Taking a white lily he placed it next to her place-mat, then changed his mind. He didn't want it to look like some corny, over-the-top *Blind Date* dinner. Intimate? Yes. Slushy? No. Taking a gulp of wine he looked at his watch – 8.15. She was late. Perhaps she was still getting ready? Or Vivienne was keeping her chatting, no doubt filling her in on the latest sexual victim. He finished off the contents of his glass and poured himself another. Maybe she'd decided not to walk and ordered a cab? Getting up, he went to check on the food. Everything was ready for action. The minute hand of the mahogany wall clock inched towards half-past. Where was she?

The phone rang, a series of shrill beeps over the mellow

Cuban CD on the stereo. Picking up the handset he squashed it against his neck as he tossed the salad with the dressing. 'Hello?'

'Sam, is that you?' It was Delilah's voice. She sounded as if she was on a mobile.

'Yeh, sure. What's up? Are you waiting for a cab?' Unable to hear properly, he put down the wooden serving spoons and held the receiver.

'No, I'm actually with Charlie. We're going to an art gallery opening or something . . .' There was the sound of a man's voice and Delilah giggling. 'I hope you don't mind about tonight. I know you were going to cook some dinner, but then Charlie called . . .' More giggling. 'Well, he'd called already but Vivienne forgot to tell me. I meant to call you but it completely slipped my mind. Sam, can you hear me? Sam?'

Sam realised he'd gone silent and was rigidly gripping the telephone. 'Er . . . yeh, I'm here.'

'Oh good. Look, I'm sorry. You didn't go to any bother, did you?'

'No, I was just cooking up some pasta or something.' He glanced at the food, the wine, the flowers. 'It doesn't matter.'

'Maybe some other time, oops . . .' The line went crackly. '. . . We're going into a tunnel so I'll have to go. I'll call you tomorrow. Bye.'

'Sure, bye.' Sam placed the receiver back on the bracket and stood, frozen to the spot. *Some other time.* Her words replayed in his head like a voiceover. *Some other time.* He looked at the lilies standing sadly in their makeshift vase, the tealights twinkling softly – his pathetic attempt at lighting – the aroma of his painstakingly prepared food wafting around the café like a painful taunt. Jesus, he felt like such a fucking idiot. He'd got it completely wrong. Completely and utterly fucking wrong. How could he have been so stupid? How could he have thought he stood a chance? Delilah wasn't interested in him, she never had been. It was Charlie that she loved.

Dejectedly, he drained the wine from the glass and poured

himself another: a jilted man with only three bottles of vintage merlot for company. Swigging down ruby-red mouthfuls he felt a blurred rush of alcohol. There was nothing else for it – it was time to drown his sorrows.

Chapter Twenty-Three

'How do you turn it off?'

'The red button.' Charlie laughed affectionately as Delilah fumbled with his mobile phone.

'Oh, yeh.' Smiling sheepishly, she ended the call and leaned back on the soft black leather seat of his silver convertible Z3 BMW.

'So, who's Sam?' Revving the engine, Charlie shifted the car into fourth as they raced down Ladbroke Grove.

'Just a friend,' she breezed, trying to downplay their relationship. She didn't want Charlie getting the wrong idea.

'Yeh, I bet he's got the hots for you.' Winking sexily he moved his hand off the gearstick and onto her leg. 'Does he often cook you dinner?'

'No,' she answered defensively. 'It was no big deal. He's a chef and just wanted to try out a few recipes on me.' She thought about Sam and his offer of dinner. A slight doubt started to creep in. He wouldn't be pissed off with her for cancelling – would he?

'I bet that's not all he wanted he try out.' Charlie squeezed her thigh suggestively. Delilah giggled, slightly embarrassed. His touch sent shivers down her body, making her feel deliciously jittery.

'Don't be daft. Sam's a good mate. It's nothing like that.' She dismissed her fears. Of course Sam wouldn't be annoyed. In fact he was probably really pleased for her – he knew how much she'd wanted Charlie to call.

'I think my lady doth protest too much.' Charlie stared ahead, a crooked smile hovering on his lips. Delilah said nothing and looked out of the window, watching the houses race past in a streaky blur. She would never have admitted it, but she was enjoying his mild display of jealousy.

Zooming around a mini-roundabout they swung a hard left into a tree-lined street. Jamming his foot down hard on the accelerator, Charlie glided over sleeping policemen, dodging potholes and pedestrians. Suddenly he braked hard and, like a silver ball-bearing, catapulted the car with expert precision into a tiny parking space between a shiny green E-type and a Mercedes sports.

They'd come to a full stop outside what appeared to be an old post office, shoehorned between a row of old Victorian houses. Red-brick council flats loomed opposite and a group of tracksuited teenage boys jostled for space on the wall by the bus stop. Swigging from six-packs of Tennent's Extra and sharing a packet of cigarettes, they greedily eyed up the rows of flashy cars parked back-to-back along the road. To a group of lads who had just passed their driving test, it was as if Christmas had come eight months early.

'What is this place?' asked Delilah, clambering out of the car. It reminded her of the red-light district in Bradford. She'd driven through there a few times, making sure she kept her eyes on the road and not on the prostitutes who guarded their territory like bulldogs. Standing on the kerb in a skirt and high heels (that she'd borrowed from Vivienne, whose sprawling shoe collection was nudging Imelda Marcos proportions) she suddenly felt like one. She folded her arms defensively.

'It's Perfect Package, the art gallery I was telling you about.' Charlie pulled on his old leather jacket and got out of the car. 'Come on, I'll introduce you to the artists, they're a couple of friends of mine.' Putting his arm tightly around her waist he kissed her gently on the end of her nose. 'Don't look so nervous. You'll have fun.' He looked deeply into her eyes. Delilah nodded, feeling apprehensive, as he pressed the buzzer and, hearing the whirr of the intercom, pushed open the heavy steel door.

Inside was a mass of people and champagne glasses.

Chinking and chattering, they mingled around large multi-coloured canvases displayed on four walls and lit by giant spotlights. Charlie ushered her into the middle of the room. Grabbing two glasses of Moët from a frosty-looking waiter, he thrust one at Delilah. 'Don't move. I'll be back very soon,' he whispered in her ear, his hot breath tickling her neck.

'But where are you . . .' – her voice tailed off as she watched his broad back disappearing through the throng – '. . . going?' Abandoned centre-stage, she nervously took a gulp of champagne and swivelled 360 degrees on her stilettos, taking in her surroundings. The place was heaving with celebs. In one corner a couple of children's TV presenters in push-up bras and trainers were giggling and sharing a joint, while in the other a clique of society It-girls were quaffing back their second case of champers and admiring each other's pashminas. Nobody seemed to have noticed the paintings.

Delilah drained her glass and immediately reached for another. It felt very weird to be in a room full of people she recognised from the telly and the pages of *Hello!* She knew everyone, but no one knew her. After years of sharing many a pleasant evening with these people – her on the sofa, them on the telly – she felt as if she was one of their best friends. She'd even been privy to their deepest darkest secrets, thanks to regular *News of the World* exposés. But tempting as it was to butt into their conversations and laugh 'remember when', she couldn't because a) she hadn't been there, b) to them she was a complete stranger, and c) they'd think she was a raving loony.

After two flutes of champagne she'd got rid of her nerves and was feeling restless. Bored with waiting for Charlie she began circling the room, poncing yet another drink from the frosty waiter and wolfing down a handful of smoked salmon vol-au-vents. In fact she was just getting the hang of this art gallery malarkey when she became aware of someone's eyes burning into her forehead and realised she was on course for a head-to-head collision with the Elvis Costello lookalike from *Adventure.* Deftly scooting sideways, Delilah hid behind what looked like a woolly mammoth, but which was in fact a portly, middle-aged and alarmingly bearded female journalist from the society pages of a national newspaper.

While waiting for the coast to clear, it was impossible not to eavesdrop on Ms Hirsute, who was discussing a particular piece of artwork with a gangly man half her age. Decked out in a black velvet suit, frilly shirt and a manicured goatee, this interior-designer-cum-media-celebrity was waving his lacy cuffs around as if he was conducting the London Philharmonic.

'I simply love the sheer force of the orange marker,' he declared in his luvvy voice, wrinkling his brow in an academic kind of way.

'Absolutely, absolutely. Though I must say the blue ink intermingles terribly well. Almost like a Pollock, wouldn't you say?' gushed Ms Hirsute, licking her jammy lipsticked mouth provocatively and moving closer.

Delilah looked at the canvas. At first glance it appeared to be covered in squiggles of marker pen and inky smudges of Bic biro, rather like those jotter pads you keep at the side of the phone. On closer inspection she realised it *was* lots of scribbles. She squinted at the title: 'Boredom' by Petal Plummer. Delilah knew how she felt. Charlie had been gone for nearly three-quarters of an hour. At this rate she'd be inclined to grab a packet of felt-tip pens and start doodling herself.

'Delilah, I want to introduce you to two very good friends of mine.'

She spun round to see Charlie, each arm glued around the twenty-inch waists of two Amazonian beauties. He flashed her a smile. 'Pollen and Petal Plummer, this is Delilah.' Gripped by a horrible shrinking feeling, rather like Alice when she'd polished off the contents of the bottle labelled 'Drink Me', Delilah suddenly felt about two inches high. The tanned and tousled identical twins towered above her, chewing gum and smoking herbal cigarettes. These were the famous twenty-something daughters of an even more famous sixties actor and his ex-model wife, and were always being photographed in exotic locations around the world wearing frangipani flowers in their hair and not much else.

'Hi,' squeaked Delilah, trying and failing to be all nonchalant and pretend she didn't know who they were.

The Plummer siblings grinned lazily and blew a fog of perfumed smoke down their nostrils.

'The pictures are great, especially "Boredom" . . .' grappling for something to say Delilah nicked Mr Frilly-Shirt's line. 'I simply love the sheer force of the orange marker.' She cringed. It didn't have the same effect when spoken in a broad Yorkshire accent.

Nodding vaguely, Pollen and Petal dragged on their cigarettes and nuzzled closer to Charlie.

Delilah shut up. The twins were interested in Charlie, not her. Feeling ignored, and now irritated, she snatched another glass of champagne from a passing tray and fired them a dirty look. If all else failed, she might as well get completely pissed at their expense. Pulling a desperate let's-get-out-of-here face she stared at Charlie, who was making no attempt to disentangle himself. On the contrary, he looked to be enjoying every second of it.

'I think I'll pop to the loo.' She forced a smile. 'Do you know where it is?'

'To your left, darling.' Reaching out, Charlie brushed his hand against hers, taking her champagne glass. 'I'll look after this for you.' Grinning sexily he took a long, lingering sip. 'Don't be long,' he winked boyishly. Delilah's annoyance melted away. The alcohol was making her paranoid. Charlie and the twins were mates. They were being friendly, not flirting. Appeased, she winked back and unsteadily began making her way through the crowd of pashminas in the direction of the ladies' loos.

The queue for the toilets snaked around the washbasins. Delilah sighed. She was bursting for a pee: the result of too much champagne and not enough food. A large woman with an even larger beehive sat in the corner, surrounded by hairspray, perfume, Constance Carroll make-up and half a pound of Mint Imperials. She kept waving various items around for general usage. Delilah politely declined the bottle of Tweed and Impulse body spray.

Some of the women were clutching credit cards. Blimey, thought Delilah, how much does a few squirts of Vidal Sassoon hairspray and a dab of translucent powder cost? She felt the loose change in her top pocket – probably a couple of quid if she was lucky. That wouldn't even buy her a coat of mascara. Crossing her legs, she leaned against the wall and waited. Two girls appeared from a cubicle, sniffing violently and looking very pleased with themselves, causing the rest of the line to giggle conspiratorially. Delilah was nonplussed. Fuelled by alcohol, she moaned impatiently. 'What's taking everybody so long?'

The peroxide blonde next to her smirked knowingly. 'Are you gasping for it?'

Delilah grimaced and nodded painfully. Her bladder had doubled in size. If she didn't get to a toilet soon her waters would break.

'Me too,' hissed the blonde, bending closer. 'If you're interested I can do you a gram.' Sliding a cellophane packet from her wallet she pressed it into Delilah's palm. 'Only fifty quid.'

The penny dropped. *Cocaine. Everybody was doing cocaine.* Delilah balked. Despite living in a society rife with it, and with a media that was obsessed with it, she'd never actually come across the real thing. Coke wasn't something you were offered down at the Dog and Duck – unless you put ice and lemon in it and had it with a packet of pork scratchings. And when she'd been clubbing it had been more Es and acid. Not that she'd ever bothered with those. In fact she'd never done any hard drugs – unless you counted the amyl-nitrate poppers she'd found in Tupperware Sandra's drawer when she was fifteen.

A cubicle door swung open. Shoving the packet back at the

startled blonde, Delilah managed to gasp, 'Not today, thanks,' before scuttling inside the sanctuary of the loo, leaving what little remained of her attempts to appear cool firmly behind.

She found Charlie by himself, leaning against a table stacked high with empty Moët bottles. He looked as pissed as she was.

'Can we go? I'm bored,' whispered Delilah, who was feeling like a complete prat after her *faux pas* in the ladies' loos.

'Sure,' grinned Charlie, grabbing her denim jacket and pulling her towards him. He buried his nose in her hair. 'I'm sorry about this evening, darling. I got talking to a few people and couldn't get away. Were you okay?'

'Yeh, fine,' fibbed Delilah, resting her head on his shoulder and inhaling the warm, pungent scent of his leather jacket and aftershave. She wanted to stay there for ever.

'Come on, let's go. Do you want to stay at mine?' Charlie kissed her ear gently.

She nodded dreamily.

'Well?'

'Yeh . . . I'd love to,' she murmured softly. This time she didn't have any doubts. There was nothing she wanted more than to spend the night with Charlie.

Chapter Twenty-Four

Delilah rested her head on Charlie's chest. Floating on a post-orgasmic high, the elusive buzz she'd assumed only existed in the pages of *Cosmopolitan*, she ran her hand over his smooth, walnut skin and sighed blissfully. *They'd done it.* Bonked. Shagged. Made love. Call it what you like – they'd done it. Twice in fact. *They'd had sex and it had been bloody fantastic.* Even despite the bit where she'd got her tights wrapped around her ankles and dive-bombed on top of him, narrowly missing kneeing him in the bollocks.

Pissed and horny, they'd grappled on the duvet, Delilah's inhibitions disappearing as fast as her underwear. Not that Charlie had been shy. Smothering her with kisses, he'd swiftly exited his jeans and T-shirt, revealing a body she'd thought only existed on boxes of Calvin Klein underpants. After ten years of being faced with Lenny's body – pale, hairy and sagging like an old settee – Delilah had been lost for words. Which probably explains why she spent the next hour and a half enthusiastically grunting and groaning.

Not that it had all gone without a hitch. After two bodged attempts at putting on a condom (being on the pill with Lenny she'd never used them before and was all fingers and thumbs – Delilah didn't remember it being as fiddly when she'd practised on test tubes in fourth form biology lessons) Charlie suffered an attack of brewer's droop. Luckily she'd remembered her St John Ambulance training, and, after a spot of mouth-to-mouth, brought him back to life – saving both his pride and the situation.

*   *   *

Charlie was lying on his back, eyes closed. Delilah tilted her head to look at him. God, he was handsome. She wriggled closer, breathing him in. The room had finally stopped whirling. All that sex must have sobered her up. Bonking was the perfect hangover cure – much nicer than a couple of Nurofen and a fried bacon sarnie. She smiled to herself in disbelief. It didn't seem real, being snuggled under the king-size duvet with Charlie Mendes. Any minute now her alarm would go off and she'd wake up next to Lenny.

But she was there. And so was Charlie, with his long muscular legs, six-pack stomach and dark brown hair flopping in damp strands over his forehead. Sweating faintly, his tanned skin glistened under the dim bedroom lamplight like a race-horse. She traced the long blue vein down his forearm, snaking downwards to his wrist and into his hand. His fingers closed gently around hers.

'Hi.' Lifting his heavy eyelids, he gazed at her.

'Hi.' She smiled, a mixture of happiness and nerves. What happened now? Was she supposed to play it cool? Or be loved-up? She wasn't exactly a seasoned pro when it came to jumping into bed with blokes. Cheating, she asked him first. 'How are you feeling?'

Gently stroking the side of her face, he grinned. 'Sleepy. How about you.'

'Me too,' she lied, staring alertly into his pale-blue eyes.

Charlie stared back, before curling his arms and legs tightly around her. Rolling her sideways he started kissing her neck. Delilah closed her eyes contentedly, feeling his lips tickle her ear, her shoulder, her chest. He didn't seem so sleepy now. Smirking, she moved her hand stealthily under the covers. There was no mistake, he definitely seemed to have something other than sleep on his mind.

'I seem to have woken up,' he breathed heavily into her ear, moving his mouth across her chest and latching firmly onto her right nipple.

'Me too,' she gasped. This time she wasn't lying.

*   *   *

Sunlight glowed through the white muslin curtains, faintly illuminating the bedroom. Peering through her eyelashes, she squinted at her surroundings. White. Everything in the vast shuttered bedroom, from the walls, curtains, duvet – even to the few minimal pieces of furniture – was white. And not a matt-emulsion white, but a creamy, smooth, alabaster white that you find in museums and art galleries. It gave the impression that she was lying in a large white cocoon.

Sliding out of the bed, she grabbed the white fluffy bathrobe and, pulling it around her, padded quietly across the floor. In the far corner was the steel spiral staircase, twisting downwards to the open-plan living room. Gingerly she climbed down it, smirking as she remembered how they'd staggered up it the night before, clinging onto the railings and each other. No easy task when you've swapped your sense of balance for a wicked case of the spins.

Charlie's flat was spotless. The highly polished wooden floor ran throughout the kitchen and living room – forty feet of the latest electronic gadgets, designer furniture and a television screen that would rival the one at the multiplex cinema in Leeds. Delilah's head turned 360 degrees like a barn owl scanning its domain. It was just as she'd imagined. No hideous swirly carpets or Formica kitchen, no gas fire with fake plastic coals and a shiny brass hood, no tassled lampshades and Laura Ashley wallpaper borders. It was the picture-perfect pad, straight out of a glossy magazine. A homage to interior design and the kind of apartment she'd always dreamed of.

Flicking the switch on the shiny silver kettle, she started cautiously investigating the sleek, stainless steel cupboards, on the lookout for coffee. A jar of Nescafé would do, even Gold Blend at a push, but there was nothing. No instant, freeze-dried granules, no teabags, no sugar, nothing. The shelves were stacked neatly with pristine white plates and long-stemmed wine glasses. A far cry from Vivienne's units, cluttered with overflowing bags of gluten-free muesli, Third World fruit teas and packets of organic crumbs, brazenly masquerading as chocolate-chip cookies.

It was as she was crouching on all fours, head in the fridge, that she felt his touch on her shoulder. 'Can I give you a hand?'

Delilah jumped up, banging her head on the freezer compartment. 'Oh . . . er . . . I was just looking for some milk . . .' The kettle boiled and clicked off. '. . . And some coffee – if you've got any.'

Wearing only his jeans, Charlie scratched his chest and face, yawning. 'Oh, I'm sorry darling. I'm clean out of all that kind of stuff. My cleaner normally gets me a few things but I've been away such a lot recently it hardly seemed worth it.' He pulled her close. 'Unlike you.' He kissed her hungrily. Delilah squirmed, feeling embarrassed. She didn't exactly look her best first thing in the morning. Last night, soaking up the alcohol like a trifle, she'd felt like a fifties Brigitte Bardot, curvaceous, kohl-eyed and pouting. Now she looked like the nineties version. Sleep, sex and plenty of snogging had smeared her lipstick around her lips, and as for her eyeliner – what wasn't on the white linen pillowcases had formed a large ring underneath each eye, as if she'd done a couple of rounds with Prince Naseem during the night.

'I need to wash my face.'

'No you don't, you look beautiful.'

Delilah couldn't remember the last time someone told her she was beautiful – not counting baggy-arsed workmen and randy lorry drivers she used to serve at the motorway café. Feeling suddenly shy, in contrast to the earlier display of bedroom acrobatics, she changed the subject. 'You've got a lovely flat.'

'Thanks. I only moved in a couple of weeks ago.' Charlie grinned. 'So you approve of my choice of accommodation?'

'God, yeh, I'd love to live here . . .' She stopped. She didn't want him to think she was trying to get her feet under the table.

'So why don't you?'

'What?'

'Live here. You said earlier that your friend's house is only temporary. And this place is too big for one person.'

'But . . . we hardly know each other . . .'

'I wouldn't say that, would you . . . ?' Slipping his hand inside her dressing gown he pushed her up against the grill and started kissing her face.

'But . . .' Delilah tried to resist, then gave in. Resisting Charlie was like resisting a bar of Cadbury's Fruit and Nut the day before your period. Bloody impossible.

He pulled gently away. 'So, what do you say?'

She couldn't say anything. To describe Delilah as being stunned would be more than a slight understatement. She was well and truly flabbergasted. Shocked. Amazed.

Bloody delighted. She swallowed hard. Was this really happening? *Could* this really be happening to a girl from Bradford, with only a clapped-out Beetle, a Tom Jones collection and a whippet who snored, to her name? Talking of Fatso . . .

'I've got a dog.'

'So, I've got a cat. They'll love each other.' Cupping her face, he tenderly kissed the hollow of her neck. He was being very persuasive. Not that he needed to be. This was what she'd been dreaming of since they first met. It had just happened a hell of a lot sooner than she expected. Out of the corner of her eye she spotted a row of empty test-tube vases attached to the wall. Just like she'd imagined. It must be fate. They were poised, waiting for her to fill them with gerberas, those primary-coloured daisies that long-haired women in sports cars bought by the dozen at the florist round the corner from Vivienne's. Wrapped in brown paper and tied with bits of raffia, they cost a fiver a flower – daylight robbery, thought Delilah, who was used to buying pastel-pink carnations and frothy gypsophila in patterned cellophane from the local garage: two quid a bunch, or three for a fiver.

'Well, as long as you're sure it's okay,' she said hesitantly.

Charlie gave her a big bear hug. 'Of course it's okay, silly! It's more than okay.' And scooping her up he carried her, Rhett-Butler style, into the living room. As he lowered her down onto the sprawling sofa, she sank into the soft velvet material. Charlie crawled next to her, laughing. 'I didn't think I'd be able to make the stairs.' Delilah beamed happily and took a deep, jubilant breath. She'd done it. She'd reeled him in. Uncle Stan would be proud.

Chapter Twenty-Five

'I'm moving in with Charlie!'

Vivienne spat a mouthful of rosehip tea over her new copy of *Brides* magazine. 'You're doing *what*?' she squawked, her vocal chords screeching upwards like a strangulated cockatoo. Delilah winced. Bubbling with excitement, she'd just returned from Charlie's, shagged out and loved-up, to find Vivienne sitting at the kitchen table, elbow-deep in wedding paraphernalia. A copy of Debrett's *Speeches and Toasts* lay on a pile of veil netting. Swatches of ivory silk were scattered all over the floor, Fatso and his tartan designer doggy basket – a present from Vivienne.

'I'm going to live with Charlie. You know, as a couple.'

'Have you gone stark staring mad?' spluttered Vivienne, hastily wringing out the free gift of confetti, which had been sellotaped to the front cover and had now turned into a soggy red pulp.

'No,' scowled Delilah, feeling miffed at Vivienne's less than enthusiastic reaction. 'I said we're going to live together. I didn't say we were getting *married*.' She glared pointedly at Vivienne.

'All right, all right. Point taken. I'm just . . .' Vivienne jumped up from her stool as a globule of rosehip tea trickled down the edge of the table and onto her Prada palazzo pants. 'Fuck,' she shrieked, grabbing the first thing that came to hand and scrubbing her trouser leg vigorously. Unfortunately she'd grabbed the sodden confetti packet. The tiny pink spot spread into a very large scarlet one.

*   *   *

Seized by panic, Vivienne continued scrubbing, oblivious to the fact she was making matters worse. Each sweep of the hand was accompanied by 'fuck', 'bugger' or 'bollocks'. Delilah's earlier annoyance rapidly changed to amusement. It was like watching a classic *Fawlty Towers* sketch; Vivienne *was* John Cleese – albeit wearing Prada and not a nylon pinstriped suit. 'These are brand, spanking new. Hot from the catwalks!' She looked woefully at Delilah who fought hard to keep a straight face. 'I've only just had them altered. They're practically bespoke.' Slumping back onto her stool, she stroked them lovingly, like one would a cat.

Delilah interrupted Vivienne's mourning. 'I just wanted to thank you for putting me up the last couple of weeks. I really appreciate it. I don't know what I'd have done without you.'

Vivienne stared at her blankly. 'You mean you're moving out. Now. *This instant?*'

'Well, Charlie said he'd call by in a few hours and pick up my stuff. What with my car being out of action again.' After the Brighton trip, Delilah's Beetle had wheezed its last carbon monoxide breath and was now resting peacefully in its kerbside grave.

'But what about our girly chats and shopping trips and . . .' Suddenly tearful, Vivienne's voice trembled. '. . . Evenings spent with a weepy video and a carton of organic popcorn?'

'You don't have a video recorder.'

'Don't be facetious. You know what I mean. I shall miss you.'

Delilah softened. 'I'm only moving down the road. I'm not emigrating. It's a different postcode, not a different country.'

Vivienne nodded glumly.

'And you're getting married in a couple of months. I would have had to start looking for a new place to stay soon anyway.'

'Nonsense. You could have stayed here.'

Delilah laughed. 'Oh, come on, Vivienne. You, me and Harold?'

Seeing the funny side, Vivienne stopped sniffling and started to snigger. 'I suppose it would have been rather ridiculous.' She cackled loudly like a goose. 'Harold, the darling, has a secret penchant for threesomes. Always has. Though I rather think he's got his hands full with me, don't you?'

Delilah nodded, trying not to shudder at the thought. Empty or full, she didn't like to think of Harold's mouldy old hands. They reminded her of Danish Blue, veined and aged.

Regaining her composure, Vivienne patted her eyes with the veil netting. 'But seriously, are you absolutely sure you're doing the right thing?'

Delilah remembered how Charlie, half-naked in a pair of faded Levi's had smothered her with kisses as she left his flat that morning. Just thinking about it made her spine tingle. 'Yeh, I'm sure.'

Vivienne shrugged, her palms facing upwards. '*Que sera, sera*,' she sing-songed.

Delilah rolled her eyes to the ceiling. Vivienne was getting all amateur-dramatic on her. 'I'm going to start packing my things.' She scooped up Fatso who, having just greedily finished off a plate of lamb chops, was feeling stuffed and showing a complete lack of interest in the proceedings.

Vivienne lit up a cigarette, wafting away the smoke with the veil. 'Okay, sweetie. I'll just sit here planning my wedding. *Alone*.'

Up to her usual tricks, thought Delilah, ignoring Vivienne's attempts at self-pity and grinning to herself. Stepping over the scraps of silk material she opened the door into the hallway.

'Before I forget, I spoke to Sam this morning. Not a happy chap.'

Delilah swung round. In her excitement, she'd completely forgotten about Sam. 'Is it because I cancelled dinner. Is he pissed off with me?'

'Not in so many words. But then you know Sam.' Vivienne looked pointedly at Delilah. Surely she knew how Sam felt about her. Hadn't he told her in Brighton?

'I didn't think he'd mind. I know he'd arranged to cook

dinner, but then you told me Charlie had called and, well, Sam knows how I feel about Charlie . . .'

Opening and closing her mouth like a goldfish, Vivienne blew a sequence of pale-grey smoke rings. Obviously he hadn't told her. She didn't have a clue. 'Perhaps you should pop round and see him. I know he's suffering from a ghastly hangover, the result of all the wine he bought – *especially.*' Vivienne knew she was being cruel but couldn't help herself. Sam was a dear friend, and she knew he'd be gutted when he found out that Delilah was moving in with Charlie. Delilah had to be the one to break the bad news. That was one job Vivienne didn't want to be lumbered with. Talk about shooting the messenger.

'I'll get my stuff together and then go round to the café and apologise.' Feeling horribly guilty, Delilah pulled on her denim jacket. 'See you later.' She waved half-heartedly, reminding Vivienne of a helium balloon that had just been punctured and was slowly sinking back down to earth.

'Chin up.' Vivienne brandished her teacup in mock salute as Delilah disappeared glumly into the hall.

Sam was busy making eggs Benedict – 'sauce on the side' – for six very large and very rowdy American tourists. He looked hassled. Delilah hovered nervously by the counter with Fatso, who was trying to nod off against her ankles. This is ridiculous, she thought, as she deliberated for the umpteenth time what to say. What was she scared of? Vivienne was probably exaggerating the whole thing anyway.

'Hi, Sam.' She bit the bullet, trying to sound breezy.

Glancing over his shoulder he saw Delilah. 'Oh, hi,' he muttered flatly, turning his back and continuing to stir the hollandaise sauce.

Delilah bit her lip. Maybe Vivienne hadn't been exaggerating after all. Fiddling with the end of Fatso's lead she cleared her throat. 'Erm, I'm sorry about last night. I hope you didn't go to too much trouble.'

'No,' he monosyllabled, his voice muffled by clouds of steam as he ladled the poached eggs onto thick slices of granary toast. Balancing plates on the full length of his arm, he marched brusquely past her towards the salivating Yanks, who had polished off their sixth bread basket and were practically licking out the butter portions.

Should she tell him that she was moving in with Charlie? With the mood he was in at the moment, now probably wasn't a good time. But did she have any choice? She could hardly leave Vivienne's without telling him. They were friends, weren't they?

'I've decided to move in with Charlie.'

Sam dropped a salt cellar. It smashed, scattering small white crystals all over the floor. The café buzz hushed as customers stopped mid-sentence and mid-mouthful to crane their necks. The lull lasted a few seconds. Disappointed that it was nothing more serious than a spilled condiment they quickly resumed their banter, clattering knives and forks against their plates. Frozen, Sam and Delilah stared at each other. It was Sam who broke the deadlock.

'When?'

'Today.'

He looked crushed. 'But you hardly know him.' The voice of reason.

Delilah sighed. Sam was acting like the mother she didn't have. 'But I hardly knew Vivienne and look how that worked out. We get on great.'

'So why leave?'

'Because she's getting married. And anyway, her place was only ever temporary until I sorted myself out.'

'And now you have?'

'Well, yeh. I guess you could say that.'

Leaning against the cappuccino machine, Sam rubbed his stubble defeatedly. He knew she liked this Charlie bloke but he'd never imagined it was serious. Never thought for a moment that she'd want to move in with him. He felt gutted. Knowing she was seeing some other bloke was bad enough – *but living with him?* He couldn't bear to think about it. Unfortunately he had to. After all, he didn't have much choice. 'Well, if that's what you want to do . . .'

Delilah allowed herself a small smile. 'I do.' She fingered the fraying cuffs of her jacket. 'Oh, come on, Sam. I don't want to have a row about this. I want you to be pleased.'

Struggling to swallow the disappointment which stuck in his throat, he bravely forced a smile. He was being selfish. He had to stop thinking about what he wanted and start thinking about what Delilah wanted for a change. Whether he liked it or not, if she wanted him to be pleased about her moving in with this bloke, then he'd try his damn hardest to look as if he was. 'So when's the housewarming?' He pretended to be cheerful, but his voice had a hollow ring to it.

Delilah didn't notice. Relieved they were friends again, she forgot her northern roots and, flinging her arms around him, gave him a big hug. 'Very soon,' she laughed happily, burying her face into his butcher's pinny.

A silver sports car drew up outside. Delilah caught the glint of the bonnet out of the corner of her eye. It was Charlie. She pulled away.

'I'd better go, Charlie's waiting outside.'

Pushing down the horizontal slats of the Venetian blind at the window with his forefinger, Sam looked out onto the street. His face tensed. 'That's not Charlie Mendes, is it?'

Delilah was puzzled. 'Yeh, why?'

With a snort of disgust he released the blind, letting it rico-chet angrily against the glass. 'You mean that's Charlie, *your Charlie?*' Incredulous, he raised his voice – and the customers' eyebrows.

'Yes. I just said so, didn't I?' Delilah suddenly felt annoyed. What the hell had got into Sam? Nice, kind Sam was suddenly shouting at her. 'Why's it such a big deal, do you know him or something?'

Sam paced up and down in front of the deli counter, blatantly ignoring the bill-waggling customers who were forming a queue by the cash register. 'Oh yeh, I know him all right.' His nostrils flared and he shook his head in disbelief. 'I can't believe it. I just can't believe that's the other bloke.'

'The other bloke?'

'The bloke you've been seeing. Going out with. *Moving in with!*' Grabbing a fistful of fivers from the Americans, Sam shoved the notes in the till and threw a saucer of loose change back at them. They stared, shocked by his bawling. A teenage boy with teeth braces and Bermuda shorts started loading his Nikon. A picture of this would go nicely with all his other photos of quaint British things: Big Ben, Houses of Parliament, eccentric Englishman with a shaved head and a lousy temper.

'I just can't believe that all along it's been him. Charlie Mendes. Charlie fucking Mendes, in his stupid poncy sports car. What the hell do you want to go out with him for?'

Delilah clenched her jaw in defence. 'Because he happens to be really nice.'

'Nice? You must be joking. He's a right wanker.'

Delilah had been trying to stay calm, but it was impossible. Charlie was the man she was going to spend the rest of her life with. She couldn't just stand there and let Sam call him a wanker. 'I don't give a shit what you think. I can go out with who I want. I don't need your permission. Who the hell do you think you are, anyway, talking to me like that? You're talking to me as if I'm some kind of idiot.'

Sam reddened. 'Well, you're acting like one going out with him. I thought you were intelligent. Don't you know he's one of the biggest sharks around?'

'Why don't you just shut up, Sam, you don't know what you're talking about.' She tried to steady her voice but it was useless. It was trembling with anger.

'Oh, don't I?' Sam marched back to the window and, yanking open the blind, stabbed the window with his forefinger.

'That's what I'm talking about. That loser. He's only out for himself, you know. He'll screw you . . . If he hasn't already,' he added to himself, muttering under his breath so that she wouldn't hear him.

But she did and the colour seemed to disappear from her face, leaving her lips white and pinched. 'Fuck you,' she spoke quietly, her eyes brimming with angry tears.

For Sam the words were like a slap round the face. He sobered up from his ranting and fell silent. Looking at Delilah he suddenly regretted saying all those things, but it was too late now. He couldn't take back any of it.

Delilah picked up Fatso and clutched him to her chest. 'You might think you know Charlie, but you don't. You're just jealous.'

'Jealous?' Sam's heart missed a beat. So his cover was blown. She'd guessed. She'd guessed that he was in love with her.

But Delilah had no idea. No inkling of what had fuelled his anger. No clue that it was only because he was utterly loopy about her that he'd said all those hurtful things. If she had, she would never have said what she did next.

'Yeh, jealous, jealous that he's successful and you're here, running a poxy little café. If anyone's the loser it's you.'

Sam's face crumpled. So that's what she really thought of him. A loser in a poxy little café. He suddenly felt sick. How had it come to this? All this nastiness and anger between them. Unable to look Delilah in the eye he turned away. He wasn't angry with her anymore, he was angry at himself. If only he hadn't lost his temper, if only he hadn't got so wound up . . . His shoulders slumped forward wearily. It was ironic, really. By trying to protect her he'd only ended up hurting her. And himself.

The Americans held their breath. Waiting.

'I think we've both said enough. I'd better go.' Delilah's voice was quiet, drained of emotion. Weaving her way silently through the tables of customers, her footsteps loud on the tiles, she made her way towards the door. The door swung shut, jingling the bell. Numb, Sam watched her climb into the BMW, which immediately accelerated away from the kerb. A silver bullet – straight into his heart.

Chapter Twenty-Six

Vivienne gingerly eased herself onto the seat, which was covered in a vicious purple and red swirly nylon fabric, numerous fag burns and a half-eaten packet of cheese and onion crisps. Summoning all her courage, she picked up the packet, using just her thumb and forefinger and held it at arm's length.

'Sam, please, take this away . . .' Unable even to bring herself to look at the offending blue and yellow plastic packet she shuddered and turned to face the other direction.

Shaking his head, Sam snatched it from her and stuffed it in the already overflowing ashtray.

'How could you bring me to this hovel?' Vivienne hissed loudly as he sat down beside her. 'We're surrounded by . . .' she lowered her voice '. . . the *working class*.' She glared at a curly-haired man at the bar who had his nose buried in a copy of the *Big Issue*.

'Don't be such a bloody snob.' Sam sipped his pint as Vivienne folded her arms and crossed her legs defensively, her Jimmy Choo stilettos sinking into the beer-sodden carpet. Why on earth had she agreed to meet Sam at this godforsaken hellhole of a drinking establishment? How could he have even suggested it?

The Ram's Head in Shepherd's Bush was a lurid mix of slot machines, horse brasses and Sky Sport on big screen TVs. Vivienne scowled at the landlady, a ruddy-cheeked, big-bosomed brunette who was wearing a leopard-print T-shirt and the UK's quota of gold bullion around her neck. She was leaning over the bar, trying to flirt with the *Big Issue* reader while

provocatively nibbling on a packet of salted cashews and stroking the torpedo-shaped handle of the Guinness pump.

'Do you want anything to eat? Lunch is on me.' Sam tried to
coax a smile from Vivienne's pursed lips. It had no effect. She
cast a withering glance over the pub menu, written on the
blackboard in coloured chalks – a futile attempt to make it both
interesting and appetising. It boasted – if boast can be used to
describe two uninspired offerings – steak and kidney pie
(microwaved and passed off as homemade) or a Ploughman's
(a French stick, a dollop of Branston's pickle and half a pound
of cheddar). For someone who thought cheese only came in
parmesan wafers arranged artistically on the top of a rocket
salad, Vivienne wasn't to be tempted.

'I seem to have lost my appetite.' She picked up her luke-
warm tonic water, wiped the second-hand lipstick from the
edge of her glass with the cashmere cardigan that had been
casually thrown over her shoulders à la St Tropez, and took a
tentative sip.

'How's your drink?' asked Sam, still pursuing a conversation.

'Wet,' snapped Vivienne, piercing the tired and wilting wedge
of lemon with her stirrer and discarding it on the table. 'So,
come along, spill the beans. On the mobile you said it was
urgent.'

'It is.'

'So, what is it? You'd better have a good reason for waking
me up at some unearthly hour and dragging me all the way out
to this wasteland.'

'It's Delilah.'

Vivienne sighed. She wasn't surprised. 'I thought so. I
suppose she told you she was moving in with Charlie.'

'Yeh, she certainly did.' Yesterday's argument flicked, like a
deck of cards, through his mind. He stared dejectedly at his
pint.

'Do I sense that you're not best pleased?'

'*Pleased?* That she's moving in with Charlie Mendes? Do me
a favour.' Draining the lager dregs from his pint glass, Sam

slammed it bitterly onto the table. Just saying the name Charlie Mendes made his blood boil. The table of leather-clad motorbike couriers stared territorially across. This was their local watering hole. Any trouble from the poofter and his posh bird and they'd be only too happy to throw a few punches in their direction.

Not wanting any trouble – or a huge dry-cleaning bill from a brawl involving spilled beer and flying steak and kidney pies – Vivienne restrained Sam's wrist and hissed loudly, 'Did you say Charlie *Mendes*, as in *the* infamous Charlie Mendes whose father, Lord Reevesbury, died a couple of years ago?'

Sam glowered sulkily. 'The very same one.'

Vivienne fell back against her chair and clapped her hands in excitement. 'Goodness, how thrilling! Didn't he inherit a couple of stately homes, a rather healthy Coutts bank account and a list of property in London that sounds like a game of Monopoly?' Blindly trampling over Sam's feelings she whooped in delight, catching the attention of the *Big Issue* reader, who glanced up from the classified section and began staring at Vivienne's bare legs.

'Along with the lease for the café?'

Vivienne looked nonplussed. 'The café?'

Sam nodded, teeth clenched, eyes narrowed.

Suddenly it dawned on her. '*Your café?* Café Prima Donna?'

It was at this point in the conversation that Mr *Big Issue*, who had slowly sidled off his bar stool, decided to interrupt.

'Excuse me.' He stooped his bulky six-foot-five frame over the table and put his face close to Vivienne's.

She shrank back. 'Pardon?' she barked, fixing him with a steely look. Moving away had brought him into focus and her initial shock was replaced by the realisation that this fortysomething male bearing down upon her was actually rather handsome. Strong jaw, ink-black hair that spilled across his forehead in a Byronic kind of way, those heavy-lidded bedroom eyes and a statuesque figure that towered upwards, incorporating one of the biggest chests she'd ever seen. In fact he was very handsome indeed.

'Would you be Miss Pendlebury?' Nervously he brushed back his hair that had fallen sexily over one eye.

He knew her? 'Er, yes.' Frantically she tried to work out how this devilishly good-looking *Big Issue* reader knew her name.

'Reverend Giles McTaggart. I believe we met briefly at St Mary of the Abbot's to make an appointment to discuss your impending marriage to your fiancé Harold?' His voice was full-bodied and incredibly low, with the faint lilt of a Scottish accent. He held out his hand tentatively, his impressive forearms bulging from the cuffs of his jumper, pink and sturdy, like two prize-winning hams.

Realisation struck in the form of a religious thunderbolt. This was the horny vicar she'd met with Harold last week when they'd decided to set the date. She remembered him being very attractive – *but not this attractive.* 'Reverend McTaggart, I do apologise, I didn't recognise you without your . . . er . . . habit.' She noticed the dog collar around his broad neck, peeking out from underneath his Shetland jumper, and proffered her manicured hand. Gently he wrapped his giant-size fingers around it and shook it nervously.

'I hope you don't mind me interrupting your conversation with you and your . . . er . . . friend . . . er . . .' He smiled self-consciously at Sam, waiting for an introduction.

'Sam – my *very good friend* Sam,' Vivienne quickly interrupted. She dreaded to imagine what the Reverend was thinking. There was she, the not-so-blushing bride-to-be knocking back drinks at 11 a.m. in a crusty old pub *with another man.* She looked like a harlot.

Reverend McTaggart grasped hold of Sam's hand in his huge shovel of a palm and pumped it enthusiastically. 'Pleased to meet you!' He grinned his huge square-jawed grin. 'I have the good fortune to be marrying Miss Pendlebury.'

'Great,' smiled Sam, mesmerised by this huge giant of a man.

'Oh, er, not that I mean I'm to marry her, of course,' Reverend McTaggart blushed, the apples of his cheeks turning a Cox's red, 'but that I'll be conducting the ceremony between these . . .' He looked at Vivienne. 'I mean this young lady and her fiancé.' He finally let go of Sam's hand and spoke to Vivienne. 'I'm really delighted you chose St Mary's.' He stopped smiling, his face suddenly serious. 'And once again I wish to thank you on behalf of the parish for your donation for the new church roof – it was more than generous.' He turned to Sam, who was being entertained by Vivienne's rather dazed expression. 'Would either of you mind if I pulled up a chair?'

'Not at all,' gushed Vivienne, before Sam had a chance to speak.

He sat down next to Sam. 'So, are you good friends with both the bride and groom?'

'Er . . .' He was just about to say no, when out of the corner of his eye he saw Vivienne nodding frantically. 'Yes. We're very good friends,' he lied, nodding his head in rhythm with Vivienne's. The nearest he'd got to meeting Harold was the time he'd popped round to Vivienne's for a cuppa and come face-to-face with a set of his acrylic dentures grinning at him from next to the kettle.

'Splendid. Then I'm sure I'll look forward to seeing you at the wedding.' The Reverend leaned back in his chair and nodded towards Vivienne. 'I'm sure there'll be a lot of men nursing broken hearts when Miss Pendlebury walks down the aisle, wouldn't you agree?'

Sam nodded and watched with amazement as hard-faced Vivienne began blushing fiercely.

'Please, call me Vivienne.'

'Vivienne . . . what a lovely name.' He stared at her as she fluttered her eyelashes and smiled coyly. Sam knew those warning signals. He'd seen them with the surfer, the bricklayer and a million other unsuspecting males. Vivienne was on the prowl – and this time it was with the bloody vicar.

'Well, I really must be going.' Reverend McTaggart made as if to get up, trying and failing to break her gaze.

'So soon?' she panted, doing her damsel-in-distress impression. It always worked. But this time the pull of the parish was too overpowering. Even Vivienne couldn't beat God in the devotional stakes.

'I really must.' He didn't look as if he wanted to move.

'But don't we need to discuss the arrangements for the wedding? I really need to talk to you about the service and the choice of hymns.' She threw down the gauntlet – it was her last-ditch attempt.

'As a matter of fact we do.' He looked at his watch. 'Well, I suppose another ten minutes wouldn't make much difference.'

Reverend McTaggart swapped places with Sam to sit next to Vivienne, and Sam used the diversion to make his escape and order another pint from the landlady, who winked tartily and began pumping the Guinness with gusto, jangling her gold jewellery. From the safety of the bar he watched Vivienne and the vicar huddled together in conversation. They made an odd couple: her tiny frame squeezed into the latest designer gear and teetering on her Jimmy Choos; his huge body coerced into a shrunken Shetland sweater and a down-at-heel pair of brogues. But after a few minutes, the Reverend glanced at his watch and reluctantly pulled away, adjusting his dog collar and waving cheerily at Sam as he walked backwards out of the pub, narrowly missing the table of Hell's Angels and eight pints of cider.

'Jesus Christ, Vivienne, he's a vicar!' Sam sat back down and took a gulp of his pint.

'Don't take the Lord's name in vain.' She leaned back against her seat, adjusting the hem of her skirt and looking very pleased with herself.

'Since when did you get religion?'

'About ten minutes ago.' She pursed her lips piously.

'Anyway less about me,' she retorted, flicking back her curls and checking her make-up in her gold Chanel compact. 'You were talking about Charlie and your café.' She snapped the lid shut and looked pointedly at Sam.

He ran his fingers over the week-old stubble on his head and sighed wearily. The row with Delilah had left him exhausted. 'Charlie Mendes is the double-crossing bastard who inherited the lease on the café when his father died.'

'You mean he was the landlord who doubled your rent?' The penny dropped.

'And the rest. Every time he gets a new motor my rent goes up. And before he got that arty-farty job in TV he was always swanning into the café, helping himself to food, ordering rounds of coffee for all his cronies and never paying for them. I even caught him with his hand in the bloody till. You'd think he owned the place.'

'Well, I suppose he does,' murmured Vivienne, sucking the last bit of watery tonic from what was left of an ice cube.

Sam slammed his fist down on the table, spilling his pint and causing Vivienne to swallow the ice cube. She choked loudly. 'No he bloody doesn't. It's my café. I've built that place up from nothing. It was a fucking launderette!'

Vivienne jumped at the sudden outburst. 'Didn't he go off with one of your waitresses . . . ?' Tact was not something she'd learnt at finishing school.

'Yeh, and he treated her like shit, like he does everyone else. The two-timing bastard.'

They both looked at each other, thinking the same thing: Delilah.

'Well, I'm not going to tell her.' Vivienne folded her arms defiantly, mind made up. 'And she won't thank you for telling her either.'

Sam rubbed his forehead. 'I know, I've already tried.'

'When?'

'Yesterday.'

'And?'

'We had a huge row.'

Vivienne groaned loudly. 'Well, that's hardly surprising, is it? You can't tell a girl that the man she's just fallen in love with is a two-timing, double-crossing cheat.' Catching her reflection in one of the horse brasses, she tweaked the faux-fur collar on her cashmere cardigan. '. . . Even if he is a millionaire and one of the most eligible bachelors in Britain . . . Is it true he's got a collection of Ferraris?'

'*Vivienne!*'

'Sorry, darling, you know me . . . always getting carried away.' She stuck out her bottom lip beseechingly. 'Look, I'm terribly sorry about the ways things are between you and Delilah at the moment, but I'm sure things will soon take a turn for the better. Let her calm down for a while. If what you say about this Charlie person is true, she'll soon change her mind about him.' She smiled brightly. 'Sorry, I'm babbling. I'm afraid I'm a rather poor excuse for an agony aunt compared to you.'

Sam smiled wearily.

'Anyway, I really should be off. I did promise Giles I'd pop over, to discuss a few things.'

'Oh, so it's Giles now?' Sam couldn't help smiling.

Vivienne narrowed her eyes. 'Just because he's a vicar it doesn't mean we can't be on first-name terms.'

'Okay, okay.' He held up his hands in mock surrender, but he couldn't resist adding, 'So what are you going to discuss? The size of his organ?'

'Ha, ha, very funny.' She rolled her eyes. 'You can be very childish sometimes,' she huffed. 'And anyway, all that kind of behaviour is firmly behind me. I'm an engaged woman, for God's sake.'

'Yeh, right,' grinned Sam disbelievingly.

Vivienne caught his expression. 'I'll see you later. Call me.'

And with that she gathered together her artefacts – Chanel handbag, mobile, Hermès scarf, Mulberry umbrella – pecked Sam on both cheeks and, like an escaped prisoner, thankfully dashed out of the dingy pub, snagging her stilettos on the nylon carpet and giving herself a shock of static electricity. Sam watched her jump into a black cab and disappear into the dense London traffic. Resigned to his own gloomy company he looked back at his empty pint glass. Should he get another? If he did, it would be the second time in three days that he'd got drunk. He deliberated for a moment. The landlady stared over, chewing suggestively on the straw of her Taboo and lemonade. Oh, what the hell. He stood up and walked over to the bar.

Chapter Twenty-Seven

As the mega-watt, mega-bucks, twin-turntable stereo blasted out Tom Jones's greatest hits, Delilah jigged, twirled, skipped and boogied up and down Charlie's penthouse flat. Wiggling her hips, she gyrated along with Tom in her M&S forget-me-not-blue knickers that had turned forget-me-not grey after too many washes on a hot cycle, and grinned like a Cheshire cat. Okay, so the underwear might not yet be Calvin Klein, but her dream of a different life, an *Elle Decoration* flat and a gorgeous bloke were firmly in place. And she was loving it!

Singing at the top of her voice, she drowned out Tom's vocal cords, which were vibrating the glass test-tube vases like a xylophone. Finally the record finished and, knackered and out of breath, she collapsed in a heap onto the huge caramel-coloured sofa and began licking the froth from her cappuccino. After twenty-four hours at Charlie's she'd ditched her lifelong addiction to instant black coffee in favour of these cups of weak, milky froth. Feeling her heart-beat beginning to return to normal she lay back and drank in her new habitat: three huge French windows gave a spec-tacular view of London's skyline, blond wooden floorboards so shiny you could see your reflection in them, and a giant glass dining table that could seat an entire football team. Most of all there was space. Metres and metres of space. She giggled to herself in disbelief. It was unreal. Like being in a five-star hotel. Not that she'd actually ever *stayed* in a five-star hotel but she had used the loos in the one in Harrogate and even those had been amazing: marble floors, piles of real fluffy towels – not like the reusable revolving tea-towel you normally find attached to the wall – and individually wrapped pieces of soap embossed with the name of the hotel. Of course she'd nicked a few, along with an ashtray and a handful of boiled sweets from the china urn in the foyer. Well, everyone does, don't they?

Now here she was in her very own five-star accommodation – with an indefinite reservation. And she could get used to it. Even if did mean foregoing her beloved Nescafé for the frothy stuff from Charlie's cappuccino machine. Smiling, she closed her eyes blissfully. If she had been a cat she would have purred.

The latch clicked open. Keeping her eyes closed, Delilah sucked in her stomach and tilted her chin, pretending she was asleep. With any luck Charlie would bend over and give her a big kiss.

'And who are you?'

She blinked. It wasn't Charlie. It wasn't even a man. It was a woman in her sixties carrying two Harvey Nichols bags and a chihuahua. She sat bolt upright, all thoughts of snogging evaporating at the sight of a pair of bulging eyes and snarling mouth . . . and that wasn't even the dog.

Suddenly she remembered Charlie telling her that his cleaner would be arriving at lunchtime. Not that this woman was dressed like a cleaner. Delilah had been expecting something more along the lines of a checked pinny and a pair of rubber gloves, not a maroon twinset and a double string of pearls. Still, they were in a posh part of London.

'Oh, hi, I'm Delilah,' she gasped, jumping up from the sofa and sticking out her hand. The woman ignored it. Delilah squirmed uncomfortably in her M&S bra and knicker set. 'I suppose you know where all the cleaning stuff is.' She tried to sound authoritative, as if greeting cleaners in her underwear was a daily occurrence. Instead she was a bag of nerves. Usually she was the one taking orders, not giving them.

'Pardon?'

'The dusters, bleach . . . you know . . .'

'*Bleach?*' The woman's jaw hit the floor along with her snuffling dog. It scampered across the wooden boards, sniffing out Fatso, who was curled up in his tartan doggy basket, paying no attention to his fellow canine, and began slavering all over him. Charlie's cat Karma, however, wasn't so chilled out. Arching her scrawny Siamese back, she let out a bloodcurling screech and, snapping out her claws like ten miniature flick knives, skidded across the room, leaving a trail of Freddy Krueger scratches on the polished wooden floorboards.

'Yeh, bleach. You'll need it for the toilet,' suggested Delilah, trying to be helpful. Jeez, at this rate she might as well find the loo brush and do it herself.

The woman fixed her with an icy stare. 'My dear girl, I think there's been some mistake.'

'Mistake?' Warning bells started to ring. 'You are Mrs Baxter, Charlie's cleaner – aren't you?'

Arching her back, the would-be cleaner brushed an imaginary speck of dust away from her shoulder. 'I most certainly am not. I'm Mrs Mendes, Charles's mother.' She glared at Delilah. 'And who may you be?'

The moment was freeze-framed. Delilah was mortified. How on earth had she made such an appalling error of judgement? And with his *mother*! Every girl knows that to get on the wrong side of your boyfriend's mother was like getting on the wrong side of the Godfather. Fatal. Luckily, before Mrs Corleone could chop off her head, horse-style, Charlie appeared brandishing a huge bunch of bright-yellow sunflowers. They were meant for Delilah, but when he caught sight of his mother, nostrils flaring and hissing like a viper at a startled and semi-naked girl, he changed his mind. Putting his damage-limitation plan into action he thrust them under his mother's nose, causing enough distraction for Delilah to take the coward's way out and scurry upstairs to the loo, leaving him with a hell of a lot of explaining to do.

'I'm sorry about Mother. She just gets a little protective.' Charlie and Delilah lay sprawled on the sofa, arms and legs entwined, finishing off a magnum of champagne. Letting the bubbles gently fizz against the roof of her mouth, Delilah couldn't help grinning as she remembered how he'd plied Mrs Mendes with a cocktail of compliments and half a bottle of Scotch, before bustling her, half-gassed and beaming with cheery benevolence, into the back of the Bentley and instructed her driver to take her and her snuffling dog directly home. Mission accomplished, he'd then fed Delilah a selection of sushi (eating raw fish was a new and not entirely pleasant experience for her. She much preferred it dipped in batter and deep-fried) and watered her with vintage Dom Perignon. For dessert they made love.

'I missed you,' he murmured, burying his nose in her hair.

Delilah closed her eyes. Pinch me.

'Work was lousy. All I kept thinking about was you here, all by yourself.'

'Don't worry about me, I'm fine. I've been trying to get to know the place.' And you, she thought, remembering how as soon as he'd left for work that morning she'd had a good look in his bathroom cabinet, bedroom drawers and laundry bin for anything that might be cause for concern. Not that she'd found anything of any interest. No alarming ointments for sexual diseases, no photos of ex-girlfriends (in fact no photos), no embarrassing items of clothing. Nothing. There were no chinks in Charlie's armour, he really did seem to be perfect.

'Are you still upset about yesterday?'

'Yesterday?'

'The argument you had with Sam. Your so-called friend.'

'Oh *that*.' She'd got into the car close to tears. Still angry and in shock, she'd poured out what had happened during the drive back to his flat. How he'd said she was an idiot, all the names he'd called both her and Charlie, the way he'd shouted at her. Incredulous, she told him all the things Sam had said about him. 'Can you believe that he said that? Can you believe it?' she'd ranted, shaking her head and wiping her eyes with a trembling hand. But Charlie had been wonderful – calming her down and telling her to forget about it. Pulling into his off-street parking space he'd switched off the engine and leaned towards her: 'Look. I'm pretty well known in this area, and even though I don't know who this Sam person is, he obviously knows who I am. Most people do.' Softly he'd stroked the side of Delilah's face. 'And it sounds to me like he's jealous. Jealous of my lifestyle, my sports car, my career and . . .' – he'd put his arms around her and kissed her gently on the lips – '. . . my beautiful girlfriend.' And miraculously, snuggled into Charlie's leather jacket, her breathing had relaxed, her tears had dried up, and suddenly things hadn't seemed so bad.

'I'm okay. I just hate rows.' She'd tried not to think about it, it was too upsetting. Pouring herself a top-up she took a large gulp. The bubbles shot up her nose.

'I know, darling, but don't think about it – or him. He doesn't sound like the sort of friend you need anyway. Too much negative energy isn't good for anybody, least of all you.'

'But . . .' She was about to protest that Sam wasn't usually like that, when Charlie started unbuttoning her shirt, turning her mind onto different things.

'It's just you and me now. Don't worry about anybody . . . or anything.'

She gave a small sigh of pleasure as he tickled her belly-button with his tongue before slowly peeling down her jeans. Charlie was right. She didn't need to worry about anything. He was the most important person in her life now, and that was all that mattered. She let out an involuntary moan. Who cared what everybody else thought. They could all go to hell. At this moment she was well on her way to heaven . . .

Chapter Twenty-Eight

'So, we're meeting at one o'clock at Harvey Nicks.'

'In the bridal section. It's next to soft furnishings on the fourth floor. You can't miss it – there'll be lots of plump Sloanes swanning around in apricot satin and diamanté tiaras.'

'What?'

'My bridesmaids are having a fitting, sweetie. Harold's insisted on having his nieces Hilary, Hermione and Harriet, even though I'd already asked a couple of my old school chums, Penny and Virginia. I just hope we don't have to alter the dresses again. They're five terribly nice girls, but they seem unable to say no to pudding. They've already cost me a fortune in extra material due to their ever-increasing girths.'

'Look, I've got to go. I'll see you this afternoon.' Delilah put the phone down, grinning. It was good to hear Vivienne hadn't changed.

Delilah was looking forward to seeing her ex-flatmate. It had been ages since they'd last got together, mainly due to Vivienne's recent illness: a serious bout of wedding fever. The symptoms of this debilitating disease included arguing with caterers, screaming at florists, crying at the discovery that the pre-booked string quartet would be on tour in China on the day of the ceremony, and near hysteria when she accidentally dropped the five-tier cake with butterscotch frosting and gold leaf onto the kitchen floor. In contrast, Delilah had been enjoying the honeymoon period of her relationship, walking around with a silly grin on her face and cheerily emptying her pockets for people who rattled charity boxes outside the Underground.

Nearly five weeks had passed since she'd moved, lock, stock and barrel, into Charlie's flat. Thirty-three days of enjoying an intoxicating merry-go-round of expensive restaurants, dinner parties and designer bars by night, and Ledbury Road shopping trips, hairdresser appointments and yoga lessons by day. And it showed. Cinderella had finally been allowed to go to the ball. Gone was the crumpled chestnut hair, daily uniform of fraying jeans and faded T-shirts. In their place were side-split skirts, cashmere cardies and a glossy mane of honey highlights.

Not that it had been her idea. It was Charlie who'd suggested the makeover. At first she'd had second thoughts, but now she loved it – a new look to go with her new life. And it was the kind of life she'd dreamed about. A life that didn't include a daily routine of work, Indian takeouts, and a night in front of the telly. Charlie had also suggested she should pack in her job at the Pantry so they could spend more time together after all, it wasn't as if she needed to earn money. He had enough for both of them. She'd been over the moon. For the first time in years she didn't have to do a job she hated, a job that left her knackered and bored to tears. Without wasting any time she'd borrowed Charlie's BMW and driven over to the Pantry to hand in her notice. Poor Vince. It was romance, not her resignation, he was after. Leaning over the delivery of Schweppes tonic water, he'd pressed his clammy hand into hers and whispered conspiratorially, 'For you, my door is always open, *bellissima.*' Along with your flies, she'd shuddered, as her eye caught sight of his half-mast zipper and she was treated to an impromptu display of his striped and heavily bulging underpants. That was one door she wanted to keep firmly closed.

The cab dropped her off in Sloane Street. Clutching Fatso and her new Louis Vuitton handbag, she pushed open the glass doors. Striding past the perfume counters she was bombarded by lab-coated women with heavily lacquered hairdos and scarlet fingernails, falling over themselves to squirt her pulse points and offer free samples. Quite a change from her pre-makeover days, when she'd been either totally ignored or eyed disapprovingly, as if she was about to nick the testers.

Gliding up the escalators, she checked out her reflection. Would Vivienne recognise her? She hardly recognised herself these days. Whereas once she felt and looked skint, now she looked and felt rich, especially with Charlie's American Express card in her pocket. Fastening the top button of her cardigan, she checked her lipgloss and eyeshadow – items from her new, subtle make-up range. The only thing that wasn't subtle was the price. Yesterday, while having a blow-dry at a trendy hair salon in Knightsbridge, she'd been swooped upon by Charlene, one of the resident make-up artists, who'd tutted pitifully at her heavy-handed blusher application. Describing her as a 'victim of colour', Charlene had proceeded to bombard her with 'free make-up advice' – an hour of trying to flog two hundred quid's worth of cream eyeshadows and light-reflecting pigments. Delilah couldn't remember much of what she'd been wittering on about, except that she used the words 'blend and smudge' a lot. Rather ironic seeing as Charlene appeared to have applied her make-up with a trowel.

'Delilah, you look sensational!' Arms outstretched, Vivienne stumbled towards her in an ivory silk crinoline with matching bustier. She reminded Delilah of the doll Sandra used to hide the loo roll underneath. 'I hardly recognised you!' Grabbing her by both shoulders she spun her around. 'It's truly a miracle.'

'Steady on,' laughed Delilah, feeling five sets of bridesmaids' eyes bearing down upon her. 'I wouldn't go that far.'

'Oh, I would,' insisted Vivienne, nodding vigorously. 'Before, your look was, well, how shall I put it – provincial.'

'Thanks.' Not sure how to take that comment, Delilah decided to take it as a compliment. 'So, how are the wedding preparations?'

Vivienne pressed the back of her trembling hand to her brow and flopped onto a chair. 'I can't begin to tell you,' she whined feebly, before launching into a tearful monologue on the trials and tribulations of organising a wedding. It was akin to a military manoeuvre, with everybody and everything having to be ready to jump into action at the given signal. If one section messed up, months of preparation would be rendered useless and 'the best day of her life' would be ruined.

'Well, the bridesmaids look nice,' said Delilah, trying to inject a note of cheeriness.

'No they don't. They look positively huge,' hissed Vivienne in despair. Delilah looked across at Penny and Virginia, big-boned mothers-of-two from the country with jiggly bits under their arms and bottoms as big as sofas. Excited by their jaunt into town, they were happily chomping through a tray of puff-pastry refreshments while the harassed seamstress tried to stretch another couple of inches out of the apricot satin. A stark contrast to Hilary, Hermione and Harriet, three sulky pubescent teenagers with pimples and puppy fat who bulged uncomfortably out of their Bo-Peep frocks. They sat slumped in the corner, gorging on family-size bags of mini Mars Bars and squabbling over whose turn it was to listen to Boyzone on the Discman.

'Maybe you should have a drink,' suggested Delilah, having second thoughts.

'Good idea,' gasped Vivienne, eyes brightening as she scooped up her petticoats and began waddling off in the direction of the escalators. Gliding regally down to the lower-ground floor, she sashayed into the bar, plonked herself onto a stool and ordered a Virgin Mary, oblivious to the stares from the ladies-who-lunch, who couldn't make up their minds whether she was an actress starring in the sequel to *Four Weddings and a Funeral*, or a real-life bride who'd just been jilted. They decided on the latter.

'Perhaps you should have changed,' suggested Delilah.

'Whatever for?' breezed Vivienne, as if propping up a bar in duchess satin embroidered with seed pearls was the most normal thing in the world. 'It's only bad luck if the groom sees you, and Harold's clay-pigeon shooting up in Shropshire.' She knocked back her drink. 'Aah, that's better. Food for the soul.'

Licking her lips, she cast her beady eye over Delilah. 'So, is Charlie responsible for this sudden change in appearance?'

Delilah blushed, feeling self-conscious. 'No, I just decided I needed a new image.' She didn't want to admit to Vivienne that it had been Charlie's idea.

'Hmm,' Vivienne pursed her lips disbelievingly. 'Still, I must say it's definitely an improvement.' She nodded appreciatively. 'So, are things still hunky-dory?'

'Yeh,' gushed Delilah, breaking into a shy smile. 'What about you and Harold?'

'Oh, you could say we're ticking along. Literally. He's had to have a pacemaker fitted.'

'He's got a pacemaker?'

'Yes. Dodgy heart, I'm afraid. Which unfortunately rules out the Viagra from now on.' She beckoned to the barman for another drink. 'It's heavy petting or nothing, which doesn't bode well for the honeymoon. I presume we'll have to make do with Scrabble, although there's always my vibrator for emergencies.'

The barman, who'd been hovering around the counter arranging ashtrays, went bright red and knocked over the container of straws. Delilah didn't know what to say. Never mind the bloody honeymoon; what about the rest of their lives? They couldn't spend the next forty years trying to think of words with the letter Q. But on the other hand, Harold didn't look as if he'd last out the wedding, never mind still be around at the ruby anniversary.

'Anyway, less about my problems. How about a top-up?' boomed Vivienne, trying to muster up some enthusiasm.

'Yeh, why not. I'll have a Kir Royal.' Delilah had recently discovered the existence of this delicious drink on one of her many nights out with Charlie.

'Ooh, my kind of girl,' whooped Vivienne, who, even though

she had to settle for the non-alcoholic version, was delighted that her friend no longer insisted on supping horrors such as vodka and *Courke*, or, even worse, cider and black *in pint glasses*.

They chatted for over two hours, moving from aperitifs to appetizers. Vivienne complained she was starving, but refused to let more than a lettuce leaf pass her lips. She scowled jealously at Delilah, who was tucking into the complimentary focaccia.

'I need to lose fifteen pounds before the wedding.'

Delilah paused from dipping her bread into the olive oil and looked at Vivienne's tiny figure swamped under the blancmange of ivory silk. 'And how are you going to do that without chopping off an arm or a leg?'

Vivienne scowled. 'It's all right for you, Miss Slimhips, but the Pendlebury women are cursed with a bottom half like Fergie's. Which was all very well a hundred years ago when child-bearing hips were today's equivalent of double-D breasts and every self-respecting female wanted them. But now they're the anatomical version of a ra-ra skirt – people point and snigger at them in the street.'

'So what are you going to do?' Delilah moved on to her starter. She wasn't even going to try and talk sense into Vivienne. Her mind was made up.

Vivienne lit a cigarette and dragged heavily. 'Liposuction. It's the only solution. I've tried everything else, even colonic irrigation, which was useless but fascinating. I couldn't believe what came out the other end. It looked remarkably like foie gras.'

Delilah put down her fork. Her crab pâté and crudités had suddenly lost their appeal. 'So have you made an appointment?' Humouring Vivienne was the only option.

'A week on Thursday. Apparently you're in and out in less than an hour.' Her mobile rang. Delilah could hear Hilary, Hermione and Harriet yelling down the handset. Vivienne barked back. 'No, you can't go to Planet Hollywood for burgers and fries. I've still got to sort out the wedding list with Margot from soft furnishings.' There was a howl of despair as she cut them off. 'Brats,' she muttered under her breath.

Lunch was over and they settled the bill with the very handsome Mediterranean-looking waiter. Vivienne left a hefty tip and, when she thought Delilah wasn't looking, her telephone number.

'And what about Sam. Have you heard from him?' Delilah couldn't leave without asking. They hadn't spoken since that terrible argument five weeks ago and she'd tried to put him out of her mind. But it wasn't so easy. It was like a dull ache. She could ignore it when she was enjoying herself with Charlie at a restaurant or a club, even forgetting about it when she was busy indulging her new hobby – shopping for designer clothes. But sometimes, when she lay awake at night, not able to sleep because of the noise of the traffic outside the bedroom window, the nagging ache would become a stabbing pain and, unable to ignore it any longer, she'd be forced to think about him and her mind would flit between memories of their time together in Brighton to that bloody awful row. How she wished she could just call him, apologise and they could go back to being friends again. Except of course she couldn't. Things had changed between them. There was no going back.

'Briefly,' lied Vivienne. Could you call three times a day for the past month briefly?

'How is he?'

'Fine,' she lied again. Well, she wasn't going to be the one to tell her how he'd spent the last month foul-tempered and foul-mouthed.

'Oh, good.' Delilah smiled weakly. Why did she get the feeling Vivienne was fibbing? And why couldn't she stop feeling so bloody guilty about Sam? He was the one who'd started the argument, it was his fault she'd got angry and said all those things she now regretted. 'Did he tell you we had a row?'

'I think he mentioned it.' This time Vivienne cringed. Three questions, three lies. She felt like Judas Iscariot. 'Look, I'd better be getting back before the little buggers go AWOL in my apricot satin.'

Delilah tried to hide her disappointment. 'Oh, okay. I'll call you on Thursday to see how the operation went. Bye.' Forcing a smile, she picked up Fatso who'd been hiding from the *maître d'* under Vivienne's skirts, and headed towards the exit.

Vivienne waved goodbye. She felt guilty about lying to Delilah, but it wasn't up to her to act as a go-between. Sam had given her strict orders not to meddle, which meant that if Delilah wanted to find out about him she'd have to call him herself. Which begged the question, if she was so in love with Charlie, why the hell was she so interested in Sam?

Chapter Twenty-Nine

'Be a darling and sort out some food. I'll sort out the drinks.' Charlie grabbed a couple of bottles of Dom Perignon from the fridge.

'But Charlie . . .'

He wasn't listening. 'Thanks, sweetheart.' Kissing Delilah distractedly on the forehead he scooped up a handful of champagne flutes and disappeared back to his friends, leaving her in the kitchen by herself. She sighed. Over the last three weeks things had stopped being so hunky-dory. It was the fourth time that week that Charlie had invited a menagerie of would-be actors, musicians and B-celebrities back from the Westshire pub and held an impromptu drinks party at the flat; the fourth time that week she'd found herself stuck in the kitchen arranging crackers and a selection of Harrods cheeses while everybody else had a good time. Delilah had always imagined being a party hostess meant flitting around the room in a strapless evening dress serving vol-au-vents and chit-chatting over After Eights. Not skivvying around, emptying ashtrays, filling glasses and crawling around on her hands and knees mopping up spills with a dishcloth.

From the living room came the sound of corks popping and glasses chinking as Charlie dished out the bubbly.

'Cheers, mate,' boomed Ruben, a six-foot-tall by four-foot-wide Jamaican whose party trick was to introduce himself as a dealer in Portobello and wait for people to jump to the wrong conclusion. And they always did. At which point he would roar with laughter and tell them he dealt in antiques, not drugs, and the only thing he could sort them out with was some nice

Victorian china or a turn-of-the-century grandfather clock. Gulping the champagne, he fiddled with the knobs on the state-of-the-art Bang & Olufsen stereo, bobbing his head to the drum'n'bass beat while using his left hand to spin imaginary discs on an imaginary mixing deck.

'Yeh, cool man,' murmured two long-haired musicians who lay sprawled and stoned on the sofa next to Pippa and Amelia, a couple of plump PR girls. Smiling nervously, they were perched uncomfortably on the edge of the cushions, sucking extra-strong mints and trying to make sure no one could see up their skirts. Zak, the lead singer (alias Edward from the Home Counties), had his stoned eye on Amelia and was trying to seduce her by reciting the lyrics to his yet-to-be-recorded-never-to-be-released album, *Poverty*. 'Working at the factory, the daily grind, the daily grind; Working at the factory, going out of my mind, going out of my mind.'

Wide-eyed, Amelia nodded sympathetically as he spouted passionately on about his socialist beliefs. Beliefs that in five years' time would be ditched, along with his Jobseeker's Allowance and patchouli-oiled biker's jacket for a job in the City and a Porsche 911. Taking a tortured drag of his soggy joint he offered it to her. Pippa's eyes stood out on stalks as her friend nodded eagerly. Mummy and Daddy would be furious with her, but all this political talk was making her feel rebellious.

'Do you want any help?' gushed Nickii as Charlie topped up her glass. 'You look as if you've got your hands full.' Sidling up to him she stroked his forearm suggestively.

He grinned and slyly squeezed her bottom. 'Maybe later.' Nickii giggled. Charlie was so much more fun when that boring girlfriend of his wasn't around.

Unfortunately for Nickii she was. 'Grub's up,' announced Delilah, plonking a plate of cheese and biscuits unceremoniously on the table – the signal for people to swarm around it like gannets. Late-night munchies after an evening of drinking.

'*Deeelicious!*' panted Ruben, cutting himself a large wedge of Cheddar.

'Well, at least we should be thankful it's not cheese and pineapple on sticks,' tutted Nickii, prodding the Brie with a cheese straw as if she was looking for signs of life.

Delilah overheard and gritted her teeth. It hadn't taken her long to suss out that Nickii wasn't thrilled by her appearance on the scene, the simple reason being that Delilah had got something she wanted – Charlie – and she was determined to get her hands on him. But Delilah was doing her best to try and ignore her. Whether she liked her or not – and it was definitely the latter – Nickii was one of Charlie's oldest friends and was always hanging around. In fact, for the last three weeks Nickii had been hanging around at their flat doing nothing but whingeing and sniping, apart from when she was flicking ash on the carpet or doing her giggly best-friends routine with Charlie.

Talking of which . . . 'Thanks, darling,' he whispered, sliding his arm around Delilah's waist. 'What would I do without you?' He winked sexily and passed her a glass of champagne. 'Now, have a drink and enjoy the party.' She smiled and took a sip. Charlie was right. For years she'd spent her evenings next to Lenny on the sofa, watching videos in her pyjamas and wishing she was at some trendy London party. Now here she was – she should be having a ball. Delilah drained her glass and surveyed the room. So why the hell wasn't she?

'I'm bored. Can't we dance?' After four glasses of Dom Perignon Nickii had moved swiftly onto the Margaritas and was getting well and truly hammered. 'Come on, this is supposed to be a party.' Ignoring Delilah she grabbed hold of Charlie and dragged him into the middle of the room. He glanced back apologetically at Delilah and raised his hands in the air. What could he do? Delilah watched Nickii gyrating against him. She had a few ideas, but none that wouldn't involve charges of manslaughter.

'Way to go,' whooped Ruben, delighted that people were

starting to boogie. Whacking up the volume until the French windows rattled he began flinging himself enthusiastically through a sequence of bumps and grinds until the sweat dripped off his forehead and onto his Hawaiian shirt. 'Come on everybody,' he bellowed, blowing his whistle in time to the beat and roaring with laughter: a booming Barry White of a laugh, that shook his belly and flashed his gold front tooth.

Soon the room had turned into a dancefloor: Rob, a gangly TV presenter, bounded around, exuberantly flinging his limbs to a beat that only he could hear, while Pippa jigged around self-consciously. Rhythmically bending her knees, snow-plough style, she nervously sipped her champers while pulling down the hem of her skirt. She desperately needed Amelia to dance with, or a handbag to dance *around*. But she had neither. Her handbag was in the boot of her Golf GTI and Amelia was in the corner, legs akimbo, snogging Zak.

Everyone was having a good time, everyone except Delilah, who'd been cornered by a drunken clubber called Howard, who was 'currently working on his first screenplay'. Howard was wearing a 'Never Mind the Bollocks' T-shirt, a pair of Cutler & Gross sunglasses and woven bracelets around his wrist from his recent backpacking trip to Thailand. He thought he was the epitome of cool.

'So, where y' from?' he slurred.

Delilah groaned inwardly. 'Bradford,' she deadpanned.

'Oh . . . I went to a wicked club there . . . I think . . . or m'ybe it wor Birmingham . . .' He scratched his groin and let out a yawnful of marijuana smoke.

Delilah forced a smile. Riveting stuff.

Swaying backwards and forwards he steadied himself on the door frame. 'I'm Irish,' he spluttered. In his drug and alcohol addled mind, it was the only thing he could think of to say.

Delilah nodded disbelievingly. He didn't look Irish and he certainly didn't sound Irish. Which was hardly surprising seeing as Howard's tenuous Irish ancestry amounted to a distant great-grandmother, having himself been born and bred in

Middlesex. His only brush with the Emerald Isle was a recent trip to see The Corrs in concert. Not that he could admit that to anyone. Scriptwriters hailed from The Streets, not a semi-detatched in suburbia.

'So how do you know Charlie?' She might as well make an attempt at conversation. If nothing else it would drag her attention away from the activities on the dancefloor.

'I dunno. I just met the geezer t'night in the pub.' Howard let the ash from his spliff drop onto the floor and watched as the ember glowed brightly, burning through the antique wood. 'But he's a cool dude. His chick's pretty cool as well.'

'His chick?'

'Yeh, the bird he's with.' Howard strummed an imaginary guitar.

Delilah's mouth went dry as she looked over his shoulder. In the far corner Charlie had stopped dancing and was sitting crosslegged on the floor like a Buddha, entertaining his posse with one of his anecdotes – the one where he won ten grand at blackjack in Monte Carlo and ended up skinny-dipping with Princess Stephanie. Wendy, Mandy, Andy, Jamie and Johnny were laughing hysterically at all the right moments, while Nickii was draped all over him, giving him a neck massage that appeared to involve sticking her hands down the front of his shirt. Delilah took a deep breath. That was it. She could put up with the bitchy comments about the food, she could even put up with her Mata Hari impersonation on the dance-floor, but she couldn't stand back and watch as she groped her boyfriend. There was a fine line between we're-just-good-friends flirting and get-my-knickers-off flirting. And Nickii had just crossed it.

As Delilah approached there was an explosion of laughter as Charlie got to the punchline. Hooting loudly, Nickii lay back against the sofa and lit up a joint.

'Having a good time?' Delilah tried to act as if nothing was the matter. It wasn't easy.

Nickii blew out a ring of smoke. 'Fabulous, thanks.' She held out her empty glass. 'Is it possible to have another Margarita – and with a little more ice this time?'

Delilah counted to ten. She couldn't lose her temper in front of everyone. She wouldn't give her the satisfaction. Instead she clenched her jaw firmly closed and, snatching the empty glass, stomped back across the room towards the kitchen.

Nickii burst out laughing and slid her hand across Charlie's shoulder. 'That girlfriend of yours is being such a party pooper. She needs to lighten up a little. Enjoy the party.'

Charlie closed his eyes, his head lolling back, and inhaled on the joint Nickii had just passed him. 'Yeh, I don't know what's got into her lately. She keeps nagging me, getting all serious . . .' He coughed out smoke. 'I just want us to have some fun together, you know. Nothing heavy.' He began giggling as the effects of the marijuana kicked in. 'I don't think I'll ever understand you chicks.'

'C'mon, we're not all like that, Charlie. She's just . . .' Nickii had to select her words carefully. Even though she'd known Charlie a long time, Delilah was still his girlfriend, whether she liked it or not. And if she stood any chance of getting in with him, she didn't want to appear as if she was being bitchy. Men didn't like that. '. . . Different. Not like you and me.' She edged nearer, her lips slightly apart.

'Yeh, I guess you're right. She is different.' Charlie eased himself back against the edge of the sofa. 'But that's probably why I like her.'

Nickii's mouth clenched firmly shut, wishing she'd swallowed her words before they'd been able to backfire on her.

Trying to stay calm, Delilah shoved the empty glass onto the kitchen surface. She could kill Nickii – and Charlie for that matter. He hadn't exactly been fighting her off. Yanking open the freezer drawer she wrestled with the ice-cube holder. A dozen ice cubes shot across the work surface and smashed against the mixer taps. 'Shit!' she muttered, scooping up the pieces and stuffing them into the glass. She was totally pissed off. They were supposed to be a couple, enjoying the party together – not apart, with her in the bloody kitchen doing her Tom Cruise in *Cocktail* impression, while Charlie was getting stoned, smashed. And if Nickii had anything to do with it, seduced. Grabbing the tequila and triple sec she half-filled the glass and looked for the fresh lime juice. It was all gone. So was the lime cordial. Undeterred she scanned the sea of bottles for another mixer. She was about to give up when she spotted just the thing lurking next to the sink.

In her defence it must be said that any female would have been tempted. But whether or not they'd actually have done what she did is another matter. Delilah, on the other hand, wasn't just any female. Grabbing the innocent-looking plastic bottle she gave it a hefty squeeze. A liberal squirt of thick green washing-up liquid filled up the glass. Delilah gave it a satisfying swirl with her finger. Very realistic. Nickii was so pissed she'd never know the difference.

'Here you are. Hope it's not too strong.' Delilah held out the drink and smiled sweetly.

Nickii blew a gust of fag smoke down her nostrils. 'Oh, I'm sure I can handle it. I've had some wicked Margaritas in my time.'

The posse giggled knowingly. Delilah smiled serenely. For once she was in on a secret that they weren't. Nickii put the rim of the glass to her heavily outlined lips and took a swig. Would she spit or swallow?

What happened next was something Delilah would never forget. Neither would the disgruntled partygoers who were unfortunate enough to be near Nickii as she finished off this particular Margarita. Within minutes her complexion had changed from healthy tan to not-so-healthy green and without any warning she threw up all over a heavily petting Zak and Amelia, splattering the posse and narrowly missing the cheese and biscuits. Pandemonium broke out and the party broke up as she was carried, retching, down the stairs and driven home by a disgruntled minicab driver. It was all over in less than fifteen minutes, but, as Andy Warhol once said, everyone can be famous for fifteen minutes.

Chapter Thirty

The outer shell of milk chocolate melted in her mouth revealing the soft orange fondant. Delilah chewed it slowly while dipping her hand back into the packet. This time she picked out a Malteser. Popping it between her teeth she bit into the crisp honeycomb centre. She smiled to herself. Her favourite.

Delilah was recovering from her first row with Charlie, an exhausting afternoon of yelling, swearing, finger-wagging and sulking. It had started when he'd accused her of being responsible for Nickii's rather sudden departure; in return she'd accused him of flirting. He'd called her a jealous cow, she'd called him an arrogant bastard. It hit a nerve. Cue bulging neck veins, a smashed wine glass, and him storming out of the flat, slamming the door so hard it nearly came off its hinges. Which is why, two hours later, she was sitting on the sofa with a box of Kleenex, watching *Friends* on video and determinedly working her way through a family-size packet of Revels.

Things weren't turning out how she'd wanted them to. Not that she was deeply unhappy, but, put it this way, it wasn't turning into the fairytale she'd imagined as she'd waved goodbye to L'Escargot, Lenny and a life of boredom. And Charlie wasn't her Prince Charming. Well, not after this afternoon's argument, anyway.

At first it had all been wonderful – lying in bed until midday, shopping until late afternoon, spending every night at a different restaurant or party until 3 a.m. – but now, nearly two months later, the novelty had worn off and she was starting to feel . . . well . . . *bored.* It sounded ludicrous, but it was true. Not working wasn't so much fun when she was by herself all day with only a credit card for company, neither was spending every evening watching her boyfriend getting pissed with his mates. Delilah had discovered very early on that going out with Charlie meant going out with the rest of his crowd. At first she hadn't minded, she'd wanted to meet his exciting friends with their exciting careers and exciting lives. Except when she got over her initial awe she discovered they were anything but exciting. The fluid assortment of wannabes, trust-fund babes and hangers-on, were all talk and all of it was about themselves. Delilah had lost count of the times she'd tried to look interested as another man with stubble and sunglasses on his head told her about his plans for a screenplay or found herself in a restaurant next to a model-cum-singer-cum-actress, bored to tears as they talked her through their fascinating resumés. Not only that but they treated Charlie as a free meal-ticket: providing the champagne, picking up their share of the restaurant tab and inviting them back to his flat for a party. Even worse, he didn't seem to mind. On the contrary, he seemed only too happy to oblige – *every night of the week.* When Delilah had finally plucked up the courage to complain he'd made her feel like the nagging girlfriend. Maybe she was. She wasn't sure what she was anymore.

Sighing miserably, she finished off the Revels and snuggled down next to Fatso, who was chewing frantically, trying to remove the chocolate toffee which had stuck to the roof of his mouth. She was fed up and lonely. What she needed was Vivienne to turn up with copious amounts of white wine and Marlboro Lights. Unfortunately Vivienne wasn't on hand with the alcohol, having retired to the country to convalesce after her liposuction. But although she couldn't be there in the flesh (what little she had left after having most of it siphoned off on the operating table) she could still be there in spirit, thanks to her trusty mobile.

★ ★ ★

She dialled Vivienne's number. Somebody picked up. There was a lot of groaning and then a faint croak.

Delilah pressed the phone to her ear. 'Vivienne, is that you?'

Silence. And then a gasp. 'Yes.'

'Vivienne, are you okay?'

Another pause. She seemed to be having trouble speaking. 'Yes.'

Delilah frowned. Something in Vivienne's monosyllabic conversation told her things were still a little tender. 'How are you feeling?'

'Fine.' Her voice was tight. The operation hadn't been as pain-less as she'd been led to believe, due to the surgeon having 'forgotten' to tell her that the procedure involved relentlessly ramming a rod backwards and forwards under the skin of her bum cheeks, as if he was sweeping under the bed with a broom handle.

'So has it been a success?'

Vivienne paused to adjust the inflatable rubber ring she was gingerly sitting on. 'Put it this way. Before I had the liposuction the surgeon described my bottom as reminding him of "porridge in a string bag".'

Delilah shuddered. 'And what does it remind him of now?' she asked tentatively, not sure if she wanted to know.

'Two scoops of ice cream.'

Delilah stifled a giggle. Vivienne was being deadly serious.

'Anyway, how are things at your end?' Briskly changing the subject, Vivienne missed the irony.

'Not too good. I've had a row with Charlie,' said Delilah flatly.

'Why, what's happened?'

'He had a party back at the flat and I poured washing-up liquid into someone's Margarita. They threw up everywhere.' She cringed. She still couldn't believe what she'd done. Spiking someone's drink – *and with washing-up liquid*. What had got into her?

Vivienne squeaked down the phone. '*Washing-up liquid? What on earth were you doing at this party? The dishes?*'

'No, but I might as well have been,' she muttered sulkily, remembering how everybody had been having a good time while she'd been stuck in the kitchen feeling like the hired help.

'Correct me if I'm wrong, but I get the slight feeling it wasn't an accident.'

Delilah didn't say anything. She was too embarrassed to admit that she'd done it on purpose. Last night it had seemed like a good idea. Twelve hours later and it had turned into a very bad one. Okay, so Nickii was a right pain in the arse and she had been out of order, but even so, she'd overreacted. She always used to be so laid back about things, but now she was behaving like the bunny boiler from *Fatal Attraction*. The jealous woman out for revenge. She groaned miserably. Hanging round with Charlie and his friends was turning her into a psycho.

Vivienne took the silence to mean yes. 'So, what's her name?'

'How did you know it was a she?' Delilah sounded surprised.

'Experience, sweetie.' So Sam had been right. Charlie was a lecherous love rat. 'So, tell me all the gory details.'

Delilah sighed. 'There's not much to tell. Her name's Nickii and she's a pain in the arse who works with Charlie. She's always flirting with him and normally I just ignore her, but last night she went just that bit too far.'

'Is she skinny?' Vivienne was a fattist. A female's potential threat was graded by her dress size. Size 8–10 was serious cause for concern and demanded immediate action (gym workouts, buttock-reducing polythene wraps and a diet consisting solely of Marlboro Lights), 12–14 could be a potential rival, depending on whether you're talking Latin curves or a classic English pear. As for 16 and over – breathe a sigh of relief, you're home and dry.

'I guess so.'

Vivienne's heart sank. So she was a Class-A threat. 'What are you doing now?'

Delilah glanced at the scrunched-up packet of Revels. 'Eating chocolate and watching *Friends*.'

Vivienne shrieked. 'No wonder you're depressed. What a distressing combination: Jennifer Aniston and a week's worth of calories. You need alcohol, darling. Preferably a 1967 Cabernet Sauvignon.

'I thought you didn't drink.'

'I don't, but I have fond memories . . .' She tailed off wistfully, remembering the good old drunken days. Unfortunately her reverie was interrupted by the sight of Harold entering the drawing room in his tweed shooting jacket and flat cap. Beaming proudly he marched towards her, dangling a brace of pheasants. Her spirits sank. 'I have to go.'

'What?'

'Something's come up.' Or rather it hasn't, she thought, glancing bitterly at the pheasant, hanging limp and lifeless, and then Harold's crotch. Luckily a mail-order package had arrived for her that morning – King Kong was twelve inches long, had four speeds and a rotating head. It promised to enliven the dullest of evenings. 'By the way, tomorrow I'm going to stay with a friend in Spain. Thought I'd recuperate from my operation and at the same time acquire myself a tan for the wedding. I'll call you from the villa.'

'Oh, okay. Have a nice time.' Delilah put the phone down. She stared at the TV screen. Jennifer was skipping around showing off her newly toned midriff and flicking her perfect hair around. Grabbing the remote control she switched it off. Sod *Friends*. Vivienne was right. She needed a drink.

Chapter Thirty-One

It was 6.30 and the wine shop on the corner was full of office-weary people fleecing the shelves of red wine. Delilah looked at the half-empty fridge, trying to appear as if she knew what she was looking for. She didn't have a clue, apart from the fact it had to be white and have 12.5% written on the label. One of the trendy male assistants hovered nearby, ready to offer his expert advice. She moved from South African to Australian and back to Italian. The assistant approached. Just in time she grabbed a bottle of Pinot Grigio.

'Are you okay there?'

'Fine.' She smiled and waved the bottle cheerily. Phew. A minute longer and she'd have been pinned against the display of Asti Spumante, trying to look interested as he gave her the benefit of his vast wine knowledge and recommended a 'full-bodied, oaky merlot' or a 'fruity, flowery chardonnay'. Translated, it meant she'd have ended up with a bottle of plonk that cost twice what she wanted to spend and tasted like paint stripper.

She joined the queue at the cash register and waited. In front of her, a middle-aged businessman was droning loudly into his hands-free headpiece, telling his wife he'd be working late at the office. Strange, seeing as he was in an off-licence clutching a dozen red roses and buying two bottles of Moët. Trying to ignore him she began idly reading a newspaper over some-body's shoulder, waiting for the line to move. Except it didn't. Tutting, she craned her neck to see which idiot was holding everybody up.

'I'm sorry, I don't seem to have enough. I'm a quid short.'

A hand squeezed her stomach. At the front of the queue was Sam, mumbling apologies and fishing around in his pockets for loose change. He wasn't having much success.

Pushing the man with the headpiece out of the way, she held out a pound coin. 'Is this what you need?'

Sam swung round. '*Delilah!*' Two spots of colour burned bright on his cheeks.

She smiled sheepishly. 'I was in the queue . . .' She motioned to the line of people who were fidgeting impatiently.

'Oh, right,' he nodded, looking flustered. He'd been thinking about Delilah for weeks, planning what he'd say if he saw her. Now that moment had come and he was struck dumb.

'Can you please get a move on. I'm in a rush,' grumbled the man with the headpiece.

'What? To get home to your wife?' Delilah gave him a dirty look. The man glared and puffed himself up, rather like a cockerel when it feels threatened. She glared back. After the kind of day she'd had, she was in no mood for unfaithful husbands.

She turned to Sam. 'I don't know about you, but I think I'll forget the wine. Do you fancy a drink at the pub instead?'

He stalled for a second before breaking into a smile. 'Yeh, why not.' Dumping their bottles they pushed open the door and stepped onto the pavement, leaving behind a flustered assistant trying to do a void on the till, and a shop full of hot and bothered people.

They decided against the Pantry. Delilah made up some excuse about wanting to avoid Vince, but really she was worried she might bump into Charlie and his cronies. Instead they walked to the Albert, a down-at-heel pub in the grotty part of Portobello, where the organic cafés, designer clothes shops and fashionable restaurants finished and the betting shops, minicab offices and Woolworths began. Inside, it was nearly empty, apart from a couple of grey-haired Rastafarians who sat in the corner playing dominos.

They sat at the bar. It was a bit awkward at first. Neither of them mentioned the argument – or Charlie. Which made things a bit difficult, seeing as everything Delilah had been doing for the last couple of months involved Charlie. Instead they circled around it, making polite conversation about neutral topics such as Gladys's health, how warm the weather was for that time of year and Vivienne's forthcoming nuptials. But after a few vodka-tonics their body language relaxed and their tongues loosened.

'I'm glad we bumped into each other. I wanted to apologise.' Delilah looked down at her drink and fiddled with her straw.

'Me too.' Sam nodded. He didn't regret what he'd said about Charlie, but he regretted falling out with Delilah. 'I didn't mean to fly off the handle at you. I know I did go on a bit.'

'Just a bit,' she smirked.

'Sorry, but sometimes I get so wound up. I just go into one.'

'And I didn't?'

Sam smiled, remembering Delilah's wrath. 'Yeh, you did give as good as you got.'

Delilah grinned sheepishly.

Suddenly Sam started laughing.

'What you laughing at?'

He didn't answer.

'Are you laughing at me?' Delilah leaned forward.

Sam shook his head, still laughing. 'No. I was just remember-ing the look on the faces of those American tourists.' He held his belly and laughed even more.

It was infectious. Delilah started giggling. 'And the guy with the camera,' she squeaked, trying to speak between fits of giggles.

Sam wiped his eyes on the back of his sleeve and motioned to the barman. 'A couple more drinks, please. And make them doubles.' He grinned at Delilah. She smiled back. She'd forgot-ten how much fun Sam was.

After the fifth round, Delilah was feeling very pissed and very emotional. It was like being on a rollercoaster. She'd gone from an exhilarated high, laughing her head off and feeling as if she didn't have a care in the world, to plunging into an out-of-perspective gloom when she'd remembered the row she'd had with Charlie. But she wasn't alone. Sam felt the gloom too. After all, he'd come along for the ride.

'So, how are things with Charlie?' It killed him to ask, but he had to. Even if it meant hearing something he didn't like.

She forced a smile. 'Great.' His heart sank. 'Well, actually no, they're far from great.' Sighing, she stirred her drink. 'We had a massive argument today.'

His heart bobbed back up to the surface. 'What happened?'

'Oh, you don't want to know.' Sucking up the last of the vodka, she put her glass back on the bar. 'Maybe I should have listened to you after all.' The alcohol was making her feel depressed. The row with Charlie had seemed like a kiss-and-make-up row when she was sober, but now – five double vodka and tonics later – it felt like a pack-your-bags-and-leave one.

Sam felt guilty. There was no satisfaction to be gained in being proved right about Charlie. Not when it meant seeing Delilah so miserable. On impulse he leaned forward and put his arms round her. 'Cheer up,' he whispered, holding her tightly. God, she felt wonderful.

Delilah leaned wearily against his chest. Her head was heavy with alcohol and the tears she'd cried that morning. It was so nice to be hugged. Closing her eyes, she breathed Sam's familiar smell. It reminded her of laughter, kindness and happy days out to Brighton. Of being cared about and made to feel as if she was important and special. Charlie didn't think she was special. He thought she was a jealous cow who spiked people's drinks.

'I've missed you.' Sam lifted her chin and looked into her eyes.

'Me too.' She bit her lip. The rollercoaster was slowing down and after all its ups and downs she was shaken and vulnerable. She felt as if she was going to start crying. Her eyes filled up with tears.

'Please don't cry.' Bending towards her he kissed her gently, tentatively. She didn't pull away. Instead she pulled him towards her, pressing her body against his as he kissed her deeper, passionately, exploring her mouth with his tongue and moving his hands across the sides of her face, through her hair and slowly down her back.

The Rastafarians stopped playing dominos and watched the young couple kissing. Dragging on a spliff, they looked at each other and smiled. Young love, eh?

Chapter Thirty-Two

For a moment she couldn't remember where she was. The room was in darkness and she had difficulty recognising anything. Everything was unfamiliar. Even the sound of her own breathing.

Then she realised. It wasn't *her* breathing she could hear, it was Sam's and he was lying next to her under the duvet. She snapped her eyes shut. Ohmigod, this couldn't be happening. She was in Sam's flat, in Sam's bed, with Sam. Gingerly she opened her eyes and peeked under the covers. *And neither of them had any clothes on.*

Now it was all coming back to her. Drunkenly snogging at the pub, staggering back to his flat with their hands all over each other, drinking whisky and making love. *Making love!* Jesus Christ, what had she been thinking? One minute she'd been having a drink and a bit of a natter, and the next she'd been stark naked doing her Sharon Stone impression. She looked at her watch. It was 5 a.m. If she was quick she could probably get home before Charlie returned from another night of partying.

Trying not to disturb Sam, she quickly pulled on her clothes which lay scattered around the floor, foregoing her knickers, which had disappeared into the black hole of the duvet, and tiptoed out into the hall. Lifting the latch she pulled open the door to Sam's flat, making sure it didn't slam behind her, hurried into the dimly lit communal hallway, down two flights of stairs – trying not to trip on the threadbare beige carpet that was coming away from the edges – pushed the security buzzer until the heavy panelled front door clicked open, and stumbled out into the street. Standing on the doorstep in the damp morning air she breathed a sigh of relief – and then groaned. Her immediate panic may have subsided, but it had been replaced with a horrendous hangover which struck up a thumping beat inside her head.

Pulling her new velvet jacket around her, she set off, scuttling down the pavement. An electric milk float whirred past her, its driver leaning out to have a good gawp. 'Pervert,' she muttered, holding her tousled head high and trying to look as if it was perfectly normal to be roaming the streets at daybreak wearing no knickers and a pair of Prada mules. A lone black cab turned into the street, its orange TAXI light glowing faintly. 'Thank God,' gasped Delilah, breaking into a hundred-metre sprint down the middle of the road, gesticulating wildly in a desperate attempt to flag it down. 'Please stop, please stop, please stop,' she chanted as she stumbled and wobbled on her stiletto heels towards the flickering orange light. But it didn't stop. In fact, for a moment she thought it was going to run her over, until suddenly it swerved and pulled into the kerb.

'I was just about to finish for the evening,' hollered the cabbie. 'Where do you want to go?'

'Thirty-four Kildare Villas. It's really close, in fact it's practically round the corner.' She crossed her fingers, praying he'd skipped that bit of his A–Z when he was doing the Knowledge.

'Oh, okay. Hop in.' The central-locking system clicked open and Delilah yanked on the door, thankfully flinging herself onto the back seat. That was the easy bit, now for the hard part.

She'd just crawled into bed when she heard keys in the front door and Charlie clattering up the spiral staircase. He emerged, drunk and disorderly, and began staggering across the room towards her, hastily trying to pull off his clothes. Unfortunately in his drunken haze he'd forgotten to take off his shoes and, as his jeans gathered in a knot around his ankles, he lost what little sense of balance he had left and tumbled on top of her.

'Sorry, darling,' he whispered loudly. Delilah shrank back. If she'd had a box of matches she could have ignited his breath. 'I didn't mean to wake you up.'

'It's okay.' She cringed. If only he knew.

'And I'm sorry about today. You were right, I was being an arrogant bastard.' Hauling himself up, he slobbered Sambuca kisses all over her face.

Delilah was mortified. He was being so nice to her. *He was even apologising.* Unable to look him in the eye, she turned away. She felt so bloody guilty. Why the hell couldn't he be horrible? She deserved it.

'What's wrong. Are you still angry?'

'No, of course not.' Did he suspect? She tried to smile, but it wasn't easy. Any minute now he was going to guess what she'd been up to. How could he not? She felt as if I'VE BEEN UNFAITH-FUL was tattooed across her forehead in two-inch-high scarlet letters.

'Where's my hug then?' Hoisting himself up onto the pillows he stared blearily down at her, his pale-blue eyes puffy and bloodshot: the by-product of too much partying and not enough sleep. Delilah reached up and gingerly put her arms around him. 'That's better.' Snuggling into her neck he held her close as she lay, tense and rigid, praying that he wasn't going to try and initiate sex. How ironic. Only a few months ago she'd been in Bradford dreaming of him making love to her; now here she was hoping he wouldn't. Thankfully he was so plastered he fell asleep within seconds, still lying on top of her with his jeans around his ankles. Hearing his breathing deepen, her body slowly began to relax. The panic was over, at least for the moment. Taking a deep breath she looked down at Charlie, his head cradled in the nook of her shoulder, his long tanned arms wrapped around her, the way they'd fallen asleep so many times before. But what had seemed so natural twenty-four hours ago now suddenly felt so odd. It was as if she was hugging a different person. Except she wasn't. Charlie was. It wasn't Charlie who had changed, she had. Closing her eyes she concentrated on the sound of her own breathing, in, out, in, out, until finally she drifted into an uneasy sleep.

Over the next couple of days Charlie sent Delilah a lavish bouquet of flowers – or rather he gave his credit card number to one of his production team and asked them to sort it out – and came home with an expensive pair of Tiffany earrings. Wracked with shame, she thanked him profusely. She didn't have the heart to tell him that she didn't have pierced ears. Which was probably just as well, seeing as they were an identical pair to the ones he'd bought Nickii for her birthday last year.

A week passed and it looked as if everything had returned to normal. On the surface things were the same between them: they drank at the same bars, ate at the same restaurants, hung out at the same parties and slept in the same bed. But it was as if an invisible wall had been built between them. Not that Charlie noticed. Assuming they'd patched things up and he was off the hook, he ceased showering her with presents and affection and concentrated his energies on the person he loved the most – himself.

Charlie was happiest when he was surrounded by his cronies, enjoying being the centre of attention, flirting and getting drunk. He was young, rich and handsome, and he was out to have a good time. He liked Delilah a lot, she was pretty and funny and they'd had some good laughs together. In fact he liked her more than most of the other girls he'd gone out with and ended up living with for a few short months. That's why he'd given her those flowers and earrings. He didn't want to be arguing with her and falling out, even if he did still have his suspicions about Nickii's Margarita. He didn't want the hassle. Okay, so he could understand how she'd got all jealous about him and Nickii, but she shouldn't have made it into such a big deal. He didn't fancy Nickii, never had, he just enjoyed the attention. That's just the way he was and he wasn't going to change. He wasn't going to stop partying with his friends, getting drunk and having a bit of a flirt. And that's all it was, flirting. Well, apart from the time he'd ended up shagging Petal in the toilets at that club in Covent Garden – but that was only because she'd been giving him the come-on all night. Anyway, Delilah didn't know about that, which was a relief, otherwise she'd really freak out. She was one of the faithful types who'd probably never cheated on anyone in her whole life. At least it meant he didn't have anything to worry about in that department. That was one of the reasons he'd stopped her working at the Pantry. He didn't want all those other blokes eyeing her up in that sexy little costume. Anyway, he liked Delilah to be there when he got home, liked it when she was all dressed up and smelling gorgeous, it made him feel good. What guy wouldn't want a girl that was crazy about him? And, argument or not, nothing had changed. She still felt the same way about him. Meaning he could carry on partying in a state of ignorant bliss.

But things had changed, and Delilah was a nervous wreck. Guilt was ripping her in two. She felt guilty for what she'd done to Charlie and guilty for what she'd done to Sam. Not only had she cheated on her boyfriend by having a one-night stand, she'd had it with her friend and done a runner before he woke up. It wasn't exactly the best situation to be in.

But she was in it, and all she could do now was find a way to deal with it. Easier said than done. At first she tried not to think about what had gone on between her and Sam, as if by blocking it out of her mind she could pretend it had never happened. And she deliberately avoided Vivienne's calls, letting them click onto the answering machine, so that she wouldn't be tempted to reveal her guilty secret. But after a while she had to face facts. It wasn't working. She *was* thinking about it. She was thinking about it every hour, every minute, every second of every day. How could she have been unfaithful? How could she have slept with Sam? She asked herself the same questions time and time again. And she kept coming up with the same answers. She'd been drunk. She'd felt vulnerable and upset and wanted affection. It could have been anyone, but Sam just happened to be there.

But was that true? Could it have been anyone? Or was there more to it than that? Once the initial shock of what had happened wore off, she found herself thinking less and less about Charlie and more and more about Sam. She owed him an explanation, not that she could give him one, and an apology for running off at 5 a.m. Taking her courage in both hands she called him – but dialled 141 before his number and put the phone down as soon as he'd answered. What was she going to say? 'Hi, sorry about the other night. Oh, and by the way, I was wondering if you'd found my knickers?' Not exactly the kind of chit-chat you have on the telephone. And to be honest she was probably the last person he wanted to speak to. No doubt he regretted what had happened more than she did. Not that she could remember much of what exactly *had* happened that night. Except for one thing. One thing she'd tried desperately hard to ignore but which kept coming back to taunt her, making her feel more confused than she did already. It was the feeling she'd had when Sam had first kissed her in the pub. When he'd first put his lips against hers. She didn't know if she'd imagined it, or if it had just been the effects of the booze, but it had felt as if a thousand flashbulbs were going off in her brain. As if someone had turned on a very bright, very intense light. And she'd sure as hell never wanted to switch it off.

'Are you ready yet? We're supposed to be there for 8 p.m.' Charlie stood by the door, jangling his car keys.

Reluctantly, Delilah pulled on her new red velvet jacket and adjusted the collar. The last thing she felt like doing was going to the opening of Iceberg, a poncy restaurant in Piccadilly. She wanted to wipe off her make-up, slap on a face pack and sit in front of the telly in her pyjamas. Exactly, she realised, what she used to do in Bradford.

'For God's sake get a move on.' His voice rose up the spiral staircase. Charlie was in a stroppy mood – somebody had slashed the roof of his new BMW.

Kissing Fatso, Delilah took a final glance at her reflection before teetering unsurely down the stairs. She never had learnt how to walk in those bloody high heels.

The paparazzi were gathered in rowdy clusters outside the restaurant, jostling for photos of people who would turn up to the opening of an envelope if it meant publicity, but then go on breakfast telly to complain about press intrusion. Climbing out of limos, they were pretending they didn't want to be photographed, but at the first sight of a zoom lens began fluffing up their feather cuts and showing off their best sides. Delilah put her head down and kept behind Charlie, who had swapped his earlier scowl for a mega-watt smile. Well, they were hardly going to want pictures of her, were they?

Inside, Iceberg was crammed with all those people who haven't yet reached the B-lists. Marbella-tanned footballers and their obligatory blondes, ex-soap stars turned would-be pop stars, TV chefs, gardeners and handymen, and random 'models': dolled-up girls from Essex who once did a bit of topless modelling but who now earned a living from cashing in on their tabloid newspaper affair with a Tory MP/married footballer/ageing rockstar or all three.

Charlie quickly located the posse, who were lingering thirstily around the complimentary champagne.

'Hello there,' purred Nickii, sucking in her stomach and manoeuvring next to him. Pouting, she passed him a drink, purposely ignoring Delilah, who stood empty-handed. 'We were wondering where you were.'

Charlie smiled and took a sip of his champagne. 'Oh, you know how long you ladies take to get dressed.' He winked roguishly.

'Not me. I take less than a minute to get dressed . . . and undressed.' Nickii giggled playfully and squeezed his arm.

Delilah pretended not to hear. It was going to be one of those evenings.

'I *thought* that was you.' Wendy with the gift for regional accents sprang forward, bursting with excitement. 'I'd recognise that coat anywhere!' She beamed triumphantly, pleased as punch with her powers of detection.

Delilah looked down at her coat and then back at Wendy. 'I'm sorry, you've lost me.'

'The other morning. Trying to hail a cab on All Saints Road. I thought you looked familiar but I'd just woken up and didn't have my contact lenses in. I live in the flat above the bookmaker's . . .' Her voice tailed off as she noticed Delilah's face drain of colour.

'It can't have been me, I haven't been in that area,' she lied, trying to think fast. The last thing she needed was for blabbermouth Wendy to start broadcasting her secret.

'No, it was definitely you. In fact I'm positive.' Wendy nodded vigorously.

'It can't have been,' Delilah insisted, gritting her teeth.

'No, I'm sure it was.' Wendy grinned even wider.

Delilah resisted the urge to scream with frustration. Instead, she frantically tried to think of a way to shut her up before she went gossiping to Charlie.

'This isn't my jacket. I've just borrowed it for tonight.' A flash of inspiration.

'Oh.' Wendy looked disappointed. 'Silly me, there was I thinking you were up to no good.' She giggled girlishly.

'Me, up to no good?' Delilah laughed nervously, crossing her fingers behind her back. That was a close one.

They were shown to their table, which was supposed to be shaped like a lifeboat. Charlie sat at the helm, with Andy, Nickii, Mandy, Jamie and Johnny down one side, and Wendy, Delilah, a TV hypnotist and two members of a boy-band down the other. Everything had a shipwreck theme, with flares as candles, salt and pepper pots made out of driftwood, and a cocktail menu which offered drinks with inspired names such as Desert Island Ice Tea, SOS on the Beach and Ship on the Rocks. You could just imagine the team from the trendy Soho design

230	*Alexandra Potter*

agency patting each other on the backs at their wit and ingenuity.

Charlie ordered a round of Desert Island Ice Teas.

'Not for me,' whispered Nickii. 'I'll just have some Evian.' She snuggled close to him, rubbing his thigh suggestively under the table.

'Not drinking tonight?' smiled Delilah brightly across the table. She knew it was wicked but she couldn't resist having a dig. Especially when Nickii still insisted on flirting outrageously with Charlie as if she didn't exist.

Nickii turned her head stiffly. 'No, I'm doing a two-week detox. Just fruit and water.' Scowling, she shoved the half-eaten breadstick back into its packet.

Three rounds of cocktails later and Delilah wanted to go home. As usual Charlie was having a great time, fooling around with his mates and paying no attention to her, while she was forced to make small-talk with Gary, the TV hypnotist. Gary was in his late thirties and pleasantly boring. After half an hour spent droning on about his penthouse flat and soft-top Mercedes, he was trying to concentrate his powers of persuasion on getting her to agree to a date. She politely refused. Hypnotist he may be, hypnotic he wasn't.

'So what do you do?' Realising he was getting nowhere by boasting about the size of his bank balance, Gary decided to switch tactics and ask Delilah about herself. Maybe that would work.

Delilah laughed, trying to cover up a feeling of slight embarrassment. She realised she was ashamed to admit that she didn't actually *do* anything. Well, nothing that didn't include shopping, having her hair done and staying in bed till lunchtime watching daytime TV, and she could hardly confess to that gruelling schedule. 'Before Delilah met Charlie she sold cigarettes in a restaurant, but now she doesn't do anything, do you?' sneered Nickii who'd been earwigging on their conversation.

Put like that, Delilah didn't know what to say. She might not like what she heard, but for once Nickii was telling the truth.

Fiddling with her menu she looked the other way. As did Gary who, realising his chances of chatting her up had just taken a nosedive, fidgeted uncomfortably and started dishing out the jugs of Desert Island Ice Teas.

Meanwhile, Wayne and Shane from the boy-band had started to act their age – sixteen and seventeen respectively – and were throwing bread rolls at Jamie and Johnny. They missed and hit Nickii. 'I think we should order,' she snapped, flicking a green olive and a few crumbs from her ciabatta-flecked fringe and beckoning one of the waiters by snapping her fingers.

'Good evening, can I take your order?'

Delilah froze. That voice. She'd recognise that voice anywhere. Slowly she lifted her head and looked at the Armani-clad waiter who stood at the end of the table. It couldn't be. It wasn't. *It was.* Sam. First her friend, then her lover, *now her waiter.* Putting her head in her hands she took a deep breath. Just when she'd thought the evening couldn't get any worse . . .

Chapter Thirty-Three

'Do you have any fruit?'

'For dessert? Yes, we have a compote of strawberries, lemon mousse—' Sam was interrupted.

'Not for dessert, idiot, for my entrée. I'm in detox. I need fruit.' Nickii flung down her napkin in a hypoglycaemic tantrum.

'I'm sure the chef can arrange something.'

'Well, I should hope so, this is supposed to be a bloody restaurant.' Now it was Gary's turn to join in.

Sam stood firm, trying to control a baying crowd. He hadn't noticed Delilah, who was hiding behind her menu wondering what the hell he was doing dressed up as a waiter and desperately wishing the ground would open up and swallow her. To make matters worse everyone was being so bloody rude. The boy-band had moved on to the breadsticks and were firing them at him like darts, Andy, Jamie and Johnny were taking the piss out of him, while Charlie was sat at the helm grinning and revelling in the whole shameful débâcle.

'And for you, Madam?'

Delilah was still cowering behind the iceberg-shaped menu, unable to surface. She was pretending to read the entrées while trying to work out how she could escape, unseen, through the nearest fire exit.

'Come on, what are you going to eat? *Delilah.*' Was it her imagination, or was Charlie deliberately emphasising her name.

Lowering her menu inch by inch, she lifted her eyes apprehensively. They met Sam's. He didn't flinch.

'What about the grilled seabass? That looks pretty tasty.'
Charlie looked directly at Sam. 'What do you think? *Waiter*.'

Still in shock, Delilah cringed. God, this was awful. Charlie
was behaving like an arrogant twerp and Sam was having to
stand there and take it.

'I *said*, what do you *think*, waiter?' Charlie repeated the
words, spitting out the consonants.

Delilah watched the muscle in the side of Sam's jaw start to
twitch. She had to do something. Charlie might not know who
he was talking to, but Sam definitely knew who he was having
to listen to. And she knew only too well how he felt about *that*
subject.

'Shut up, Charlie.' There, she'd said it.

There was a sudden hush. Nobody had ever told Charlie
Mendes to shut up. Especially not one of his girlfriends.

'What did you say?' Charlie put down his drink, his face
hard and stony.

Delilah bristled, her stubborn streak rising to the surface. 'I
said, shut up and stop being so rude.'

Charlie looked around the table, like a king seeking the
approval of his courtiers. 'Was I being rude?'

His posse waggled their heads like puppets. 'No, of course
not. It's the bloody staff,' tutted Nickii, deliberately ignoring the
ashtray and flicking her cigarette onto the tablecloth.

'You see? I'm not the one being rude. It's the waiter.' Charlie
folded his arms behind his head and leaned back in the chair.
'In fact, he's being so rude I think I'm going to have to call the
manager.'

Delilah didn't know what to do. Perhaps Charlie would shut
up if she told him that the waiter was her friend Sam. But
perhaps that wasn't such a good idea, seeing as she'd told
Charlie all about Sam slagging him off in the café. Far from
appeasing matters, it would just make everything worse.

As she sat there chewing the side of her thumb, Delilah had
no idea that Charlie knew exactly who Sam was. In fact, he'd
known exactly who he was since he'd inherited a stack of

property leases from his father, including one for Café Prima Donna. For years Charlie had disagreed with Sam about the rent and his own perks as a landlord, and belittled his tenant's ambition to be a chef by turning the café into a restaurant. In fact he'd viewed Sam as a source of mild entertainment, until he'd discovered that he was Delilah's best friend. If that hadn't been bad enough, she'd then told him – word for word – exactly what Sam had been saying about him. No doubt trying to turn her against him. And he couldn't have that, could he? So, biding his time, Charlie had waited until the lease had come up for renewal and then he'd doubled the rent. He knew Sam would never be able to afford it and would have to close the café down, which he had done, after a couple of blazing rows between them. Not that Charlie had cared; in fact, he'd revelled in Sam's anger and frustration, and calmly put the phone down on him. That would teach anyone who thought to call Charlie Mendes a wanker. He'd expected that would be the last he ever heard or saw of Sam. Unfortunately, like the bad penny he was, he'd turned up. Still, if Charlie had his way he'd soon lose that job as well.

'I demand to see the manager.'

Delilah looked at Sam, who was struggling to keep his cool. He'd wanted to sort Charlie Mendes out for a long time, and there was no better time than now.

'Be quiet, Charlie.' Delilah stood up from the table.

'Delilah, sit down,' he barked angrily.

The posse giggled nervously. Delilah ignored them and started squeezing past Gary, who was apparently unable to move, so hypnotised was he by the unfolding drama.

Charlie stood up to make a grab for her as she walked past him, when Sam, poised like a coiled spring, snapped. 'Keep your filthy hands off her.' He pushed Charlie sharply.

'What the hell . . .' He swayed backwards, surprised and faintly drunk.

'You think everybody has to do what you say. Well, they don't.' Sam pulled off his Armani tunic and, screwing it up, stuffed it in Charlie's face. 'You might be able to take my café away, but that's all of mine you're taking.' He glanced at the subdued table and back at Charlie, who was still reeling with shock. 'Call the fucking manager. You can't get me sacked. I've just quit.' Turning round he began walking stiffly out of the hushed restaurant, pushing past the crowd of stunned onlookers.

His departure from the scene gave a signal to the rest of the restaurant to begin whispering and pointing at Charlie who, realising he'd become the centre of attention, recovered his senses and quickly smoothed his ruffled hair and straightened his collar. 'Poxy waiter,' he sniffed loudly, trying to hide his embarrassment at being made to look a fool. 'Jumped-up little shit. Who the fuck does he think he is?' Knocking over a champagne bottle, he grabbed his drink and took a large swig, trying to regain his composure.

Delilah stood for a moment in shock. What did Sam mean? *Took away his café?* She looked at Charlie, flushed and flustered. She used to think he was so handsome, but now his pale-blue eyes looked grey, a hard, stony grey, and his mouth was screwed up, tight and bitter. Before, he'd always looked so laid back and sure of himself, exuding an air of self-confidence that only truly rich and good-looking people could have, casting a spell over everybody he met. And that's what had made him so attractive. Now he stood bathed in a different light. A harsh light that had nothing to do with the halogen spotlights in the restaurant. The handsome surface that charmed and captivated her had been peeled away and for the first time she saw what was underneath. And she didn't like it. The spell had been broken.

Whirling round, she saw Sam's broad back quickly disappearing through the restaurant. 'Sam, wait.' Tottering on her heels she ran after him.

Chapter Thirty-Four

Outside it was pouring with rain. Delilah pushed open the glass doors. The street was empty, the paparazzi having long since bored of the soap stars and footballers and retired to the pub for a swift half before the next assignment – a tip-off from a waitress at a restaurant on the King's Road that a well-known actor was turning up with his new mystery girlfriend. A lone bouncer stood by the door, scanning the wet London night for possible gatecrashers.

'Sam, wait. Please.' Delilah ran down the steps and onto the pavement. 'Sam!'

Across the street Sam paused, the rain drenching his T-shirt and making it cling to his skin in soggy, navy-blue wrinkles. He hesitated before turning to look at her. 'What?'

Delilah swallowed. The curtain of rain splashed onto her hair and trickled down her forehead, quickly soaking her face, her clothes, her body. 'What were you doing in there? What happened in the café?'

Sam shook his head. 'Don't pretend you don't know. Don't pretend you don't know what's been going on,' he yelled across the noise of a passing taxi. His voice was hard, cutting through the rain.

'I don't know what you're talking about.' Delilah was taken aback. He'd never spoken to her like that before. 'I don't understand.'

Sam laughed bitterly. 'Well, ask your boyfriend to explain. He's the one with all the answers.' He stood for a moment, staring, before starting to walk away.

'Please, Sam, please talk to me.' Her voice broke.

He stopped dead. 'Oh, so it's different when you want to talk, isn't it? What about last week when I wanted to talk?' He stared, his face screwed up against the stinging rain. 'But you wouldn't know about that, would you? You couldn't wait to run away, run away from your mistake.'

She tried to speak but couldn't. Tears welled up and spilled down her face, merging with the rain into heavy streams. 'It wasn't like that.' Her voice was barely audible. 'I didn't think.'

'That's just it, isn't it? You don't think. You don't think about anybody but yourself.' There was to be no respite. He'd had enough.

'But Sam . . .'

'Go home, Delilah. Go home to your rich boyfriend.' He looked at her bedraggled, designer-clad figure with contempt. 'I don't know who you are any more.' Turning his back on her he began walking away, blindly tramping through the puddles and overflowing drains. Distraught, Delilah stared after him, watching as he strode up the street, gradually getting smaller and smaller until suddenly he was gone, swallowed up by the heavy evening traffic. For what seemed like ages she stood there, a pathetic figure standing alone in the night. Until, drenched to the skin, she sat down on the edge of the pavement and put her head in her hands, her sobs mingling with the rain and flowing like a river of tears into the gutter.

After what seemed like an eternity, the bouncer took pity on her and put her in a cab. The journey back to the flat she spent in a trance, staring miserably out of the rain-splattered windows not knowing what to think. Everything was going wrong. She'd had another row with Charlie and now she'd fallen out with Sam again. Slumping against the seat she pressed her cheek against the cold pane of glass. His words kept swirling around in her head. '*I don't know who you are any more. I don't know who you are any more.*' He'd sounded as if he hated her.

It wasn't until she'd turned her key in the lock and Fatso had appeared, jumping all over her and enthusiastically licking away her tear-streaked foundation, that she stopped feeling numb. She sat on the sofa, cuddling him tightly and wearily resting her head on his soft, skinny body. Which was how Charlie found her when he arrived home not long after. Feeling remorseful he'd gone outside to look for her, and when she wasn't there he'd taken the unprecedented step of cutting short his evening and hailing a cab. When finally he saw her on the sofa, safe and asleep, he felt a sense of relief. For a moment there he thought he'd lost her. And he didn't want to. In his own selfish way, he loved her, whatever anyone might say.

Over the next few days there was an uneasy truce. Charlie apologised, so did Delilah. She didn't want to argue with him. In fact she was sick of arguing with him. What had happened to how it used to be? When they'd spent their whole time in bed, whispering babytalk into each other's ears, giggling at corny jokes and making love until they'd fallen asleep curled up together. Then it had all seemed really simple. Now it was a lot more complicated. Lust and blissful affection had given way to doubts and accusations, thoughts left unsaid, resentments left to fester.

She asked him about Sam. About the café. And Charlie swore his innocence, reiterating what he'd always said. That Sam was jealous. That people like Sam blamed people like Charlie for all their misfortunes.

'I don't know what the hell he was talking about. Taken his café away?' His voice rose an octave as he threw his arms in the air with exaggerated surprise. 'Okay, I can understand why he's pissed off about losing his job at Iceberg. But it's not my fault. The stupid waiter resigned, didn't he?' He stared at her like a man wrongly accused. Except he wasn't. What he was was a very convincing liar.

'He's not a waiter, he's a chef,' mumbled Delilah sulkily.

'Okay, whatever,' snapped Charlie impatiently. 'But whatever he is, I don't want him to come between me and you.'

Leaning forward he curled his fingers around hers and softened his voice. 'I love you.'

Three words. Three little words she'd longed to hear since she first caught sight of him in Bradford General. Three little words that once upon a time she'd have given anything for him to say. Three little words that once they are spoken are like a gift that's been unwrapped. The surprise is over, but is it what you want? Delilah stood motionless as Charlie softly brushed the hair away from her face. Closing her eyes she felt him press his lips gently against hers, his tongue slowly parting her mouth. She wasn't so sure any more.

The next morning Charlie packed a small holdall. He said he was going to Cornwall to film some new documentary and wouldn't be back for two days. Delilah lay in bed, listening to his footsteps clattering down the staircase, the door closing, the revving of the engine of his car. Relief swept over her. She needed the space and time to think about things, get her head together after everything that had happened. She lay there for an hour, staring up at the white expanse of ceiling, tracing the shaft of light that flickered through the curtains. Eventually she dragged herself out of bed, padded over to her Tom Jones collection that she kept at the bottom of the wardrobe, selected one of her favourite albums and, easing it lovingly out of its paper sleeve, put it on the record player. 'It's Not Unusual' started playing.

Turning up the volume she pressed her nose against the large French windows and stared out over London. Normally those lyrics would turn back the clock and make everything better, a big fat sticking plaster covering up her worries and fears, but this time it didn't work. Her mind was too much of a jumbled mess, a thick ball of knotted string, without an end or a beginning, just a jumbled blur of images: Nickii flirting with Charlie, spiking Nickii's drink, sleeping with Sam, the rows, Charlie saying 'I love you', Sam's face as he'd shouted at her in the rain, his café . . . She stood motionless as the song finished and another began. And another, and another, until the whole of one side of the album stopped and the needle clicked off. The silence jolted her back to reality. She knew what she had to do.

At the first opportunity she left the flat and walked with Fatso towards the café. She wanted to find out what was going on, to understand what Sam had been talking about. And the only way to do that was to go and see for herself. Normally it took about fifteen minutes to walk to the café, but today it took twice as long because Fatso insisted on lagging behind on his lead, sniffing every inch of the pavement and circling every lamp-post. It was almost as if he was playing for time. A delaying tactic. Did he know something she didn't? Stopping short of the café, she loitered around the corner. She didn't want to bump into anyone she knew, least of all Sam. But when she saw Café Prima Donna she knew there was no chance of that. Gone was the red and white striped awning, the wooden tables and chairs that spilled out onto the pavements on warm days, the smell of freshly baked croissants and brewing coffee. In their place were large ugly squares of chipboard covering the windows and the door that had always been open. Someone had already graffitied 'Say No to McDonald's' over them in black spraypaint, and fixed high up on the brickwork was a sign: TO LET. Delilah stared at the red and blue lettering, a mixture of sadness and bewilderment. What the hell was going on? It wasn't that long ago that Sam had been talking about setting up a restaurant. Why would he simply pack up and leave?

A drop of rain landed on her face. She looked up at the sky. The sun had long disappeared and it had turned a feisty grey, brooding with thick, heavy clouds. It looked as if there was going to be a storm. Pulling up her collar she tugged on Fatso's lead and started to head back to the flat. There was a loud rumble of thunder and crack of lightning ahead. Fatso whimpered and tried to tangle himself around her legs. 'Don't worry, boy, we'll be home soon.' She quickened her pace. But it was too late. The patter of rain on the leaves of the trees suddenly increased to a rapid drumbeat and with a burst of energy the clouds emptied their pockets, throwing down a powerful wall of water.

'Shit! Run!' yelled Delilah to Fatso, who scarpered, ears down flat against his tiny skull, paws skimming on the slippery pavement, but it was useless – within moments they were drenched. The streets quickly cleared of people, leaving them empty apart from one girl and her dog, who zig-zagged between the cracks in the road that had suddenly filled up with huge puddles of water.

Squinting through the rain, Delilah suddenly caught sight of a large Victorian red-brick building at the end of the street. The library. Luminous strip-lighting shone out from inside and the door was slightly ajar, promising shelter from the rain. Bending down, she scooped up Fatso, and clutching his shivering body charged across the pavement and dived into the entrance.

The stillness came as a shock. Squeezing drips of water from her hair, she pulled off her faded denim jacket, now navy blue from being soaked, and strung it across one of the large grille radiators. Shivering, she looked around her. The entrance hall was large, separated from the main library by two fire doors, and it smelled warm and damp from all the wet bodies that had come through it. She thought about going inside, but a NO DOGS sign and the sight of a grumpy-looking librarian changed her mind. Instead, she leaned against the doorway, watching the weather outside, noticing how dark it had become. A chill ran down her back and she moved further inside, idly looking around her. A large noticeboard ran along the far side, full of the usual library stuff: planning application forms, cards about private tuition, a poster advertising a church jumble sale . . . And then something caught her eye. At the far left, slightly hidden by a notice about the local swimming baths, was a pamphlet for Westminster College of Higher Education. Removing the small brass drawing pin she plucked it down from the wall and, crouching down to warm her back against the radiator, she flicked through. Accountancy, Business Studies, Design. Her finger stopped at the page showing a photograph of someone leaning over a drawing board. Her eyes scanned down the list of courses: fine art, sculpture, design. She read the blurb underneath: 'The college welcomes applications from A-level or mature students considering either the one-year or three-year courses, taken either as full- or part-time.'

Her mind flicked back through the last few months, flashing up moments: the night in the restaurant when Gary the hypnotist had asked her what she did and she'd been struck dumb, too embarrassed to admit she did nothing; sitting alone in the house bored out of her brains with the TV remote control; that night on the beach with Sam talking about her dreams of going to college; then back to when she was a child of seven or eight, sitting on dustsheets watching with fascination and longing as Uncle Stan painted a room.

She looked back at the pamphlet. Interior Design. The words swam invitingly in front of her eyes. This was fate, this was meant to happen, the pamphlet was what she'd been looking for. Feeling a sudden surge in her mood, she folded it carefully and put it in the top of her jacket pocket, still damp from the rain, and looked out of the doorway. The rain had stopped, the sun had broken through the clouds and people were swarming back onto the streets. Things had suddenly brightened up, they were going to be much better.

Back at the flat she decided to call Vivienne, the only person other than Sam himself who would know what was going on with him and the café. She hadn't spoken to her since before she'd slept with Sam, but now it was time to bite the bullet. Dialling her mobile she listened to the ringing tone. Eventually someone answered. But it wasn't Vivienne. It was Harold.

'Vivienne's not here, my dear. She's otherwise engaged,' he spluttered, puffing away like a pair of wheezy old bellows down her mobile.

If only she was, thought Delilah. Perhaps then she'd be able to get some sense and find out what was going on. Harold, bless him, was about as much use as a chocolate kettle. His hearing aid was suffering interference from the mobile's signal and emitting a high-pitched whine, making it impossible for him to hear what she was saying. This, coupled with her Yorkshire accent, and they might as well have been having two completely different conversations.

'When will she be back?' she yelled, pressing her mouth to the phone.

'Oh, my back's much better now, thank you. Although it did play up at yesterday's shoot.'

Delilah groaned. This was impossible. She gave up. 'Well, I'll say goodbye, but when you speak to Vivienne, will you ask her to give me a ring. I just want to make sure everything's all right.' She remembered the pain she'd heard etched on Vivienne's voice after the liposuction ordeal.

'Tomorrow night? Yes, she's returning from Spain for your get-together on Thursday night,' Harold bellowed jovially down the phone. Alas, just as he'd managed to provide her with some information he was unceremoniously cut off.

Heaving a grateful sigh of relief Delilah put down the phone. Of course! Vivienne wasn't ill, she'd gone abroad to get a tan for the wedding and wasn't due back for another twenty-four hours. How could she have forgotten? Tomorrow was Vivienne's hen night.

Chapter Thirty-Five

'I must say, you look very chi-chi.' Vivienne was scrutinising a photo of Delilah, a paparazzi shot taken at the opening of Iceberg which had somehow found its way onto the society pages of an upmarket glossy with the caption: 'Eligible bachelor Charles Mendes and mystery girlfriend'. 'Is that coat from Adventure?' She dragged on her cigarette.

'You must be joking,' laughed Delilah scornfully, momentarily forgetting that Vivienne was an Adventure devotee. 'Do I *look* like the kind of person that would shop there?'

'Well, yes, you do, actually,' replied Vivienne who, completely oblivious to the sarcasm, thought she was paying Delilah a compliment.

Horrified, Delilah snatched back the magazine and took another look at the photograph. Vivienne was right. She looked exactly like one of those women she'd always taken the piss out of. Honey-blonde highlights, lipglossed pout and head-to-toe designer gear. Delilah groaned. Oh my God. Somehow during the last few months she'd turned into Tara Palmer-Tomkinson.

The doorbell rang. 'That'll be the taxi,' whooped Vivienne excitedly, jumping up and down and clapping her hands together. 'Come along, it's time to party!' Hauling Delilah off the chaise-longue and out of her doldrums, she slipped on her kitten heels and did a quick twirl. 'How do I look?' she beamed, knowing only too well how she looked.

Eager to show off her new liposuctioned physique, Vivienne had splashed out on a brand new Versace number that would have made even Liz Hurley blush. With a neckline that grazed her navel, cutaway sides and strategically placed splits that revealed two perfectly honed thighs, the dress was certainly eye-catching. But the fact that it was made entirely from thousands of red sequins, normally the preserve of fake-tanned ballroom dancers on BBC2, gave it that extra phwoar-factor. Or, to put it another way, this was a dress that was less *Come Dancing* and more Come and Get Me.

'Gorgeous,' smiled Delilah. It was certainly a change from the usual hen-night garb she'd seen her friends back in Bradford wearing. Where was the plastic tiara, the veil made from net curtains and the tacky L-plates, so much favoured by brides-to-be? Delilah had never understood this unexplained phenomenon. What causes an attractive, fashion-conscious female to want to make herself look as unattractive and ridiculous as possible *and then go on a pub crawl around the town centre*? Perhaps the bizarre tradition was invented by would-be grooms as a ruse to ward off other suitors. Vivienne, however, had stuck two fingers up at tradition, swapped the veil for Versace, and opted for drop-dead gorgeous.

'Come on, the taxi's waiting,' chivvied Delilah, as Vivienne began preening herself in the mirror. As it was Vivienne's hen night, she'd decided it wasn't the right time to tell her about what had happened at the restaurant or ask her about Sam's café. Tonight they were out to have fun, and she didn't want to spoil things by talking about men. Linking arms, they hurriedly clambered over the debris in the hallway – Vivienne very nearly splitting her dress even further as she skidded on an old copy of *Tatler* – and fell, in a cloud of cigarette smoke, onto the pavement and into the back of the taxi.

It was just like old times.

First stop was the Pantry. Vince was at the bar chatting up someone's girlfriend, but as soon as he saw Delilah he rushed over, waving his Cuban cigar feverishly and jangling his assortment of gold bracelets.

'Delilah, Delilah,' he beamed, smacking his lips together as if she was a tasty dish he was about to eat. 'What have I done to deserve this honour?' Grasping her hand he pressed it to his fleshy lips, covering it in wet, slobbery kisses which swiftly moved upwards past her wrist and towards her elbow. God knows where he would have ended up if he hadn't spotted Vivienne in *that* dress.

It was like a red rag to a bull. Pumped with pent-up testosterone, Vince hastily dropped Delilah's hand and charged towards Vivienne. '*Bellissima, bellissima*,' he panted excitedly, nearly bursting out of his shiny black silk shirt. 'Where have you been all my life?' Pulling himself up to his full height of five-foot-two, he stood, arms outstretched, revealing two large sweat patches that were rapidly spreading out from under his armpits.

Vivienne smiled stiffly. This was not the kind of male attention she'd had in mind when she'd written out a cheque for ten grand at Versace.

'Hands off, Vinnie, she's getting married on Saturday.' Delilah couldn't resist dampening his raging hormones. Vince's face collapsed. 'Terrible, terrible.' He shook his head, showering them both with globules of perspiration. 'What a terrible waste.' He stared gloomily, like a man who'd been condemned to a life of celibacy, before suddenly brightening. Vince wasn't a man to mourn for long over a woman. Less than a minute in fact. 'Never mind,' he smiled broadly, flashing his gold molars, 'let's have a drink together, on the house!'

They left the Pantry after half an hour. It took that long to prise themselves away from Vince, who'd slid a chubby arm around each of their waists and kept pinching them intermittently, as if checking for ripeness. Despite their unease, he was in his element and would have happily stayed like that all night if their prayers hadn't been answered in the form of two large-chested blondes in leather trousers. Unable to resist a cleavage, Vince had immediately switched his affections, giving Delilah and Vivienne the opportunity to make their escape, and leaving him free to continue his carousing in the shadow of two pairs of silicon breasts.

Next stop was the South Kensington Arts Club. This members-only establishment was Vivienne's old stomping ground and where she'd arranged to meet Penny and Virginia. Delilah was excited. She'd never been to an arts club before and was expecting to encounter broodingly handsome Rupert Everett types lounging around in button-back leather armchairs reading scripts and smoking roll-ups. She was disappointed. Instead there were lots of jowled men in gold-buttoned blazers and old school ties tucking into roast dinners, while their gingham-skirted wives sat outside in the garden drinking subsidised Pimm's. Suddenly Delilah remembered that this was where Vivienne had first met Harold. She should have known.

Peering through the pipe smoke, Vivienne spotted Penny and Virginia at the bar sipping Babycham and comparing outfits: busy mum Virginia had plumped for a dip-dye viscose sundress from M&S – 'it's so easy, the creases just drop out' – while weight-watcher Penny had lost a few pounds and managed to squeeze back into a suit she'd bought before the birth of her twins. Wonderful news, except the twins were now thirteen, and Penny looked like an extra from *Dynasty* – big shoulderpads, even bigger hair and frosted lipstick.

Vivienne sashayed across the room towards them, causing more than one member to choke on his roast beef.

'Darling, you look sensational!' Penny gave her a jolly good hug and beamed brightly. 'I must say, next to you I feel rather under-dressed!' She broke into a snorting laugh before turning to Delilah. 'Do forgive me, we weren't introduced at Harvey Nichols. I'm Penny.'

'I'm Delilah.'

'And I'm Virginia, but please call me Ginny.' Ginny held out her hand and gave Delilah a firm no-nonsense handshake. As Guide Leader and president of the residents' committee she didn't believe in any shilly-shallying around.

They ordered a round of drinks: pineapple juice for Ginny, dry sherry for Penny, white wine for Delilah and Vivienne's usual, tonic on the rocks, and enjoyed the attentions of married men who wore pinstriped shirts with cufflinks and signet rings on their little fingers. Or rather didn't enjoy, as was the case with Delilah, who had unfortunately attracted Oscar, a ruddy-cheeked architect in his early thirties.

'Can I buy you a drink?' Reeking of whisky, he leered hungrily at her chest.

'No, I've got one, thanks.' Delilah took a sip of her wine and looked to Vivienne for moral support. But Vivienne didn't notice. She was too busy showing off her new thighs to Malcolm, a property developer from Chelsea.

'Why can't I buy you a drink?' Oscar spluttered, annoyed that his advances weren't being greeted with enthusiasm. What was wrong with the gal? He was a jolly handsome fellow.

'Because I've already got one, thanks.' This time she spoke louder. Perhaps he was deaf as well as drunk.

'Suit yourself,' he huffed, puffing out his pigeon chest and gulping back his last mouthful of whisky. 'I don't want to talk to you anyway, you're from the north.' And clutching his empty glass he stumbled haughtily away. Delilah was aghast. For a moment she thought about storming after him and having an argument. Then decided against it. What was the point? Not only was he a pompous oaf, he was a very pissed one.

'Well, isn't this a hoot?' beamed Penny, who was getting very tipsy on her sherry. 'I must say, I was rather nervous about this evening but this is all rather jolly.' She hiccupped loudly and broke into her snorting laugh.

Vivienne frowned. 'It hasn't even started yet,' she muttered, taking away her glass. Penny had been renowned at boarding school for peaking too quickly and had suffered the ignominy of being known as Piss-Artist Penny.

'I think we should catch a cab to Soho.' Delilah stood up. She'd had enough of the stuffed shirts at the Arts Club. She wanted to party.

'Hear, hear,' trilled Ginny, finishing off her pineapple juice and slamming it down with gusto on the bar. 'Let's be on our way.'

Despite its shaky start, the evening soon accelerated into fifth gear. Soho was alive and kicking, buzzing with all the ingredients needed to make a brilliant girls' night out: drinking, dancing and lots and lots of men. Vivienne didn't waste any time. Diving out of the cab before the meter had even stopped, she sprinted into CO_2, a glossy bar full of glossy people, and began chatting up the tight-T-shirted barman. He was to be the first of many. Forget a pub crawl, this was more a sprint, as the merry gang followed Vivienne from karaoke bars to gay bars to salsa bars, high on adrenaline and tequila slammers.

For the first time in ages, Delilah let her hair down and really had fun, drinking vodka and *Courke*, dancing to Abba and making a complete fool of herself by karaokeing with Ginny to Gloria Gaynor's 'I Will Survive'. She felt like herself again, and for the first time in ages she didn't think about Sam or Charlie. Grinning, she looked across at Penny who, left to her own devices, had discovered the cocktail list and was slowly working her way down it – and the bar stool – while Vivienne was surrounded by a flock of male admirers. Like moths to a flame, they were knocking into each other as they flapped their biceps, vying for her attention. Not that she minded. On the contrary, she was flirting like crazy, playing to her eager audience.

But all too soon it was time for last orders and reluctantly they finished their drinks and staggered outside.

'Where to next?' asked Delilah, looking at her watch. It wasn't even midnight.

Penny leaned a crumpled shoulderpad against a post box and mumbled something about her bed, while Ginny suggested Chinatown. 'I'm rather peckish. I vote for a Chinese.' She fanned herself with a cocktail menu, her mouth watering at the thought of all that delicious MSG. She'd never admit it, but she was actually feeling rather tiddly.

Neither suggestion was met with much enthusiasm by
Vivienne, who was drunk on male attention and craved more. 'I
want to dance,' she announced, striking her Shirley Bassey pose.
'I want to dance the night away in a club.' She twirled around a
lamppost, head back, laughing throatily. Delilah grinned wearily.
This was Vivienne sober? No wonder she'd given up drinking.

'So, suggest somewhere to dance,' she said, calling her bluff.
Vivienne hardly ever went out in Soho, she wouldn't have a clue
where to go.

She was wrong.

'I know a super club, it's just around the corner.' Vivienne
did a quick two-step. 'Follow me.'

With hindsight, Delilah should have suspected there was something dodgy about Secrets when the woman with pierced
eyebrows in the neon-lit entrance booth asked them if they
were dancers. Dancers? *Penny and Ginny?* Penny was so pissed
she could hardly stand up, while Ginny was dressed as if she
was about to go on the school run. Of course Vivienne, who
looked like something out of *Cabaret*, said she was and wangled
herself free admission, scooting inside and leaving the three of
them to pay twenty quid each. Ginny nearly fainted. 'Twenty
pounds. Good heavens, that's daylight robbery,' she gasped
loudly, her matronly bosom heaving dangerously as she struggled to keep up with Delilah and Penny, who had rushed inside
trying to find Vivienne. Navigating their way down the dimly lit
staircase they headed towards the thumping music, finally
catching sight of Vivienne who had eagerly rushed ahead,
impatient to shake her thang on the dancefloor.

'Hang on a minute,' yelled Delilah above the beat of Whitney
Houston's 'I Wanna Dance'. 'Wait for us.' Vivienne came to a
halt by the saloon-style swing doors.

'Hurry up, I want to dance.' She sang along to Whitney and
practised her wiggle.

Delilah caught up, as did a very red-faced and short-of-
breath Ginny, and Penny, who'd suddenly got a second wind

and was excitedly applying another coat of frosted lipstick. Full of anticipation, Vivienne pushed open the swing doors – and stood rooted to the spot. It was certainly a club. And there were certainly lots of people dancing. There was just one snag. They were all half-naked women, and the only place they were dancing was in men's laps.

Chapter Thirty-Six

'Good Lord, this place is full of strippers.' Ginny's eyes rolled into the back of her head. She looked as if she was about to collapse.

'Actually, they're lap-dancers,' whispered wide-eyed Penny who was peering over her shoulder.

'Does it matter what they're called?' bellowed Ginny. 'They've hardly got any clothes on!'

Delilah tried not to laugh. Here they were, four women on a hen night, *in a lap-dancing club*. It was difficult not to see the funny side. She looked over at Vivienne, who was mesmerised by one of the dancers onstage: a brunette in a PVC catsuit and zip-up-to-your-thigh kinky boots, gyrating around a fireman's pole. 'Vivienne, when exactly did you last come to this club?'

'I think it was about 1987,' answered Vivienne, not taking her eyes off the stage. 'Although it does seem to have changed somewhat.'

'I'll say,' interrupted Ginny, who began fanning herself grumpily. 'I think I need to sit down.' As a sensible mother-of-two she was not amused at discovering she'd parted with her housekeeping money to get into a strip joint. She scowled at Vivienne.

'So what shall we do?' Delilah didn't want to stand in the doorway all night watching Ginny pass out and Vivienne doing impressions of *Dirty Dancing*.

'Go in, of course.' Vivienne was surprised. Wasn't that obvious? 'I must say, I've always rather fancied myself as a lap-dancer, I'd like to see what they get up to.'

Penny nodded in agreement. 'Me too,' she whispered shyly. Delilah did a double-take. Vivienne with her bedside drawers full of suspender belts and rubber corsets maybe, but calorie-controlled Penny in her Krystle Carrington shoulderpads? Surely she was more sports bras and waist-huggers than tassled bras and spangly G-strings? Perhaps Uncle Stan was right after all – there's nowt so queer as folk.

They took a vote on it. Vivienne was adamant, Penny was rather keen, and Delilah? Well, she was as intrigued as the next girl. It was Ginny who needed a lot of persuading, but once Vivienne had helpfully pointed out that as a responsible Guide Leader she owed it to her girls to find out what evils could lead them astray, she had to agree. At which point her desire to take charge took over and, folding her arms firmly across her bosoms to stop any ogling, she led them bravely into the club.

It wasn't as bad as Delilah had expected. The decor was actually rather pleasant, in a bland Trusthouse Forte kind of way, and it was dimly lit, apart from a few strobe lights and the obligatory glitterballs to help get the punters in the mood. Through the mists of cigarette smoke and dry ice, Delilah could make out a stage on which there was a girl in a frilly basque and fishnet stockings doing a rather lame version of the Can-Can. Around the edges, tables were crammed full of every type of bloke you could imagine, from groups of arrogantly handsome City boys to the nerdy types in half-mast trousers you see filling shelves at your local supermarket, all peeling off wads of £20 notes and happily stuffing them down different girls' G-strings.

Thanks to Ginny's orienteering skills, they managed to find a spare table without having to circumnavigate the club, and Delilah plonked herself down, trying to look as inconspicuous as possible. It wasn't easy when the only other women in the club were wearing crotchless knickers and doing the splits. Ignoring the stares from all the tables around them, she leaned across to Vivienne.

'Can you imagine taking your clothes off in front of all these men?' Delilah was incredulous. She felt embarrassed topless sunbathing – on a beach, lying down.

'Yes I can,' grumbled Vivienne jealously. She didn't want to sit on the sidelines, she wanted to be one of the teamplayers. Opening her fifth packet of Marlboro Lights that evening, she lit up a cigarette and blew smoke rings at Penny, who was jigging around in her seat like an excited child at the circus. She certainly had plenty of acrobatics to watch, not least from a girl on the stage who was doing cartwheels in a leather bikini. Ginny, meanwhile, was perspiring heavily with embarrassment. Ordering some iced water, she nervously glanced around her, catching the eye of a tattooed bulldog of a woman. It was the house 'Muvva' who was leaning against the wall, drinking a pint of snakebite and glaring at them suspiciously. They weren't exactly her regular clientele – in fact they were probably lesbians, especially the one in the dip-dye sundress.

Trying to look like a cool, modern-thinking woman and not a shockable prude, Delilah watched the entertainment. She was surprised to see that the dancers came in all shapes and sizes. For some reason she'd been under the impression that they would all look like Pamela Anderson, with fake boobs, fake hair and *Playboy* figures. In fact, once they'd taken off their costumes, most of them looked pretty normal: stretchmarks, thread veins, a generous smattering of cellulite. None of the dancers was embarrassed about their less-than-perfect bodies, and there certainly weren't any complaints from the men. On the contrary, they couldn't get enough of all those dimpled bottoms, small boobs and fleshy bits. Which was a bit of an eye-opener. Delilah had always thought a lap-dancing club would make her feel inadequate about her body, but in fact it gave her a confidence boost. Never again would she dash naked across the bedroom with her back against the wall, trying to get into bed before her boyfriend glimpsed her arse.

Just as Delilah was patting herself on the back for not going to the gym to work on her fleshy bits, she saw a leggy, DD platinum blonde, dressed up as a cowgirl, wandering towards her, scanning the tables for any interest.

'Lisa?' Delilah craned forward to get a better look. Yes, it was Lisa, aka Fifi, the cigarette girl from the Pantry.

Lisa stopped and turned around. She squinted under a strobe light. 'Delilah, is that you?' She strutted towards the table. Ginny took a gulp of her iced water. One of them was coming over! 'Hey, honey.' Bending closer to Delilah, she whispered, 'I'm called Kelly in here, as in Cowgirl Kelly, from the Wild, Wild West.' She rolled her eyes and smirked. 'Sorry, I can't stop and chat but I'm supposed to be working.' She looked over her shoulder at the army of bouncers. 'Pretend to stick some notes in my G-string and I'll do you a two-minute turn. That way we can have a chat.'

Delilah nodded, trying to look as if she was *au fait* with this kind of thing and fumbled nervously with the sides of Lisa's suede knickers.

Immediately, Lisa began to wiggle her tassled miniskirt hips. 'So, where've you been?' She twirled a six-foot-long leather lassoo in between her legs.

'Nowhere, I moved in with my boyfriend.'

'I suppose he made you give up your job at the Pantry? Men can be so jealous sometimes, they just can't deal with you having your independence, can they?'

Delilah nodded distractedly. She'd never thought of it that way before. Charlie had suggested she give up her job so they could spend time together, not because he hadn't wanted her to have her independence. Anyway, she hadn't liked her job at the Pantry, so what did it matter? She brushed the thought away, but a seed of doubt had been sown. The little woman at home, is that how he wanted her? That was as bad as Lenny had been.

'So how long have you worked here?'

'About three weeks. The money's amazing, much better than the cigarette lark.' She took off her cowboy hat and put it on Penny's head. Penny giggled nervously, but didn't take it off. 'Especially when you get customers like that guy over there. He tips fifty quid a time.'

Delilah looked over to where she was pointing. A blast of dry ice from the stage obscured her vision, but as it slowly cleared she saw who Lisa was talking about. She froze. In disbelief she saw Charlie at a table with several others, drinking champagne while a redhead stuffed her bottom in his face.

'Excuse me.' Apologising to Lisa, who was doing the grand finale with her spurs, she jumped up. Blindly stumbling through a sea of push-up bras and suspender belts she marched around the side of the stage. She was livid. Charlie had told her he was in bloody Cornwall, filming some TV programme or other. What the hell was he doing in Secrets?

'So, what's this documentary going to be about? Women's underwear?' Delilah stood, hands on hips, in front of Charlie, who had a spangly G-string between his teeth. He groaned and released the elastic back into its resting place. 'Darling, I can explain . . .'

Delilah fumed. She'd heard that one before.

'We're doing some filming on nineties culture, I'm here with the crew . . .'

'Oh, really?' she said sarcastically, glaring at the redhead who was trying to retrieve her knickers. 'So who's that? The bloody camera man?'

Charlie opened his mouth, and then closed it. There was no way he was going to be able to charm his way out of this one. He'd been caught red-handed, or in fact red-bottomed. The question was, how? How on earth had Delilah known he'd be there? Defeated, he decided to wave the white flag, or in his case a glass of champagne. 'Here, have a drink.' He held out a cheap tumbler full of Moët. Secrets wasn't the kind of place you found cut-glass champagne flutes.

Amazed at his cheek, Delilah was just about to reel off as many four-letter words as she knew and some she didn't, when she was distracted by a flash of red sequins on the stage. It was Vivienne, with her dress around her thighs, gyrating wildly to Prince's 'Kiss'. 'Shit,' muttered Delilah, covering her eyes. She couldn't bear to look, but then she couldn't bear not to. Peering through her fingers she watched Vivienne, who'd finished sliding up and down the fireman's pole and was beginning some kind of limbo dance. 'What *is* she doing?'

Vivienne was doing what she loved the most. Being the centre of attention. Bored of being part of the audience, she'd decided she'd much rather be the performer and climbed onto the podium. The exhilaration was amazing, and she had thrown herself into a routine which, until now, she'd kept between herself and the bedroom mirror. In fact she was so good at strutting her stuff that she'd practically wiggled her way through the entire Prince number before the bouncers twigged she wasn't actually one of the dancers. With perfect timing they lunged at her just before she was about to let it all hang out and bundled her off the stage, 'escorting' her to the entrance amid a slow handclap, wolf whistles and shouts of 'We want the lady in red.' It was a fitting climax to the evening.

Chapter Thirty-Seven

It was the morning of Vivienne's wedding and she was having a crisis. Despite strict diet instructions, bridesmaids Hilary, Hermione and Harriet had gained several pounds since the last fitting and were literally bursting at the seams of their Bo-Peep dresses.

Which meant that with only half an hour left before they had to leave for the church, Vivienne's mother, Cynthia, was on her hands and knees in the kitchen with a needle and thread, doing her best to sew them back into the apricot satin, while Vivienne paced around her bedroom chainsmoking and on the verge of tears. It was not what you'd call the best start to a wedding day.

'Calm down, everything will be okay,' soothed Delilah, trying to dampen the hysteria. She wasn't having much success. Vivienne fiddled impatiently with her tiara. 'Everything will not be okay, everything will be ruined. I've already had those dresses altered three times – any more silk and we could have made a bloody parachute. I knew those three lumps were a mistake from the beginning, but bloody Harold insisted.' Fighting back the tears she tugged the tiara out of her hair and threw it onto the bed. 'Fuck it. The stupid thing can stay in its box.'

Delilah rolled her eyes. Vivienne was having one of her tantrums. In fact she'd been having one of her tantrums on the hour, every hour, for the past few days and unfortunately Delilah had witnessed them all.

She'd been staying at Vivienne's since the hen night's unforgettable finale when, along with Ginny and Penny, she'd been unceremoniously thrown out of Secrets by the house 'Muvva'.

Afterwards she'd stormed back to the flat and waited for Charlie. He didn't come home. Not that it would have made much difference if he had. Her mind was made up. The next morning she'd pulled on her old faded jeans and T-shirt, packed up her stuff for the third time that year, and turned up on Vivienne's doorstep expecting a shoulder to cry on, only to discover that she was the one providing the shoulder.

The next few days had been a frenzy of last-minute wedding preparations and Vivienne had been like a woman with twenty-four-hour PMT, veering out of control between snappy irritability and tearful outbursts. Delilah never did get the chance to talk about Charlie or Sam, in fact she never got the chance to talk to Vivienne at all. When she hadn't been busy making cups of herbal tea for Vivienne's eccentric relatives, who kept arriving with bizarre, oversized wedding presents from overpriced antique shops in Highgate, she'd been roped into helping to decorate the church, collecting the bridesmaids' dresses and trying to reason with Miranda the harpist, who'd flounced around the house in a peacock-blue ballgown adamantly refusing to play 'What's New, Pussycat?' at the reception.

Not that she'd minded. It had given her time to think about a few things and to see that she was being hypocritical – Charlie may have been at a lap-dancing bar, but she was the one who'd been unfaithful. Once she'd calmed down she realised that she'd been using the lap-dancing incident as an excuse to leave him. Seeing him with a G-string between his teeth wasn't the real reason she had to finish their relationship, it was discovering that she wasn't in love with him. And she'd only really decided that when she'd left him. Of course, she'd known their relationship hadn't been right for a long time, but she'd played the ostrich game, choosing to ignore things rather than to face up to them. After all, it's not easy to admit that the lifestyle and the man you'd thought were so right for you are so wrong. And it's even harder to accept it. But once Delilah had, she felt an enormous sense of relief. She may have lost

Charlie, but in return she'd found her sense of identity, of who she really was and what she wanted – and what she didn't want. The dreams she'd had about Charlie and his life were just that – dreams. Finally she'd woken up and realised that what she'd been searching for had been under her nose all along. It wasn't living in a penthouse, or wearing designer clothes, or going out to ludicrously expensive restaurants with the jet-set crowd. It wasn't even about money or hitching up with a drop-dead handsome eligible bachelor-about-town. She'd had all that and was more than happy to give it all back. None of it had filled that big black hole deep inside her. In fact, in the long run it had made the hole seem blacker and deeper. It was just as her mum had always told her. It's not getting what you want that's the hard part, it's deciding what you want. And now she had.

Unfolding the crumpled pamphlet she'd kept in her jacket pocket, she'd taken a deep breath and dialled the number of Westminster College. The line had been engaged, but she'd tried again and again, until eventually she'd got through and nervously asked for an application form. 'For which course?' had answered the harassed female voice.

There'd been a pause as Delilah had tried to steady her nerves. 'Interior Design.' Despite her voice, breathless and squeaky, she felt a wave of relief. She'd said it. And now, feeling bolder, she repeated it, this time her voice steady and determined. 'I want to do the degree course in Interior Design.'

The woman let out an impatient tut, well rehearsed from days of answering the same query. 'I'm afraid you're too late to apply. The course begins in less than six weeks and we've already been inundated with application forms. Perhaps it would be better if you waited until next year.'

'But I want to apply this year.' Delilah wasn't going to be put off. Now she'd made up her mind there was no going back.

'But the course is full—'

Delilah interrupted. 'Are you going to send me an application form or not?'

'Well, if you insist, but I really can't see there's much point, as I said earlier—'

But the woman never got a chance to finish her sentence as Delilah was already spelling out her surname and address, thanking her ever-so-politely for her help and putting the phone down. Padding into the kitchen in a pair of her old sheepskin slippers, she'd heaped three large teaspoons of instant coffee into a mug and switched on the kettle. Waiting for it to boil she'd stared out of the kitchen window, jammed firmly shut from being painted over too many times. So what if the course was full? She was going to apply anyway. Who said there wouldn't be room for one more? And anyway, she'd come this far, she wasn't about to start giving up now. Steam rose from the spout as the water began to boil, and, too impatient to wait until it clicked off, Delilah lifted the hissing kettle and filled her cup, stirring in the brown frothy granules. Since leaving Charlie's she'd happily dumped the cappuccinos and switched back to her beloved Nescafé. Smiling to herself, she took a mouthful, the coffee scorching her tongue as she swallowed, inhaling its strong, hot aroma. Yep, she'd definitely woken up and smelled the coffee. And it had never been so good.

'The Rolls-Royce is here.' Cynthia's voice shrilled down the hallway. 'My word, doesn't it look marvellous? Just look at that satin ribbon!' Clutching her wide-brimmed hat – which screamed 'I'm the bride's mother' – she made a dash for the door. 'Yoohoo!' She waved excitedly at the chauffeur, who was giving a final polish to the flying lady on the bonnet of the Silver Shadow. 'We'll be there in two hoots of the horn.'

In the bedroom Vivienne stubbed out her cigarette. 'Well, I suppose this is it.' With slightly trembling hands, she smoothed down her crinoline skirt which billowed around her like an ivory silk marquee and looked at Delilah. 'Do I look like a bride?'

Delilah had never seen Vivienne so nervous. She smiled encouragingly. 'Of course you do, you look beautiful.' And she did. Brides always do.

'Have you got something old, something new, something borrowed and something blue?' suggested Delilah. Brides loved all that rubbish – blue garters, antique lace, borrowed hanky, you know the kind of thing.

'Superstitious nonsense,' dismissed Vivienne, adjusting her veil.

'Oh, come on. No self-respecting bride can get married without all that stuff,' coaxed Delilah, grinning. 'Look, borrow my watch.' Unbuckling the worn leather strap, she passed Vivienne the Timex her mum had bought her one Christmas. 'What about something new?'

Furrowing her forehead, Vivienne tried to think. 'Well, I'm wearing some new La Perla underwear. And it's very blue – if you know what I mean.' She smiled wickedly. This was actually rather fun.

'Great. That only leaves something old.'

They both fell silent, deep in concentration, before looking at each and breaking into wide grins. 'Harold!' they shrieked in unison, and burst out laughing.

'We must have a photograph of you leaving the house, darling.' Cynthia scampered ahead of the bridesmaids, narrowly avoiding tripping down the front steps. 'Just think, next time you return you won't be a spinster.' She beamed delightedly in her lilac two-piece.

'Mother!' scowled Vivienne, trying to negotiate her way through the potted geraniums while Penny and Ginny, glowing proudly in their apricot dresses and matching headbands, struggled to stop her skirt trailing on the floor. 'I am not a spinster. I'm a single, affluent, attractive woman in her thirties.'

'Whatever,' trilled Cynthia, paying no attention and fiddling with the zoom lens. 'In my day we called women like you spinsters.'

'*Women like me* . . .' Vivienne's voice lurched upwards.

'Smile!'

The flash went off, forever freeze-framing the scene for

posterity – the bride and her bridesmaids. It was a photograph that Vivienne would keep for years, until the colour had faded away to a pale yellow and the edges had started to curl. A photograph that, every once in a while, she took out of her top drawer to show her children, and their children, and they would laugh at the funny clothes and the comical expressions. The picture said it all: Hilary, Hermione and Harriet squeezed into dresses that were stretched tight like satin balloons, picking their spots and squinting in the sunlight; Penny and Ginny beaming proudly and clutching their posy baskets; and Vivienne, standing in the middle with her hands on her hips, scowling into the lens.

The guests were still going into the church as the vintage Rolls-Royce approached.

'Would you like me to do a detour for a few minutes, Madam?' The chauffeur looked at her through the rear-view mirror. A retired bus driver from Epping, he was trying hard to sound posh. Too hard. Not content with simply sounding his aitches, he was putting them in front of every word.

'I suppose so.' Vivienne fiddled with her bouquet and glanced at Delilah. There was just the two of them in the back of the car. Vivienne's father had died when she was a teenager and she'd politely turned down Great Uncle George's offer to give her away. It was a load of sexist claptrap anyway. '"Giving away" is something you do to your old clothes, not thirty-five-year-old women,' she'd lectured. Instead, she'd planned to travel to the church with her mother and walk up the aisle by herself, but at the last minute changed the plans and asked Delilah to accompany her in the Rolls, squashing a disgruntled Cynthia into the Bentley with the bridesmaids.

'Are you okay?' Delilah leaned back against the soft leather seats.

'A little nervous.' Vivienne drummed her fingers on the walnut fittings. She could murder a cigarette.

Delilah smiled supportively. 'Don't worry. It's just wedding jitters, every bride gets them.' Though perhaps not as badly as you, she thought, watching Vivienne beat out a drumroll.

'Yes, quite likely.' Vivienne swallowed. She didn't seem convinced.

Delilah looked out of the window. The sun had disappeared and it had started to drizzle. The chauffeur turned right at the traffic lights. They were heading back to the church and Delilah could still see the last few guests making their way up the path. As the Rolls got closer she realised one of them was Sam, dressed in a morning suit, with his arm around a suntanned blonde in her early thirties. She blinked. Who the hell was that? She felt a stab of jealousy.

'We're here, Madam.' The chauffeur turned off the purring engine and stepped out of the car. He opened the door with his white-gloved hand. Delilah clambered out first, her mind whirling with the image of Sam and that woman, distractedly stepping on the hem of her bias-cut dress. It ripped. 'Shit,' she muttered, that was all she needed. Bending down she fussed with the fraying material, waiting for Vivienne to climb out. Except she didn't.

She peered into the car. There was no movement. Vivienne was wedged against the far door, a mound of duchess silk and ivory veil.

'What's up, do you need a hand?' Delilah leaned inside the car.

Vivienne's complexion had turned the same colour as her dress. 'I can't go in.'

'What?'

'I can't go in. I've changed my mind.'

Delilah's heart joined in the drumroll. '*Vivienne!*' She tried not to panic. 'But everyone's here. The bridesmaids, guests . . . *Harold.*'

'Exactly. That's why I can't go in. I can't marry Harold.' Vivienne's face began to turn mottled and a large tear streaked down her carefully applied make-up.

Delilah stared. My God, she was actually crying. Vivienne

must be serious. 'Are you *sure* you don't want to get married?' She gave it one last go.

Vivienne nodded, wiping her smudged mascara on her antique veil. 'Absolutely.'

'I suppose now's not the time to ask why.'

Vivienne's bottom lip trembled and she shook her head, beginning to snivel.

'Well, I guess that's that then,' announced Delilah matter-of-factly, trying to be practical in a highly emotional situation. What was the point of crying over spilt milk – or jilted grooms, for that matter. Squeezing Vivienne's gloved hand she forced a smile. 'C'mon, it's not the end of the world.'

Vivienne gulped. 'I know, but somebody's got to tell Harold.'

Delilah froze. Somebody? There wasn't anybody. *Everybody was in the church.* 'You can't mean . . .' She stared horrified at Vivienne, who was sniffling dejectedly. 'You don't mean . . .' But she did. Delilah was that somebody.

Chapter Thirty-Eight

'*She said what?*' blustered Harold, his face taking on a purplish tint.

Delilah hesitated and cleared her throat before nervously leaning forward. 'She said she's changed her mind.' She whispered loudly into his hearing aid, trying to avoid any eye contact with him, or the congregation who had stopped chatting among themselves and were staring at her suspiciously.

'Well, I'll be buggered,' he bellowed, shaking his jowls. 'Changed her mind! She can't change her mind. We're getting married. Look!' He flung out his arms in the direction of the pews, startling a couple of people, who jumped in their seats. Whispering to the person next to them, they began spreading the gossip like a bad case of Chinese whispers, until the rows of guests were a sea of different coloured hats bobbing up and down like a Mexican wave.

Delilah sighed. Harold seemed to missing the point. 'But she doesn't want to get married.' She raised her voice over the sound of Mendelssohn's 'Wedding March'. The organist was pounding away on the pedals, trying to disguise the sound of speculation that was rushing through the church.

Harold fixed her with his watery grey eyes. 'Do you have any idea how much I've spent on this wedding?'

Delilah ignored him. She was watching Cynthia as she 'Excuse me'd her way through the front row and began trotting up the aisle towards them. She looked flustered.

'*Well, do you?*'

Any sympathy that Delilah had felt for Harold disappeared. All he was bothered about was his bloody money.

'No, I don't. And to be honest I don't care. It's not important,' she snapped.

Harold visibly shook at the impudence. 'It bloody well is, young lady!' he puffed angrily and lurched towards her shaking his fist. Luckily he was restrained by Cynthia, who appeared from behind his tailcoat, out of breath and clutching on to her hat.

'What's happening? Where's Vivienne?' she gasped anxiously, her head flicking from side to side like a bird.

'Outside in the car. She doesn't want to go through with it.' Delilah was growing weary of explaining.

Harold spluttered noisily. 'So she's outside, is she? Well, let's see what madam has to say for herself.' And before Delilah or Cynthia could stop him, he brusquely pushed his way through the bridesmaids who were gathered fretfully by the door, wedging his top hat firmly onto his wispy pink head, and stomped, nostrils flaring, down the gravel path towards the Rolls-Royce.

Vivienne was sitting in the car waiting anxiously for Delilah to return. She dragged heavily on the cigarette she'd cadged from the chauffeur, trying to get as much nicotine into her bloodstream as possible, while plucking the petals off her bouquet. Suddenly, out of the corner of her eye, she saw Harold, tailcoat flaring and purple face bulging as he marched towards her. 'Oh fuck,' she muttered under her breath, pulling the door shut. She prepared to do battle.

'Get out of the car.' Harold stood shouting at the Rolls-Royce. A woman with a pushchair and several Tesco bags walked past, staring at the crazy old man in his top hat and tails. Vivienne sat tight inside and prayed he'd go away. There was no point trying to talk to him when he was in a temper.

'I said, get out of the car.' He stamped his foot repeatedly on the pavement, startling a couple of pensioners waiting at the bus stop with their shopping trolleys.

Vivienne relented and opened the door a chink. 'Harold, please calm down,' she hissed, aware that a small crowd of pedestrians had gathered across the road and were having a good old gawp. 'You know what the doctor said about your heart.'

With an alarming burst of agility, Harold seized his chance and made a grab for the door. But Vivienne was too quick, slamming it shut and trapping his fingers.

Delilah heard the strangulated howl as she ran out of the church. So did Cynthia, who was scampering along behind her, providing the backing vocals. 'Dearie me, dearie, dearie me,' she shrilled in a tremulous high-pitched voice, holding on to the rim of her hat. Harold was bent double at the kerbside, clutching the knuckles of his right hand. A trickle of blood fell onto the pavement.

'Good heavens. Are you all right?' gasped Cynthia, ignoring her daughter in the Rolls and fussing maternally over him.

'I think I need to go to hospital.' His voice quivered.

Delilah glanced at Vivienne. 'Are you okay?' she mouthed through the glass of the car window.

Nodding, Vivienne wound down the window. 'Oh dear, have I broken his fingers?' She didn't sound repentant. 'I didn't mean to, but I had no choice. He was like a wild animal.' She raised her eyes imploringly. Vivienne was well practised in getting out of tricky situations.

Delilah gave a wry smile. 'Oh, he'll be fine, but I think we're going to have to take him to Casualty.'

Vivienne paled. '*We?*'

'Well, we can't just leave him at the side of the road.' Not that she didn't want to.

Vivienne looked across at Harold who was being comforted by Cynthia. 'Oh, if we must,' she tutted, sounding annoyed. 'But don't ask me to apologise.' She sniffed stubbornly, arching her back in her ivory, seed-pearled bodice.

Sighing, Delilah walked reluctantly over to Cynthia and helped the pathetic figure of Harold onto the front seat of the Rolls. All the stuffing had been knocked out of him, and he lolled dejectedly like a crumpled pillow against the chauffeur, whimpering and nursing his hand which had been carefully bandaged in Cynthia's lilac hat ribbon. Delilah carefully shut the door and squashed up on the back seat, making sure she was between Vivienne and her mother. They weren't speaking.

'St Mary's Hospital in Paddington, please,' instructed Delilah, looking out of the window as the car pulled away from the kerb. A small group of guests were mingling outside the church, along with a photographer and Reverend McTaggart, who was looking rather confused. 'Oh shit,' she groaned, closing her eyes and sinking into the upholstery. In all the panic, she'd forgotten to tell the vicar.

St Mary's casualty department was jam-packed. Saturday afternoons always signalled a rush of injured husbands who'd tried to be handy around the home and doctors were used to dealing with these men who'd nearly chopped off limbs doing a spot of DIY with their brand-new power tools, or half electrocuted themselves while mowing the lawn. What they weren't used to dealing with were geriatric grooms with crushed fingers.

'Please, come this way Mr and Mrs . . .' the staff nurse hesitated as she saw Vivienne in full bridal regalia, still clutching her bouquet of antique roses.

'Mr Gosborne and Miss Pendlebury,' prompted Vivienne.

'Ah, yes,' smiled the nurse briskly, glancing down at the notes on her clipboard. 'Cubicle Five, please.' She walked ahead, helping Cynthia to support Harold, while Delilah and Vivienne tagged behind, Vivienne's skirts sweeping the linoleum floor of the hospital corridor. Entering the cubicle the nurse eased Harold onto the trolley bed and briskly pulled on the blue curtain, making it very squashed and claustrophobic inside.

'So, what seems to be the matter?' The nurse spoke loudly into his hearing aid and smiled benevolently. The kind of smile always reserved for old people.

Cynthia answered for him. 'My daughter trapped his fingers in the door of the Rolls-Royce.' She patted Harold's leg tenderly and glared at Vivienne, who was slumped sulkily against the blood-pressure machine.

'I see,' said the nurse, not seeing at all and jotting something down on the clipboard. Delilah tried to see what it was. It probably said 'Mad People'.

'Actually, I didn't trap his fingers,' interrupted Vivienne. 'He put them there.'

'Pardon?' The nurse looked up.

'He was trying to grab hold of the door so he could pull me out of the car and march me up the aisle. It was self-defence.'

'Now, Vivienne, stop being a naughty girl and tell the truth,' chastised Cynthia, who'd developed rather a soft spot for Harold, and was intent on defending him, seeing as he couldn't defend himself. With all the arguing, she'd only just noticed he'd dozed off and was snoring contentedly.

'I *am* telling the truth, *Mother*,' Vivienne hissed loudly.

It was Delilah's signal to leave. 'I think I'll get a coffee,' she muttered quietly, lifting up the edge of the curtain and making a sneaky escape.

At the end of the corridor she found a vending machine. Sliding two 20p pieces into the slot, she pressed the button for strong black coffee. With the kind of day she was having she needed a caffeine fix. Exhausted, she watched the brown liquid squirt into the beige plastic beaker. It slowed to a trickle and then stopped. Picking up the beaker, she leaned against the wall and lifted it to her lips. The coffee tasted bitter and watery. She sipped it anyway, idly noticing the pale mustard-coloured walls which seemed to be an interior design feature of NHS hospitals across the country, and breathed in the mingling smells of disinfectant and the food trolley, which was doing its rounds. It reminded her of the night she'd met Charlie in Bradford General and how her stomach had flipped over when she'd first seen him. He'd looked so gorgeous. She smiled to herself, remembering how bloody awful she'd looked, with streaky mascara and blotchy skin. It seemed like years ago.

Her jaunt down memory lane was cut short by a nurse's voice from the cubicle directly in front of her. It was breezy and efficient. 'Now, as the doctor said, the X-rays have shown two fractured ribs and a severe spiral fracture of the fibia and tibia. Which means that for a couple of months there will be no gallivanting around for you, young man.'

There was a groan from the patient. Poor bloke, thought Delilah pityingly. During her childhood she'd suffered a broken leg and could still vividly remember how long and boring the weeks had been, hobbling miserably around on crutches.

'Now, come along. After a car accident like that, you're very lucky to be alive.'

'I know, I know.'

Delilah screwed up her forehead, straining to hear better. The patient's voice was similar to Charlie's. She tutted to herself for being so silly. Her mind was playing tricks. It had been a long day.

'Now, I want to check this admittance form with you before we take you up to the ward. Is it Charles Mendes, or would you prefer Charlie?'

'Charlie.'

Delilah nearly choked on her coffee. That couldn't be a coincidence. There couldn't be two Charlie Mendes in West London. Hastily dropping her beaker in the plastic swing-bin, she pulled back the curtain with trepidation.

'Excuse me, but this is a private cubicle.' The nurse scowled impatiently at her through her bifocals.

'Delilah . . .' gasped Charlie in surprise, struggling to sit up on a stretcher. Beneath his A&E tunic his body was strapped with large crêpe bandages, holding together his splintered bones.

'I'm sorry, do you two know each other?' The nurse adjusted the bed so that it elevated Charlie's head slightly.

'Yes, she's my . . .' he faltered, correcting himself '. . . was my girlfriend.' He smiled limply, his bruised and cut face groggy with painkillers.

'Well, I think I'll leave you two to have a little chat for a moment.' She nodded briskly and, smoothing down her uniform, wafted through the cubicle curtain.

Delilah stared at Charlie in disbelief. They had come full circle.

Chapter Thirty-Nine

'What the hell happened?'

'I smashed up the car.'

'How?'

'Driving back from a party this morning. I lost control and crashed into the front of a chemist's. Luckily, there was nobody on the pavement.' Charlie smiled feebly, hoping for sympathy.

But Delilah didn't give him any. It made her think about her mum. She hadn't been so lucky. She *had* been on the pavement when the drunken lorry driver had lost control and careered into her. 'Were you over the limit?'

Closing his eyes, he nodded. 'Yeh.' His voice was a faint whisper.

She sighed. 'Oh, Charlie . . .'

'I know, I know. Please don't be angry with me, Delilah. I couldn't bear that. Not after everything that's happened.' He tried to hold out his arm, but the pain was too much. He dropped it limply onto the scratchy, thin blanket embroidered with ST MARY'S. It looked about fifty years old.

So did Charlie.

'I wanted to call you, but I didn't know where you'd gone.' He gazed at her with his pale-blue eyes, bloodshot and bleary with morphine. 'Why did you leave?'

Delilah leaned against the side of the bed, fiddling self-consciously with the mother-of-pearl buttons on the sleeve of her jacket. 'You know why I left.'

'Because of that stupid lap-dancing club?'

'No . . .'

'Well, what then? Was it Nickii?' He waited for her to say

something but she didn't. 'There's nothing going on between us. We just flirt, have a laugh. You know me.'

She nodded. Yes, she did know him, but he didn't know her. That was the problem.

'So what is it? Is it somebody else?' It was a wild guess. He didn't think for a moment it was.

Her stomach flipped like a pancake. 'What are you talking about?' she snapped, her voice strained. Charlie watched as she fidgeted uncomfortably. Surely he hadn't got it right. *Had he?*

'Who is it?'

'No one, there's no one else,' she gabbled. Why was she gabbling? There was no way he could know she'd slept with Sam, and even if he did it didn't matter. That wasn't the reason she'd left him.

Charlie stared. Despite her repeated denials, her agitation gave her away. *He was right.* There was another bloke. But who? Charlie felt stunned. It was the last thing he'd suspected. Delilah didn't know any other men, apart from Vince the slimy Italian or that stupid friend of hers, Sam. He rewound. *Sam.* It couldn't be . . . He remembered the scene at the restaurant and how she'd defended him, running after him into the rain. It all fell into place.

'It's Sam, isn't it?'

'Of course not.' She felt her cheeks beginning to burn. This was crazy.

Charlie shook his head in astonishment. She'd chosen a waiter over him? What the hell was going on? 'Are you in love with him?'

'Of course not.' She denied it emphatically. Too emphatically. Who was she trying to convince? Herself or Charlie? 'Look, it's got nothing to do with anyone else. It's nobody else's fault. It's between you and me.' Pausing, she gently put her hand on top of his and lowered her voice. 'We're just not right for each other.'

How ironic. That was normally his line. When he'd got tired of a relationship he'd use it as the perfect get-out clause. But now the tables had turned. He gazed at Delilah, her hair falling in waves against the side of her face, and felt a blow to his male pride. It wasn't just his body that was bruised and broken, it was his ego.

'But we had a good time, didn't we?'

'Yeh, we did . . . for a while.' She picked at the unravelling cotton on her buttonhole. 'But I stopped having a good time, Charlie.'

'What do you mean?'

'All your friends, the restaurants, the parties. It just wasn't me. At first it was exciting and new, but after a while I was bored – bored and lonely. I tried to pretend I enjoyed it all. I even tried to fit in by making myself look the part, with all those clothes and the hairstyle . . .' She smiled ruefully, remembering the paparazzi photograph of her. 'But in the end I just got fed up of trying to be something I wasn't.'

'So what are you?'

Sighing, she stood up and walked over to the window, looking out across the busy side street full of black cabs and double-parked cars. 'I'm just a girl from Bradford. I'm not the daughter of some rich rock star like Pollen or Petal, I don't have a trust fund like Nickii, I don't want to be a model or an actress and I certainly can't sing. I've got a whippet and a Yorkshire accent and I like drinking instant coffee and listening to old Tom Jones records . . .' She breathed faintly onto the glass, a cloud of condensation spreading outwards, and with childlike concentration used her finger to draw the letter 'D'.

Charlie's head drooped sleepily against the pillow, his eyes half-closing as the effects of the drugs began to take hold. 'What's the "D" for?' His voice had lulled to a faint whisper.

She hesitated for a moment. 'D is for Delilah,' she murmured quietly, before turning to him, her eyes bright with determination. 'Because *that's* who I am.'

The curtain scraped back and an attractive young Irish nurse bustled in carrying a kidney-shaped silver tray. Glancing at Delilah she smiled politely, and then looked at Charlie. Her face flushed. After a shift spent tending to Black & Decker casualties, she'd expected to see yet another middle-aged husband and father of two, not a single, handsome male in his early thirties.

'You'll probably want to ask your guest to pop back in a few minutes, Mr Mendes.' She gestured to the tray. 'We need a urine sample.' She looked embarrassed.

Despite being pumped with painkillers and dressed in a regulation hospital gown, Charlie still managed to look sexy. He gave her his 007 smile. Even half-comatose he knew a pretty girl when he saw one. 'In there?'

'I'm afraid so, Mr Mendes. We can't move you until the surgeon has operated on your leg, and until then this is probably the easiest way . . .' Slightly flustered, she began fiddling with the bedclothes and turned to Delilah. 'Would you mind?'

'No, of course not.' It was time to leave anyway. She glanced at Charlie. He didn't waste any time, he was already flirting with the nurses. Some things never change. 'If you need anything I'm staying at Vivienne's.' Bending down, she kissed him gently on the forehead. 'Take care.'

'Don't worry, I'm sure Staff Nurse Murphy will take good care of me.' Charlie winked, his broken heart miraculously mended. Delilah nodded. She didn't doubt it for a minute.

Closing the curtain behind her, Delilah loitered outside the cubicle for a moment. In front of Charlie she'd tried to appear calm, but inside she was reeling. What had he been talking about? Being in love with Sam? Of course she wasn't. It was ridiculous, they were just friends. Her mind jumped back to when she'd seen him earlier at the church with his arms around another woman. But if they were just friends, why did it make her feel so knotted up inside? And why couldn't she stop thinking about that kiss, that night?

Feeling suddenly weak, she put a hand against the wall, trying to steady her legs which felt as if they were going to buckle under her. She had the weirdest feeling. It was as if she was one of those heroines she'd seen in black and white movies, the ones that were always tied to the railway tracks, watching as a steam train charged straight towards them. There she was, tied on one of those very same tracks, trapped and helpless. Except it wasn't a train that was heading towards her, but her feelings for Sam that were stronger than she'd ever imagined. So strong, in fact, that it was useless trying to ignore them, to pretend they didn't exist, to try and stop them. They were inevitable. All she could do was lie on that railway track and let those feelings engulf her whole being. And finally accept she was in love with Sam.

Turning away, she heard Charlie's voice. 'Staff Nurse Murphy,' he was murmuring sleepily, 'what's your first name?'

Hesitating, the nurse answered shyly, 'Mary.'

'As in the Bible?'

Delilah couldn't help smiling. Trust Charlie. Shaking her head, she walked back up the corridor.

Chapter Forty

Delilah and Vivienne left Harold at the hospital with Cynthia, who was cheerfully plumping up his pillows and diluting tumblers of Ribena, and were chauffeur-driven home in the Rolls-Royce. It was a dismal journey. Boyfriends in cars stared nervously and their girlfriends gazed wistfully as they pulled up next to them at traffic lights, a bus driver on the No. 9 gave them the thumbs up, and a group of Chelsea supporters on their way to a match stopped belting out rowdy football songs and started singing 'Here Comes the Bride'. Delilah cringed and looked the other way, while Vivienne pulled down her veil and scowled. What was supposed to be the best day of her life had turned into her worst.

After a painfully slow journey, the Rolls made it through the Kensington traffic into Notting Hill and glided into Vivienne's street. In the distance Delilah noticed a huge man with a bicycle leaning against their gate.

'I think you've got a visitor.' She glanced across at Vivienne, who huffed loudly.

'Who the bloody hell is it? If it's Uncle George you'll have to tell him I'm not receiving visitors today!' Like a spoilt child she flounced against the cream leather armrest and petulantly looked the other way.

Delilah leaned forwards, peering out of the window as they slowed. 'He looks like a vicar.'

There was a knee-jerk reaction. Vivienne twirled around, hastily pulling up her veil. 'Dear Lord, it's Giles.' Grasping for the handle she flung open the door and, hitching her dress up around her knees, scrambled out of the car while it was still moving.

Delilah watched her scuttle across the pavement towards Giles, who straightened up nervously, his corduroy trousers with faded knees bunched at the ankles with bicycle clips. He towered above Vivienne, his Goliath-size frame casting a shadow across the Rolls. They exchanged a few words – Delilah couldn't hear what they were saying – and he squeezed her hand consolingly, before dutifully following her up the path and into the house.

Wonder what that's all about, mused Delilah, getting out of the car and saying goodbye to the chauffeur. No doubt he was offering her a bit of godly advice. Being a vicar and all that.

She was just putting her key in the latch when the door was flung open and Giles pushed brusquely past her. 'I do apologise. Please. Excuse me,' he gabbled in a fluster, his Scottish accent much stronger than before. Flattening down wayward locks of hair with the palm of his hand he mounted his bicycle and set off jerkily down the street, ringing his bell furiously at pedestrians.

Delilah squinted in the sunlight. What the bloody hell was going on? Closing the door behind her, she negotiated her way down the dimly lit hallway and into the living room. In the corner was Vivienne, strewn across the chaise-longue, whimpering loudly.

'What's the matter?' Rushing across the room Delilah crouched down beside her. 'What's happened now?'

Vivienne hiccuped and snuffled into her veil. 'It's too terrible. I can't tell you.'

Delilah grabbed a tissue from the top of a nest of tables – a wedding present from Cynthia – and passed it to her. 'Of course you can. We're mates, aren't we?'

Vivienne blew her nose violently and nodded.

'Well then?'

She sniffed. 'You wanted to know why I didn't marry Harold. Well, it's partly to do with something you said.'

'Me?' Delilah was alarmed. Christ, what had she and her big mouth gone and done now?

'Yes, when you were talking about being in love and all that. When you asked me if I was in love with Harold and I said I didn't know, that I didn't know what being in love was like . . .' She stopped talking and blew her nose. 'Well, you were right. I wasn't in love with Harold and so I couldn't marry him . . .'

Delilah nodded sympathetically. 'Then you made the right decision not to go through with it.'

'But it's not just that—' Vivienne broke off, her eyes welling up with smudge-proof-mascara tears. 'I knew that I couldn't possibly be in love with Harold because I realised I was in love with someone else . . .'

Delilah lost her balance and put a hand on the floor to steady herself. Vivienne looked down at her, her bottom lip quivering. 'I'm in love with Giles.'

There was silence as Delilah tried to take it all in. Today was certainly a day for revelations. Hoisting herself up, she sat down next to Vivienne on the chaise-longue. 'The *vicar*? You've fallen in love with the vicar?'

Vivienne nodded miserably.

'Since when?'

'Since we started having the banns read.' She peered glumly at Delilah through the grubby antique netting. 'I tried to convince myself that it didn't matter. That I could marry Harold without being in love. After all, how could I miss something I'd never had? I've never been in love, you see, not ever. That's probably why I've had so many lovers, looking for the right one, I guess. Still, I can't say it hasn't been fun, and I've had some brilliant sex . . . and some not so brilliant, but in the end it didn't mean anything. It was all just a game, like the flirting. And I'm an expert at playing that game. But when I met you, and I saw how you felt about Charlie, how your eyes lit up when you mentioned his name and you got that flushed look on your face, I wanted what you had, I wanted to feel how you did. But it's true what they say, it's the one bloody thing that money can't buy. If you could, I'd have put it on my credit card by now . . .' She smiled ruefully. 'I so wanted to get married, to live happily ever after. The whole fucking fairytale bit. I even desperately tried to make myself fall in love with Harold, but of course it was useless. You can't make yourself fall in love, just as you can't choose who you fall in love with. Goodness, I should know more than most. I should know because when I finally felt that flushed look creep onto my face, when I finally experienced that feeling you described and I knew that I was in love for the first time in my entire life, it was when I was with Giles. Can you believe it? I've fallen in love with the vicar.' Tugging off her engagement ring, she threw it with frustration into the fire-place. It rattled dismally against the marble, rolling around in ever-decreasing circles. 'What vicar's ever going to want me? An atheist nymphomaniac in her late thirties. Giles is never going to fall in love with me, is he? And if I can't have him, I don't want anybody. I'm going to end up growing old by myself, sad and lonely . . .' Her imagination ran away with her. 'Oh, Delilah, what am I going to do?'

Delilah took a deep breath, thinking about her own predica-ment. 'What am I going to do?' she muttered, her voice sounding like a faint echo.

Vivienne was jolted out of her self-pity. 'Oh my goodness, I'm being terribly selfish, aren't I? What with everything that's been happening, I haven't had a thought for anybody else but myself.' She sat up straight, flattening down her voluminous skirts, and tugged off her veil. Folding her arms she peered closely at Delilah. 'You must tell me everything that's been happening. *Everything!*'

It was the green light that Delilah had been waiting for. Relieved that she could finally unburden herself of everything that had been bottled up inside her for the past few weeks, she let it all come tumbling out in a mass of words and unanswered ques-tions. Vivienne listened in amazement. As a self-confessed Queen of Gossip, she was rather miffed that all this had been going on under her nose – and she hadn't known about it.

'So, after the terrible argument with Sam at Iceberg, I went to see him at the café but it was all boarded up. I just don't understand what's going on . . .' Taking her first breath, Delilah paused and looked desperately at Vivienne, hoping for answers.

And she got them. Vivienne pushed a blonde curl behind her ears and slowly licked her lips, allowing the tension to build. Her frustrated acting ambitions always surfaced when she had a captive audience. 'Café Prima Donna closed down because Sam's lease wasn't renewed.'

Delilah was puzzled. In Brighton Sam had told her all about his plans to make it into a restaurant. 'Why?'

Vivienne paused. There was no alternative. It looked as if she was going to have to be the one to break the bad news. 'Charlie threw him out.'

'*Charlie?* What's he got to do with it?'

'He was Sam's landlord. Had been for years, though I don't think either of them liked the arrangement. From what I've gathered, Charlie was always putting up the rent, using the place like a free hotel to entertain his friends, even two-timing the waitresses. Which probably explains why Sam was so upset when he found out you were moving in with Charlie. And at a wild guess, I imagine Charlie wasn't too happy about your friendship with Sam either. Too much competition.'

Delilah stared in disbelief. 'But that can't be true. I asked Charlie and he denied it.'

'What did you think he would do. Confess?' Vivienne lit up a full-strength Marlboro and inhaled deeply until the embers had burned halfway down the cigarette. Satisfied that her lungs were at full capacity she breathed out, emitting a fog of smoke, and leaned back against the sofa, enjoying the head-rush.

Delilah tried to digest all this new information. After weeks spent fumbling around in the dark, it was as if someone had switched on a 100-watt bulb. It all made sense. From the beginning Sam had tried to warn her about Charlie, but she hadn't listened. Instead, she'd told Charlie everything he'd said. She groaned at her naivety. That was probably the reason why he didn't renew Sam's lease. It also explained why they'd argued in the restaurant – and why Sam had assumed she'd known what had been going on. In fact, he probably blamed her for it. And he'd be right. After all, if it hadn't been for her, he'd still have his café.

'Why didn't you tell me?' she asked indignantly, fixing Vivienne with an accusatory look.

'Would you have believed me?'

Delilah crumpled. 'Probably not,' she muttered gloomily. She'd been so sure of what she wanted that she wouldn't have listened to anyone. Shit. Why did she have to be so stubborn sometimes?

'Perhaps you should call him,' suggested Vivienne, trying to sound bright and breezy. It was her turn to try and offer practical advice.

'And say what? Sorry for ruining your life?'

'Nonsense. You weren't anything to do with it.' Vivienne motioned to the hallway. 'Go on, call him. Promise I won't listen.' She put her fingers in her ears and started humming the bridal march. Delilah looked at her. Who was Vivienne trying to kid? As soon as she picked up the handset, Vivienne's ear would be superglued against the door. 'Okay, but definitely no earwigging.'

'On my mother's grave.' Vivienne smirked wickedly. She should be so lucky.

Chapter Forty-One

Delilah dialled the number. Her stomach was fluttering around like a trapped bird and her hands had started sweating. She noticed her knuckles were white from gripping the handset so hard. Ohmigod, Ohmigod. Ohmigod. Listening to the dialling tone, she took a deep breath. If she didn't calm down, Sam would think he'd got some dirty old man panting down his line. To try and relax she picked up a pile of photos that had been left on top of the *Yellow Pages* and started flicking through them. There were lots of Vivienne in a silver string bikini posing on various sun loungers. She peered at the date in the corner – they must have been taken last week when she was in Spain.

The phone picked up and clicked onto the answering machine message. His voice sounded kind and friendly, not like that night outside the restaurant. 'Hi, this is Sam. Sorry I can't take your call, but if you'd like to leave your name after the tone, I'll call you straight back. Bye.' Nervously she listened to a jingly electronic version of Beethoven's *Für Elise* before there was a piercing beep. She opened her mouth. No words came out. She swallowed, trying to say something. Just as she could feel a phrase forming there was another piercing beep and the answering machine clicked off.

Frustrated, she stared into the mouthpiece. Why hadn't she left a message? But on second thoughts, why did she have to leave a message? Where the hell was he? Her mind raced. Probably having a good time somewhere with that bloody blonde he'd been practically snogging at the church. Dropping the phone miserably she glanced at the photos still in her hand. Vivienne and another woman on a speedboat, posing seductively with the bare-chested captain who was wearing mirrored Ray-Bans and a pair of very tight white shorts. *Hang on a minute*. The other woman looked exactly like the blonde she'd seen with Sam. She took a closer look. *It was the blonde!*

'Vivienne,' she yelled, slamming open the door and stomping back into the living room, brandishing the photo.

Looking embarrassed, Vivienne jumped back, startled, from behind the door. 'Er, yes?' she replied, trying to appear blasé about having just been caught with her ear wedged in the keyhole. 'No joy on the phone then?'

Delilah ignored her. As if she didn't know. 'Who the hell is this woman?' She shoved the photo under her nose.

Vivienne blinked. 'That's Jackie, the friend I stayed with in Spain.'

'So what was Sam doing with her at the church?'

Vivienne smiled cheerily. 'Was he really? Oh, that's wonderful.'

Delilah gasped. 'How can you say that? It's not wonderful, it's terrible.' Snatching back the photo she turned it towards the light and undertook a critical inspection of her rival.

Watching her, Vivienne suddenly cottoned on. 'Silly me, I should have explained. No wonder you're upset. But you've simply no need to be . . .' She smiled, feeling delighted at the news she was about to tell her. 'Jackie's Sam's stepmother.'

'*What?*'

'His stepmother. Jackie's married to Sam's father.'

Delilah scowled. She didn't believe her. 'But he hates his stepmother.'

'Not any more. It would seem they've patched things up.' Hoisting herself onto one of the kitchen buffets, Vivienne balanced on a cushion made of £12,000 of satin skirt, which was beginning to look as jaded as she did. Tapping the last Marlboro out of the packet, she lit up. 'It's all rather a long story.' She blew out a cloud of grey smoke. 'Sam's stepmother is one of my oldest friends. We went to finishing school together in the early eighties, a very dull little chalet in Switzerland where we embroidered doilies and learnt how to make pot-pourri.'

She rolled her eyes sardonically. 'And when we both came back to London she got herself a rather good secretarial job at a solicitor's in Chancery Lane, while I just lounged around wearing crucifixes and lacy gloves, trying to look like Madonna, getting drunk and sleeping with unsuitable men. Jackie was always the sensible one, which was why it took me by surprise when she confessed to her affair with one of the partners, Richard, a man twice her age, and who just so happened to be Sam's father.' She paused to flick the ash into a teacup.

Delilah sat down on the buffet opposite. 'Go on.'

Vivienne frowned. She didn't like being made to hurry when she was telling one of her stories. 'Well, of course I didn't know Sam very well at the time. He was just a boy then, all teenage angst, acne and New Romantic hair . . .' She glanced at Delilah's surprised expression. '. . . Yes, in those days he had plenty of hair. It was probably all that back-combing and hairspray that killed it.' She smirked at the memory. 'He was about to go to university and would often pop up to town to see his father – Richard was terribly keen for him to go into the family business, you see – and I'd bump into him in the lift on my way to meet Jackie. At first we just said hello, but it wasn't very long before we'd struck up rather a friendship, and started going for a few drinks by ourselves. Nothing romantic, I hasten to add. I thought he was rather sweet, a refreshing change from all the ageing Lotharios I was hanging around with.'

She broke off, remembering Ronnie, the drummer of a sixties band who used to take her to Tramps and have sex with her under the tables.

'Anyway, it was during this time that Jackie and his father dropped the bombshell and ran off together. Sam was dreadfully upset, as you can imagine. And so was I. Jackie left without saying goodbye or returning my Hermès Kelly bag. Which reminds me, I really must ask for that back . . .' She tutted at the memory.

'So what happened with you and Sam?' Delilah was impatient.

'Oh, we lost touch. He went off to university . . . or was it cooking school? Anyway, I didn't see him for a couple of years, until one day I bumped into him at the café. We've been friends ever since, but I've never mentioned his father, or Jackie, even though we've kept in touch. He didn't want to have anything to do with them. But all that changed when I was in Spain last week and Jackie told me she was three and a half months pregnant – her and Richard have been trying for a child for ages – and as the baby will be a little half-brother or -sister for Sam, his father feels it's time to heal the rift. It's been over ten years and it's long overdue. Of course, being me I didn't want to interfere,' she paused dramatically, 'but I suggested Jackie came to the wedding and used the opportunity to try and patch things up with Sam. Which, by the sound of things, seems to be what's happened.'

Looking very smug with herself she stubbed out her cigarette and glanced at Delilah. 'You don't seem very pleased.'

'I am,' she protested feebly. 'I'm just fed up about everything that's happened. Sam must hate my guts.'

'Good heavens, don't be stupid. He's in love with you.'

Delilah's heart lurched. 'Did he say that?'

'Well, not exactly,' added Vivienne as an afterthought. 'And it was rather a while ago that I spoke to him, what with all the wedding preparations . . .' Her voice tailed off.

Delilah sighed dejectedly. 'Well, that's it then.' She chewed her manicured fingernail gloomily. Any hopes she'd had of getting it together with Sam were over. For ever.

The atmosphere in the room sunk to an all-time low, the bride and her best friend both bemoaning their situations. Their clothes might be ones you'd wear to a wedding, but their expressions were ones you'd wear to a funeral. Vivienne sighed glumly and slumped over the table, sneaking a look at Delilah, who was peeling off the layers of her French manicure in the pits of depression. She felt partly responsible for Delilah's unhappiness; if only she hadn't kept her big mouth shut this time, things might have been so different.

Screwing up her skirts, she clomped over to the mirror and peered at her reflection. Her face reminded her of one of those chalk drawings on pavements that had been smudged by the rain. It looked exactly like she felt. Washed out and washed up. Thirty-five years old and still single. *A spinster.* She scowled. What a hateful word. It made her sound as if she should have varicose veins and a hairy chin, and spend her days reading large-print novels and making her own pickles. But is that what the future had in store for her? A lifetime of being by herself, a sad, lonely old woman rejected by future lovers only interested in young, fertile twenty-somethings? She felt a tear balancing on an eyelash and watched as it swelled and tumbled down her cheek and plopped off the end of her chin. In an act of rebellion she lifted up her hem and used it to wipe off the rest of her make-up. Get a grip, girl, she told herself, smearing traces of bright red lipstick over the seed-pearl embroidery. What was she talking about? All this wedding malarkey was making her maudlin. She wasn't a bloody spinster. *She was an eligible bachelorette.* A woman in her prime. A woman with everything going for her. She smiled defiantly at her reflection. Who cared if she wasn't married? Who cared if she was the wrong side of thirty? All she needed was something to cheer her up. Something to make her feel alive, carefree, happy.

As if she could read her thoughts, Delilah let out a heavy sigh. So did she.

Suddenly Vivienne had a flash of inspiration. Clapping her hands together, she spun round in excitement. 'I've got just the thing!'

Delilah cast a weary eye upon her. She'd had enough of Vivienne's surprises for one day.

'The honeymoon.' Vivienne's chest swelled. It looked as if she was going to pop out of her bodice.

Delilah looked nonplussed. 'So? Harold's in hospital.'

Vivienne gasped, exasperated. 'I know that, silly. You don't think I want to go with him, do you? I mean for us two. You and me. A week in Bali. Forget men, what we need is a holiday. Just

think! We can mend our broken hearts while getting a suntan.'
She whooped delightedly. 'What do you say?'

The thick black cloud shifted from over Delilah's head and a
chink of light peeked through. So this was the silver lining. She
hesitated, but only for a moment, before smiling ironically. 'I
do.'

Chapter Forty-Two

That evening they left Fatso grumbling in kennels and, courtesy of Harold, jetted off in first-class seats to the five-star
Aman Puri Hotel, set high on the terraced paddyfields of Bali.
On arrival they were greeted by the hotel manager, who
congratulated them with a bottle of champagne and garlands
of lotus flowers and courteously showed them to the sumptu-
ous bridal suite, before nipping back to reception and
gossiping with the rest of his staff about this very unusual
honeymoon couple.

Not that Delilah or Vivienne cared. They spent seven glori-
ous days chilling out with wind-chimes and scented candles,
eating coconut curries and shopping for sarongs and those
twiddly woven-string bracelets – the ones that look great with a
tan and all those brightly coloured vest tops you've bought in
three-packs, but start looking very dodgy when you're back to
your usual pasty white and trussed up in a polo-neck and
hooded fleece in the middle of a British winter. They put the
world to rights over multicoloured drinks decorated with interesting shapes cut out of pineapple, and swore to each other that
they didn't need men to get on with their lives. In fact they
didn't need anything, apart from SPF15 and Vivienne's duty-
free fags.

Of course, it was just holiday bravado. And secretly,
neither of them was looking forward to going back to
London. Vivienne had to face the music, the sound of 250
disgruntled guests demanding the return of their wedding
presents, and Delilah, who'd diligently filled in her college
application form, would find out if she'd been successful. If

she hadn't, then what? Wait until next year and reapply? And what would she do in the meantime? She couldn't bear the thought of waitressing, but maybe she'd have to go back to it. As the end of the holiday loomed, the unanswered questions in her life multiplied until she couldn't sleep for thinking about them.

That was two months ago. Two months since Delilah had arrived home to find two envelopes waiting for her on Vivienne's doormat: the first had confirmed her worst fears – it was a standard rejection letter from the college. Gutted, she'd sunk into a heap in the hallway, reading and rereading the polite blurb: 'Thank you for your interest . . . The course was over-subscribed . . . Please apply next year . . .' She'd stared at the headed notepaper for nearly an hour, wondering what the hell she was going to do, before she remembered the second enve-lope. It was one of those thick brown A4-size ones and the handwriting on the address was familiar but she couldn't place it. She studied the postmark – Monte Carlo. Who would send her a letter from Monte Carlo? Intrigued, she'd ripped it open, never once imagining that inside would be a folded document with the words 'No hard feelings, hey?' scribbled on the back. It was the lease for the café. Charlie had signed it over to her as a parting gift.

It was eight weeks since she'd received that lease and following her gut instincts climbed unsteadily up a ladder and with her bare hands pulled down the FOR LET sign outside Café Prima Donna. Fifty-six days since she'd sat down and given everything she had, every idea, every dream, every concept she'd ever idly dreamed of, to design a whole new interior, full of light and colour, textures and fabrics, cleverly concealed lighting. And she'd watched, breathless with excitement, as an army of workmen followed her instruc-tions and knocked down walls and built new ones, ripped out fittings and installed different ones. Slowly it all began to come together, especially with the help of Uncle Stan, who'd arrived back from Benidorm on the same day as he'd received a phone call from Delilah. Tanned and bored after too much sun and dodgy sangria, he'd been only too delighted to come out of retirement, and without further ado he'd thrown on his paint-splattered overalls, kissed a powdery Shirley ta-ra, grabbed his packed lunch and headed off down the M1 in his trusty van.

It was like old times, Stan and Delilah. Except this time she wasn't sitting on the dustsheets, she was in charge, deciding on paints, experimenting with different textures, loving every minute of the 1,344 hours since she'd made the unshakeable decision to turn the café into a restaurant. With no experience and even less money, she'd had to work bloody hard and learn bloody fast. Luckily, Vivienne had happily solved the financial problem by offering a large injection of cash from her trust fund and in return was now a sleeping partner. Which, as a title for her first job, was rather apt. Sleeping with partners had always been the one thing she was good at.

Not that things had turned out so badly for Vivienne either. In fact they'd turned out pretty damn great. Never one to change the habit of a lifetime, she was once again sharing her bed with a member of the male species, except this time it wasn't just about sex, it was about love. Being totally, completely, head-over-her-Gucci-heels in love with the man snuggled next to her under the duvet – Giles. It was Giles who, after admitting to himself that he was as mad about Vivienne as she was about him, decided he'd risk the wrath of his congregation for the love of a good woman and had spent two days at Terminal 4 waiting for her to return from Bali. No sooner had her woven sandals touched the tarmac at Heathrow, than he'd whisked her off to Gretna Green and they'd officially been declared Mr and Mrs McTaggart – or rather, in Vivienne's case, Mrs Pendlebury-McTaggart. And she couldn't have been more delighted. She was married and in love for the first time in her life, and it felt wonderful. There was also an added bonus – she'd always loved playing tarts and vicars, and now she could do it for real.

The restaurant was due to open in two weeks. The sign had been hoisted above the door: 'Tom's', in homage to her mum's idol, and the staff had been hired. Except for the head chef. Delilah couldn't bring herself to fill that position. It was Sam's. Except Sam hadn't been seen or heard from since the wedding. Nobody knew where he'd gone. Delilah was heartbroken. When she'd found Charlie's letter she'd called Sam for days, but he'd never answered his phone. All she'd heard was that bloody answering machine, and after a while she didn't even hear that anymore. Just a continuous beep. Eventually she'd plucked up the courage to go and see him, deciding that even if he told her to get lost it would be better than being ignored. Except there was no answer when she'd rung the buzzer to his flat, and, peering through his letterbox, she'd seen piles of unopened mail.

Nobody likes to accept it's over, but it was. It was over before it had even begun. And as she sat on his front doorstep, watching the traffic stream endlessly past, gangs of teenage boys loitering outside the bookie's smoking cigarettes and trying to look hard, and a pregnant woman waddling down the pavement, she realised that it was too late. Life doesn't hang around, it keeps moving and if you don't keep up you can lose things. Just like she'd lost Sam. He'd gone and it was too late to talk to him. To say sorry. To tell him how she felt.

Over the passing weeks she'd tried to get on with things and put him out of her mind. But it was impossible, especially at night when she'd stay late by herself in the restaurant, putting the last lick of paint to the skirting boards and listening to Tom Jones albums on an old record player that one of the electricians had rigged up for her in the corner. For the first time in her life she felt fulfilled, proud of what she'd achieved. A reporter from the *Daily Mail* had been over to see the restaurant before it opened and had written a glowing report about the design, calling Delilah 'a new raw talent . . . innovative and bold . . . one to watch out for'. Thrilled to bits, she'd cut out the newspaper article and stuck it next to her mum's photo. But just when she thought things couldn't get any better, she'd had another surprise. It came two days later in the form of a telephone call. It was Westminster College saying they had reconsidered her application in light of her recent publicity and obviously exceptional talents, and there was a place waiting for her on the course if she wanted it. Wanted it! Of course she wanted it. Still clutching the handset she'd jumped up and down with excitement, shrieking her head off. It was a dream come true. Her dream – and she was over the moon.

Everybody had been so happy for her and the phone had never stopped ringing with different people wanting to congratulate her. But the only person who didn't call was Sam, and he was the only one who really mattered. He'd believed in her and by doing so he'd made her believe in herself. He'd given her the courage to apply to college, and the confidence to take the plunge and redesign the café. But turning it into a restaurant had been Sam's idea, she was just the designer. It was Sam who should be devising the menus, choosing the ingredients, making it his. Her role in the restaurant was over now. She was about to embark on a degree course which would give her the qualifications she needed to follow her dream. Now it was time for Sam to follow his.

'Hurry up, you're going to miss the beginning of the procession.' It was August bank holiday and Notting Hill Carnival was in full swing. Delilah was getting pleasantly drunk on the flat roof of Tom's, watching the crowds of partygoers below, baking in the August sun, blowing whistles and getting well and truly pissed on whatever booze the tattooed blokes were flogging on the unlicensed stalls. It was the perfect place to enjoy the party – you got all the atmosphere but you didn't get squashed in the crowds of drunken revellers. 'C'mon, you two,' she shouted eagerly to Vivienne and Giles, who were lolling on deckchairs behind her, rubbing suntan lotion into each other and giggling annoyingly, like newlyweds always do.

'Okay, okay,' grumbled Vivienne, disentangling herself from Giles and hauling herself out of her chair. After being a Notting Hill resident for fifteen years, Carnival had long since lost its appeal. In fact, she usually joined the other residents who fled with their Mercedes full of their most valuable possessions at the first sight of the metal barriers being put in place, and didn't return until the last empty beer bottle and streamer had been swept up by the street-cleaners. Except this year Delilah had begged her to stay. This was her first Carnival and for ages she'd been looking forward to the weekend-long party, full of tinsel-covered floats, thumping sound stages and dancing in the streets.

'Ah yes, Carnival,' boomed Vivienne, closing her eyes and breathing in the aroma of barbecued corn-on-the-cob, goat curry and jerk chicken. Opening them, she caught sight of a couple of red-faced policemen with their arms around a Jamaican woman in a feather headdress and sequinned costume, jigging around self-consciously. Privately wishing they'd swapped their beats for ones in Putney, they smiled stiffly for the harassed tabloid photographer who was trying to get the classic 'Local Bobbies in Carnival Spirit' picture.

'This brings back memories.' She turned to Delilah. 'Did I ever tell you the time I danced naked, apart from silver body paint, on the back of one of the floats?'

'No,' smirked Delilah, glancing backwards at Giles, who was jigging around in his deckchair to the echoes of a distant salsa beat, shaking his hands as if he was holding a couple of maracas.

'I was only eighteen at the time, and going through my wild stage. I got as far as Ladbroke Grove before Mother spotted me from her friend's dining-room window and phoned the police. I was arrested for gross indecency.' Vivienne was still annoyed with her mother, who, after striking up a friendship with Harold at the hospital, had wasted no time in moving herself into his house in the country. Publicly she told everybody how she thought it was disgusting, her own mother going out with one of her ex-lovers, but secretly she admitted to Delilah that they did seem terribly well suited.

'I say, can you hear that music?' Giles jumped out of the deck-chair and started shaking his hips and waving his hands in the air. Determined to get into the spirit of things – carnival rather than holy – he'd swapped his dog collar and Shetland jumper for a glow-in-the-dark whistle and a tie-dye T-shirt. Very Glastonbury. 'Isn't that a tune from that chap you both like?'

'What chap?' snapped Vivienne impatiently. Giles was ador-able, but he did have an irritating habit of being very unspecific.

'That chap. Tom Whatsisname.'

Delilah and Vivienne screwed up their foreheads and listened hard through the cacophony below. In the distance they could make out the faint strains of Tom Jones's 'Delilah'. It was coming from one of the floats.

Delilah grinned. 'Can you hear what I hear?' She looked at Vivienne, a warm feeling tingling up inside her.

Vivienne shrieked. 'Good heavens, they're playing "Delilah" for you.'

The three of them looked at each other, grinning like idiots as the first of the decorated floats edged past them, stacked high with a sound system blasting out 180 decibels of reggae from the six-foot-tall speakers. But in the distance Delilah could hear wafts of her song, and it was growing louder and louder.

And then she saw it. A lorry covered in hundreds of gold and silver helium balloons, carrying a steel band energetically drumming out a rendition of 'Delilah', Caribbean style, and surrounded by sequin-spangled dancers in bikinis and ostrich-feather headdresses, clapping their hands and joining in the chorus.

For a few brief seconds, Delilah could only watch, paralysed with amazement. But then the energy grabbed hold of her and she began swaying to the music. She knew all the words and she started singing them at the top of her voice. Until something made her stop. And stare. For there, standing in the middle of the band, was Sam. And he was smiling up at her, holding out his arms and serenading her.

'Well, what are you waiting for?' Vivienne screeched in her ear. Delilah didn't hesitate. She wasn't going to lose him a second time. Grabbing Vivienne by both shoulders, she gave her a big kiss on the cheek and ran to the fire escape. Vivienne fell back laughing and snuggled up to Giles. Together they watched her disappear from view, Fatso scrambling after her, barking loudly.

In a mad rush, Delilah clattered downwards, two steps at a time, until she reached the bottom step and flung herself onto the pavement. She groaned with frustration. The fire escape came out onto the side street full of people jostling for views of the procession. Taking a deep breath she picked up Fatso, squashing him close to her chest and, sticking out her elbows, began pushing forwards through the crowds – women with toddlers, girls with exposed midriffs, blokes with shaved heads and huge joints, an outside broadcasting crew with fluffy mikes and hand-held cameras, making yet another documentary. 'Excuse me, excuse me,' she panted, wriggling through spaces, trying to see over shoulders and in between elbows. In the distance she could see the floats had moved further up the street, but she couldn't see Sam.

Then she heard him.

'Delilah!' Over the roar of the crowd she could hear her name being called.

'Sam!' she shouted, as loud as she could. A woman wearing a pair of fairy wings turned round and gave her a dirty look for shouting in her ear. She didn't care. 'Sam!'

And then suddenly she could see him. He was outside Tom's, clambering towards her and grinning like crazy. He held his hands above the heads of the crowd and holding Fatso with one hand she reached out, straining, until she felt his fingers against hers and she grasped them. He pulled her towards him until they were opposite each other, gasping for breath and smiling crazily like a couple of lovesick teenagers.

And neither of them could do anything but stare at each other.

'Where've you been?' Delilah finally asked, her voice hardly audible against the music.

'In Spain with Dad, sorting a few things out.' His dark brown eyes looked deep into hers. 'I saw a newspaper out in Spain . . . the picture of you and the article about the restaurant. I had to come back.'

She bit her lip, feeling suddenly shy. She had all this stuff she'd planned to say, but she couldn't say any of it.

'So, have you found yourself a chef yet?' He nodded towards the sign on the restaurant door.

'No, why, are you interested?'

'I might be.' Nervously he pulled a crumpled bit of paper from out of his back pocket and gave it to her. 'How about I find you a chef, if you find someone who'll come with me to Las Vegas.'

What was he going on about? Confused, she looked at the paper. It was a British Airways ticket valid for a flight that afternoon to Las Vegas. 'Why, what's happening in Vegas?'

'The usual – blackjack, roulette – oh, and there's a singer giving a concert in one of the casinos. I don't know if you've heard of him. Some Welsh geezer called Tom Jones.'

Even the whistles couldn't drown out her scream of delight. And, boy, did she scream. Hanging on to Fatso with one arm, she threw the other around his neck and hugged him, never wanting to let go. Neither did Sam, who held on to her as if she was the most valuable thing in the whole world. Two people and a skinny whippet clinging to each other in the middle of thousands of revellers. Looking deep into his eyes she kissed him. Yep, she'd been right. There were those thousand flash-bulbs again. 'I bloody love you, Sam.'

Sam grinned. It was what he'd been waiting to hear since that first night in the café. 'And I love you, Delilah.'

Epilogue

So that's what happened.

Notting Hill changed my life. And even though it's now full of bankers, designer boutiques and expensive restaurants, some of the old places remain. You've just got to know where to look.

Turning down a side street I see a red awning: *Mario's Cobblers*. It's been here forever, tucked away in a tiny hole in the wall. Mario's standing in the doorway chatting to a customer. He cuts a familiar figure; his pinafore, streaked with polish and tied tightly around his generous middle, his glasses teetering on the edge of his large Roman nose as he inspects a pair of stilettos.

I ring my bicycle bell as I pass and he looks up. His face splits into a smile.

'Hey Delilah, when are you going to bring in your boots?' he booms in his thick Napoli accent.

'Summer's coming!' I smile and, taking my feet off the pedals, I wave my Havaianas in the air.

'I can put a nice sole on them, give them a polish,' he suggests with his characteristic enthusiasm.

'Mario, they're flip-flops!' I laugh and he chuckles and waves after me good-naturedly as I cycle away down the street.

Though some of the old places have been given a bit of a makeover, I reflect, turning the corner and glancing across at what used to be Sam's old Café Prima Donna, now a sleek restaurant, its rows of smart white-clothed tables filled with diners enjoying lunch. My eyes flick to the sign above the door-way – *Tom's* – and I feel a swell of pride. It's been through some changes over the years, the menu has evolved and the interior has been completely redesigned, but it's still really popular. Like the singer himself, he's gone grey now, who would have ever believed it?

Yet, he's still the same Tom Jones. Just like I'm the same Delilah. Well, a few things are different . . .

Nearing the coffee shop where we'd planned to meet I scan the crowds. Oh, there he is! Half-hidden by the hordes of people I spot a man standing just ahead of me, further along the pavement. He's got his back to me but I'd recognise him anywhere. He's wearing his usual uniform of T-shirt and jeans and his head is still shaven, though now it's more because he's losing his hair than a fashion statement. Which is fine by me, I always liked it shaved anyway, always liked how it felt beneath my fingertips. So soft it's almost like velvet.

'Sam!' I call his name and he turns around. As does Fatso, who he's holding on a lead, and who begins wagging his tail – not as manically as in the old days, but he is fourteen now, with fur that's almost completely white.

Seeing me, Sam's eyes crinkle into a smile. 'What took you so long?' he grins as I hop off my bicycle and hurry towards him.

'I know, I'm sorry, it took me forever—' I begin apologising but he silences me with a kiss. 'Where's Tom?' I ask, reluctantly breaking free but no sooner is the question out of my mouth than I hear a rasping baritone, 'Cuthbert, Peregrine, Rupert! Behave yourself on those confounded scooters, you'll kill someone!' and twirl around to see a blonde-haired woman dressed in fuchsia pink and surrounded by three blond shrieking boys, in decreasing sizes like they came from a Russian doll.

'Vivienne!' I grin as her sons scoot out of the way like a marauding army of mini-Viviennes to reveal she's holding hands with another small boy – one with bouncy brown curls and pinch-red cheeks.

'My darling Delilah—' she begins theatrically, but is interrupted by a delighted squeal of 'Mummy!'

Breaking free of her hand, the little boy runs towards me and scooping him up, I hug him tightly and shower him in kisses. This is Thomas – my three-year-old.

Well, what else was I going to call him?

It was Tom Jones who brought me and Sam together, who serenaded us on our honeymoon to Vegas all those years ago, before we came back to Notting Hill and started on our new adventure. And what an adventure it's been. Sam started working as a chef at the new restaurant, building it into the success it is today as well as writing several bestselling organic cookery books. Meanwhile I started the design course that would lead me to setting up my own business, Delilah's Designs, and appearing on TV as a 'design specialist' in makeover programmes.

Okay, it's only been a couple of times, but even so. *Me!* On the TV! Can you believe it? No, neither can I. As for my Uncle Stan and Auntie Shirley, they now think I'm some kind of mega celebrity. It's actually a bit embarrassing as Shirley will insist on starting every sentence with, 'Well, our Delilah has been on the telly you know . . .'

Speaking of whom . . . 'What time are Stan and Shirley arriving this afternoon?' I ask Sam.

'Their flight from Spain lands at four. We've got plenty of time, I've already been to the market for ingredients.' Plopping several large carrier bags in the bicycle's basket he glances over at Vivienne. 'Are you coming over for dinner tonight?'

Her face lights up. 'Oooh, what are you cooking?'

'Linguine con vongole, warm pear and rocket salad, home-baked focaccia, flourless chocolate truffle cake to finish . . .'

'Sounds absolutely divine,' she gasps.

'Shirley will have her tambourine,' I remind her with a grin.

Vivienne blanches. 'You northerners with your home entertainment.'

'Well you know how Uncle Stan likes a sing-along.'

'Be careful – he might get you doing karaoke,' warns Sam.

'What's karaoke?' asks Thomas, looking at me wide-eyed.

'A modern torture device, darling,' coos Vivienne, ruffling

Thomas's hair and planting a ketchup-red lipstick kiss on his cheek.

'Vivienne!' I gasp.

'What?' she wide-eyes innocently. 'Don't worry, I'm sure Giles will love an excuse to flex his vocal cords. He's forever singing in the bath and rivals the choir in church. He's quite the baritone, you know.'

'Well, that's sorted then,' laughs Sam, lifting Thomas from my arms. I shoot him a grateful look. Thomas might only be three but he's getting increasingly heavy. 'See you tonight.'

'I can't wait,' Vivienne grins wickedly, then reaches inside her handbag and pulls out a packet of Marlboro Lights.

'I thought you were going to stop,' I chastise.

'I am,' she protests. 'Just a couple of sneaky puffs while the boys are mowing down pedestrians.'

I smile. See, not everything has changed.

And giving her a hug, I take Fatso's lead as Sam lifts Thomas high up onto his shoulders. 'I can see the whole world,' he says, giggling with delight.

'I know,' I smile, wrapping my arm around Sam's waist. 'I can see it too.'

And, as I breathe in the sights and smells and sounds of Notting Hill, I know more than ever that this *is* my whole world. Here, in this tiny corner of the globe, is everything I've ever wanted.

'Come on, let's go home,' says Sam, and with his free hand he grabs hold of the handlebars of the bicycle and we set off walking. Weaving through the crowds.

A couple with their adorable little boy, a not-so-skinny-anymore whippet and their whole lives ahead of them.

ALEXANDRA POTTER

You're the One That I Don't Want

How do you know he's The One?
Are you getting butterflies just thinking about him?
Have you dreamt of marrying him?
Do you just *know*?

When Lucy meets Nate in Venice, aged 18, she knows
instantly he's The One. And, caught up in the whirlwind of first
love, they kiss under the Bridge of Sighs at sunset. Which
– according to legend – will tie them together forever.

But ten years later, they've completely lost contact. That is,
until Lucy moves to New York and the legend brings them
back together. Again. And again. And again.

But what if Nate isn't The One? How is she going to get rid of
him? Because forever could be a very long time . . .

*A funny, magical romantic comedy about how finding The One
doesn't always have to mean happily ever after.*

HODDER

ALEXANDRA POTTER

Who's That Girl?

If only you knew then what you know now . . .

Imagine you could go back ten years and meet your younger self
– would you recognise her? And what advice would you give?

- Wear sunscreen
- Back away from those PVC trousers?
- DON'T give that idiot your phone number
- Lemon juice won't bleach your hair – it just attracts wasps
- He's The One – don't let him get away

For Charlotte Merryweather, there's no need to imagine. She's
about to find out for real. With some surprising consequences . . .

*Alexandra Potter's deliciously funny and enchanting
romantic comedy looks at life, love and what might happen
if you could turn back time . . .*

HODDER

ALEXANDRA POTTER

Me and Mr Darcy

He's every woman's fantasy . . .

After a string of nightmare relationships, Emily Albright has
decided she's had it with modern-day men. She'd rather pour
herself a glass of wine, curl up with *Pride and Prejudice* and
step into a time where men were dashing, devoted and
honourable, strode across fields in breeches, their damp shirts
clinging to their chests, and *weren't* into internet porn.

So when her best friend invites her to Mexico for a week of
margaritas and men, Emily decides to book a guided tour of
Jane Austen country instead.

She quickly realises she won't find her dream man here. The coach
tour is full of pensioners, apart from one Mr Spike Hargreaves, a
foul-tempered journalist sent to write a piece on why Mr Darcy's
been voted the man most women would love to date.

Until she walks into a room and finds herself face-to-face with
Darcy himself. And every woman's fantasy suddenly becomes
one woman's reality.

HODDER

ALEXANDRA POTTER

Be Careful What You Wish For

'I wish I could get a seat on the tube . . . I hadn't eaten that entire bag of Maltesers . . . I could meet a man whose hobbies include washing up and monogamy . . .'

Heather Hamilton is always wishing for things. Not just big stuff – like world peace or for a date with Brad Pitt – but little, everyday wishes, made without thinking. With her luck, she knows they'll never come true . . .

Until one day she buys some lucky heather from a gypsy. Suddenly the bad hair days stop; a handsome American answers her ad for a housemate; and she starts seeing James – The Perfect Man who sends her flowers, excels in the bedroom, and isn't afraid to say 'I love you' . . .

But are these wishes-come-true a blessing or a curse? And is there such a thing as *too much* foreplay?

HODDER